STORYBOUND

ALSO BY EMILY McKAY

Creative Hearts Series

Weddings, Crushes, and Other Dramas
How Willa Got Her Groove Back

The Farm Series

The Farm
The Lair
The Vault
The Before

STORYBOUND

EMILY MCKAY

Entangled Publishing, LLC
10940 S Parker Road
Suite 327
Parker, CO 80134
rights@entangledpublishing.com

Entangled Teen is an imprint of Entangled Publishing, LLC.

Visit our website at www.entangledpublishing.com.

Edited by Brenda Chin
Cover design by L.J. Anderson, Mayhem Cover Creations
Cover images by
vadimphoto1/Depositphotos
SergeyNivens/Depositphotos
Vertyr/Depositphotos
den-belitsky/iStock
MelashaCat/Depositphotos
artant/AdobeStock
Interior design by Toni Kerr

ISBN 978-1-64063-656-9
Ebook ISBN 978-1-64063-657-6

Manufactured in the United States of America

First Edition May 2020

10 9 8 7 6 5 4 3 2 1

entangled teen
an imprint of Entangled Publishing LLC

This one is for the all the dreamers in the world. The hopers and the wishers. The space cadets. The dads at Disney wearing goofy T-shirts. And Goofy T-shirts. Anyone who lives more in their own head than in the outside world. I truly believe that story is the magic that weaves the world together and you are all wizards.

Also, Club Oreo: Adi, Anisha, Avyu, Diya, Emma, Katelyn, Miranda, Nastasia, Tati, & Unnathi. Thank you for letting me be part of your lives.

PROLOGUE

*T*he *Traveler Undone*, the final book in The Traveler Chronicles, was released on the same day the movers delivered our boxes to the new apartment—the ninth in six years.

The Traveler Chronicles was my favorite series. Ever. I loved Kane, the hero from those books, more than any other hero. More than Harry Potter. More than Aragorn from Lord of the Rings. More than Wade Watts from *Ready Player One*.

According to interviews with the author, Chuck Wallace, *The Traveler Undone* would be the last book.

I don't know what sacrifices Mom made to the bookstore gods to get a book delivered on release day to an apartment we'd lived in less than twenty-four hours. I didn't ask.

But when the I saw the box, I knew exactly what it was.

A beginning and an ending all in one day.

It felt auspicious.

"What do you want to do now?" Mom asked, as I clutched the box.

Yeah. Like she didn't know.

I wanted to crawl into bed with my book. I wanted to not move again until I was done.

"We're finally close to a Cheesecake Factory, she offered.

I squeezed the box to my chest. I could almost feel the beating heart of the book through the cardboard. "Maybe for dinner?"

Her lips twitched with a smile more resigned than amused. "Sure, kiddo."

Pretending I didn't notice how sad her eyes looked, I crossed the living room of the garage apartment, heading for the single bedroom Mom and I would share. I didn't want to open it in front of her. I wanted to be alone when I saw the book for the first time. When I ran my fingers over the embossed cover. I wanted to make a ceremony out of it.

I had almost escaped to the bedroom when Mom said, "I just want—"

She cut herself off, either unwilling or unable to finish her sentence. That's what stopped me.

She was still by the front door, threading her keys in and out of her fingers. The apartment was so tiny that we were barely ten feet apart. The living room held a sofa and a chair, both pushed too close to the center to accommodate the boxes stacked against the wall—all of the stuff we'd hauled from one place to the next as we followed Mom's job across the country. The effect was claustrophobic.

Once again my mom's gaze dropped to the box in my hands. Self-consciously, I tucked it behind my back. Mom wasn't a reader. Not like me. She'd never understood the need to escape reality.

I wanted to live in a world where the monsters were hellhounds and demons, not isolation and bullies. In a world where the bad guys could be slayed. Where a valiant hero—or better yet, a snarky, reluctant one—would always step in to win the day.

"I just want to give this place a shot."

"Sure."

"The doctors give Ms. Polinski a year or more. And Seattle could be a real home for us. Especially after…"

Regret flickered across her expression. Then she crossed

over to me and gave me a fierce hug.

Her voice trembled, even though her hands didn't. "You could make friends here."

Thank God she was hugging me too tightly to see me roll my eyes.

The last place we lived, somehow, someone found out about Dad. I don't know how, because I sure as shit didn't tell them. After that, friends were low on my list of requirements.

Still, I knew what she wanted to hear. "Yeah. Of course."

"You don't have to spend your whole life reading. You can go out. Be around other people more. Go to parties."

"I can't wait."

My voice sounded falsely high. Too optimistic.

What Mom didn't understand, what she had never understood, was that I didn't want those things. Even if I knew how to make new friends, I was happy where I was. At home with a book.

Mom was a palliative care nurse—one of the best in the country. Which was a fancy way of saying she took care of rich people who were dying.

She had an important job and she was amazing at it. I knew she felt guilty about moving us around so much, but it wasn't her fault. A single mom did what she had to.

And an introverted, book-loving loner like me did what she had to do, too. I gave my mom an I-love-you-but-back-off hug and then retreated to the bedroom.

The garage apartment came furnished in fancy-shmancy, rich-people guesthouse luxury. So I kicked off my Converse and spread my Hufflepuff blanket out on the velvet chaise lounge before curling up with the box. I sliced it open with the very tip of my scissors. No way I'd risk scratching the cover.

Since I'd been stalking the Chuck Wallace blog tour, I'd seen the cover a ton of times—it featured Kane, standing in profile, wearing his black leather duster, his blackthorn blasting rod in his hand.

I traced the line of his arm before flipping the book over. There were no words printed on the back—only an outstretched feminine hand and the fluttering hem of a petal-covered skirt. It was as if Kane were watching a woman leave. Would this be the book I'd been waiting for? Well, me and every other female reader. Would Kane finally get a love interest?

I eased the book open to read the blurb on the front cover flap.

You don't want to read this book.

Sure, maybe you're one of the millions of Dark Worlders who've read the first four books. It might be too late for you.

But in case you're not one of those fools, I'll bring you up to speed.

The Kingdoms of Mithres are a mess. The High King died a year ago. As far as everyone knows, he doesn't have an heir. Since then, the seven remaining High Courts have been duking it out for power. The Curator—the one person who could restore the balance of power—went looking for the lost heir and hasn't been seen since. Rumor is she crossed over to your world to search there.

But me? I've got bigger problems. Closer-to-home problems. A princess of the Red Court has been kidnapped. If I can find her and get her to Saint Lew in time for her wedding, the reward is substantial—buy-my-own-private-island substantial.

Maybe I'll even retire from this life of thieving, cheating, and bounty hunting I've been doing since my mom died when I was thirteen. Then I wouldn't have to spend every waking second looking over my shoulder.

If I'm going to save the princess, I need to stay one step ahead of everyone else. And ten steps ahead of Smyth, his pack of hellhounds, and his army of Sleekers who guard the thresholds between this world and the Dark World.

Oh, by the way, Smyth killed my mother, the High Queen. He's been hunting me ever since.

Why, you ask? Because I'm a Dark Worlder.

I'm a changeling. A human, swapped as an infant for the High Queen's own dying Tuatha baby. Which, coincidentally, also makes me the missing heir everyone is looking for.

How can I be a Dark Worlder changeling and the missing heir to the most powerful magic legacy in the Kingdoms?

This is Mithres, where the thread of magic connects every living being, where the Tuatha practice elemental magic you can't even imagine, where Sirens swim the oceans and dragons soar the skies.

Here, anything is possible.

I read the words before closing the book and squeezing it tight to my chest. Yeah. Hugging that book brought me more comfort and joy than hugging my mom. A greater sense of peace. Of belonging.

Mom would never get that. But I never even questioned it.

I'd lived a thousand lives through books. I'd had adventures she couldn't even imagine. The world between the pages of a book was as real to me as this world was.

Of course, I didn't know then what I know now. I didn't know that the world of Kane the Traveler really was real. I didn't know that in that world, I was more powerful than I could ever imagine.

And I never dreamed it was real for my mother, too.

Excerpt from
Book Five of The Traveler Chronicles:
The Traveler Undone

Sure, I have a binding name, but if you're stupid enough to ask me what it is, I don't want to work for you. Most people just call me Kane the Traveler.

I'm a smuggler, a thief, and a wand for hire.

I've never started a fight I couldn't win or broken a law that wasn't meant to be bent. I fight hard, but dirty — for the right price.

If you need me, just ask around in the sleaziest parts of town and in the seediest bars — the kinds of places no one wants to walk into alone. Eventually, you'll meet someone who knows how to summon me. But conjure me at your own risk.

I can solve almost any problem, but trouble always finds me. And I promise you this: whatever your problems, mine are worse.

CHAPTER ONE

One year later

As a lifelong reader, I'm something of a connoisseur of monsters. Dragons, vampires, hellhounds. I know all their strengths and weaknesses. I know how to defeat them, (Elven-forged steel, ebony stake, run like hell—respectively). But this monster has me stumped. *Mean Girlia Wealthipithica.*

This particular *Mean Girlia Wealthipithica*—Chelsea Banks—is crushing my windpipe with her forearm. She is about to kick my ass, and then hand it back to me in pieces—all sanctioned by the school's Phys Ed program.

I've been in this school only a handful of days, but I already know Chelsea is the queen bee. So far, she's played nice. All smiles, rainbows, and kittens. But I've been in enough dojangs that I know the type. The competitive gleam in her eyes tells me she likes having an excuse to kick ass.

She's also a politician's daughter—and she knows how to play the game.

"I'm sorry, Master Flores," Chelsea says, her eyes wide and innocent. "I can't do it. It just doesn't seem right." Chelsea stands and offers her hand to help me up. "She hasn't been to your weekly Tae Kwon Do classes."

Oh, so she can kick ass *and* kiss ass. No wonder she's

the queen bee.

"Besides…"

"Besides what?" I ask blandly.

She gives me a smile that's the equivalent to a pat on the head. "Besides, you're smaller than I am."

Smaller than her runway-model-worthy five foot ten?

Um, yeah. I'm five four. I don't have a lot of body fat, but every ounce I do have has settled on my ass and hips. Basically, I look like Judy Hops from *Zootopia*. So yeah, my body type is cartoon bunny. But I'm no weakling.

"I can defend myself."

Master Flores looks at me, her gray-capped head cocked to the side pensively. It's like she's never met anyone just trying to fly below everyone's radar long enough to graduate from high school.

Who knows, maybe she hasn't. After all, AIBS is the school of choice for the daughters of politicians, ranching magnates, and rich foreign nationals. And then there's me. The new student, shoehorned in to assuage my mother's guilt over my spotty high school transcript. I'm just trying to be invisible until graduation.

Finally, Master Flores says, "Edena Allegra Keller, step forward."

Someone behind me snorts at the formal pronunciation of my name, and I cringe. It's a lot of name.

I step forward. "Most people just call me Edie."

She gives a tight nod, clearly unimpressed.

She's a tiny woman—several inches shorter than even me—but I can tell she's a badass even without counting the gold stripes on her black belt. But I have counted. There are six of them.

I cross to stand before her and bow. With a name like Flores, she could be from almost anywhere—South or Central America.

Spain. The Philippines. Though her looks and her accent are unusual, I can't pin down either one.

She holds out her hand.

Oookay. I take her hand to shake it, but she clasps both her hands around mine. The fingers of her right hand press hard against the inside of my wrist.

After a very long moment, she releases my hand. "I have seen your transcript."

"Yes, Master." Behind me, the girls snicker. I ignore it.

"You have earned your black belt in Tae Kwon Do."

"Yes, Master." I'd been taking Tae Kwon Do for seven of my seventeen years. It's the one thing I asked for, no matter where Mom's job took us—a decent dojang.

"You could have defended yourself against Ms. Banks."

"Yes, Master."

Chelsea frowns. She definitely doesn't like the idea that I might be better at sparring than she is.

"Then you are a coward."

"No." Not picking a fight with the most popular girl in school isn't cowardice. It's common sense.

"Then show me what you can do." Obviously, common sense isn't something Master Flores understands. "Chelsea, get out the bō staffs."

"Yes, Master," Chelsea coos.

A moment later, Chelsea tosses a bō staff at me. I barely have time to snatch the six-foot length of polished wood out of the air before Master Flores barks, "*Si-Jak*."

"Wait. What?"

I've used a bō staff before. In my old dojang, we'd done forms and sparring with foam bō. But I'd never *fought* with a wooden one.

Before I can protest, Chelsea twirls her bō with flare. She swings the tip toward me, but I get my staff up in time and deflect it away from me.

I'd been okay letting Chelsea fake choke me—I hadn't been in any real danger—but there's no way I'm letting her beat me with a piece of polished walnut. A girl has her limits.

The bō feels solidly familiar in my hands and I spin it around with ease, knocking aside her strikes.

Chelsea's willowy build gives her a long reach, but after only a few minutes of sparring, I can tell she's not as good as she thinks.

We fall into an easy rhythm. Strike, parry, retreat. Strike, parry, retreat.

Every time I deflect one of her blows, her gaze hardens even more. People in power rarely like skilled opponents.

Then Master Flores barks out a word, something I don't quite catch. I pause, glancing at Master Flores, thinking it must be *kumon*, the Korean word for "end."

That moment of inattention costs me. Something in Chelsea changes and her eyes blaze—not with malice but with fierce determination. Instantly, her inexperience falls away and she becomes a skilled fighter.

She spins, feinting to the left then lunging forward to swipe her bō at my legs. I barely manage to leap out of the way, but she brings her bō up with lightning speed, knocking my own staff out of my hands. It clatters to the floor, several feet away.

Which should have ended the match, but Chelsea keeps coming at me.

"What the hell?" I ask.

"Fight me," she growls.

"You won." I stumble back. *What the hell is going on?* "You disarmed me."

She twirls her bō, her gaze cold and distant. "Grab it," she orders.

I take my eyes off Chelsea long enough to look for Master

Flores, thinking she must not see what's happening. But she is standing there, her expression intense, her gaze focused on me.

"Get your bō," Master Flores barks when she meets my eyes.

"I can't reach it."

"You were made to want things beyond your reach," Master Flores says, coldly. "Now grab your bō."

"I can't."

Chelsea feints to the left again, but as soon as I dodge out of the way, she clips my left shoulder. Pain blazes down my arm.

This is bullshit and I've had enough. I'm getting that bō staff.

I drop into a roll, but Chelsea's bō slams down on the ground mere centimeters from my hip.

"Fight me, damn it!" she roars.

An instant later, my bō spins across the floor and slams into my palm, just like a lightsaber propelled by the Force. Except, this isn't Dagobah and I'm no Skywalker.

So what *the hell* just happened?

I don't even have time to worry about it, because Chelsea's right on top of me and not letting up.

"You are useless." Her voice is a low snarl as she swipes her staff to the left. "You may be Untethered, but you are no child of the Kingdoms of Mithres." She sweeps at my calves, knocking my feet out from under me.

I fall onto my ass.

"You have no hope of finding the lost *Ivah*."

I get my bō up just before she slams her staff down, straight at my head.

But even my bō isn't enough to protect me. It splinters beneath the force of her blow. Her staff smashes into my skull with bone-jarring force. My vision blurs and goes black.

Excerpt from
Book Five of The Traveler Chronicles:
The Traveler Undone

I don't like Sleekers very much.

For one thing, they use their magic as a weapon.

Okay, I knew that sounded ironic coming from someone who got in as many fights as I did. But when I used magic in a fight, it was to protect myself or someone I love. Occasionally it was to protect someone who hired me to do it.

It was never—never—to impose my will on someone else. It was never because I was a control freak who thought things had to be done my way or else.

And it sure as hell wasn't because I wanted more power than I already had.

I was powerful enough, thank you very much.

As far as the Council of Sleekers was concerned, there was no such thing as too much power…as long as it was all in their hands.

CHAPTER TWO

I wake up, flat on my back, staring at the fluorescent lights of the gym.

What the hell just happened?

I just had the shit beat out of me by Chelsea-freakin'-Banks! While she was muttering a stream of utter nonsense. Except it wasn't nonsense—it made sense to me. At least some of it had. Had she suffered some kind of psychotic break? Had she been possessed by demons?

Given the things she'd said, demons seemed more believable. If, you know, I believed in that kind of thing. Which—despite my reading habits—I did not.

I cautiously push myself up onto my elbows. I feel a little woozy, but that's it. I raise a hand to the crown of my head expecting to feel a knot, but there's nothing.

I hear an unfamiliar voice say, "Can you call her mother?"

That gets me to my feet, because the last thing I need is my mother freaking out.

Most of the other girls are waiting by the gym doors, like they can't wait to make a run for it. Chelsea's surrounded by a cluster of concerned-looking girls. Like *she's* the one who's been traumatized.

The school nurse has pulled one girl aside and is obviously about to send her off to the office.

"Wait!" I step forward, surprised that I'm as steady on my feet as I am. "Don't call my mom. I'm fine."

Nurse Graw, who I met the first day of school, hurries over, a sympathetic frown on her face. Master Flores is standing by the door, her expression unreadable. Turning to the other girls, she waves them out. "You may go change."

Only Chelsea looks at me before leaving the room.

"How are you feeling?" Ms. Graw asks.

I rub at my forehead again. "Okay, I guess."

"But you don't want me to call your mom?"

If Mom knew I'd been hit on the head with a bō staff, she would freak.

"I don't want to bother her at work," I fib. "Why don't you check me out for signs of a concussion? If you think I'm okay, I'll just tell her about it tonight."

I give Ms. Graw my most winning smile.

Frowning, she pulls out one of those little flashlights and shines it in my eyes.

"You look okay. Any nausea?"

I follow the light with my eyes. "No."

She flicks the light off. "From what Master Flores says, one of your classmates caught you when you fainted, so you didn't hit your head very hard."

"When I fainted?" I ask. "Is that what they're calling it?"

This is bullshit.

I get the crap beat out of me by the school's most powerful and influential student and they're going to look the other way? I want to say something. I'm itching to say something.

But what? The truth is, I feel fine. I'm not hurt. Chelsea may be a bitch, but she didn't do any lasting damage. And if I throw a fit, who is it going to hurt?

Not Chelsea. Not that weirdo Master Flores.

No, it'll hurt me. And my mom.

The reason Mom accepted this job in Austin is because the daughter of her patient got me admitted to this school on scholarship. AIBS is one of the top private prep schools west of the Mississippi. Spending my junior year here will grease the wheels of my college applications. But not if I throw a fit about Chelsea Banks.

I know how these things work. Teachers and school admins are no more immune to mean girls than the rest of us. Maybe less. If I demand she be punished, her dad—the governor—will just come down here and shit all over my credibility. Or maybe he'll have an army of lawyers do it for him.

So I let it go. There's no point in making waves for Chelsea when it's my boat that will end up capsized.

When I head out of the gym to go change, there's a girl waiting just outside the doors. She has pale, freckled skin and bright red hair dyed with chunky black strips. She's like Emo Strawberry Shortcake. She's dressed in the same yoga pants and tee that I'm wearing, so she must have been in the Tae Kwon Do class, but I don't remember seeing her before.

"You're okay?" Her voice is high-pitched and delicate… and just as cute as the rest of her.

"I'm Brena," the girl says, holding out her hand and smiling.

I shake it. "I'm Edie."

"Yeah. I know." She blushes, like she's said something she didn't mean to give away. "I mean, in a school this size, everybody knows when someone's new, right?"

So far, she's the only person I've met who seems like a real person and not just a walking Instagram feed.

"You weren't out long. If we hurry, we'll have time to change before the next class." She flashes me a smile as we head for the changing rooms. "So Master Flores says you're a real Tae Kwon Do badass. Like a black belt, right?"

"Yeah." Second degree black belt, but I don't correct her. I don't want to be that person.

Besides, now that I'm not stressing about a head injury anymore, those moments right before Chelsea knocked me out are circling around in my mind.

I shove aside my baseline WTF reaction and think through what happened.

What had Master Flores said? *You were made to want things beyond your reach.*

What did she mean by that? And why does it sound familiar?

As for the rest, the stuff Chelsea said? That I definitely remembered. *You may be Untethered, but you are no child of the Kingdoms of Mithres.*

The Kingdoms of Mithres. The Traveler Chronicles are set in the Kingdoms of Mithres.

Does Chelsea Banks even know what they are? She does not strike me as a hard-core fantasy fan. If she was going to have a breakdown, I'd have expected her to be yelling about shoes or K-pop.

Brena reaches for the door to the dressing room, but I stop her, putting a hand on her arm. "When Chelsea and I were sparring, did you hear what she said to me?"

Brena looks startled by my question, but shakes her head. "No. I...I wasn't very close to you."

Which explains why I don't remember seeing Brena until I walked out of the gym.

Before I can press her for more details, she slips into the dressing room. Chelsea and all the other girls from the class are changing already.

When Brena and I walk in, Chelsea gives me this look like I'm a slug on the sidewalk. Then she leans over to one of her minions and whispers. The other girl titters.

I don't need this shit. People like Chelsea Banks are so

not worth my angst.

I walk right past them to my locker and put in the combination. Thirty-six right. Seven left. Sixteen right.

The lock pops open. See? Ignoring them is easy.

Except my clothes are gone. The locker is empty.

Giggles erupt behind me.

Of course, it's not just my clothes that are missing. It's my backpack. My cell phone. My school-issued iPad.

Shit.

It's been in my possession less than forty-eight hours.

I whirl around. "Where are my clothes?"

"Is there a problem?"

"Yeah, there's a problem. Where's my stuff?"

"Have you looked in your locker?" Chelsea asks, all dewy-eyed innocence.

Behind her, one of her minions giggles. Another kicks the giggling girl, as if she's honestly afraid the giggling is going to give them away. These are real mental giants I'm dealing with.

I fling the locker door open and gesture. "Yeah. I checked my locker. It's empty."

"Are you sure that's the right locker?"

The chime rings, signaling the end of the class. Suddenly, I'm just done. I've had it. Forget flying under the radar.

I stalk across the changing room aisle and get right in Chelsea's face. "I'm done playing your games. You want an easy target? Find someone else. So you thought it was funny to go all psycho when we were sparring and hurl some random insults at me. Whatever. But you took it too far when you knocked me out with the bō. I could have been hurt. And stealing my stuff? That's against the law. And don't think I won't press charges. Because—"

"Stealing your stuff?" Chelsea sneers. "Like I'd want your cheap-ass stuff. And I didn't knock you out. You fainted."

"After you hit me in the head."

Just for an instant, Chelsea's bravado flickers. It happens so fast, I almost don't see it. A spark of confusion. She doesn't know what I'm talking about.

Then she rolls her eyes. "Whatever. You fainted."

"I didn't faint," I insist, even though my mind is reeling and I'm not really talking to her. "You broke my bō. You hit me in the head and knocked me out."

She shoves past me. "I didn't even touch you."

Despite her words—and the way she shoves past me—there's panic in her voice. Not because she's afraid she hurt me, but because she knows she didn't.

I can see it in her eyes. She believes she's telling the truth.

Suddenly, I'm the one freaking out. I grab her arm. "What did you say to me when we were sparring?"

"Let go of me, you freak."

She wrenches her arm, but I cling to it like a lifeline.

"When we were sparring. What did you say to me? Did you say I was untethered? Did you say I was a child of the Kingdoms of Mithres?"

Her eyes are wide now, her gaze fearful. "I said you were a social climbing weirdo and you would never fit in here."

I let her go. The other girls—Chelsea's followers and the awkward bystanders—grab at their clothes, tugging on shirts and zipping up skirts.

Dazed, I sink onto one of the benches.

When the chime signals the beginning of the next class, everyone has cleared out.

Alone, I search the dressing room until I find my stuff. It's in locker number 00. Some imaginative person wrote the letters *L* and *SER* on either side of the zeros. Chelsea's minions can't spell for crap, because I'm guessing they thought they were spelling *loser*, not *looser*. Idiots.

Not that I care.

Their opinion of me matters a lot less now than it did fifty-five minutes ago.

Chelsea and I have completely different memories of what happened in the gym.

I remember sparring with her until she went all freaky weird and called me Untethered and a lot of other crazy shit. And then she broke my bō and knocked me out. She thinks she called me a misfit and then I fainted.

There's no way both of us are right.

I can't let Chelsea or her friends know they've gotten to me, so I try to look cheerful and serene as I go to my next class, but inside, I'm wailing.

Because there's only one logical explanation for why Chelsea and I have different memories of what happened in the gym—one of us was hallucinating.

And, since everyone else remembers Chelsea's version, chances are, it's me.

Excerpt from
Book Five of The Traveler Chronicles:
The Traveler Undone

Demons aren't very smart. And they do not play well with others. You never see more than two of them working together.

So when I rounded the corner and saw a pair of Vargon ice demons standing between me and the exit, I wasn't worried.

"Surrender," one hissed. "You're outnumbered."

"I'm outnumbered? By two demons?" I shook my head. "I've been fighting demons since I was twelve. I can do this in my sleep."

The male launched himself at me. I raised my blasting rod. This was almost too easy.

Then something hard smashed down on the back of my head. An instant later, everything went dark.

I woke up with my head throbbing and my muscles screaming. The room was dark, but from a distant corner, I could hear the scratch of demon claws on concrete.

Huh. Guess I couldn't fight demons in my sleep after all.

CHAPTER THREE

As of last weekend, Mom and I share a six hundred and eleven square foot "guesthouse" located behind the Buford mansion owned by Mom's latest patient.

I've been home from school about ten minutes when Mom strides across the back lawn of the mansion toward the guesthouse. Mom works long hours, but tonight Mr. Buford is leaving for D.C. and she's going with him. It's not surprising that she wants to squeeze in a little time with me before she leaves, but after the day I've had, I'm not ready to deal with her yet, so I take sanctuary in the shower.

The water is still heating up when she knocks on the bathroom door.

"Everything okay?" she asks.

"Great!" I blurt.

Please don't let her have heard about the fainting spell. Please, please, please.

"I got sweaty in gym and need a shower," I call out.

"Okay," she answers.

In the shower, I let the water wash over me and my *please, please, please* mantra gives way to a stream of curse words so long and repetitive, I wish I knew more languages to cuss in. #Lifegoals.

But the scalding blast of water isn't enough to sear away

the panic that's been building inside me all day. No matter how you slice it, hallucinations aren't good. Especially given the fact that my dad has a history of mental illness.

All of Dad's mental stuff, it wasn't the kind of thing you see in those "Talk to your doctor about…" ads on TV. Not to minimize any of that stuff, but Dad's sickness was full-blown, hearing-voices-seeing-demons schizophrenia that struck out of the blue. One day he was fine. The next, he was holding Mom and me at gunpoint and SWAT had to take him out with a Taser.

Which makes all of this that much scarier. Because, hell, yesterday, *I* seemed fine. Mildly antisocial and insecure, with a touch of anxiety. But basically, okay.

Today, not so much.

Whatever happened in class, me freaking out won't help. Mom finding out won't help.

Ever since the incident with Dad, Mom has been "a little overprotective." That's her description, not mine.

She makes your average helicopter parent look like a Buddhist hippie.

For example, two years ago, my high school went into lockdown for like five minutes because a homeless guy tried to panhandle in the front office. Mom pulled me from the school, and I've been in private schools ever since.

So if she found out about this, she would lose her shit.

By the time I get myself together enough to face her, the water is icy. Which, in the heat of Austin, is just fine.

I dry off, then put on clean yoga pants and a T-shirt. I find her in the bedroom, frowning at the open suitcase on the bed.

"That's it. I'm not going," my mother says, reaching into the suitcase and pulling out the folded clothes.

This is what I was afraid of. I take the clothes from her before she can do too much damage to the neat stack. "You have to go."

"I don't want to leave you here alone."

"I'm not alone. And you have to go." I carefully return the clothes to the suitcase. "You knew when you took this job that you'd have to travel with Mr. Buford. At least for the next few months."

She frowns. "I don't know, Edie. It's our first week here. You just started school."

"It's going great," I assure her, but she gives me the stink eye. She knows I have trouble making friends.

She stands over the suitcase, wringing her hands. "I don't like leaving you alone."

"You'll be back by brunch on Sunday."

She's about five seconds away from throwing up her arms and insisting she's going to take a job with hospice so I can have a "normal life." This argument is familiar territory. I don't need Google Maps to help me cross this terrain.

"Don't worry, Mom." I fish my phone out of my back pocket and waggle it at her. "I'm making friends already. I will text them."

"Really?"

"Yes. Everyone there is super nice." Since lightning doesn't strike me where I stand, I spin the lie out a little. "One girl, Brena, said she might even have me over on Saturday night."

"But—"

"Nothing is going to happen to me," I reassure her. "Dad has no idea where we are. And you and I both know he's not looking. There's no reason I can't have a normal junior year."

A normal junior year? After today?

God, if she knew…

Feeling vulnerable, I throw my arms around her in an impulsive hug. She squeezes me so tight, I can hardly breath.

It's crazy how serene and calm Mom can be when she's dealing with a patient. She has this Zen-like acceptance about death's inevitability.

But when it comes to me? When it comes to my safety? She's full-on Mama Bear. All the time.

If her hugs make it hard to breathe, her smothering makes it impossible. Finally, she steps back, surreptitiously wiping her eyes. I think it's the first time she's ever pulled away first.

"I'll be fine," I say again. This is my new mantra. "Other than hanging out with Brena, I'm going to spend the entire weekend on the sofa, eating pizza and rewatching Game of Thrones."

She holds up her hand in protest. "Do we have—"

"Yes, we have pizza in the freezer."

Forty minutes later, I watch as Mom climbs into the limo waiting in the driveway with the Bufords, and I wave goodbye with a smile. It's not until I head back into the tiny apartment, locking the door behind me, that I see what Mom left me on the counter—a slim stack of twenties. A Post-it note rests on top. *Go ahead and order delivery. For luck.*

I'm afraid I'll need it. And not for any of the reasons my mom thinks.

Excerpt from
Book Five of The Traveler Chronicles:
The Traveler Undone

No one likes to work with Vargon Ice Demons. They're untrustworthy, disagreeable, and just plain mean. Besides, they're ice demons. Their breath could freeze your nose off.

Only one guy is enough of an asshole to hire them.

Smyth.

"I know you're there, Smyth, you might as well show yourself," I call out.

For several seconds, I hear nothing but the scuttling of demon claws on concrete. Then, from behind me, I hear the clu-clunk *of expensive oxford shoes. And I catch a whiff of cinnamon.*

Curse the Thread, I hate it when I'm right.

CHAPTER FOUR

L ying to my mother is hard.
 Despite her tendency to hug too tight and hold on too long, she is my best friend. My lodestone. My cool, creamy center when life goes Ding Dong on me. Deceiving her just about kills me. After that, everything else is easy. Well, easy-ish.

Once she's gone, I head into the bathroom. I sit on the floor and pull out a box labeled "Medication" from under the sink. I pull out the prescription bottles, one by one, until I find the Xanax my doctor prescribed for me after my school went on lockdown.

Okay, yeah, it was harder on me than I like to admit. It brought some stuff up. I started having panic attacks. Whatever.

I eye the Xanax for a few minutes before tucking the bottle, unopened, into my messenger bag. I'm panicky, but just knowing it's nearby helps. Besides, my therapist taught me a lot of tricks to deal with panic. Logic and reason are my friends here.

First things first. I google "hallucinations."

A quick glance at Web MD is not reassuring.

You know it's a shit day when you're pulling for Parkinson's disease.

I clear my browser history, just in case. Then I make a list. And then another. The first contains questions I need answers to.

- Did I faint or was I knocked out?
- What did Chelsea say to me?
- What does *untethered* mean?
- What the hell is an *Ivah*?
- Why would Chelsea lie to me?

The second is my to-do list. The one that's going to help me hunt down the answers.

The first question, I might need to let go. I have no way of proving Chelsea's bō made contact with my head.

I tuck my feet under my legs, staring at the list, trying to remember who else was in the gym besides Brena who might confirm my version of events.

But here's the weird thing… Okay, the weirder thing…

When I think back, I don't remember anyone else being there.

I remember Chelsea growling and swinging her bō. I remember Master Flores, her expression fierce. I remember my bō staff, laying several feet away and out of reach…and then sliding across the floor into my hand. But that's it.

Me, my bō, Chelsea, Master Flores. Everything else is just a blur. I'm chasing down a memory that's slipping further away.

So at the top of my to-do list, I write down, *Talk to Master Flores*.

I don't know what to think about Master Flores. She seemed frustrated with me. Disappointed, even. But why would she care about a student she'd never met before?

Then below that, I write, *And Brena*.

So far, she's the only student I've met who doesn't seem to be under Chelsea's spell. Surely she can tell me something.

The second question on my list…that's pretty much the same. Chelsea's word against mine.

Another question with no answer.

I move down the list. What does *Untethered* mean?

For this one, there is something I can do. I log on to each of the four Kingdoms of Mithres forums.

I've been active on all the Traveler fan forums from the time I was old enough to get online. I followed all the gossip, all the fan theories, all the Easter eggs. Then, in the last book, Wallace left Kane, dead on the Cathedral floor, with the love of his life, Princess Merianna of the Red Court forced to marry another in a last-ditch effort to keep power out of the hands of the series Big Bad, a Sleeker named Smyth.

On a logical, intellectual level, the ending felt wrong. Badly planned. Poorly executed and incomplete. Those were phrases the reviews had used.

On an emotional level, I'd been devastated. Kane had been my hero. His death felt like a profound betrayal. It left a hole in my life that nothing had been able to fill.

The night I finished *The Traveler Undone*, I stayed up until four on the fan forums, confirming what I already knew, what had been said throughout the blog tour leading up to the book's release. *The Traveler Undone* was the last book that would be published in the series.

Before Wallace killed Kane, I used to read lots of fanfic set in the Kingdoms of Mithres. I loved Wallace's unique take on elemental magic—how mages had an affinity to control specific elements from the periodic table, rather than the elements of fire, earth, air, and water. I loved the haughty beauty of the Tuatha, the wicked deviousness of the Sleekers, the sinister intelligence of the Kellas cats, the amiable charm of Sirens. But without Kane there, what was the point?

I hadn't been on the fan forums again since reading the last book. Apparently, not everyone was in it solely for Kane, because there are lots of people still visiting the sites. Thank goodness.

As Kanesgirl345, I post the question: *Have you ever heard the term Untethered Sleeker? What about the lost Ivah (sp?)?*

I don't wait for an answer, but open another tab and Google the term *untethered*. I come up with information about diabetes treatments, instructions for hacking your iPhone, and a self-help book about how to untether your soul. Basically, I draw a blank.

I want to thumb through my copies of The Traveler Chronicles. Unfortunately, all my books are still in storage. This apartment is seriously small. We don't have room for books. We barely have room for people.

For a moment, I consider buying the books electronically, but my account is linked to my mom's. Mom witnessed my grief over the last book and knows I've stayed away from them since then. So if I run out and buy digital copies of all the books at once, she'll know something is up. I'll have to hit a library tomorrow. We haven't even been here long enough for me to get a library card, and the Austin Public Library won't let me log in to check the books out digitally until I've been there in person.

In the end, I go to bed. I lay there a long time with my phone, scanning through posts on Tumblr about the Kingdoms of Mithres, searching for answers no one seems to have.

I'm up long before dawn, prowling the forums again.

This time, there are several answers in the thread.

SmartBookBitch: *Sleekers are like normal Tuatha, but more powerful. They guard the thresholds between worlds. They've been genetically engineered to have these crazy long arms that sprout from their backs. They can reach for anything they want. That's how they make sure that only the things and people they want can cross over from the Dark World.*

TravelerObsessed476: *I think she was asking about the term Untethered Sleeker, not Sleekers in general. Also, genetically engineered? Over countless generations, they were bred by the Curator herself to have the magical will to reach for things no one else could. That's not genetic engineering.*

    SmartBookBitch: *Duh. The Curati curated their bloodlines to make them more powerful and stronger and to give them their Sleeker arms. If that's not genetic engineering, I don't know what is.*

    TravelerObsessed476: *Anyway… The term Untethered appears in an ARC of The Traveler Arrives. When Kane meets the Curator, she gives this prophecy to him: "Beware the Untethered Sleeker of the Dark World. She may be the only one who can find the lost Oidrhe but she brings chaos. She has the power to unlock all the thresholds between the worlds, and you will be unspun."*

I read the line over and over again, playing out my memory of that scene. The Dark World is the world parallel to the Kingdoms of Mithres—the world Kane is from. In the books, the Sleekers are government agents. They guard all the thresholds between the two worlds. They keep Dark Worlders out and kill any who accidently cross over.

Which means there is no "Sleeker of the Dark World" in the books. At least, not one that survives for very long. I seem to remember Smyth killing some random Dark World kid in the first book, but that's the only Dark Worlder who crosses over. Other than Kane himself, whose mom brought him over as a changeling.

I recognize the prophecy, but not the term "Untethered." So I send a message back.

    Kanesgirl345: *ARC?*

By the time my eggs are done and I've eaten, I have a response.

    TravelerObsessed476: *Advance Reading Copy. I'm a*

blogger and I got it from the publisher. I don't think the term Untethered was used in the final version, though.

Kanesgirl345: *What about the lost Ivah?*

SmartBookBitch: *I think you mean lost *Oidrhe**

Kanesgirl345: *???*

TravelerObsessed476: *Oidrhe is Gaelic. Aloud, it sounds kind of like I've fah.*

I Google it, because that seems unlikely.

Still, TravelerObsessed476 and SmartBookBitch are right. According to the Irish guy Google pulls up, *Oidrhe* sounds like *I've fah*. And it means heir.

By the time I glance back at the forum, TravelerObsessed476 and SmartBookBitch are going at it.

TravelerObsessed476: *But we still don't know what Untethered means.*

SmartBookBitch: *That's obvious. Untethered means that this person isn't tethered to the Dark World or the Kingdoms of Mithres. He or she is a child of both worlds.*

TravelerObsessed476: *How is that obvious?*

SmartBookBitch: *A child of the Dark World who could unspin the magical threads of Kane's fate must belong in the Dark World and the Kingdoms of Mithres.*

TravelerObsessed476: *No, the prophecy says Kane will be unspun. Not that this person has the power to unspin him.*

SmartBookBitch: *It's implied.*

The dueling ellipses on the screen tell me they're both typing. I log out. I've seen enough flame wars on the forums to know this isn't going to end anytime soon or give me the answers I need.

Some fans think the prophecy means the Child of the Dark World has the power to kill Kane. Some think that the Dark Worlder was supposed to change his fate, to make him king. Most fans think the prophecy is just a clunky red herring, in a crappy ending to an otherwise great series. After that prophecy, the Curator disappears. No Child of the Dark World shows up. And Kane is killed by an unknown assassin who is never brought to justice.

All of which makes Chuck Wallace one of the most hated authors in the world.

Which is neither here nor there. I can't just sit in the apartment obsessing, so I head to school.

The Bufords live on an estate near Lake Austin, not too far from downtown. I ride my bike through the neighborhood, cross over Lamar at Windsor, and then catch a bus up to an area of town called The Triangle, where AIBS is located. By the time I hop off the bus, I'm running late. I dash to the academics building and make it to calculus just before the bell chimes.

Chelsea and her minions snicker.

Brena offers me an encouraging smile, though, so I go to the back of the room and sit next to her. "I didn't know you had this class," I whisper.

Brena just shrugs. Chelsea turns around to give me another one of her "you're crazy" stares. I ignore her. I officially have bigger problems.

I try talking to Brena at lunch, but she can't tell me what actually happened.

After lunch, I swing by the campus gym one more time, but I still don't see Master Flores. But that's not surprising, since the Tae Kwon Do classes are held only on Thursday. Phys ed rotates through a schedule of things like yoga, kickboxing, and tennis.

It's not until I'm leaving the gym that I think to Google how to buy an ARC.

Except—holy LEGO Batman—a signed copy of Chuck Wallace's *The Traveler Arrives* goes for over eight hundred bucks on eBay. I do not have that kind of money to spend.

I dig deeper and it turns out there's an ARC on display at

Book People as part of the Texas Book Festival.

I look up the directions. Book People is only a few stops away on the bus I'm already taking home.

There's no question. Of course I'm going.

I had been begging Mom to take me to a Chuck Wallace book signing since…forever. Mom was always a firm pass on any of the hard-core fan stuff.

After the incident with Dad, Mom had waged an all-out war on my love of fantasy, particularly The Traveler Chronicles.

In her mind, Dad's massive psychotic break with reality was linked to his love of fiction. She seemed to think my love of reading was a sign I might be similarly unhinged.

I won't lie. That thought occurred to me, too.

Was there something wrong with me because the friends I met in the pages of a book were more real to me than the simpering, Snapchat obsessed girl who sat in front of me in trig?

Why did I love my book boyfriend more than any guy I'd ever met in real life?

The Great Book War—as I had come to think of it—ended in a knock-down, drag-out fight between my mom and me. One in which she'd literally torn apart my copy of The Fellowship of the Rings, ripping the pages from the spine and stomping on them as they fell to the ground.

It's the only time I've seen my mom completely lose her shit. The only time.

But that moment was when I won the war. I stood there, watching her destroy my beloved book that Dad had given me for my previous birthday, the last gift I'd ever gotten from him.

It broke me. But it broke her more.

After that, we never fought about books again. We barely even talked about them. She knew she'd crossed a line.

We both did.

She could never understand why I loved being in a book

more than I loved being with her. And I could never understand what was supposed to be so flippin' great about the real world.

So when she'd told me we were moving to Austin, neither of us mentioned that an alternate Austin was the setting of The Traveler Chronicles. Or that I could finally make my pilgrimage to Book People. Maybe she just assumed that The Traveler Chronicles didn't have me in their grasp anymore. Until yesterday, she was right.

Excerpt from
Book Five of The Traveler Chronicles:
The Traveler Undone

"What do you want?" I asked. I'd be tempted to spit on those
fancy shoes of his, but I didn't have time for formalities.

"I want what anyone who contacts you wants. I want to hire
you to do a job." Smyth smiles and the already cold room drops
another thousand degrees.

"Too bad," I snarled. "I'm not a Vargon Ice Demon. I won't
work for just anyone."

The demon behind me scuttled closer. Smyth waved him off.

"Oh, I think you'll work for me."

"Don't you have enough lackeys on the Council of Sleekers
to run errands for you?"

"Oh, this isn't a job just anyone can do." Smyth attempted to
smile again and I prayed the hypothermia would get me before
he bored me to death. "I need someone with your unique talents
and your particular opportunities."

"Maybe you should hire the Curati to breed you an underling.
Someone who can stomach being in your presence."

Smyth ignored my quip and kept pacing. I used the moments
he wasn't facing me to slide my blasting rod down the length
of my sleeve. Between Smyth and the Ice Demons, there was
no way I could blast my way out of this, but this is why I had a
blade on the end of my blasting rod. At the very least, I could
cut through the leather and free my hands.

I knew one thing. Whatever Smyth had planned for me, I
didn't want to face it with my hands tied.

CHAPTER FIVE

I get off the bus at 6th and Lamar in front of the biggest Whole Foods I've ever seen. It's a sprawling metal and glass temple to Austin's hippy roots. I cross 6th Street and head for the three-story building that — according to Maps — houses Book People.

I have to walk around to the other side of the building to reach the entrance. As I approach the door, anxiety tunnels my vision. The burst of excitement I felt when I decided to come here has given way to stomach-churning nausea. Somewhere, just beyond those doors, are the answers I need.

I can feel it in my gut with a clarity that stuns me. Every step in my life has led me here. Mom's career choices, my love of The Traveler Chronicles, even my acceptance into AIBS.

At some point in the past three months, I stepped off a cliff and the gravitational pull of destiny has been hurtling me toward this moment ever since.

I close my eyes, take a deep breath, and shake off that bullshit.

I don't believe in destiny. Or prophecies. Or fate. I never have.

That's the stuff of fantasy novels and fairy tales.

Despite my love of both, I know exactly where all that airy-fairy crap belongs. In my imagination.

Still, I feel compelled to keep moving. I step forward, only to be hit by a wave of dizziness. Like someone painlessly punctured my eardrums and siphoned out the inner ear fluid that keeps me upright. Instinctively, I squeeze my eyes closed and stumble forward until I reach the counter by the door.

"Need something, pet?" says a gravelly voice.

The guy behind the counter has a greasy Duck Dynasty beard. The visible parts of his face are the color and texture of shoe leather. His smile reveals teeth only a shade lighter. He reeks of dust and sour socks. Or maybe it's the store that smells like that. Honestly, I can't tell.

Everything is wrong.

I'm not in the store I glimpsed through the doors. I'm... somewhere else. But where?

I push away from the counter. "I'm good. Thanks."

I scan the room. Book People is one of the largest independent bookstores in the country. I have seen pictures of it online. There should be tables of the latest best sellers and hardcover cookbooks. Dump displays of paperbacks. Cute gadgets, tchotchkes, and toys. I see none of that.

Instead, this place is a dump.

To the left of Creepy Guy's counter, there is a bookshelf of tattered books. Beside that, there's a bookshelf with glass doors which are padlocked, bearing a sign that reads: RARE AND EXTREMELY DANGEROUS. DO NOT OPEN. EVER.

What the...?

What kind of books are extremely dangerous?

I squint at the bookshelf, trying to make out the titles through glass that's foggy with age. As I turn away, I swear something scuttles inside the cabinet. I look back; everything is still.

The rest of the room is small and cramped. There's a rack of dingy clothing. Beside it, there's a table loaded with junk. Over it hangs a sign that reads: DANGEROUS ARTIFACTS. TOUCH AT YOUR OWN RISK. ABSOLUTELY NO RETURNS.

Dangerous? It's a decrepit stereo, a toaster, and a bin of

old flip phones. Between the Goodwill rejects and the creepy locked bookshelf, puce velvet curtains hang in front of a door. I swear, the weight of my glance alone causes dust to rise up off the curtains, as if the dust mites don't even like being looked at.

This cannot be the right place.

Shuddering with disgust, I turned to leave—and bathe in hand sanitizer.

But the second I touch the door, I am hit with another wave of nausea. I brace my hand against the grimy glass and wait for it to pass. Before it does, the door beside it opens and a small figure scurries through. It's my teacher, Master Flores.

Stifling my nausea, I call out, "Master Flores?"

The woman's steps falter, but she doesn't turn around. Instead she glances at Creepy Guy.

She doesn't say anything, just looks at him, and he asks, "You know your way in?"

"Of course," she snaps in her familiar voice.

Acting on instinct, I follow her. I catch up to her just as she walks through the puce velvet curtains.

Hard to believe, but this part of the store is even creepier. It's a maze of towering shelves.

To my left, there's a shelf of rusty car parts labeled, A TOE MOBILE PARTS. In the far corner, I glimpse a staircase leading up to the next floor. To the right, there's another glass-fronted, padlocked bookshelf, except, instead of books, this one contains row upon row of human skulls.

Statistically speaking, the leading cause of death for people my age is car accidents. If I had to guess, wandering into places like this would be number two.

Master Flores veers to the left toward the staircase and I follow her.

"Wait, Master Flores." I sprint to catch up with her. "I have to talk to you."

She whirls on me and I'm surprised by the annoyance in her eyes. Gone is the stoic, Yoda-like martial arts instructor from school. "You," she says in disgust. "Go back. You don't even want to be here."

No one would want to be here without a hazmat suit. Instead of pointing this out, I say, "I have to know what really happened yesterday, in class."

"You don't want to know."

I grab her arm. "Yes! I do."

Master Flores gives me a hard, assessing look, one that I feel deep in my bones, along with the unease that comes when a stranger stares too deeply into your eyes. But I don't flinch. I don't move away, not even when she reaches up and presses the first three fingers of one tiny hand along my temple and the fingers of her other hand on my neck right at my carotid artery. After a second, her eyes drift closed.

"I know what you are," I whisper. "You are one of the Curati."

It's a ridiculous thing to say. The Curati aren't real. They're part of a fictional universe. And yet…somehow it feels like the truth. And somehow, instead of scoffing or shaking me off, her eyes flicker open. "Yes."

She breathes out the word, but I get the feeling that she is not answering my question, so much as confirming something for herself.

Which makes sense, I suppose. The Curati are part of a special race in the Kingdoms of Mithres. An ancient people who can read someone's bloodlines through their pulse. They can feel a person's genetic makeup through their skin. Predict how the thread of magic will weave through a person's life.

I think of the moment back in the gym that first day, when Master Flores grabbed my wrist before handing me the bō staff. Whatever she was searching for then, she has clearly confirmed now.

"Yes," she says again. "You are Sleeker bred. The Dark World is the world of your birth, yet you are meant for more." She gives me a piercing look that I feel all the way to my soul. "You know the truth of this."

She is right. I do know the truth of this.

I *have* always believed that I didn't belong in the world I'd been born to. I *have* always believed I was different. And not just because my father is certifiably crazy. Like, legally, certifiably crazy.

Even before my father's mental illness carved away pieces of my life and my soul, I was different. Even before it sliced my family to shreds and marred my body, I was different. I *am* different.

And she is right about something else as well. I have always believed in the Kingdoms of Mithres. From the first page of the very first Traveler Chronicle, I have believed. I believe in the mighty and awesome power of the High King. In the feckless whimsy of the Red Court. In the wealth and ambition of the Han Court. In the guarded fortress of the Court Arcadia, high in the Eastern mountains. I believe in the great thread of power that connects all living and nonliving things and in the woven magic of time and space.

Most of all, I believe in Kane himself. From the moment I first met him on the page, I believed he was real. Just around the corner, just out of my sight, waiting for me to meet him.

If, on some level, I've always believed in this world, then why is it so hard to imagine that someday I would make it here?

Excerpt from
Book Five of The Traveler Chronicles:
The Traveler Undone

"This afternoon, you have a meeting with the Red Court," Smyth
said, as he paced in front of me.

*I was only mildly surprised he knew about the meeting. The
guy had spies everywhere.*

*"Now that you mention it, I did have somewhere to be today.
Maybe you should check with my secretary the next time you
plan to abduct me."*

*"You will take the job the Red Court offers you. However,
instead of escorting the princess to Saint Lew, you will deliver
her to me, at the Council of Sleekers' detention center on Gull
Veston Island."*

"Funny, I don't remember taking orders from you."

*Smyth whirled around, his expression suddenly furious.
"Your insolence grows tiring, boy."* Then his lips curved into
another one of those creepy smiles. *"Your mother should have
taught you better manners."*

*Rage flooded me, and I bucked against the leather straps
holding me down.*

*This asshole dared to even mention my mother? Five years
ago, he murdered her in front of me and called it justice.*

"Manners," Smyth snapped.

*As he said the word, his extra pair of Sleeker arms
materialized. They were long and thin and sprouted from his
shoulder blades.*

*This was the magic that made Sleekers unique among Tuatha.
His Sleeker arms were the physical manifestation of his will.*

*One of those long, slimy things wrapped around my chest,
holding me to the chair, pinning me more tightly than the leather*

straps ever could.

"You will work for me," he snarled. "Because I have something you want."

Before I could ask what that was, his second Sleeker arm unfurled from behind his back to dangle something before my face.

A flash of gold hanging from a thin silver chain. My mother's medallion.

"Now," Smyth says, "unless I'm very much mistaken, this medallion is your most prized possession. Bring me the princess and I'll return it to you."

He was right. That medallion was the most important thing I owned. But I still wasn't going to trade the princess for it. There was nothing in the world that would make me work for Smyth.

Besides, he was wrong about my meeting with the Red Court. They hired me weeks ago, and the princess was already safely stashed away where Smyth would never find her.

So now all I had to do was figure out how to get my medallion back.

CHAPTER SIX

"Wait, the Kingdoms of Mithres are real?" I ask.

"Yes." She gives a curt nod.

"Like, *real* real?"

At her look of frustration, I make a give-me-a-second gesture.

This can't be right. It just can't be.

I squeeze my eyes closed and suck in a few deep breaths. I must be dreaming. Or hallucinating or something. Because this can*not* be real.

Except...

Except why couldn't it be?

The idea of parallel universes is pretty much accepted scientific doctrine. And it's also true that one of the things most scientists agree on is that there is so much about the world and the universe that we don't know yet. So who's to say you can't walk through the doors of a bookstore in Austin and end up in another world?

"I'm not imagining this? I'm not crazy? I'm really here?"

"Yes. I have said that."

"Oh my God, I have so many questions." Excitement races through me, but it's still not fast enough to keep up with my racing thoughts. "If the Kingdoms of Mithres are real, does that mean other story worlds are real? If I'd opened a wardrobe in

England, would I have ended up in Narnia?"

She gives an impatient wave of her hand. "This is all very complicated. Yes. Your world—the Dark World—and this one, are deeply connected."

"Connected by what?" I interrupt her.

"By the thread of energy that stretches between all living things." She isn't the kind of person who would say, "Well, duh," but it's there in her expression. "The Thread connects all worlds. Stories are magic. Every time one person shares a story with another, that energy grows. It is that power the Tuatha pull from when they do magic."

I take a step back, my mind reeling. "The energy of stories is the magic that connects all the worlds," I say aloud, rolling the idea over in my mind.

When I was ten, when we lived briefly in L.A., Dad took me to Disneyland. Neither of us liked roller coasters, but we loved sitting outside the ice cream shop, watching the constant stream of tiny princesses, couples in matching Minnie and Mickey ears, burly middle-aged men in Star Wars shirts. Total strangers, made friends by their shared love of a story.

Of course the magic of stories is real. Of course it connects all of us.

"But, wait. Is it just my world and this world? Or are there others?"

The Curator gives me an appraising look. Like she's trying to decide if it's worth her time to even answer. "The Thread flows through many worlds."

"Star Wars?"

"Yes."

"Harry Potter?"

"Yes, of course."

"Game of Thrones? Star Trek?" She keeps nodding. "The Walking Dead?" I ask, my voice rising. She nods. "Oh my God.

Those poor people."

"You are missing the point."

"What point?"

"*This* is the story you have a connection to. This is the story you were meant for."

Anticipation skitters up my spine and out along my nerves. "I knew it."

This is why those books spoke to me, why I felt them in my soul. Why reading them was like coming home. Because they were mine in a way no other books were. *Are.*

They *are* mine.

Haven't I always known that, on some level? That I had some deep, gut-level connection to the Kingdoms of Mithres, to Kane's world?

But Kane is dead. Whatever connection I have to this world, it can't involve him. He died at the end of the fifth book.

"Back in class, you said I need to find the lost *Oidrhe*." Now that I know how it sounds, I pronounce it *Iv-fah*, the way she did. "With Kane dead, the lost—"

"Kane is not dead."

"What?"

"Kane is not yet dead."

"What?" I repeat stupidly, as shock tilts the world beneath my feet. It's stupid, I know, that entering another universe didn't surprise me…but this does. "How can Kane still be alive? He was shot at the end of the fifth book. He bled out on the floor of the cathedral. Wallace even said—"

Even as the words are tumbling out of my mouth, I realize how idiotic I sound. It doesn't matter what Wallace—the "writer" of The Traveler Chronicles—has said in interviews. Not if the Kingdoms of Mithres are real. Not if Kane is a real person.

I shake my head. "I don't understand."

"Wallace is merely the conduit for Kane's story. He is not

its creator."

"What do you mean, he's the conduit?"

"The story threads of the universe exist independent of the one who tells them. They are all there. Written in the tapestry of the universe. Storytellers from your world weave those threads into your books, your movies, your video games. Without the thread of magic woven between the many worlds, stories would not exist in the Dark World, and magic would not exist here."

"Wait. Video games? Please don't tell me *Grand Theft Auto* is real."

"I do not know this tale. But have faith. Many storytellers see only the story they want to see. Or they see an incomplete story. A fraction of the whole. Some even glimpse stories that are not meant for them at all. Those stories are told very badly. I do not know why Wallace ended his book the way he did. The story Wallace told is incomplete."

"So Kane's alive? He won't be assassinated at the cathedral in Saint Lew?"

"That I do not know. The thread of Kane's life is woven deeply into the fabric of this world."

"Cut the crap. Is Kane alive? Right now?"

"Yes."

"Then if someone warns him about the assassin, he can protect himself. He'll live."

Master Flores doesn't immediately agree. "Perhaps. But if he is to be warned, it must be by me and at the correct time. Twisting the threads of time is treacherous work. If it is not done with care, an entire life can be unspun."

Unspun did not sound good.

"Edena Allegra Keller, you must promise me—"

"Oh my God! Is that my binding name?"

She sighs. "Edena—"

"It is, isn't it?" I step closer to Master Flores, almost as if she's already used my binding name. As if magic is already weaving me into the story of this world. "How do you know my binding name? You used it then, too, didn't you? Is it like, in my school records? Did you—" I cut myself off.

Master Flores looks ready to strangle me.

"Why don't I just let you finish your thought." I try to contain my smile. I mean, a binding name! How cool is that?

Okay, sure. Anyone who knows it can use it to summon me or bind me to their will. So it's actually a little terrifying. But as long as I don't tell anyone what it is, what could go wrong?

Master Flores seems to be waiting to make sure I'm really done babbling. Finally, she says, "Edena Allegra Keller, you must not tell Kane of the death that fate has woven for him."

And this time when she says my name, I feel a tingle of electricity weave through the air between us.

"If no one tells him, how will he avoid it?"

"Promise me."

"Are you going to tell him?"

"When the time is ripe," she murmurs. "But you must promise not to interfere."

"Only if you promise me you're going to tell him first." Binding name or not, I'm not letting him die.

She narrows her gaze at me.

I narrow mine right back.

"You'll tell him before the day of his assassination," I say, pressing her. "I'll need your binding name to secure the promise."

"Very well." She once again reaches up and puts her fingers to my temple. "My binding name is Mahalia Diwata Flores."

I carefully place my fingers on her temple, mirroring her. I repeat her name, trying to mimic her exact pronunciation.

Finally, she nods. "I give you my word."

"And I give you mine."

The second half of the binding pledge comes easily to my lips, as if I had been swearing oaths in the Kingdoms of Mithres all my life. The magic in the air tightens around us, binding us to the promise.

Or maybe I'm just excited. I am embarking on a grand adventure.

I am in the Kingdoms of Mithres. Kane is somewhere nearby. And I have exacted a promise from a powerful Curati that she will help prevent Kane's assassination.

Even as powerful as she is, I know she's wrong about one thing—it's not my destiny to find the lost *Oidrhe*. Kane is the lost *Oidrhe*. He may not be much older than I am, he may not believe it yet himself, but he is meant to be the High King.

When he claims the throne, he will pull this world back from the brink of civil war. I know it in my soul. Just like I knew I was meant to walk through the doors of Book People and into this world.

For the first time in a very long time, I have a purpose.

If Master Flores is correct and I do have Sleeker blood, then I really was made to want things beyond my reach, to want impossible things. Saving one guy's life and altering the course of destiny seems about as impossible as it gets.

That's good enough for me. This is what I was made for. Saving Kane is my destiny.

Excerpt from
Book Five of The Traveler Chronicles:
A Traveler Undone

After escaping from Smyth and his goons, I went home.

My apartment had so many wards placed around that a hellhound could lift a leg and take a piss on it and still not realize it was there.

I had spent the past six years of my life making sure Smyth could never find it and wouldn't be able to get in even if he did.

Since that was where I'd stashed the princess, I knew beyond a shadow of a dowtless Kellas cat that she was safe.

I was wrong.

CHAPTER SEVEN

B efore I can say anything else, the curtain rustles behind me. And there he is.

Kane.

In the flesh. Living and breathing.

Emphasis on living.

There's no question it's him. From the tips of his scuffed leather work boots to his worn leather jacket, to the scruffy, too-long brown hair, to the sharp intelligence blazing in his eyes, I recognize him. And he's *tall*. Taller than I thought six four would be.

Still, he's not *exactly* what I expect. He's younger than I thought. The jacket's wrong. His hair is the right length, but lighter than I expect. His jaw is lean, with hard edges like Wallace described, but his lips are too full.

My reaction to the sight of him is physical. Visceral.

Like nothing I've ever felt before. Like every cell in my body has been in cryogenic stasis until now and the second I saw him, they all leaped to life and started vibrating.

It's not just that I'm glad he's alive. It's not just that he's real, or that he's actually here. It's more than that.

It's that I've been in love with him since I was eleven. He's everything I've ever wanted in a guy. He's smart and clever. Strong, but sometimes vulnerable. He's an outcast, like me.

He's been abandoned by his father, like me. He's cynical and bitter, but never enough to outweigh the goodness at his core. He's tough. A fighter. But in the end, he always, *always* does the right thing.

The biggest difference between us is that his life has thrust the chance for greatness upon him. I've never had the chance to do anything that's of value to anyone.

If he lives long enough to take the throne, he will rule a vast magical kingdom. If I make it back to my world...? I'll just go back to English class.

Jesus, my life feels small sometimes. Insignificant.

But it feels bigger with Kane here.

Not just here. But alive.

He is not going to die. Not on my watch.

For a second, he just stares at us, his scowl deepening until he practically growls, "What are you doing here, Curator?"

I gape at Master Flores. I'd figured out she was one of the Curati, but...

"You're *the* Curator? As in, the most powerful of all the Curati?"

Kane still glares at Master Flores—holy shit, the Curator! "You know I'm not magically bound by protocols of high court. I'm not going to bow and grovel and tell you how your very presence makes my soul blossom or any of that other shit. So you might as well just tell me why you're here."

Master Flores wraps her fingers around my arm and tugs me forward, presenting me to Kane. "I bring you an Untethered Sleeker."

For the first time, I feel the weight of his gaze. It's not so much that he didn't notice me before, but rather that he didn't think I was worth his attention. Now he looks at me, taking a few steps closer and studying me with the tilted head. I shiver under the intensity of his gaze, my pulse racing. I'm afraid he can read everything in my eyes. My hopes and dreams. My deepest fantasies. My very soul. I can hardly breathe when he looks at me, because—OMG!—he's Kane-the-frickin'-Traveler! And he's looking at me. And—

"A bit stubby, isn't she?" he says, arching an eyebrow at Master Flores. "For a Sleeker, I mean."

Wait. What?

Kane the Traveler just looked me up and down, gazed intently into my eyes, seemed to assess my very soul. And all he could come up with was stubby?

Stubby?

"Perhaps," Master Flores says.

"I'm five four," I interject. "Which is average." I definitely prefer my own cartoon-bunny analogy.

They both ignore me.

"I have felt the Sleeker blood coursing through her veins." Master Flores continues. "And she is Untethered, something even you cannot dispute, since she stands before you now."

Since I'm still unsure about this whole Untethered thing, I hold up a finger to interrupt. "Can someone—"

Kane ignores me. "I don't dispute it. But I don't need a Sleeker, Untethered or otherwise. I don't need someone who can cross freely between worlds, because I'm not going to waste my time trying to cross over to the Dark World to search for the lost *Oidrhe*. The lost *Oidrhe* is a myth. If she was still alive, you'd have found her by now."

"Wait, you think the lost *Oidrhe* is a girl? That's insane. Kane is obviously the lost *Oidrhe*!"

This time they both turn and glare at me. Kane even rolls his eyes.

"Your doubts are irrelevant," the Curator says to Kane. "Smyth is amassing power and will act soon. Neither of you will be safe until—"

This time, Kane doesn't just cut her off. He grabs her by the shoulders and gives her a little shake. "Don't you dare say—" He stops abruptly to glare in my direction. Then he releases Master Flores's shoulders. "I will not discuss this here. Not in public. And not in front of this scrawny Dark Worlder."

He abruptly lets go of Master Flores and walks past her. She follows him.

I scurry along behind them. We take the same path as before, but this time we end up at a staircase. Kane pauses in front of it. He raises his hands before him and traces a shape in the air. A faint pulse of energy surges through the narrow aisle.

"Oh! I know what you're doing," I exclaim. "You just pulled a rune to take down your wards."

Kane pauses long enough to give me a "well, duh" look.

I can feel the heat rising in my cheeks. "It's just...I've read about that."

"Seriously? This is the Sleeker that's going to help me find the *Oidrhe*?"

The Curator bristles defensively. "She still needs training."

"Obviously."

"You—" He points to the Curator. "Can come with me. We have things to discuss. But you..." This time he points to me. "Stay here."

"What?" I protest. "You really expect me to just stay here? That's not—"

But before I can finish the sentence, he and the Curator are gone. I try to follow them, but the wards snap back into place, like there's a wall of Jell-O between me and the stairs. When I lean into it, it gives, but no more than an inch or so. And when I stop pushing, I spring back again.

Well, this sucks.

I can't believe I actually met Kane.

My hero. My idol. My book boyfriend and literary soul mate.

And he thinks I'm stubby. And maybe scrawny. And apparently, a little incompetent.

Ugh.

Not that I expected anything…I don't know…romantic or lightning bolt-y. After all, Kane's going to fall in love with Princess Merianna of the Red Court—one of the most beautiful, sophisticated, powerful girls in his world. My expectation for romantic chemistry between us was zero, but still… Let's just say, that did not go as planned.

Not that I had a plan. I didn't imagine I'd run into Kane, here of all places, in this dump, where… Oh. This must be the building his loft is in.

In the books, he lives above an old bookstore called The Volume Arcana. The dumpy store downstairs must be that bookstore. Wow. Wallace really oversold the place.

The minutes tick by. What could be taking so long? I pull my phone out and check the time. I reached Book People around seven. It's not even eight yet. I've been in the Kingdoms of Mithres less than an hour.

Also, I have several unread texts from my mom.

Stopped at DD for an afternoon snack.

Then there's an awkward selfie of my mom holding my favorite glazed chocolate cake donut and an iced coffee.

Shit.

I hadn't thought about my mom. Not even once. I feel bad, since she's obviously trying her best to not be helicopter-y, to trust me to be safe. She would not be okay with this.

I type a quick **Bring me one?** and add a kiss-blowing emoji. It's not until I hit send and watch my phone struggling to deliver the message that it hits me. Duh. No cell service in an alternate reality.

I swipe left on the texts and see that they came through in a cluster just before I entered Book People.

I stare at the picture of my mom for a long minute before turning off my phone and sliding it back in the pocket of my messenger bag. Seeing my mom—glimpsing the real world— stirs up a mess of crap inside me.

Like the fact that I don't know... I don't really know...that this is all really real. It feels real. I believe it's real. But maybe my dad believed it was real, too.

But I can't think like that. That's a rabbit hole I've been avoiding for the past four years. I'm a pro at shutting down those thoughts.

Assuming this is real, I'm in another world. How am I going to get back? What if I *can't* go back?

What if...what if I'm trapped here?

That would... Well, that would really suck.

Being in the Kingdoms of Mithres is cool and all, but I don't want to *live* here. Plus, just being here is illegal. Most of the Tuatha like Dark Worlder stuff—artifacts, movies, etc.—but hate actual Dark Worlders.

So much, in fact, they created the Sleekers, a whole new race, to keep them out. And to track them down and kill them if they happened to make it across into the Kingdoms of Mithres.

So yeah, if I'm stuck here, I probably won't be stuck here for very long, because I'll be hunted down like the fugitive I am.

Also, what about my mom? All she would know is that she left for a weekend and I vanished. She would assume I was kidnapped and left in a ditch somewhere, dead. Or at the bottom of a pit rubbing lotion on my skin like that chick from *Silence of the Lambs*.

She would be thinking that right now if she wasn't out of town.

Whatever else happens, that gives me at least thirty-six

hours to get this sorted out.

At the beginning of the last book, Kane is hired to find a princess, Merianna, who was kidnapped by Smyth on the way to her wedding. After Kane rescues her, she hires him to escort her the rest of the way. They travel incognito and fall in love. Kane finally accepts that he is powerful enough to unite the Kingdoms of Mithres and they decide to rule the kingdoms together. However, when they enter the church, an assassin is waiting for them. Kane throws himself in front of the princess, which saves her, but he is killed.

Is there a way to honor my binding promise to the Curator *and* save Kane? After all, I don't have to actually tell him about the assassin. I just have to keep him out of that church.

I can save Kane. I know I can.

I may be insignificant and basically friendless in my world, but here, I can do something important. I can change Kane's fate.

Which sounds like a great plan, until I remember I'm still trapped in this warehouse. I hear a scuttling sound off to my left. I whirl around but see nothing but a flicker of movement in the shadows.

Oh God. I hope that's a rat.

Okay, there's a thought I never imagined having.

I call out, "Hey, Curator! I think there's something down here with me."

God, I hope that's a normal rat and not a huge, Dark-Worlder-murdering rat.

My whole body shivers with revulsion.

Okay, let's think this through.

What are my options?

Option 1: I can go back out into the store and get help from the store clerk.

Who absolutely is the kind of guy who has a dress made

out of human skin.

So that's a big no.

Option 2: I leave the store and hope that when I walk back through the doors, I end up back in my world.

But if I walk through the doors and don't go home, then I'm out on the streets by myself, with no way to defend myself from hellhounds or any of the other scary bad guys who prowl the streets of the Kingdoms of Mithres at night.

So with option 2, I have a fifty-fifty shot of going home or ending up dead.

Option 3: I find a way past Kane's wards.

That's not quite as crazy as it sounds.

The way Wallace described it, the air in the Kingdoms of Mithres is woven thick with a dense web of the threads that connect all things. Pulling a rune draws a specific thread of magic toward you—in this case, the thread of magical protection that surrounds Kane's apartment.

With my eyes closed, I try to remember the motion I saw Kane do.

I open my eyes, press my thumb and forefinger together, and then trace the shape in the air, watching my fingers carefully, waiting for a pulse of energy, a blur of magical light. Anything.

I get nothing.

No zing. No zap. No glimmer.

I try again. And a third time. Just in case, you know, that's the charm.

Still nothing.

Well, shit.

I guess it was a bit much to expect that I'd be able to do magic forty-five minutes after crossing into the Kingdoms of Mithres.

Just for giggles, I pretend it's the Room of Requirement and walk back and forth three times, hoping to get in. Big surprise, that doesn't work either.

Then, because there's no way I'm sitting down on this floor, I lean my back against the Jell-O wall.

This sucks.

The universe is being completely unreasonable.

Clearly, I'm here for a reason.

Saving Kane is up to me.

All I want is to restore justice to the universe and prevent the Kingdoms of Mithres from descending into the chaos of outright civil war. Why is that too much to ask?

Why can't—

That's when I fall backward onto my ass.

Excerpt from
Book Five of The Traveler Chronicles:
The Traveler Undone

The building that houses The Volume Arcana was designed and built in 1943 by a Sleeker architect by the name of Williams Dodgly. Dodgly was obsessed with strengthening his connection to the Dark World. He imbued every pebble of mortar, every beam, and every brick with magical energy. Then he planted the building right on top of the most volatile threshold between worlds.

Sometimes, I have to actively work to keep Dark Worlder artifacts from just floating through the front door.

CHAPTER EIGHT

O ne second, the barrier of Kane's wards is solid at my back, the next, it's gone.

No rune magic, no spark, no hint at what I did to bring it down. It's just gone.

Huh.

Well, I'm not going to look a gift horse in the mouth. I stand, rubbing the sting out of my backside, and tiptoe up the stairs.

According to Wallace, Kane lives on the third floor.

The first two floors are The Volume Arcana and its storage.

The stairs are uneven heights, the way they are in extremely old buildings. I guess the Kingdoms of Mithres don't have a lot of government inspectors.

As soon as I reach the second floor—which looks like a poorly lit maze of stacked bookcases and crates—I hear it. A noise somewhere between a whimper and a groan. It sounds like it's coming from a wounded animal.

I cringe, squeezing my eyes closed. Do I go forward and try to help or flee, like the coward I am?

I'm about to scurry back to the stairs when a voice groans, "Please. Help."

Screw it.

I may be in the Kingdoms of Mithres. I may be the least powerful person here. But that doesn't mean I'm going to ignore any creature in pain. I pull out my phone, turn on the flashlight, and head toward the voice.

I follow the sounds and find myself facing a large open space with a cage in it. It's about the proportions of a dog crate, but big enough to hold a timber wolf. Or a bear. Or…

Or a human.

I creep closer, shining the light over the shape inside. Nope, not furry. Not a dog. Just a girl, dressed in rags, curled in the corner.

"Hello?" I ask.

There's a groan, followed by a whimper. I take another step closer, shining my light on the side of the cage, looking for a way to open it. The metal is the color of brushed aluminum, but it's faintly warm to the touch. There's a latch on the outside, but there's no lock, so I guess the person inside is too weak to open it.

The mechanism on the latch is a little stiff and I have to ram my palm against it several times before it opens. She does little more than whimper and cry. Her obvious pain stirs a sick, squishy feeling in the pit of my stomach. My fingers stumble as the latch gouges deeply enough into my palm that I bleed a little, but I finally get it.

"Can you get out? Do you need help?"

"Do…I…look…like…I…need…help?"

Wow. It takes a pro to maintain such sarcasm in the face of gasping pain.

"Okay," I say, even though I am already regretting helping her. "Can you take my hand?"

"Do…I…"

"Yeah. Not this again."

I brace one hand on the top of the crate and reach in with my other one to grab her forearm. Her skin is pale, her hand thin and fine-boned, her skin splotchy with burns. Her grasp is surprisingly strong as I pull her from the crate.

She stumbles out to land on the floor, where she lies for a moment. Then, she stands, straightening into a startlingly tall, wraith-thin young woman. Beautiful, but gaunt and grimy. Then, her appearance changes. It's like watching a time lapse photography movie. The wrinkles fall away from her clothes. The dirt vanishes from her face. The burns on her hands whiten and fade. The knots in her hair smooth. For a moment, she's merely pretty. Okay, very, very pretty.

Then her hair itself straightens before springing into thick curls. The pink of her lips deepens to a glossy rose. Her eyebrows smooth into perfect arches.

Within a minute, she has gone from a girl who looked like she lived on the street to a gorgeous creature worthy of the pages of a magazine. She is dressed in a blindingly white shift dress scattered with actual flower petals.

"Whoa."

So this is what an actual fairy princess looks like.

I know who she is. Who she must be.

"You're Princess Merianna of the Red Court."

One of the most beautiful women in the world. An unparalleled master of glamour with the ability to heal anyone (including herself).

Undoubtedly, I'd just witnessed her healing powers. And she'd added a glamour on top to seal the deal. The transformation from wounded victim to glowing princess is some serious, Skywalker Ranch–level special effects.

Except that it's not illusion. It's magic she just did. Right before my eyes.

A second ago, she was wounded. Now she's…

"Hey, are you still hurt? Do you need me to call 911? Or whatever the equivalent is?"

"Do I appear to be unable to heal myself?"

"No." My hands go up in protest. "I'm a big fan of the whole strong female character thing. Obviously. Since I'm a woman. You get it. I know you have the glamour and healing power and all that stuff, but does it really work that quickly?"

I'm babbling. I do that when I'm nervous.

The princess takes a step backward, looking just a little concerned for my sanity. "How do you know of my powers?"

"Um…" Somehow, I don't think she's going to be a fan of the I-stumbled-into-her-world-by-accident-like-Lucy-in-the-fricking-wardrobe version of events. "I've heard of you?" I say tentatively. "You are famous, right?"

This seems to mollify her. She tips her chin up to reveal an even more flattering angle. "Well, yes. I suppose I am."

Whew. Dodged that bullet.

"I owe you a debt of gratitude," she says. "Ask for a boon and I will grant it."

"No, thanks."

She frowns, looking horrified. "Excuse me?"

"I don't need anything." Sure, if I ever need someone to bibbidi-bobbidi-boo me a dress for prom, I'll probably regret not accepting a gift from a fairy princess, but off the top of my head, I can't think of any way a favor from Princess Merianna will help me save Kane.

"Very well," she says, turning to leave.

Except…

While I don't need a favor from her, I do still need to rescue Kane. And I'm sure I could use some help with that.

As soon as I put her and Kane together in the same thought, it hits me.

Book Five starts with the princess being kidnapped and Kane being hired to find her…

Which means…

But she's already heading down the stairs.

I chase after the princess.

"Wait! Hang on!"

She pauses, turning back to me, her lovely brow furrowed. "Hang on to what?"

"What? No. That's just a saying. But, here's the thing—and I need you to trust me on this." My words have tumbled out so quickly, I have to pause to take a breath. "I need you to get back in the cage."

More brow furrowing. "Pardon?"

"See, here's the deal. I'm not supposed to be the person who rescues you. Someone else was supposed to do that. So if you'll just come with me, I'll lock you back in and—"

"You expect me to get back into the crate?"

"Yes! Exactly. Then I'll go get Kane and—"

"But you just freed me."

"Yes, but—"

"And being in there was extremely painful."

I cringe. "Yeah. I was afraid of that. But, once you're back inside, I'll be really fast. I'll just zip right upstairs, find Kane. Then he can rescue you and the story will be back on track."

At least, the good parts of the story.

The budding romance needed to stay intact, but I still needed to find a way to avert the assassination. But I would worry about that later.

The princess was still frowning, but she was looking less confused and more annoyed. "What story?"

"The story." See, this is why she was annoyed. I hadn't explained it properly. "You are destined to fall in love with the man who rescues you. And he's right upstairs."

The princess narrows her gaze, scanning the room. "This man I'm supposed to fall in love with lives here?"

Her tone alone implies that "here" is a rat-infested hovel. Which, in all fairness, it is.

"Not *here* here." I point up. "Two floors up." Her expression of scathing disdain doesn't even flicker, so I add in a few flourishes. "In a loft with contemporary modern decor and a stunning view of downtown."

Okay, that's not exactly how Wallace described it, but Princess Merianna looked like a woman who appreciated modern architecture.

"I find it very unlikely that I would fall in love with any man who lives above a vermin-infested storage facility."

With that pronouncement, she turns away, the skirt of her dress flaring out dramatically, before she sweeps off toward the stairs.

Okay, her bad attitude is really starting to get on my nerves.

I rush after her, bodily throwing myself between her and the stairs.

"You can't leave."

"Are all Dark Worlders this deranged?" she asks.

"No!" I follow her down the stairs, but her legs are longer and she moves *fast*. "I mean, I'm not deranged. I swear."

I break into a run and throw myself between Princess Marianna and the puce curtain. "You have to stay here and meet Kane. I'll introduce you. I won't even make you go back into the cage."

"Dark Worlder, you have neither the power nor the ability to make me do anything, least of all go back into that iron prison. You cannot prevent me from leaving this building and summoning my guards. You do not wish to be haranguing me when they arrive."

"You can't leave!"

Princess Merianna waves her hand in apparent frustration. "No wonder the Dark World is so dark. Your wits are all addled."

And before I can stop her, she marches through the front door of the shop and out into the night.

I rush after her, only to skid to a halt, looking back at the door I just passed through. The door that should have sent me back to Austin.

But it didn't.

Excerpt from
Book Five of The Traveler Chronicles:
The Traveler Undone

I work alone. I've lived alone since I was fifteen. Since loop-hopping with another person is a pain in the ass, I even travel alone.

So do I want a job guarding the princess twenty-four seven for the next three weeks?

No.

But when all seven of the High Courts actually agree on something long enough to ask you to take a job, you do it. Especially when they remind you the Kingdoms are on the brink of civil war. Basically, if the Red Court and the Han Court can agree to marry off their heirs, the rest of the courts will fall in line and accept them as High Queen and King. War will be averted. The Kingdoms will be saved. Nothing will go kaboom.

Besides, someone has to take up the mantle of responsibility and rule the world. I don't particularly care who it is, as long as it's not me.

CHAPTER NINE

"Wait!" I call out to the princess. She's on the corner by now, looking around as if she expects her car to appear out of thin air. "You can't just leave."

"Of course I can," she says, shooing me away as she marches down the street. In my Austin, the streets around Book People were full of shoppers. Here, not so much. "Now be on your way. I don't want you anywhere near me when your stench attracts the attention of a *Barghest*."

"A what?"

"A hellhound," she says with slow exaggerated pronunciation. "A beast that guards the barrier between—"

"I know what a hellhound is."

"Ah! Then you know to avoid them."

Then she raises her hand, her forefinger and middle finger extended, and swipes them through the air. Immediately, a car zips out of traffic—as if by magic—and stops at the curb.

Somewhere a few blocks away, there is a loud thud and a crunch of metal. What sounds like a car alarm goes off. The princess looks in that direction, a frown marring her perfect features.

As she moves to get into her waiting car, she glances back. Master Flores is hurrying toward us. The princess stills, looking longingly at the limo and then at Master Flores. Obviously annoyed, she steps away from the limo. When Master Flores is closer, the princess drops into a florid curtsy and says in a dull voice, "Madam Curator. I am honored by your presence."

There is another thud, another crunch, and another car alarm goes off, this time closer. Something very large is running through the streets toward us, knocking cars out of the way as it comes.

Master Flores scowls at the princess's deep curtsy. "Yes, yes, yes. Now stand up."

From her curtsy, the princess tilts her head to glare at Master Flores. Under her breath, she growls, "You know I cannot."

Ah, this must be part of the binding protocol of the High Courts that Kane mentioned.

More thuds pound down the street, so strong I feel the vibration through the ground.

Ignoring them, the princess continues, "I bow before your wisdom and age. Please gaze upon me and find me worthy of my lin—"

Master Flores grabs her by the arm and drags her to her feet. "I release you from your bonds."

Pulling the princess behind her, Master Flores swoops past me, snagging my arm on her way. Though she is smaller than either of us, she drags us bodily back down the narrow street that runs beside the bookstore, as chaos erupts behind us. "Child, why did you leave the safety of The Volume Arcana?"

I ignore her question and ask one of my own. "Exactly how big are hellhounds?"

From behind us comes the sound of crunching metal and smashing bricks. Shit. Do I even want to know what's coming after us?

I glance over my shoulder.

Yep. Big mistake.

And, no. I did not want to know.

There are two of them and they are huge. They're dogs, but only in the most general sense. They have roughly the girth and weight of a rhino. Their snouts are both too long and too broad to be dogs. Their paws are the size of footstools. Oh, and again, there's the size. I mentioned that, right? Rhino big. Think about that for a second.

Naturally, they're hellhounds. Of course they are.

The alleyway ends in the entrance to the bookstore. The princess tugs at the door, but it doesn't open.

The hellhounds thunder down the alley toward us. Except they don't really…thunder. Oh, there's all the noise, but very little of the speed. They're hampered by the tight space of the alley. Their shoulders keep bumping the walls, knocking them from side to side. Their inability to maneuver buys us precious seconds.

Madam Flores moves in front of us, stretching out her arms. "At all costs, you must protect the girl."

"Okay," the princess and I both say.

We exchange a look and the princess smirks. "She was talking to me."

Keeping my eyes on the hellhounds, I dig into my messenger bag. My right hand closes around my pepper spray. I slip my hand through the wrist strap and I thumb the lock off as I pull it out.

"I hardly need protection from a Dark Worlder."

Hellhounds are rampaging down the alley. They have teeth the size of hatchets.

I think we need all the protection we can get.

Before I can say this out loud, the hellhound has reached Master Flores.

She holds out her hands. "I am the Curator of Lineage—"

With a rumbling growl, the hellhound leaps at Master

Flores. With a brutal sweep of his head, he knocks her clear off her feet. She flies through the air and hits the wall before crumpling to the ground. He gives his head another massive shake and a tendril of slobber flies off his lips to splatter the brick wall.

"Forget this," I mutter. I thrust out my hand and jam the button down, emptying the entire canister of pepper spray up his nostril.

The creature rears back like a bucking bronco. He stumbles over the hound behind him and they both yelp.

The hellhounds have collapsed in a tangle of legs and bristly fur, but all eight feet are struggling to gain purchase, even as they snap and growl at each other.

I push the princess past the jumble of canines. "Go!" I yell. "Run!"

Her feet stumble as she turns to gape at me. "But—"

"I'm getting Master Flores. Run!"

I don't wait to see if she follows my advice, but instead drop to my knees beside Master Flores. Her chest heaves. She's still alive.

Sure, you're not supposed to move someone with a possible spinal injury, but death as chew toy has to be worse. Even if I could pick her up, we'd have to get past the hellhounds, who've untangled themselves. At the entrance to the alleyway, the princess pauses, looking back at us.

One of the hellhounds leaps after her. He doesn't even slow down. He just twists his head to the side and snatches her up in his mouth.

I suck in a pained breath, but I don't have time to worry about the fate of the princess. I have my own hellhound to deal with.

Even wounded, he's faster and stronger than I am. But I'm no stranger to fighting things faster and stronger than I am. I do it all the time in the dojang. Against humans. I know their pressure points, their weakest joints. I don't know any of that on a dog.

Then, in a burst of fur and speed, he launches himself toward me, landing directly in front of me, one ottoman-sized paw on either side of me, his snout level with my face. And all I have to defend myself is the empty can of pepper spray still dangling from my wrist.

Hell, I may not know his weakest points, but that nose looks pretty soft.

So I do the only thing I can think of: I shove the can straight up his nose.

I go in deep—like, elbow deep—past the spongy tip of his nose to the delicate soft tissue of his nasal cavity. He yelps, jerking his head back.

Unfortunately, my entire arm is still in his nose. The can of pepper spray is wedged in there and, even though I've let go, my wrist is still attached to the strap. He shakes his head side to side and my entire body goes with him. My body slams against one of the brick walls. Blinding pain blazes through my shoulder as my arm suddenly goes limp.

I feel the strap on the pepper spray snap, and my arm slides out of his nose. I drop to the ground with a bone-jolting thud only to have a massive paw land beside my head. I roll out of the way.

Above me, the hellhound howls in pain and rage. Shaking his head, trying to dislodge the can of pepper spray, he backs away, growling.

I crawl toward Master Flores. Before I reach her, she struggles into a sitting position. The hellhound looks from me to her, as if trying to decide which of us is the threat.

She is, obviously, but I'm the one he's after.

He shuffles in my direction. But before he can lunge for me, a blaze of bluish-green light shoots over my head, right into the hellhound's front haunch. It yelps, crouching low and snarling.

I look behind me. It's Kane, framed by the open door to The Volume Arcana.

He's standing, feet planted wide, the hood of his leather jacket thrown back, arm outstretched, his blackthorn blasting rod gripped in his hand.

The hellhound bares its teeth, a low growl rumbling through its chest.

Kane twitches the blasting rod and another burst of light shoots out from the end. Except it's not light, it's something else. Liquid fire infused with anger and will.

Even together, the Curator and I were not a match for this hellhound. Kane, on the other hand, is a threat to it.

The hellhound knows it's beaten. But it's still pissed off.

In what I can only imagine is angry defiance, the hellhound snatches the Curator up in its mouth before turning clumsily and galloping off.

Emotion surges through me. Frustration, anger, and exhaustion combine to wash away the fear that gripped me during the battle.

I collapse onto the ground.

Shit. My presence here has endangered everyone. The princess and the Curator have both been dragged off and I don't understand why.

The hellhounds must have been there for me. They are bred to track down and drag away Dark Worlders. Not Tuathan royalty and religious leaders. So what the hell just happened?

For a second, Kane just stares down at me, his expression inscrutable. Then, he crouches, sliding his arm under my good one and helping me up.

"Let's get you out of here," he says, his voice exasperated.

I expect him to drag me back into The Volume Arcana. He

doesn't. Instead, he cups his hands in front of him.

He mutters words I don't understand. Then he slowly pulls his hands apart, the space between his hands swirling with energy.

In the books, Wallace describes this as *pulling a loop*.

It's a power only Kane has. Rare, tricky, and dangerous as hell.

He is magically stretching open a hole in space, looping this spot to another.

When the loop is as big as a Kane-sized doorway, he once again wedges his shoulder under my arm and drags me through.

Excerpt from
Book Five of The Traveler Chronicles:
The Traveler Undone

*When I got back to my apartment above The Volume Arcana,
the princess was missing.*

*When the Red Court hired me, the job seemed simple enough.
Keep the princess safe and hidden until right before her wedding,
then escort her to Saint Lew. As long as she gets there safely, I
get paid a ton of money.*

So I'd stashed her in the safest place I knew of.

And now she was gone.

Funny thing was, my wards were still in place.

*So either she'd walked out of there on her own — unlikely,
since she knew her life was in danger — or someone I knew and
trusted was working for Smyth.*

*Which explained how he knew about my mother's medallion
and how he got his greedy Sleeker hands on it.*

So now I need to find the princess and my mother's medallion.

The list of people who could have betrayed me isn't very long.

*If I'm going to find my mother's medallion, rescue the
princess, and figure out what Smyth is up to, I'm going to need
all the help I can get. Which will mean calling up every favor
from everyone I've ever trusted.*

*So yeah, I'm going to go pick a fight with my worst enemy
and I'm going to do it knowing that one of the people who has
my back is actually working for him.*

CHAPTER TEN

I t's dark where we land.

I can see the night sky above me, but its milky gray color tells me there are streetlights on somewhere nearby.

The ground beneath me is hard and rough. And it stinks. Bile pools in the back of my throat, gagging me, until I bend over at the waist, hands braced on my knees, and let it drip out of my mouth.

Fighting my nausea, my brain works overtime to piece together all the shit that just happened, but my thoughts seem to be running around inside my head, waving their arms in panic.

When I straighten, wiping the back of my hand across my mouth, Kane is watching.

Which is perfect. Because who doesn't want to wretch in front of her dream guy?

Even though I've been reading about loops for years, I never thought I'd travel through one. Or that it would feel so god-awful. Which sort of makes sense. Thresholds are naturally occurring gateways and I got dizzy walking through one of those. A loop is a hole ripped into space by pure force. No wonder wedging yourself through that feels like shit.

This alleyway is darker and creepier than the one near Book People. I know instinctively—and from my years of reading the Traveler books—that there are hundreds of ways to die in this world. Suddenly, what seemed like a great adventure earlier, now seems extraordinarily dangerous.

Kane comes back over to me and squats so that we're at eye level, since I'm sitting on my ass.

"You always react this badly to a loop-jump?"

"Can't say that I do." I shove my hair out of my face. "So. That was a hellhound."

"Yep."

He helps me to my feet and then reaches out a hand and places it on my dislocated shoulder.

I wince, expecting searing pain.

For an instant, there is pain blazing through my body. Then there's only warmth.

"Relax," he mutters.

Yeah, right. I'm in a parallel universe, where magic is real and hellhounds want to kill me. Kane is here. Touching my arm. And I'm pretty sure I had been sitting in a puddle of human piss. This is possibly the least relaxed I've ever been.

Before I can quip my disdain for his suggestion, the muscles of my arm seem to melt. They loosen and stretch. He eases my arm down and away from my body. With a gentle pop, my arm sinks back into the socket.

When he releases me, I give my shoulder a roll. It still aches, but there's no blinding pain and I can move my arm again.

Kane stands with a disgusted grunt, all traces of the tenderness from a moment ago now gone. "If you don't want more attention from the *barghest*, you shouldn't be walking around with an open wound."

My palms are scratched and tender, dotted with blood in several places. My blood.

Right. The red blood of Dark Worlders is "tainted" with too much iron. The blood of the Tuatha is bright blue with copper. The scent of iron is how hellhounds track humans down.

I dig through my messenger bag, but don't find anything to bind a wound. All I have is my Leatherman, so I use the knife to cut off the bottom few inches of my T-shirt.

"Why didn't you bring me back to your loft?" I ask. "We'd be safe there."

He arches an eyebrow. "You think I'm going to bring a total stranger—a Dark Worlder, at that—past my wards and into my home?" He gestures to the alley in general. "This is safe enough for now. Covering that wound should buy you enough time to open another threshold into your world."

"You know," I mutter, as I fold the knife closed on my knee and drop it back into my purse. "I thought you'd be nicer."

"You think I should be nice?" he asks in obvious disbelief. "After all the trouble you've caused me?"

"Well nic*er*." I hold the fabric to my palm with my thumb and start wrapping the strip of cloth around it.

"Look, we gotta get out of here," he says. "That hellhound might come back. Can you open a threshold or not?"

It takes me a few seconds to realize the "we" in that sentence didn't mean him and me together.

"You can't leave without me."

"I already saved your ass once, Cupcake. Why should I do it again?"

"I don't need you to save me." Strictly speaking, this is probably a lie. But I run with it. "The Curator brought me to you because you need me. I can help you," I say, stumbling along behind him. "You need an Untethered Sleeker to help you find the lost *Oidrhe*."

Kane's steps slow, so I keep talking. Trying to remember the things Master Flores said. "If you can't find the lost *Oidrhe*, all you hold dear is at risk. If Smyth—"

Kane goes rigid. Then slowly he turns around. "What did you say?"

"Um…" Clearly, something very wrong. "All you hold dear is at risk?"

"After that."

"Smyth?"

His gaze goes thunderously dark. "Do you work for Smyth?"

"No! I'm a Dark Worlder." I wave my hastily bandaged hand. "My blood is red. Remember?"

"But you are Sleeker bred." His gaze is still narrowed with suspicion.

"I don't know. My parents were from Indiana, which I don't think is a hotbed of Sleeker immigration. But the Curator swears I am. There's a fan theory that the barrier between worlds was more fluid before the Iron Age and that the Tuatha used to intermingle and sometimes even marry Dark Worlders. So that certain isolated populations throughout the world have a concentration of recessive Tuatha DNA."

I break off abruptly. I'm rambling. And clearly, it's not helping.

I take another step forward. "I don't work for Smyth. I promise. I don't know if I have Sleeker blood or how to use my Sleeker powers if I do." He's so tall, I have to tip my head back to look at him. "But I promise I will help you."

There's this crazy moment when he looks into my eyes. Like, deep into my eyes. Like he's trying to read my very soul.

And suddenly, I'm painfully aware that this is *Kane.*

Kane the Traveler. Kane the warrior. The misunderstood and mistreated hero that I've loved from page one of that first book.

I feel myself sway toward him. Is this the real reason I'm here? For him?

Did his…I don't know, his gravitational pull, or something… actually pull me across the universe for this very moment? Because that's what it feels like. Like my connection to him is so strong, it could cross any distance.

But then he jerks me toward him and slams me into the wall jamming his forearm up under my jaw.

"What the hell?" I gasp.

His mouth twists into a snarl. "Here's what I don't get, Cupcake." He says the words with deadly gentleness. "Why would Smyth send you? Why would Smyth send an assassin so weak, she's never even loop-jumped? Why would Smyth send someone who doesn't know a hellhound when she sees one? Unless Smyth is smart enough to send one hell of an actress."

My vision is blurring to black at the edges. I can't breathe. My legs flail, kicking uselessly as panic eats through the part of my brain that should know how to break out of this hold.

I summon the last of my strength to swing my legs up to wrap around his waist. I hook my feet behind his back and leverage my weight against him. He drops me before I can do any more.

I fall hard on my back and instantly roll back onto my feet.

"You could have killed me."

"Exactly." His mouth twists wryly. "And if you had even a drop of magical power, you would have fought back. So maybe Smyth didn't send you."

"That's what I've been trying to tell you. The Curator brought me to you."

"Like I'm supposed to trust that old fool."

He gives his arm a shake and the blackthorn blasting rod that he stores up the sleeve of his jacket drops into his hand. It's a sixteen-inch wand of supple wood used to focus Kane's powers. He also has a three-inch steel blade bound to the side. It's deadly even if he doesn't use magic. He whips it up and presses the side of the blade to my neck.

"Who are you?" he asks.

The metal of the blade is warm against my skin, maybe from the pulse of magic coursing through the blackthorn. Maybe from being stored inside his jacket, against his arm.

Part of my brain is ticking through my self-defense moves. If it was just a knife, I could disarm him and escape. But it's not just a knife.

I saw what he did to those hellhounds. He can kill me with a single blast. Besides, I don't need to escape. I need him to trust me.

I tip up my chin and meet his gaze. "I'm Edie."

He stares at me for what seems like forever. His eyes are hard and icy, despite his warm brown irises. There is no softness in him at all.

"Smyth is just using you." Kane pulls the blade about an inch away from my neck and gives me the stink eye. "And if he thinks I'll be distracted by your beauty, he's wrong."

"My beauty? Wait. What?"

He thinks I'm beautiful?

Kane presses the blade to my throat again.

Okay. Bigger problems. I should focus on those.

"He sent you here to fight me," he says, his voice cold. "And he didn't even tell you who I am."

"I know your name." I should keep my mouth shut, but I don't. "You're Wesley Kane. You go by the name Kane the Traveler. You've been hired by the Red Court to rescue Princess Merianna."

"Wrong again. I am Kane Travers. And I never work for the government."

He spins the blasting rod in his hand and touches the blunt tip to my temple. Then the world goes black.

Excerpt from
Book Five of The Traveler Chronicles:
The Traveler Undone

If someone has enough money to hire me, they probably either robbed someone, oppressed someone, or cheated someone to get it. Or they inherited it from generations of people who did that. Or worse.

No one gets a lot of money without taking it from someone else.

Now, to be fair, when I say no one, I'm including myself. I take from a lot of people. But what do you expect? That's what all thieves do. I'm just honest about the cheating I do.

CHAPTER ELEVEN

When I wake up, I'm in a cage.

It's the same frickin' crate the princess was in earlier. My muscles hurt, I'm still a little nauseated from loop-jumping, and every bare inch of skin has the impression of the cage waffled into it. The cage isn't big enough for me to lie flat in, so whoever shoved me in here—spoiler alert: I'm guessing it was Kane—just wedged me in.

I still have my messenger bag, so there's that.

Also, on the plus side, the cage isn't in the stinky warehouse on the second floor. It's in the middle of Kane's darkened living room. At least, I think that's where I am.

In the first book, *A Traveler Arrives*, Kane wins a warehouse, in a shitty part of downtown, in a poker game. He rents the first two floors to The Volume Arcana, does business out of an office on the third floor, and lives on the fourth. As Wallace describes it, it's a dingy shithole with mismatched furniture and bad lighting. Wallace was being generous.

Something that passes for a galley kitchen sits at one end. There are a couple of threadbare chairs and some bookshelves. Then there's a vast stretch of emptiness surrounding my cage. As soon as my head clears, I look for a way out.

There wasn't a lock on it when the princess was in it, but he's added a nice big padlock. Of course.

I sit up, groaning.

If the Curator is right, I'm the only person who can find the lost *Oidrhe*. Right now, I'm so disappointed in the real Kane that I will happily go off and find some other lost *Oidrhe* to take his place.

For the moment, I'm not letting myself think about the fact that Kane the Traveler—my book boyfriend—is possibly a psychopath who locks women up in his living room. I mean, he does think I'm an enemy assassin. So possibly that counts as a good reason.

I wind my fingers through the links of the cage and I pull back my legs and ram them against the door to the cage.

It gives only a fraction of an inch, and the clang of metal against metal rings in my ears. I do it again anyway. And then again. Someone has to hear me.

The fourth time I slam my feet against the cage door, I hear a door open and a light flicks on from the shadows behind me.

I whirl around to see Kane standing in a doorway, backlit by the light in the other room. "Knock it off."

I twist around so I'm facing him. I kick the wall of the cage. "You want me to stop making noise? Let me out of this goddamn cage," I nearly scream in frustration. Instead, I just yell at him. "What the hell is wrong with you?" My voice cracks with what sounds suspiciously like despair. He is *not* going to make me cry. I push as much anger and snark into my voice as it will carry. "Is this some kind of sick joke? Or are you actually a serial killer?"

"What?"

"Do you make a habit of kidnapping girls?" I sneer.

He blinks like he's surprised by my accusation. "Actually, you're the first. And I didn't kidnap you. I rescued you, Cupcake."

Something in his tone—either his wry humor or his obvious derision—makes me look at him. Really look at him.

It's the first time I've had the chance to study him.

This Kane isn't the living, breathing representation of my fantasy. He's just a little…off. His hair is lighter. More chocolate than inky black. And there's a springiness to it. A slight wave. His jaw is narrower. He looks younger, too. Sure, Kane is nineteen in the books, but he felt older. And then, there're his eyes. In the books, they are a merciless steely gray. Here, now, in the light, they are an unmistakable honey brown.

The kind of warm brown you'd want to spend hours staring into.

You know, if the guy hadn't just locked you in a cage like some *frickin' psychopath.*

Kane squats down, which puts him almost at my eye level.

"Tell me about these books."

"What books?" I ask.

"The Traveler books. The ones that make you think you know so much about me."

My eyebrows shoot up. *Oh shit.* "You know about the books?"

"The Curator told me about them. About how she gave my stories to some Dark Worlder writer to try to lure out an Untethered Sleeker."

"Wait. She *gave* the stories to Wallace? What does that mean?"

"She's a Curati. It's what they do. They curate stories."

Something about his tone, which is so reasonable and measured, so calming, ratchets down my emotions a bit. I'm able to blink back the tears that were threatening just a moment ago.

"I thought the Curati curated bloodlines."

"Well, sure, they do that, too. But their main job is to curate stories from the many universes, to gift those stories to Dark Worlders."

"So Curati are muses?" Okay. Mind. Blown. I sit up on my knees, inching forward. "So all human creativity, all our books, all our movies, are gifts from the Curati? That's... Wait. Why do they do that?"

"To strengthen the Thread. The Thread is—"

"Yeah. I know. It's the magical cord that connects every living creature to the universe. It's the power the Tuatha use to fuel their magic. That's in the books. And the Curator talked about it, too."

"Exactly. Emotion feeds energy into the Thread, so—"

The Curator hadn't told me that part, but my brain leaps ahead and I finish the thought before he can. "The more humans care about a story, the more energy goes into the Thread."

"Yes."

"So Tuatha are just emotional vampires who use humans to fuel their magic? Ew. That's gross."

"Don't Dark Worlders use the decayed flesh of others to fuel cars?"

"No! We use gas. That's... Okay, I see your point. But that's still gross."

His lips twitch, like he might smile, and something about it unsettles me, but before I figure out what, he pulls his gaze from mine to look out the windows behind me.

"Because they curate stories, the Curati have the ability to impart visions. They find stories from the many universes that will appeal to humans. And then they give those stories to writers and artists." He pauses, shifting his eyes back to mine. "They've never gifted stories from our world. That's strictly forbidden."

"But the Curator did it anyway. She spent the past"—I do the math quickly—"six years imparting visions to Chuck Wallace? All so that she could find an Untethered Sleeker?"

"So that she could find you."

I slowly lean back against the side of the cage, blowing out a long breath. "Wow."

"That's not what she told you?"

"No. She just talked a lot about the vast tapestry of the universe and the threads that connect—" I stumble over my words, my mouth suddenly dry. I can't tell him what the Curator said. That the threads of the universe connect the two of us. I clear my throat and continue. "That connect every living thing."

"Yeah. That sounds like her. Not completely wrong, but vague and misleading." He pins me with a look. "And she brought you here to…"

He lets his words trail off, leaving me to finish the sentence.

"She says it's my destiny to help you find the lost *Oidrhe*." Kane scoffs, but I rush on before he dismisses what I'm saying. "But *you're* the lost *Oidrhe*. Aren't you?"

Kane ignores my question and stands, arching up on his toes like he needs to stretch after crouching for these few minutes. "See, this is why I have trust issues." He crosses his arms over his chest and stares down at me. "Tell me about the books."

The chill in his voice sends shivers down my spine. The not-good kind of shivers. "Are you going to throw me up against the wall and accuse me of being an assassin again?"

"I'll try not to."

"Okay." I let out a shuddering breath. "They're just contemporary fantasy books."

"Give me the details."

"Okay. They're called The Traveler Chronicles and they're about you. Or rather, about someone very much like you. His name is Kane the Traveler. He's a mercenary wizard. He carries a blackthorn blasting rod."

I look pointedly at the hand he held the blasting rod in when he pressed it to my neck. He shoves his hand in his pocket in what seems to be a conciliatory gesture.

I let out a shuddering breath and keep talking. "He lives

in Austin, in a loft decorated like this one. He—"

"I get it."

"—has grey eyes though."

Kane smirks. "Nice touch. Because he's a grey wizard, skirting the line between right and wrong. The grey wizard with grey eyes."

"It's kind of a running theme in the books," I whisper.

I used to fall asleep dreaming about Kane's grey eyes. I loved how mysterious they made him seem. How haunted. I even loved that Wallace used the English spelling of grey, instead of the dull American gray. I don't know why that mattered to me, but it did.

Now, staring into Kane's actual eyes, I can't remember why cold grey seemed romantic, when clearly honey brown is so much…yummier.

I swallow as the smirk slips from his face. That's when it hits me. The thing that bugged me about his almost smile.

"Holy shit. You have dimples."

"What?"

"Dimples. You have—" I gesture to his cheeks as his gaze narrows.

Okay. He does not seem happy about me noticing those dimples.

Wow. Dimples. I did not see that coming. Dimples seem so…whimsical. So not Kane.

This is so weird. So…awkward. Right. That's what I'm feeling. Just very, very awkward.

"I have an app," I blurt out suddenly. Because I'm not good with long silences.

"A what?"

"An app." I fumble in my bag for my cell phone, unlock it, and thumb through until I find the Traveler Chronicles app I downloaded before the third book came out.

I hand the phone through the bars. Clearly, he's seen a smartphone before, because he clicks away, his frown deepening with every click. The app has covers, blurbs, and excerpts from all the books. Links to the forums. Even links to collections of fanfic on Wattpad.

Which makes me very thankful there's no internet connection in the Kingdoms of Mithres. Because I sure as hell do not want him reading the fanfic I've "Liked."

Finally, he asks, "What else do you know about me?"

"I know—" But I break off, unsure what to say. I know every major event in Kane's life from the time he turned fifteen. I know that he blames himself for his mother's death. That he blames himself for the chaos in the Kingdoms of Mithres, that he feels guilty for not claiming the throne and feels unworthy of it all at the same time. I know that before his mother's death, she tattooed him with a complicated rune that protects him from the hellhounds. I know that he's a Dark Worlder, like me. "I know everything."

"And you read all of this in the books?"

"Yes. The Traveler Chronicles. It's a five-book series and—"

"How many people have read these books?"

"Millions. They're best sellers."

"Millions? Millions of people know all these things you know about me?"

"I—" God, when he says it like that it seems like such an invasion. How would I feel if my whole life were on display like that? "But some things are different," I argue. "Your eyes, for example. And…um…your jacket."

"My jacket?" he asks, running a hand down the front. "What's wrong with my jacket?"

Oh, now he sounds insulted?

"Nothing. It's just…" I cock my head to the side. It's made of brown leather, but not the stiff leather of my world. It's supple and thin but still tough. Like he's worn it every day for years. Like he's fought battles in it and imbued it with enough magical protection to stop a bullet. Which, if the books are right, he has. But, still… "It looks like a hoodie."

"So?" He pulls the hood up. "Of course, it's got a hood. How else would it protect the back of my neck?"

I shrug. "In the books, you wear a leather duster."

"A leather duster?"

"Yeah."

"I live in Austin. If I wear a leather duster in the summer here, I'll die of heat stroke."

"This is my point! I'm sure there are lots of things Wallace got wrong."

"Wallace is the author?"

I nod. I'm having enough trouble making all of this make sense without wondering which bits Wallace got right and which he got wrong. Or why.

"What do you know about my family?" His tone is suddenly sharp.

"About your birth parents? Your Dark Worlder parents? Nothing. No one knows who they are. The woman who raised you as her own was Queen Nerida of the Grey Court. Her infant son was sickly and dying. She crossed to the Dark World and swapped her child for you."

"What happened to the baby?"

"The queen's real baby?"

He nods, his gaze sharp.

"You never know for sure. At first, you assume that baby died. But throughout the books, you get hints that maybe Dark Worlder medicine was able to save the child."

He seems to consider this, looking worried and torn, before asking, "What about the king?"

Kane's tone is still so cold, I hardly know how to answer.

"He never knew you weren't his. He blessed you as his own, bestowed the title of heir upon you, and the queen mostly kept you away from him until you were eight. He got suspicious when you couldn't do basic spell work."

"*I* couldn't do basic spell work?" Kane snorts derisively.

"Well, you're a changeling, right? So you can't tap into the thread the way everyone else can." I nod toward his right sleeve. "That's why you need the blasting rod. To help you focus your powers. So now you can do spell work."

Kane's lips are twitching, as though it is all he can do to keep his laughter in check. "So let me see if I've got this straight. I can't do basic spell work without my blasting rod, but somehow I'm able to pull loops?"

"A lot of fans think that's a problem. They say it's lazy writing. It doesn't bother me, though. I mean, if Wallace wanted you to have a cool power, then pulling loops—"

I break off, suddenly aware of what I am saying. Wallace has nothing to do with whatever powers Kane has.

"Hey. Why can you pull loops? If it's not lazy writing, then what is it?"

Kane flashes me that sardonic smile of his. "Maybe everyone here can pull a loop, but they just prefer driving around in whatever crappy Dark Worlder car they can find."

"That's not an answer."

"It wasn't meant to be. What about siblings?"

"None. At least none here. Who knows in the Dark World? But Morgan Geroux is like a brother to you. You're also close to his younger sister, Ro. You meet Morgan in the second book, when you're both gambling on this riverboat outside Nawlins. At first you really hate him, because he beats you at poker. But then this other guy steals your mother's medallion and Morgan offers to help you get it back. There's this whole heist plot. But it goes wrong and then—"

"My mother's medallion?" he asks, sounding skeptical.

"Yeah. You wear it around your neck."

He arches an eyebrow. "Do I look like the kind of guy who wears jewelry?"

"There's nothing wrong with a man who wears jewelry." He doesn't look convinced. "Besides, this isn't jewelry. It's a charmed medallion. It protects lost things and helps them find their way back. It was the last thing she gave you before she died. It's like a compass. It's your most treasured—"

Just like that, Kane turns his back on me and walks away.

"Wait!" I call out, desperate now. Jesus, what did I do wrong? "You can't just leave me here in this stupid, frickin' cage!"

He pauses, glancing back as he scrubs at his forehead. "It's a Faraday Cage."

I blink, my mind working sluggishly. "A Faraday Cage? One of those things that blocks electromagnetic radiation that people use to protect computers from EM pulses or whatever?"

Kane looks confused for a second, but then shakes it off. "No. A Faraday Cage. One of those things that blocks and deflects magical pulses."

"Magical... But that's not what a Faraday Cage is."

"Look, I don't know what a Faraday Cage is in the Dark World, but here it blocks magic. End of story."

"But—"

"You and I both know the Tuatha borrow shit from the Dark World all the time. Sometimes it's actually stuff—cars, tech, whatever. Sometimes it's words, phrases, concepts. We don't always get everything right."

Oh. That made sense. There were things in the books from almost every cultural mythology. That was something hard-core fantasy fans bitched about. But if the Tuatha borrowed freely from all over the world, then it made sense.

"The point is, it breaks down any magical spell going in

either direction. As long as you're in there, you can't cast a spell."

"I can't cast a spell anyway," I protest. "I'm a Dark Worlder, remember? I'm a muggle!"

He stalks a few steps closer and I can see the steely anger on his face. "The Curator says you have Sleeker blood."

"Please," I beg again. "I'm not an assassin. I'm not here to hurt you or spy on you or anything like that. I promise."

He arches an eyebrow at this. "You don't honestly expect me to buy that honor among thieves routine, do you?"

I wrap my fingers around the bars of the cage. "I'm not a thief."

He shrugs. "Well, I am."

Before I can say anything else, he disappears back through the door.

"I need my phone back!" I call out.

No response. Big surprise there.

Well, that hadn't gone well.

And I'm still in a cage.

From where I am, I can't see into the room, but I'm guessing it's his workshop—where he stores all his magical artifacts and occasionally brews a potion or two.

For a few minutes, I just sit there. Too much has happened since yesterday morning when I was knocked out in gym class. It's all too weird.

But that doesn't mean I'm going to follow his orders. I don't care how hot he is.

If I was Tuathan, then putting me in a cage that deadens my magical powers would be a serious blow. But I don't have any magical powers.

I need to figure a way out of here on my own. Besides, the bars of this cage are really uncomfortable on my ass.

I still have my messenger bag slung over my shoulder, so the first thing I do is riffle through it for my keys and the LED flashlight attached to them. I flip it on and scan the contents of my purse, looking for anything else useful. There's not a lot. My wallet. My Leatherman. A nail file. A Luna bar. My bottle of Xanax.

Wish I'd remembered that I'd had that back in the warehouse when I thought I was going to be attacked.

Other than that, I have a pack of gum, a pair of earbuds, my Mac lipstick, and a water bottle. Not much with which to stage a breakout.

I slip the Leatherman into my jeans pocket, take a sip of water, and put everything back in the purse so I can focus on the cage. I check out the lock first, but the way it's hanging on the outside, I can't reach it.

I'm about to be seriously frustrated when I notice the one obvious thing I've been overlooking. The six panels that make up the crate aren't welded on. They're bolted together.

The heads of the bolts are on the inside and the nuts are on the outside. I feed my fingers through the holes and grip the nut between my index and middle finger. The metal of the bolt bites into my fingers so I use the pliers on my Leatherman to hold it still. Finally, I feel the nut give.

The work is slow, almost excruciating, but finally, I get one off. I pull my fingers back into the cage and shake out my cramping muscles. One down and—I do a quick bolt count.

Jesus. One down and three more to go.

Seriously?

I turn off my flashlight—no point in wasting the battery— and slip it back into my bag. Then I get to work.

When I get out of here, I am kicking Kane's ass.

Excerpt from
Book Five of The Traveler Chronicles:
The Traveler Undone

The apartment is a shithole.

The building was used as a warehouse sometime in the past hundred years. Everything the previous owner couldn't sell, give away, or curse someone with, he or she left behind to collect dust mites, mold spores, and chaos demons. Which means every time I walk through the front doors, I sneeze. Then cough. Then trip over something that wasn't there a minute ago.

But whatever. I won the building in a card game and, since I don't have anywhere else to live that's free, this is it. Besides, when I say I "won" it, I'm being generous. I cheated.

So if the chaos demons eventually do enough damage to kill me, I probably have it coming.

CHAPTER TWELVE

T hree bolts later, I'm ready to skip the ass-kicking and go straight for the brutal murder. My hand muscles are so cramped, I can't even straighten out my fingers, my knees have what feels like a permanent grid etched into them, and my back muscles are spasming. Oh, and I smell like dog snot.

All in all, not my best day.

By the time I slide the last bolt out and gently lower the side grate to the ground, I feel like I've been trapped in that damn cage for hours.

I climb out, cringing as I stretch. So maybe I won't be kicking his ass after all. But it sounds good in theory.

Okay, I have two options: either I can go confront him in his workshop and try to figure out exactly what's going on, or I can sneak out of his apartment and... And what?

I've been reading about this world for years, but that hasn't prepared me for being here. Only luck and Kane have kept me from becoming a hellhound's Scooby Snack.

Since Master Flores and the princess were dragged off by hellhounds, I have no way of getting home.

In the books, the princess is kidnapped and carted off to Gull Veston Island, where Kane rescues her. Incidentally, Gull Veston Island is also where hellhounds bring any Dark Worlders they catch. There's a whole Sleeker detention center there. It's very Alcatraz.

So maybe the story isn't too far off track. Maybe I just have to get Kane to go rescue the princess from Gull Veston Island. Then they can fall in love and I can rescue Master Flores. I mean, the Curator. She's the one who got me into this mess, so she can send me home. After I save Kane's life. And hopefully convince him he should be king, thus preventing a civil war that would tear apart the world I love.

It's a good plan. Probably impossible to execute, but still a good plan.

One problem: it assumes I still think Kane is worthy of being King.

You know, since he locked me in a frickin' cage!

And, since he locked me in the same crate the princess was in, there's definitely a possibility that Kane locked up the princess to begin with. Asshole.

That's right. My book boyfriend is an asshole. Which is a huge frickin' disappointment.

I blow out a breath.

Okay, I need to calm down and back up a step.

Kane is gruff. Taciturn. A truly reluctant hero.

I know that.

Sometimes, he acts like a jerk. He tries to be selfish and self-serving, for his own preservation. But at the end of the day, when shit goes bad, he always does the right thing. The selfless thing. Always.

There has to be a reasonable explanation. There simply has to be, because…

God, I've loved Kane for most of my life. Before Wallace messed up the story in the last book, I read those books over and over. I practically lived in that world. They made me believe that shitty, horrible things could happen to someone but that person could still summon the strength to do the right thing.

That is what I have always loved about Kane. The fact that no matter how much he wanted to give up on the world, deep inside, he still had hope. Because of Kane, when shitty, horrible things happened to me, when I wanted to give up, I was able to dig deep and find hope, too.

Which is what I have to do now. I have to find the hope. In me and in him.

So I'll just go to him and demand an explanation.

After I arm myself with some kind of weaponry. Just in case I'm wrong.

If the books are right, all the iron in Kane's world comes from the Dark World. None of the magical creatures here like iron much. If a metal has enough iron in it, it can burn their skin.

So no cast-iron pans. And that's why the cage was made out of that funky metal. And also why the hellhound freaked out when I shoved the pepper spray up his nose. If iron burns, then that probably hurt like hell. In my world, iron is in everything, including steel cans. And nail files.

Score.

I dig through my purse for the nail file. And just for good measure, I go back and collect the bolts and nuts off the floor. To me, they feel different from the metal of the cage. They feel like the normal steel hardware you'd find in my world. Which would mean they have iron in them.

I figure the bolts may prove useful later, so I stuff them into my jeans pocket and creep over to the laboratory door. The room is almost as long as his living space, but narrower. Shelves crammed with books and equipment line the far wall. A work bench as long as a bus dominates the center of the room. That's where Kane is. He's bent over a shallow bowl filled with a shimmering silvery liquid. His blasting rod is maybe four feet away, left carelessly on the table by a collection of bottles.

He looks up when I push open the door. In the same instant,

he holds out his hand, palm down, and his wand flies into it. He flicks his wrist and the blasting rod slides back up his sleeve just like, well, just like magic.

At the sight of me, his lips curve into a smile that's as hard and cold as the fire slate his workbench is topped with. "Well, aren't you a clever girl. How'd you break out?"

"Shoddy design work at the cage factory." I reach into my pocket, pull out the nuts and bolts, and show them to Kane. "You just can't find a well-designed cage capable of holding a human captive these days, can you? What with us having brains and opposable thumbs and all."

For a long moment he just stares at the nuts and bolts in my hand.

"What?" I ask. When the silence gets really awkward, I ask again. "What?"

Finally, he looks up at me, but there's something soft about his eyes. Like I've surprised him. Or maybe amused him.

"Oh, come on, my quip about the opposable thumbs wasn't that funny."

He leans back, eyeing the bolts in my hand. "So then, you really are a Dark Worlder."

"Why?" Slowly pieces of the puzzle slip into place. "Because I touched the bolts?"

He holds up my phone. The Traveler app is open to an excerpt from the books.

"The books got it wrong. Tuatha can touch iron, but it's definitely not comfortable. It wouldn't"—he turns the phone around and reads aloud—"'sear the skin right off his face,' but it would definitely leave red welts. So…"

I look down at my palm. "So no welts means I'm not Tuatha."

His lips curve into a smile, which make his dimples wink. My stomach dips, and I have to force my mind back to work.

"So this was just another test?" I ask, sliding my nail file into my back pocket. "Like when you nearly killed me out in the alleyway to see if I would break and use magic?"

"Pretty much."

I step forward and snatch my phone out of his hand. "You're a jerk."

A jerk, but apparently not a murderer.

"Are all Dark Worlders this prickly?"

"You tried to kill me and then you locked me in a cage. The fact that I'm upset about that is not *my* personality flaw."

"Look, Cupcake, I haven't stayed alive this long by not asking questions. If someone shows up, attracts the attention of hellhounds, and gets the Curator kidnapped, it's only reasonable to ask if they summoned it."

"I didn't summon the hellhounds! I don't even know—"

"So you keep saying."

"You know I'm a Dark Worlder!" I slide my phone back into the pocket inside my messenger bag. "You saw me bleed."

"Blood can be faked."

"Blood can't be faked."

He picks up the ceramic knife from the table beside him and he slices a shallow half inch cut into his left forearm. Blue drops of blood bead at the cut.

I gasp and take a step backward. "You're Tuatha!"

He holds up his hand so the blue blood rolls down his arm.

The Kane of the books is a child of the Dark World. Like me. His blood should be red.

Before I can stop myself, I reach out, catching the drops of blue blood on my fingertips. The blood on my fingers feels real. It is bright blue and viscous and warm. It even smells like real blood.

He reaches out and takes my hand in his. With his other hand, he draws a quick rune in the air. The blood seeping from his arm turns a warm, deep red. As does the blood on my fingertip. With another wave of his hand, the cut seals itself, but the blood on his arm remains.

I look from his face to the blood and back again. "I don't understand."

For a second, he just holds my gaze, searching for something. His hand suddenly feels too warm on my skin. He drops my hand and turns away. "Like I said, Cupcake. Blood can be faked."

When I glance down, the blood on my fingertips is blue again.

"What... How? Which is your real blood?"

Instead of answering me, he uses a towel to blot the blood from his arm. And then from my finger. Then he takes the rag with the blood on it to the sink. He drops it in, gives it a jolt with his blasting rod, and a second later, it's a pile of ash.

Instead of explaining, he starts packing his bag, loading it up with tools and bottles. The knife gets sheathed and stuffed in, along with a flask and a round gold object, like a compass. In fact, by the time he's done, almost nothing is left on the table. He's clearing out.

"Wait. Where are we going?"

He flashes me another smirk. "*We* aren't going anywhere. I'm leaving. You're on your own."

On my own?

I won't last ten minutes on my own.

I was out on the streets unprotected for less than five minutes when the hellhounds tracked me down the last time.

I have to convince Kane to bring me with him or I am dead.

I throw myself in front of him. "You can't leave me here. You need me."

"No. I don't. Even if I believed in prophecies, even if you are an Untethered Sleeker, even if you could find the lost *Oidrhe*, that's the Curator's mission. Not mine."

"It's not mine, either," I say, holding my hands palms out. "I just want to go home. And I can't do that without the Curator."

He gives me a how-is-this-my-problem look.

"I get it. I am not your problem. But here's the thing—you need me. I read your books. I know everything you're going to do in the next four days."

"No, you don't."

But I can see the flicker of indecision in his eyes. He is cocky, but he has doubts.

"You're going to rescue the princess from the Sleeker detention center, right?"

"How do you know that?"

"Because it happens in the book." I don't add a "duh" at the end. See how mature I am?

"In this book of yours, why do the hellhounds drag her off? I read about the book on that app of yours. It doesn't mention a Dark Worlder or an Untethered Sleeker."

"Well, no."

"Then why do the hellhounds drag her off?"

"In the book, she's not dragged off by hellhounds." He turns and walks away again, so I hastily add, "She is kidnapped by Smyth. He's the one who brings her to Gull Veston Island. But that's where the hellhounds bring anyone they capture, right? So that's where she'll be."

"The detention center is impossible to break into. Nobody even knows where it is."

This makes me beam. Finally, an ace up my sleeve! "I know where it is."

Surprise flickers in his eyes.

So I keep talking. "I can get you there. You need to rescue the princess. I need to rescue the Curator. We both need to figure out what Smyth is up to and stop—"

"What do you have against Smyth anyway?"

I blink in surprise as his question takes me aback. "He's the bad guy." Kane makes a keep-it-coming gesture with his hand. "Well, he killed your mom."

My dad read the first book aloud to me when I was eleven. That was back before all that stuff happened, when he was still a sane and loving father. In a book full of demons and monsters, the moment that kept me up at night was the moment Smyth killed Kane's mother. "He murdered her right in front of you. When you were just a kid."

One night, I woke up screaming because I'd dreamed Smyth had my mom, his long, black, Sleeker arms wrapped around her body, his embrace almost loving. His expression was gaunt and sad as he plunged one pointed Sleeker tentacle straight through her heart. But that was after my dad had been carted off. I had all kinds of nightmares then. The monsters had become real for me.

"That's why I hate Smyth," Kane says sharply. "He killed my mom. Why do *you* hate him?"

"I just…" I shake my head to free myself from the memory of that dream. Why had it seemed so real? "He's the villain of—"

"You said that already."

"Well, stop interrupting me. If you want answers to complicated questions, you have to let me think about them."

He smirks and gestures broadly, as if yielding me the floor.

"There are some villains we love to hate. Or even just love. Villains like Darth Vader. Or Ursula, the sea witch." Kane probably isn't much of a fan of animated movies, so I add, "She's from *The Little Mermaid*."

"I know who Ursula is," he says dryly. "And Darth Vader. In case you're worried."

"Smyth isn't like that. He isn't a fun villain. He's just horrible. Power hungry. Controlling. Willing to do things he knows are wrong to get what he wants."

"You know a lot about him."

I shrug. "Just what's in the books."

"What is it he wants? In the books, I mean."

"He wants to control everything. He's obsessed with ridding the Kingdoms of Mithres of all influence from the Dark World. He's spent the last five books hunting down every Dark Worlder he can find and destroying every artifact that makes it across the threshold between worlds. It's one of the reasons he hates you so much. Because you're an expert at finding thresholds and at tracking Dark Worlder artifacts once they've come through. You import things and sell them on the black market. They disappear into private collections before he can destroy them."

Kane chuckles.

"What?"

"That's what you think I do?"

"Isn't it?"

"I don't know." He gives a diffident huff. "The way you describe it, it sounds like a business." He rubs his hands over the back of his neck. "Sure, sometimes I'm able to sell the stuff I find. Sometimes, what I find is a piece of crap no one wants and it sits down in The Volume Arcana until Gus throws it out."

"Oh. It sounded more glamorous the way Wallace described it."

"Every once in a while, someone will hire me to find something special, but that's pretty rare. It's certainly not a business."

I'm still mulling over this new information, but Kane must take my silence for disapproval, because he sounds offended when he declares, "Sorry to disappoint you, but I'm only nineteen. I don't have any formal education. I live my life entirely off the map. I haven't exactly had time to launch a career."

"I wasn't—"

"Most days, I think I'm doing pretty good just to keep us alive. So don't—"

"Us?"

He breaks off his rant and just blinks at me for a second, like his own words are only now sinking in. Then he gives one of those sarcastic smirks of his. "Yeah. Us. Gus and me. You wouldn't believe how much that guy can eat."

"Oh. So you guys, like, hang out a lot?"

"Yeah," Kane says sharply. "He's like a father to me."

"Huh." Okay, sure. I liked it better when I thought my book boyfriend's best friend was a suave millionaire time traveler (i.e., Morgan Geroux, of the Nawlins Court), but who am I to judge a fatherly old man on appearance alone? Well, appearance and smell. And dental hygiene.

"Just out of curiosity, do you get a lot of toothpaste from the Dark World? Because that maybe seems like something some people might need more of."

The look Kane gives me would knock a lesser woman to her knees. A woman who hadn't already fought a hellhound and survived. Mostly.

Whatever I'm going to say to convince him to bring me along, I need to say it now.

"Look, the point is, you hate Smyth. I hate Smyth. He's tried to kill you in the past. He'll very likely try to kill me, too, merely because I'm a Dark Worlder. So there's no reason we can't help each other."

After a long moment, he shakes his head, slings his bag over his shoulder, and heads for the door.

"Even if I trusted you, even if I wanted your help, I'm not going to take a kid with me."

"I'm not a kid. I'm almost as old as you are."

He raises an eyebrow.

"You said you were nineteen, right?" I ask.

It takes him a beat to admit, "Yeah." He frowns. "Why? How old are you?"

Technically, I'm seventeen, but I fudge for the sake of winning the argument. That's legit, right? "I'm eighteen."

"In what? Dog years?"

"I'm eighteen," I lie again.

"You can't be. You're so…short."

"I am a perfectly normal height in the Dark World."

"Dark Worlders are all this short?"

"No, I just… Five four is well within normal range."

He smirks. "I doubt that."

"My point is, I'm a legal adult." -*ish* "I could join the army. Not that I'm going to, but still." Kane looks stunningly disinterested in my pacifist views. "I can make rescuing the princess so much easier."

He gives me one of *those* looks again. "Sure, you can."

"I can. You didn't even know that the Sleeker Detention is on Gull Veston Island."

He smirks. "Now I do."

"But you don't know where the island is. Or about the magic barriers protecting the island, or the cliffs of insanity or—"

"Man, you talk a lot."

"Wait!" I call after him. "You can't go to Morgan's."

He stops in his tracks, slowly turns toward me, and narrows his gaze. "Why do you think that's where I'm going?"

"Duh. Because that's where you go in the book. You go to his house on the lake, but there are a pair of Kellas cats staking out his place. They attack you both. Morgan is injured. He can't go with you to rescue the princess. And trust me, when you get to the island, you will wish Morgan was there."

After a second, he nods. "Okay. You can come." Then he pauses. "But first we need to do something to disguise you from hellhounds."

I perk up. "Like a rune?"

He rolls his eyes. "No. For Thread's sake, no. Something a little less permanent." He nods toward a shelf behind me. "Grab that blue bottle."

I reach for a bottle of bright blue liquid.

"No! Not that one. That's activated bluestone."

"So?"

"It'll dissolve your skin."

"Oh."

"The pale blue one. To the left."

This time I reach for a dusty blue bottle and bring it to him. "Do I drink it?"

He gives me another look like I'm a moron. "You rub it on your skin. It'll cover the scent of your Dark Worlder blood. It'll confuse the hellhounds."

"Oh. Okay." I pull off the cap and give it a whiff, only to be hit with a nose-numbing scent of mint. "What is this made of? Pure mint?"

He smirks. "It better not be. That would really piss the Kellas cats off. They do not like mint."

I pour some onto my hand, cringing as I rub it on my exposed skin. "Why would that matter? Aren't we going to Gull Veston Island to rescue the princess?"

"Nope."

"Then where—"

"We're going to Morgan's."

"But that's where the Kellas cats are."

"Exactly. If you're right and there are a pair of Kellas cats staking out the place, then we'll talk."

I don't admire a lot of people. Fearsome magical power doesn't impress me.

The High King—he had all kinds of power. Shake the earth, raise the oceans, bring down civilizations kind of power. He was also an ass. And, frankly, a little stupid. I mean, come on, his wife swapped his dying infant with a Dark Worlder changeling and it took him eight years to notice?

So no, I don't admire raw power. Wizards with raw power are a dime a dozen.

But brains? That I can get behind.

CHAPTER THIRTEEN

T he wards placed around Kane's loft make it extremely difficult to loop-jump in and out. It's one of the reasons The Volume Arcana is open to the public. Loop-jumping in public spaces is easy.

But instead of pulling a loop as soon as he reaches the first floor, Kane heads for the door.

I have to hurry to reach him before he steps out onto the street. His stupid long legs don't help, either.

"Wait, hold up."

He hesitates, shooting me a disgruntled glare. "What?"

"Aren't you going to…?" I glance toward the counter. Gus McCreeperson is behind the counter again. I make a circle with my four fingers and thumbs, miming pulling a loop. "You know."

Kane rolls his eyes. "Do you mean why are we not just going to loop-jump to Morgan's place? Yeah. Gus knows what I do. It would be a little hard to keep that from him."

"Okay then. Why aren't we going to loop-jump to Morgan's place?"

"For starters, Morgan is a prince of the Nawlins Court. He has more wards around his place than the average high-security prison. Secondly, I'm tired."

"But—"

"Those books that you claim detail every aspect of my life? Did they happen to mention that it takes a hell of a lot of energy to loop-jump anywhere?"

"Well, yes." Kane seems to take this as enough of an explanation and walks off, but I'm not done yet. "Wait—"

He pauses by the door. "Yeah?" He draws out the word like he's talking to a moron.

I cross the length of the store, all too aware of creepy Gus behind the counter. "If we're going to work together, I need reassurances."

"*You* need reassurances? Five minutes ago"—he jabs a thumb in the direction of the stairs—"you were begging me to bring you. Now you want reassurances?"

"Okay, what I meant was, I would like more information." He quirks an eyebrow, but I don't give him another chance to snark-slap me. "What exactly is your relationship with the princess?"

"I don't have a relationship with the princess. She's a princess. I'm a mercenary." He smirks, like he enjoys throwing that word back in my face. "End of story."

"But she was in a cage in your building." Gus is just standing there at the desk, looking back and forth between the two of us. I take a step closer to Kane and lower my voice. "I get that it was a Faraday Cage, so maybe it has protective qualities. But she did not seem happy to be there."

Still no response from Kane.

"I don't think I can condone that kind of behavior."

This time he turns and walks for the door. "You coming or not?"

I so don't know what to say in response. I even look to Gus, who just shrugs.

"Just give me something to work with here."

He stops so quickly, I nearly run into his back. "You want

something to work with? Work with this: I don't need you to come with me. You begged me to come. So either come or don't."

I don't have a lot of options here. So I follow him. Besides, the last time I was out on the streets, I was attacked by hellhounds. Kane may not be forthcoming, but being with him is safer than getting mauled to death. I think.

It doesn't take long to confirm I was right. This is not the kind of place a girl wants to walk around alone.

The Volume Arcana is in a neighborhood that makes Bourbon Street look like Main Street Disneyland.

The Kingdoms of Mithres have been without a ruler for over a year now. In the power vacuum left by the king's death, the seven High Courts were wrangling for position, each determined to seize power. Things might have been okay, if the Curator had been around. She was the one person who could read the blood of any contender for the throne and know instantly if he or she had enough power to rule the Kingdoms. If she declared a High King or Queen, no one—not even the princes or princesses of the seven High Courts—would dispute that person's claim to the throne.

But in the books, the Curator had disappeared right after the High King died. With no real leader and the Seven Courts all fighting among themselves, things had gotten bad. It might be different along the East and West coast, where the Red Court and the Han Court still hold so much sway, but here in the middle of the country, the cities are ruled by gangs, thugs, and minor corporations, all fighting for whatever power they can hold on to.

So I'm relieved when an older model limo pulls up beside

us almost immediately. When the vehicle pulls to a stop, Kane opens the rear passenger door and holds it open for me to climb inside. Kane gets in after me and the limo is moving again before Kane can even shut the door. I don't know how or when Kane summoned the limo, but I'm thankful to be off the streets.

There's one other person in the back, and I recognize him instantly—Morgan Geroux.

Morgan slides over to make room for us, moving himself onto the bench seat that runs the length of the limo. I end up wedged into the corner with Kane on one side and Morgan on the other. It's a good thing I'm small, because neither of them is. Their legs take up all the floor space.

If there are subtle differences between the Kane of the books and the Kane I now know, the same is not true of Morgan. Morgan is Kane's best friend and one of the few people in this world who is more powerful than Kane. Morgan is a timekeeper. He can manipulate and control the flow of time, able to travel freely within the span of his lifetime.

Morgan is exactly the way Wallace describes him. He's wearing dress pants and a crisp striped shirt with a jaunty little scarf. It's a look very few straight human men could have pulled off, but it doesn't undermine Morgan's masculinity at all, probably because he's so ridiculously handsome. His cheekbones look like they've been carved from granite. His dreadlocks fall just past his shoulders, and his eyes are a startling green that looks exotic against his tawny skin.

He looks like a young Lenny Kravitz, if Lenny Kravitz had been sprinkled with fairy dust and therefore became inexplicably more beautiful and cooler than any normal human could be.

So basically, he looks like Lenny Kravitz.

As soon as Kane closes the door behind him, Morgan flicks

on the overhead light. Then he angles himself away from me so that he can lean forward to study me through a narrowed, intense gaze.

Maybe Morgan has never seen a Dark Worlder before. Maybe my "stubby" Dark Worlder looks are repulsive to someone of his lean Tuathan heritage. I would suspect he's just insufferably rude, but after several long heartbeats, a slow, bemused smile creeps across his face. Shaking his head a little, he chuckles, seemingly delighted.

Beside me, Kane clears his throat. Morgan blinks, as if waking from a trance, then he stretches his arm out along the bench seat.

If I didn't know better—if I hadn't been reading about Morgan Geroux for the past six years—I would have sworn he was trying to play it cool.

"Well," he says, turning to Kane with an arched eyebrow. "Where'd you get the cupcake?"

Kane makes a snorting noise that could be laughter or derision. Hard to say.

Me, I'm just tired of being treated like a freak.

"Okay," I protest. "I've about had it with the cupcake thing. What is up with that?"

Morgan raises a sardonic eyebrow and then looks pointedly at my chest.

"What?" I ask.

His lips twitch. And again, his gaze drops to my chest.

Only then do I look down…and remember I'm wearing the Hello, Cupcake! T-shirt I bought from the famous Austin food truck. It's a pale green, girl-cut T-shirt with the company's logo emblazoned across the front. A giant pink-frosted cupcake.

Great. Just great. Way to be a badass.

Before I can burst into flames of embarrassment, Morgan

extends his hand. "Well, Cupcake, I'm—"

"You're Morgan Geroux. Of the Houston Gerouxes. You're known for your charm, your gambling, your wit, and your occasional disregard for the laws of the Kingdoms of Mithres."

I expect Morgan to be surprised by my knowledge, but he just turns to Kane, a glimmer of mischief in his gaze, and drawls, "Well, she's interesting. Where'd you find her?"

"I didn't. She found me."

It takes Kane a lot less time to explain the events of the evening than it would have taken me. Morgan takes it all in stride, as though Dark Worlders wandering over thresholds, powerful princesses being dragged off by hellhounds, and finding out his best friend stars in a fantasy series is just a fun diversion for a Friday night.

"Can she be trusted?" Morgan asks.

"Hey, I'm not the one who's untrustworthy here! I'm not the one who locks women up in cages."

Morgan looks from me to Kane and then back again. "I sense there's a story here."

I explain about the cage the princess was in when I found her.

Morgan looks at Kane and clucks his tongue disapprovingly. "And you let her think that you'd locked the princess up?"

Kane shrugs, looking out the window.

Morgan takes my hand in both of his and says, "My dear, the last time I saw the princess, she was in Kane's apartment, ordering him around like he was a servant. That was yesterday morning. They were supposed to leave for Saint Lew today. Then I got a call from Kane this morning to tell me someone kidnapped her from his apartment while he was gone."

"Then why was she still in the building?" I ask. Morgan starts to speak, but I answer my own question before he can. "Unless whoever was kidnapping her didn't have a chance to get her out of the building before Kane came home. Or he thought that hiding her in plain sight would make it harder for Kane to track her."

Morgan smiles at Kane. "She's very quick, isn't she?"

I twist, pulling my right leg up onto the seat beside me so I can jab a finger at Kane. "You couldn't just tell me that? 'Edie, I didn't trap the princess in that cage.' How is that hard?"

Morgan gives my shoulder a playful bump. "Don't be too tough on him. He has trust issues. Which I assume you know about, if you've read all about his life."

There's something unexpected behind Morgan's smooth charm. A glimmer of mischief in his eyes.

But he's definitely playing me. No doubt about that.

"Look," I say to him, because I don't want him to think he's getting away with it. "I know how this goes. I've read this scene in about fifteen other books."

"What scene?" he asks.

"The scene where the charming sidekick vouches for his best friend."

"Sidekick?" Morgan presses a hand to his chest. "Oh, you wound me."

"Yeah. Sure. My point is, it doesn't matter if you vouch for him if I don't trust you, either."

Morgan grins at Kane. "I think I like this Cupcake of yours."

"Hey—" I point a finger at Morgan. "Enough with the cupcake thing. In my own world, I'm a real badass." Sort of. "I know how to defend myself."

Morgan raises his eyebrows again.

Kane shrugs. "She's not entirely useless."

"Okay then, Cupcake Badass, you're in." Then Morgan looks at Kane. "Can I assume you're here because you need me to do the tracking spell for you?"

I don't give Kane a chance to answer. "Actually, I know

where the princess is."

"Then, why do you need me?"

"So Cupcake Badass here can prove she knows what's going to happen over the next few days."

I jump in to explain. "In the book, Kane contacts you and has you meet him at your house, where you're ambushed by a pair of Kellas cats."

"Kellas cats, huh?" Morgan raises an eyebrow. "Only two? Because a dowt of Kellas cats has three or more."

"In the book, it's just two."

"Well, shall we go and have a look?" Morgan taps on the glass and the window separating us from the driver parts slightly. "Drive back to the house."

A few minutes later, we pull into a residential neighborhood. Kane turns to the driver and says, "When you get half a block away, pull over and let me out."

"Wait, you can't face a pair of Kellas cats alone," I protest.

"Does it kill me?"

"Well, no, but—"

Kane gives a cocky shrug. "Then apparently I *can* face a pair of Kellas cats alone."

And before I can protest, the limo stops in front of a sprawling lakeside mansion and Kane is out the door.

Kellas cats are rogue creatures. They're smarter than hellhounds, hired muscle with bad attitudes and sharp claws. If you happen to be one of the few people with the gift of mastering cats, you essentially have to bend their will to yours. They never stop resenting their master, which means even the people who hire them don't like to be alone with them. No one voluntarily faces them alone.

Except Kane.

Shocked, I look over at Morgan. "Aren't you going to help him?"

Morgan gives an exaggerated shudder. "Oh, heavens, no. I can't stand Kellas cats. My mother had a dowt when I was a child. They used to sleep on my chest at night, hoping I'd die in my sleep so they could steal my soul. Horrid things."

"He's your best friend!" I protest. I stare out the window, dread pumping through my veins. I whirl on Morgan. "You've got to do something!"

Morgan quirks an eyebrow. "I can't imagine what you think I could do."

"Get out and help him! Fight with him! He's going up against at least two Kellas cats. No one could survive against those odds."

"My point exactly." Morgan shifts his shoulder in a gesture as apathetic as his tone. "I doubt an extra person will make a difference."

"I can't even—" I stutter. "This is bullshit."

Without thinking, I do the unthinkable. I throw open the door and run out into the night.

Despite what he just said, part of me expects Morgan to follow. He doesn't. Asshole.

Outside the car, it's dark. Only the limo's headlights illuminate the sprawling oaks. It's barely enough to give me the lay of the land. Morgan's house is a masterpiece of joyless modern architecture, all sharp metal, poured concrete, and brittle glass. The landscaping is as austere as the architecture and offers little cover. Kane is striding across the lawn with a confidence that borders on arrogance. Or stupidity.

I try to cut him off from the danger, but he's so much taller than I am that I don't even come close to matching his stride.

He's almost to the tree where the first of the Kellas cats is hiding. Before I can call out a warning, Kane stops and calls out. "Cat of the Kells, if you hear my voice, reveal yourself and speak to me."

I stop in my tracks. Holy shit. He's going to try to master it?

A faint noise rumbles across the lawn. An angry, annoyed sound.

Again, Kane says, "Cat of the Kells. If you hear my voice, reveal yourself and speak to me or find yourself banished to the void between worlds."

Excerpt from
Book Five of The Traveler Chronicles:
The Traveler Undone

*When you make your living as a smuggler and a thief, it's only
natural that you don't trust many people.*

Anyone could sell you out for a handful of gold dahekuns.

*On the other hand, when you work as a smuggler and a thief,
you need someone to watch your back. For me, that person is
Morgan.*

*He's a timekeeper, with the ability to travel throughout the
span of his life. Which, surprisingly, does not make him any
more punctual.*

Still, he is my oldest friend. I trust him with my life.

Which is ironic, since he's an assassin.

CHAPTER FOURTEEN

There's an angry grumble, followed by a whisper-faint swishing of a tail over foliage. Something flickers in the darkness and then the Kellas cat slinks into view.

Her muscular body is low to the ground. Three times the size of a domestic cat, her coat is all black, except for a single patch of white shining on her chest. Her face is broad and flat and her eyes are wide and bright green. Her lips barely move when she talks.

"You have summoned me. Now speak. I am yours to command."

My breath catches in my chest. Has he done it?

What am I doing out here? Why the hell didn't I stay in the limo? What if my very presence here puts Kane in further danger?

The Kellas cat's eyes never even flicker in my direction, but I'm sure she sees me. She's a creature of the night and her vision is perfect in this near darkness.

Her attention, however, is focused solely on Kane, who speaks to her in steady, fearless tones. "I don't seek to command you, but wish to strike a bargain."

A bargain with a Kellas cat? Is he mad?

A pact with a Kellas cat will last for generations. There is no breaking that bond. Not for the life of that cat or for the nine lives following it.

The cat inclines her head just slightly. "Tell me of your bargain, grey wizard, and I will consider it."

"I will trade you knowledge for power."

"I'm listening," she purrs. She slinks across the lawn as she speaks, circling Kane.

He moves in unison with her, never giving her his back. "Tell me the number in your dowt and the name of your master and I will free you from your service."

"It would take a wizard more powerful than you to break my bonds of servitude."

"You know nothing of my power."

She lets loose a noise louder than her purr, harsher than her words. It's halfway between a hiss and cackle.

I realize with a splash of icy dread that the noise is her laughter.

Jesus.

If this is her amused, I do not want to see her pissed off.

The Kellas cat is still circling Kane, and she's close enough to me that he can see me now, from the corner of his gaze. Exasperation flickers across his face. It's a sort of oh-great-now-I-have-to-deal-with-you-too expression.

Just then, something skitters in my peripheral. There are two more Kellas cats, slinking up the tree behind Kane. They are wickedly fast. When they reach the branch above his head, one of the cats creeps along the top, while the other skitters out along the length of the branch, clinging to its underside like a giant spider.

I have to force the words past my icy fear. "Kane! Above you!"

He looks up just as two cats drop from the tree. One lands in front of him, the other flips in midair to land, paws down, on Kane's back. He howls in pain.

I'd be more concerned about him if I didn't have problems of my own. The second I shout to Kane, the Kellas cat he'd been talking to whirls and throws herself at me.

I stumble as fifty-plus pounds of pissed off monster lands squarely on my chest. I go down hard, landing on my ass with her claws digging into my skin.

She's howling madly—an unearthly, soul-chilling sound—and each swipe leaves four long gashes in my shirt and my skin.

I shove my arms up, bucking my hips as I push her over my head and off me. I roll away, desperate to get my feet under me. The pain searing my chest has me almost doubled over.

I whirl to face her, unwilling to let her have my back and equally unwilling to run away. She crouches several feet away, back arched, fur on end, bushy tail straight up in the air. Her eyes gleam maliciously at me.

The hellhound was scary. I'm not gonna lie. The teeth. The slobber. The gaping maw. None of that was exactly what I'd call peaceful. But this? This creature, with her keen intelligence and her absolute, malicious contempt... This creature is terrifying.

And I don't have so much as a rock to throw at her.

Yeah. This was a great idea.

She makes that noise again. That bone-chilling cackle.

"This is the girl come to rescue the formidable Kane Travers? This mewling infant of a child? This insignificant Dark Worlder?"

Her glee morphs into venomous rage. She hisses and spits, arching her back even more as she scuttles sideways.

That's when I remember.

The saliva of a Kellas cat is venomous. Her attack is no accident.

She struck first with her claws and then retreated to spit at me from a distance. If any of that spit reaches my bloodstream, I'll be paralyzed.

Then all she has to do is perch on my chest and suck out my soul from my gaping mouth.

I clutch at the edges of my shirt, trying desperately to cover my open wounds. I take a step back. And then another.

And then I feel something against my back. Not the rough bark of the tree, but the solid warmth of Kane's back. From the corner of my eye, I can see the glow from his blasting rod. He, at least, is not completely defenseless.

"She get you yet?" he asks.

"With her venom? No. I don't think so. How would I know?"

I feel his shoulders move and picture him shrugging. "Searing pain, trouble breathing, near instant paralysis. You'd know."

"Great. Sounds like fun." The Kellas cat is still moving, circling us. Kane must have dispatched one of the cats who attacked him, because now, it's two against two.

"I don't suppose you have any more of that burning spray you used on the hellhounds?" he asks.

"The pepper spray? How'd you even know about that?"

"My apartment has windows. Do you have any more or not?"

"Nope." In desperation, I reach into my pocket. Maybe I have something. A Glock would be perfect, but hell, I'd settle for a can of tuna and some arsenic.

What I find is the steel bolts I took out of the Faraday Cage back at Kane's place. As weapons go, they're far from perfect—especially since iron isn't as deadly in this world as Wallace made it sound. But it's all I have.

Keeping my hand in my pocket, I palm a nut and a bolt.

Over my shoulder, I ask, "You've got your blasting rod, right?"

"Obviously."

"You think you can handle yours?"

"Yes. But I can't blast both of them. Not quickly enough."

"It's okay," I tell him.

"Just out of curiosity, how do I get out of this in the book?"

"Morgan saves you."

Kane snorts. "Yeah. Like that's going to happen."

Yeah. He's a lot less helpful than I expected.

Before I can mention this to Kane, the Kellas cat skitters closer still.

"Are you ready to die, mewling Dark Worlder?"

"Are you?" I ask, fingering the bolt in my pocket. I know it's a long shot, thinking this small bit of my world can save me, but it's the only shot I've got.

Before I can decide if my plan is brilliant or just foolhardy, the Kellas cat pounces closer, spitting viciously in my direction. Hot venom lands on my skin, as I spin into a roundhouse kick, but she leaps back before the toe of my Converse makes contact with her head.

I might have her on strength, purely because I'm bigger than she is, but she's so fast, I'll never get close enough to find out.

She moves back, watching me. She's waiting for her venom to work. So I give her what she's waiting for. I still dramatically and then sway, trying to make it look good. Then I tumble back onto the ground, my arms falling out to the side.

She pounces on me in an instant, all fifty or so pounds of her landing on my chest with such force, she must have cracked ribs. All of the air rushes out of me. She crouches there, on my chest, her head almost as big as mine, her bright green eyes peering into mine.

"You should never have come here," she murmurs in a purring voice.

Then with her heavy paws, she kneads my chest.

She wiggles closer, getting her mouth right next to mine. Her lips part. Purring now, she draws in one long, shuddering breath. She doesn't exhale, just keeps breathing in.

She purrs contentedly, her eyes narrowing as my soul pulls loose from its mooring.

Then I grab the back of her neck with one hand and shove the bolt into her open mouth with the other. I slam my palm up under her jaw, forcing her mouth shut. She tries to reel back, but I don't let her go.

She's incredibly powerful and it's all I can do to hold on as she tears at me. Pain flames across my skin and she shreds my flesh, desperate to break free of my grasp and spit out the bolt.

Then she stills and her eyes meet mine. I see so much in her gaze. Her hatred. Her resentment. Her anguish and her fear. The iron in the bolt is eating away at the inside of her mouth, making her blood boil.

Wallace may have exaggerated the effects of iron on the Tuatha—who are clearly closer to human than he made them sound—but Kellas cats truly belong to this fairy world. The iron is deadly to her. It's killing her. *I'm* killing her.

Oh God. I'm *killing* her.

My hands loosen, almost involuntarily, but before she can wrench free, there's a loud cracking noise like a bat hitting a baseball, and the Kellas cat flies out of my hands.

Morgan stands over me, with what looks like a hockey stick in his hands.

Excerpt from
Book Five of The Traveler Chronicles:
The Traveler Undone

Kellas cats obey no laws and follow no rules. They are merciless predators who suck the soul from any living being they get close to.

And they wonder why no one likes them.

CHAPTER FIFTEEN

I crawl away from the dying Kellas cat. I make it maybe five feet before puking my guts out. Every muscle in my body is trembling.

Morgan reaches out a hand to help me up. I take it, only to jerk away in pain. Blisters are forming on my palms. Welts dot the bits of skin that aren't covered in scratches. He bends over me, grasping my elbows, one of the few parts of my body not ripped to shreds, and helps me to my feet, muttering a string of curses under his breath.

Only after I'm standing do I realize tears are pouring down my face. I brush at them with my wrists, because the scratches there don't seem as bad. The body of the Kellas cat who attacked me lays maybe ten feet away, her spine broken. The fur of her cheeks seems almost to be smoldering. The bolt, covered in bright blue blood, lies on the ground beside her. Her front paws are still twitching.

I did that.

I may not have delivered the death blow, but she is dead because of me.

Morgan is standing beside me, breathing hard and fast, apparently assessing the damage. A few feet away, Kane nudges the body of another Kellas cat with the toe of his boot. That cat appears to have a hole blasted in its side. When it doesn't move, he walks over to the one I fought and points his blasting rod at it, to put it out of its misery.

I've read about this world, about these creatures, for years. I thought I knew them. I thought I was tough. But in the end, this beast nearly destroyed me.

And now it's dead because of me. Because—

"Don't," Morgan says softly. I glance at him. "You look like someone nursing doubts. Dismiss them. Given the chance, she would have sucked your soul right out of your body and eaten it for lunch."

I've never killed before. Not unless you count bugs. This isn't some scorpion I squashed. She was a sentient creature. She had a family. A dowt. Maybe kittens somewhere.

I glance around the lawn and see the bodies of the cats Kane fought. "Are they both dead?"

Kane glances up. "One is. The other's stunned."

"Are you going to…?" I leave the question dangling.

"Probably," Kane answers, at the same time Morgan says, "No."

Morgan says, "I have a friend who deals in the animal trade. A cat like that is damn valuable. I have a crate in the garage that should hold her."

I fight off another wave of nausea.

"You did what you had to do," Morgan reminds me. And then he smiles. "And you were damn impressive. By the Thread, a Dark Worlder in a fight with a Kellas cat? If I'd known how it would turn out, I'd have sold tickets."

Ten minutes later, I'm standing in the foyer of Morgan Geroux's stunning modern home, holding together the tattered shreds of my shirt.

All I want is to strip off my now ruined Hello, Cupcake! T-shirt and wash my scratches.

Instead, I'm listening to Morgan and Kane argue. Incessantly.

They're doing it in low voices, but this much I get: Kane thinks I'll be okay so long as I wash the scratches. Morgan wants to take me to a healer.

Me? I just want to do something fast.

"I am bleeding here. Lot of iron-based, bright red blood. So unless you know a healer who isn't going to have a problem with that, I suggest you just get me some bandages and get out of my way."

Kane looks me up and down, his lips twitching. "She has you there, Morgan."

Morgan doesn't even blink. "Take her into the bathroom in the guest wing. I'll get bandages."

Kane leads the way and I hobble along behind him. It's a bone-deep spasming that makes it hard to walk, and even harder to keep up with Kane's long strides. Plus, I think I twisted my ankle, because the tendon along the outside burns with every step.

Sprawling mansions are all well and good when you don't have to limp past forty feet of pretentious modern art just to get to the bathroom.

Kane is a good fifteen feet ahead of me when he realizes I've fallen behind. "You need me to carry you?"

Oh, sure. That will prove I'm a badass.

"No, I've got it."

"Because you're really slow."

Kane Travers. Master of stating the obvious.

"I'm good," I say through gritted teeth. I don't want Kane thinking I'm a liability. I can't afford to *be* a liability.

I'm tough. I can take pain.

Except, when I take my next step, fresh pain shoots up my

leg. I pause, biting my lip to keep from crying out.

Kane starts walking back toward me.

"No, it's okay. I was just…" I cast around for a lie, and my gaze lands on an enormous paint-splattered canvas. "Is that a real Jackson Pollock?"

Kane barely glances at the canvas but sweeps me up into his arms, Rhett Butler–style, and stalks off down the corridor.

He carries me like I weigh nothing. For someone so much taller than I am, I probably do. Still, I am intensely aware of how broad his chest is, how hard the muscles are beneath my palm.

Oh God. Why is my palm flat against his chest?

I snatch my hand away and clench my fists.

He looks down, and it occurs to me that he might not have noticed my hand was on his chest until I pulled it away so obviously.

Okay, Edie, say something. Anything.

"Um…" Anything at all. Words. Just so long as it's words. "Morgan really does have a lot of art, huh?"

Okay. Most of those were words.

Kane makes a grunting sound that might be agreement or might be amusement at my general inability to sound like a rational human being.

But the babbling floodgates are open.

"So do you think that really is a real Pollack? Because, I saw one in New York and—"

"Yes. It is."

"Oh."

"You don't really think every private art collector is a Dark Worlder, do you?"

"I—" Honestly, I'd never thought of it before now. "I just assumed you had your own artists."

He scoffs. "Tuatha aren't known for their creativity. Art isn't really our thing."

Isn't really *their* thing, he should have said. Because he's not Tuatha, either, even though he certainly acts like he is.

I'm still wondering about that when Kane opens the door and carries me into an austere guest room that I barely have time to glance at. At the far end of the room, there's a bathroom visible through an open door. Kane sets me down.

I step into the bathroom, but Kane tries to follow me. I hold up a hand. "Whoa, there. Where you going?"

"You need help bandaging your injuries."

I glance down at my ripped shirt. My chest, my arms, my shoulders are all latticed with scratches. There is no way I am taking off my shirt. Not in front of Kane. Not ever.

Like, not *ever*.

I plant my palm firmly on his chest—you know, on purpose this time—and give him a shove. Maybe it's my imagination, but I feel like he leans into my hand before taking a step back. Just to remind me I can't push him around.

"No way."

"Don't be stubborn. You need help."

"What I need is a shower and a whole lot of soap." I scan the bathroom. "You do have showers in this world, right?"

"Right behind you." He points to a wall of glass bricks.

"Then I'm good." I start to shut the door and then open it a few more inches to say, "Maybe some Neosporin. Or Bactine. Or whatever the Tuatha equivalent is."

There is not even a flicker of confusion in his expression. So I assume he knows what I mean, and I shut the door.

I eye my tattered Hello, Cupcake! shirt.

It's a bloody ruined mess.

I pull it over my head, wincing as the action stretches my scratches, and then drop it in the sink. Kane or Morgan will probably want to burn it later. Blood can be used to track a person. I don't even want to imagine what my iron-rich blood could be used for.

I toe off my shoes and leave them in the corner. My other clothes—socks, underwear, bra, and jeans—are in better shape. The jeans have a few rips and some blood, but maybe Morgan has a washing machine I can borrow.

The next thing I do is pee. I figure I've now been in the Kingdoms of Mithres for close to six hours—which frankly makes it impressive that I didn't wet myself when the Kellas cat attacked.

Excerpt from
Book Five of The Traveler Chronicles:
The Traveler Undone

The Nawlins Court has made and lost more fortunes than all the other courts combined. They have a reputation for being charming, lazy, and too pretty to be of any use in a fight.

Like most rumors about the Nawlins Court, that last is only partly true.

CHAPTER SIXTEEN

When I get out of the shower, my bloodied clothes have been washed, mended, and neatly refolded. My Hello, Cupcake! shirt is on top. The bottom two inches that I cut off to bind my hand are still missing. The other rips and tears have been repaired—not stitched with needle and thread, but somehow rewoven, so it looks as though the fabric was never damaged. I bring it to my nose and sniff. The fabric smells clean and faintly of lavender. Like the laundry detergent my mother used when I was a kid.

Huh.

Did someone glamour my clothes or is this all part of the Tuatha mending and tailoring service?

I quickly slip into my underwear and bra.

Whoever cleaned and folded my clothes in the ten minutes I was in the shower also left me a small jar of ointment.

I unscrew the lid of the jar and dip my finger in. I kid you not, as I rub the ointment into the wound, the bright red inflammation surrounding the scratch fades to a healthy pink.

I work quickly, hitting the deeper scratches on my legs first, and then slip into my jeans. The scratches on my arms aren't very deep, but there are several gouges on my torso and shoulders that may leave scars.

But it's not like these are the worst scars I have. That prize goes to the one just above my right breast, where the bullet exited my body. The gun was small caliber, so the entry wound scar just under my shoulder blade is so small, you hardly notice it.

The thing about bullets—at least about mine—is the physical injury never hurts as much as the mental. Being shot didn't hurt me. Knowing my father was the one who shot me? That had nearly killed me.

It was years before I could even look at my naked chest in the mirror without wanting to claw my skin off. Years before I accepted what had happened to me. Like those scars, the ones I got today are proof I survived the battle. I'm not ashamed of being a survivor.

After a few minutes, the tips of my fingers start to go numb. So I find a washcloth and dip the corner of it in the salve. I've just brought the washcloth up to my chin when the door behind me opens and Kane walks in.

I jerk the washcloth to my chest to cover my scar and the tattoo that covers it. I'm not ashamed of my scars, but that doesn't mean I want anyone seeing them, either.

"What the hell?"

"I knew you would need—" Kane breaks off midsentence.

In the mirror, I see him look down and realize I am still shirtless. Yeah, my bra covers the important bits and the washcloth covers the bit I really don't want him to see, but that still leaves a lot of bare skin. His gaze seems to linger on my reflection, and I feel my nerves prickle in response. Then, abruptly, he jerks his gaze away and clears his throat.

"Need help. Reaching the scratches on your shoulders and back." He finishes the sentence, like he didn't even miss a beat.

"I don't," I say quickly. I stretch my left hand over my back and wave it around. "Look. I can reach my back. No problem."

"Don't be stupid." He reaches around to pick the jar of

ointment off the counter.

I snatch the jar back out of his hand. "I'll be fine."

"If you don't treat these, a scratch from a Kellas cat can fester for weeks."

"Ew."

"And after about a day, they stink. And ooze."

"You're making that up."

"I'm not. The stench allows a Kellas cat to track down any prey that it didn't kill."

"Seriously?" I push the jar back into his hand. "Go for it."

Kane dips a finger into the ointment and smears it on one of the scratches on my left shoulder. His touch is brusque and quick, as if this is a task he just wants done. He doesn't look at the reflection of us in the mirror, but down at the wounds he's dressing.

He's nearly a full foot taller than I am. With his head ducked, I can still see his face, the seriousness of his expression. I'm so distracted watching him, I don't think to brace myself against the sharp sting of pain when he touches one of the deeper cuts.

I gasped involuntarily, and his gaze jerks to mine in the mirror. His hand stills.

"I'm sorry."

"No, it's okay. I can take it." I've had much worse, but I don't tell him that.

"I'm not used to"—he clears his throat again—"delicate things."

"It's really okay. I'm tough."

He nods, but still, he hesitates before barely trailing his finger across one of the scratches on my shoulder blade.

"I don't think that," he says, his voice rough.

"What?" I ask.

He clears his throat again. "That you're delicate."

I snort. "Obviously. I think the term you used was stubby."

His gaze flickers to mine in the mirror and then back down again. "No. What I meant is, I don't think you're weak."

"Oh."

"You handled yourself well out there. With the Kellas cat. You're pretty tough."

"Pretty tough for a Dark Worlder, you mean?"

"No." He looks up again and his gaze holds mine in the mirror. "Pretty tough for anyone. Dark Worlder or Tuatha."

His compliment sends another burst of heat spiraling through my chest. Kane-the-effing-Traveler thinks I'm tough. "Thank you."

He nods and then looks back down. He seems to be concentrating a bit more than he needs to, as if this conversation makes him deeply uncomfortable. I guess when you're a badass, lone-wolf mercenary, you're not used to handing out compliments.

He continues to rub that one spot, a gentle brush of his fingertips, over and over until the ointment is absorbed. And then he moves on to the next scratch and then the next.

Everywhere he touches, there's the faint numbing from the ointment. The pleasant warmth that follows has nothing to do with the salve and everything to do with Kane. I feel myself softening, my whole body relaxing, warmth swirling up through my torso and then back down again until I tingle all over.

My reaction surprises me. After I was shot, I was in the hospital for weeks. My lung had collapsed. They inserted a tube to drain fluid from it. There were multiple surgeries and then physical therapy. After a while, I sort of...detached from my own body. This physical vessel I walked around was handled and manipulated by countless doctors, nurses, physical therapists, and aides. Even when the caregivers were kind, respectful, and sensitive, the experience was dehumanizing. Later, my therapist called it a coping mechanism. At the time,

I was so broken inside, I didn't want to feel human. Either way, when that many strangers touch your body, it no longer feels like it's *your* body.

To be honest, I wasn't sure it would ever feel like my body again. Until now.

My eyes drift closed as I lose myself in the sensation of his fingertips trailing heat along my shoulder blades. One of my bra straps must have gotten in his way, because he hooks a finger under it and lowers it off my shoulder. A sigh comes unbidden to my lips. I feel his hands still and then pull away.

My eyes fly open and I find him staring at me in the mirror. I can't look away from the reflection of the two of us together. His expression is dark, shuttered. My cheeks are flushed, my lips parted and damp, like I licked them without realizing it.

Abruptly, he drops his hands. He reaches past me to set the jar of ointment on the counter and grabs the towels beside the sink. Wiping the excess ointment off his fingers he says, "I think I got the worst of them."

I nod, mutely, but I'm not sure if he even notices. He tosses the towel on the counter and goes to leave, then pauses with his hand on the doorknob.

"I'm not him, you know."

"What?" I ask, turning toward him

Now he does look up at me, and I press the washcloth more firmly against my skin.

"The character from the books. That guy you think you know. I'm not him."

"I know that," I say quickly.

"I'm not a hero. I'm not someone anyone looks up to. I'm not even particularly nice."

"I—"

"If we met under different circumstances, if I didn't need your help, I probably wouldn't even care if you lived or died."

"I know," I say for a third time, but this time Kane is already gone, closing the door firmly behind him.

Alone in the room, I turn back to the mirror.

Slowly I lower my hand, letting the washcloth drop into the sink. There, on my chest just a little right of center, is the scar from where I was shot. A puckered oval, barely visible since I got the tattoo. A tattoo in the shape of a rune. A gentle arc of three overlapping backward J's. It's a rune for protection. For disguise and deceit. It's the rune Kane has marked on his own chest.

I shiver when I remember how his hands felt on my skin. Like I was alive again. Like I was fully in my body for the first time in years.

Shaking off the feeling, I pull my mended T-shirt over my head.

Was I honest with Kane just now, or did I lie to him and to myself?

Do I know that he's not the character I fell in love with from the books? Does it matter?

Excerpt from
Book Five of The Traveler Chronicles:
The Traveler Undone

No one likes a smart-ass.
That probably explains why I don't have more friends.

CHAPTER SEVENTEEN

W hen I leave the bathroom, Kane is gone. The guest room is empty and I'm all alone.

There is a note propped on the bed.

It's late. Can't do more until morning anyway. Get some rest.

— K

Part of me wants to argue with this logic. Yes, it's late. But it's harder to do magic during the day, so if we're going to break the princess and the Curator out of jail, shouldn't we go now?

Clutching the note in my hand, I walk toward the door, but my ankle hurts with every step. I make it only halfway across the room before I turn and hobble back to the bed. I swing my legs to examine my throbbing ankle. It's starting to swell.

Kane has essentially stranded me here.

Even as tired as I am, my thoughts race. No, race isn't quite the right word. It's more like they leap from topic to topic, like a frog on lily pads. I am in the Kingdoms of Mithres. Is my mother trying to reach me? She would be texting me for sure. She must be terrified that I haven't texted back. But I am in the Kingdoms of Mithres. In. The. Kingdoms. Of Mithres.

And, apparently, I'm an Untethered Sleeker. Whatever that is.

The Curator didn't need just anyone to cross the threshold. She needed me. She'd searched for me.

And there it was—the lily pad not strong enough to support my weight. I feel the thought folding around me, dragging me underwater. Holding me there.

If the Curator believes I am of Sleeker blood, then it must be recent Sleeker blood.

Not some distant ancestor I never knew, but a parent.

The truth holds me underwater until I feel like I'm drowning.

My father.

My troubled, broken father.

What if he wasn't broken after all?

During the incident, he'd ranted and raved about monsters only he could see. What if hellhounds and Kellas cats weren't the only monsters that were real?

What if he wasn't crazy. What if he was a Sleeker?

Oh, that was a dangerous idea. It tapped into all my deepest fantasies. My darkest yearnings.

What if he hadn't really been crazy? What if he'd never meant to hurt me? What if he'd been trying to protect me from something when he'd fired that gun?

What if…?

What if…?

Those are the thoughts that hold my mind as I drift off to sleep.

I dream of the lily pads and drowning. And for the first time in years, I dream of my father.

In my memories, he is tall and thin. And always—or almost always—dressed in a meticulous iron-gray suit. He was always either coming home from a business trip or leaving on one. Even on weekends, even when he was relaxed, there was a fastidiousness about him. A contained-ness. But he loved reading, and my best memories of him, my earliest memories of him, are of sitting on his lap, my cheek pressed to his chest as he read to me. He loved the sci-fi and fantasy classics. Tolkien. McCaffrey. Zimmer Bradley.

And in the dream, I am on his lap, even though, at ten, I am too old. But it's late, and he just got in from a business trip. I'm on his lap, rubbing my cheek back and forth against the warmth of his suit jacket, while he reads aloud. And in my dream, I hear his voice starting a book.

Sure, I have a binding name, but if you're stupid enough to ask me what it is, I don't want to work for you.

Excerpt from
Book Five of The Traveler Chronicles:
The Traveler Undone

The Tuatha disdain physical violence. They think it's uncivilized.
I've used this to my advantage more than once in a fight.
Obviously.

Maybe it's my Dark World blood, but I actually like punching things. Besides, when you use a blasting rod, you need a little space between you and the guy you're blasting. You need only five inches to punch someone in the kidneys.

When I'm in a fight, I don't give a frayed Thread about being civilized. What I care about is winning.

CHAPTER EIGHTEEN

I wake with a foggy brain and a sharp pain in my ankle.

It's dark in the room, but there's a light on in the hall—just bright enough for me to see that there's someone in the room with me, sitting at the foot of the bed.

I scramble back.

"Who are you?"

The person reaches out and turns on a lamp on the bedside table.

It's a girl about my age. Her skin is lighter than Morgan's, her hair a riot of curls that have been subdued into two ponytails on the top of her head. She's dressed in a crisp white tennis skort with lime green trim and a matching polo. There is an air of comforting kindness about her. She's like Snow White and chamomile tea mixed together and poured into the body of a runway model.

"Your ankle is broken," she says gently. "Just a hairline fracture, but walking on it will make it worse." As she says the words, she reaches out a finger and skims it along my ankle.

I feel another jab of pain before I wrench my ankle out of her reach.

"Oh," she says, wide-eyed. "Did that hurt?"

"Yes." I have to suck in a few deeps breaths before I can speak. "You're Ro."

She jerks her hand away from me, looking startled, and then giggles. "Morgan is right. That is disconcerting."

"What is?"

"You are. Knowing things about us when you've never met us."

"I'm sorry," I say, feeling like a stalker again.

"No! It's okay." Ro breaks into a grin. She bounces a little, tucking one leg up under her. "Tell me more. What do the books say about me?" She leans forward, looking like a tween eager to gossip at a slumber party. "How did he describe me? Obviously, he got my physical description right, or you wouldn't have recognized me. But what kinds of powers do I have in the books?"

"You have an affinity to the alkaline elements."

"Oh," She sits back, frowning. "Well, that's a bummer."

"Why? Is that not your power in real life?"

"No, it is," she admits. "It's just, like, the dullest, crappiest affinity ever. Shifters are a drakuna a dozen."

"Shifters?" I ask. "You mean shape-shifters? Like, werewolves?"

"Werewolves?" She looks confused, but then laughs. "I only wish I had that kind of power. No, people with an alkaline affinity are earth movers. Shifters. Because they shift land around."

"That sounds pretty powerful to me."

She scoffs. "Um. No. Almost anyone can do it. It's so common. Most royalty of the seven High Courts hire teams of shifters to reshape their kingdoms. It's a power people curate out of their bloodlines, not one they put in."

"Oh." I don't know what to say to this. It's not like I have any power royalty would envy, either.

She sighs. "Whatever. I was just hoping the fictional me would have cooler powers."

I don't quite know what to say here, because no one wants to be lowest on the totem pole. And Ro definitely is—at least in terms of power.

"Do I have any other powers? Any secret abilities I keep hidden? Any mad fighting skills I pull out in the heat of battle?"

"Um...no."

"Oh." She gives a sage nod. "That's okay, I guess. Just so long as I'm funny."

Something in my expression must give me away.

"Oh, come on!" She throws up her hands. "Don't tell me I'm not even funny!"

I really don't want to disappoint her, so I say brightly, "You rescued Kane from an avalanche once."

"Hmmm," she grumbles, obviously not placated. "But I'm not funny?"

I cringe. "I'm sorry."

"No, it's not your fault," she says with a beleaguered sigh. "It's just...I'm funny and I've got fabulous hair. Those are the only two things I have going for me."

"Those aren't the only two things," I say quickly. "You're gorgeous."

She makes a *phfft* sound and waves away my compliment. "I don't have any affinity for carbon, so that means no glamour at all. Which sucks. Besides, who cares about looks?"

She looks so crestfallen.

I reach out and put my hand on her arm. "I promise you that when I get back to my world, I will track Chuck Wallace down and tell him how funny you are."

There are a lot of things I need to set him straight on. Which, I'm sure he'll be totally into. Because who wouldn't want a deranged teenager showing up on their doorstep, ranting about their imaginary world?

Still, Ro beams at me, looking a little misty-eyed. "Thank

you." She squeezes my hand, then sighs. "That's going to make this so much harder."

"What?"

"Healing your ankle."

"But you're not a healer."

"Oh! Of course not!" She smiles gently. "Not with any of the soft tissue, at least. If my parents had enough money to curate my blood for an affinity to carbon, I could numb your pain receptors and—" She snaps her fingers. "You wouldn't feel a thing when I heal your foot. Which I totally can do, because of my affinity to calcium. All those little calcium atoms... I can make those do anything I want. The really good healers have affinities to calcium, carbon, even oxygen and nitrogen. Instead you're stuck with me." Her frown deepens. "Ugh. I hate hurting people."

I laugh at that.

Which only makes her frown deepen. "I'm serious! It's really going to hurt."

"I believe you. Whatever you're going to do, I can take it. I promise."

"Maybe." She shifts her gaze from mine. "But nobody likes people who cause them pain. And I was kind of hoping you and I would be friends."

I put my hand on her arm again. "It's okay. I promise, we can still be friends."

It's a little crazy—me, reassuring her. Comforting her. Usually, it's the other way around. Nurses, doctors, therapists— reassuring me. You can do this. You're stronger than you think. This scar will fade. Your father still loves you in his own way.

I was never good at telling the truth from the lies, but I was great at forgiving the liars.

Ro is right. It does hurt.

It's a bone deep burning, like nothing I've ever felt.

Which totally makes sense, since she's rearranging the cells in my ankle, actually stitching them back together.

I try not to show it, because I don't want to freak her out. When it gets so bad I can't catch my breath, I pull over a pillow and press my face into it. So she can't see my tears.

Then, slowly, the fire in my ankle cools to a steady warmth. I force my facial muscles to relax before lowering the pillow to squeeze it to my chest like a stuffed animal.

Ro is still beside me on the bed, her hand is still on my ankle. Tears stream down her face, as she mutters, "I'm so sorry. I'm so sorry."

"It's okay," I say, between gasping breaths.

"It was worse than I thought." She turns and glares behind her. "You said it wasn't that bad."

I follow her gaze to see Kane standing in the doorway, his shoulder propped against the doorjamb.

I drop the pillow and push myself up against the ones at my back.

"I didn't think it was that bad. She was walking on it."

Ro glares at me and then back at him. Her glare is about as forceful as a kitten's. "Well, she shouldn't have been. She's lucky she didn't do any ligament damage. I couldn't have fixed that."

Kane tips his head toward me. His mouth twitches, almost like he's trying not to smile. "Hear that? Next time, don't try so hard to be tough."

"Are you laughing at me?"

"Never." The twitch doesn't go away.

"You're definitely laughing."

"This expression is amazement. Not humor. Ro has done this to me before. Two ribs and my clavicle. I know it hurts."

"You know it hurts and that amuses you?"

"No. Last time she healed me, it took four guys to hold me down."

"Oh." I don't know what to say to that. Or how to respond to the grudging respect in his eyes. After a second, we both look away.

That guy you think you know. I'm not him.

I know that.

But do I?

I should be better now at telling the truth from the lies. But am I?

Because I may not be able to forgive myself if I'm the liar.

Excerpt from
Book Five of The Traveler Chronicles:
The Traveler Undone

You think I seem a bit young to be a hardened criminal?

You think a guy who is nineteen is a bit young to do whatever job you're hiring for?

Maybe you're right.

Or maybe I have an advantage you haven't thought of. After all, everyone underestimates a nineteen-year-old. You just did, didn't you?

CHAPTER NINETEEN

"Thank you," I say to Ro. "What you did was amazing."

She waves the compliment aside. "It's nothing. Any mud slinger could have done it."

"Mud slinger?" I ask, but then realize she's using it as an insult for her own talents.

She gives a sardonic smile. "Thankfully, Morgan feels guilty that our parents spent their entire fortune curating his affinity. So he spoils me."

"Well, maybe any mud slinger could have done this, but I think you're a miracle worker."

She beams. "I think I'm going to like being friends with you."

She brushes my hair off my forehead in a way that's vaguely maternal, then pats my hand before turning to leave.

"So that's Ro," I say once she's shut the door behind her. I scoot to the edge of the bed and swing my legs off.

"I take it she's in the books, too?"

"Yeah, she—" I cut myself off. In the books, she has a crush on Kane. I guess it's reassuring that the fight with the Kellas cats isn't the only thing Wallace got right. "She's prettier than Wallace describes."

No, I am not fishing to see if this Kane feels differently about Ro.

But all Kane says is, "She does good bone work."

"How did you know it was fractured?" I ease my weight onto my foot.

"I didn't. Not for sure. But the more you walked on it, the worse it seemed to get."

I took a tentative step forward and felt no pain. My ankle was as good as new.

As much as I would love marveling at Tuathan health care, I have a job to do here in the Kingdoms of Mithres. Knowing this conversation is not going to get any easier, I blurt out, "I know you're not him, but —"

"There is nothing after the 'but' in that sentence."

"Yes, there is. You may not be exactly like that guy in the books, but you *are* supposed to be king."

"I was wondering if that was in there."

"It's not just *in there*." I make air quotes around the words "in there." "It's the whole point. The entire series is your journey from boy-who-would-be-king to King."

"*His* journey," Kane corrects me softly.

"*Your* journey. Your mother was queen, right?"

He gives an obviously reluctant nod.

"When she presented you to the king for the naming ceremony, he recognized you as his heir, right?"

I see the truth in his eyes. There are things Wallace got wrong, but that's not one of them. "The power of the high king is bound to you. If you don't —"

"Why doesn't he do it?"

I am so surprised at Kane's interruption, it takes me a second to understand his question. "He's a changeling. He doesn't think people will accept him. Or that he's worthy of power."

"No offense, but your Kane sounds like kind of a douchebag."

"He is *not* a douchebag."

"Really? All the Kingdoms of Mithres are descending into chaos, civil war is about to break out, and he doesn't step up because he's wallowing in angst?" He gives a shrug. "Sounds kind of douchey to me."

"Okay, then." This is a common topic of debate among the fandom. But hearing it from Kane (this version of Kane, anyway), well, it stings a little. "So what are *your* reasons for not taking power?"

"My reasons..." He lets the words hang there in the air between us for a second. "Are none of your business."

Ouch. That stings. Still, I'm not letting him assassinate Kane's character. "The point is, Kane...I mean, my Kane... In the end he steps up. He does the right thing."

Kane looks as if he is about to say something else, but before he can, Morgan walks in carrying a drink.

"Ah, Cupcake is alive and well."

Kane takes the opportunity to bug out, and he's gone before I can say anything else. Damn it.

"I can tell from your expression that Kane is being annoying. Don't take it personally. It's what he does best."

I jab a finger in his face. "You have no room to talk."

Morgan holds up his free hand, in a universal sign of surrender. "Whoa, there. Whatever I did, I apologize."

I give him the stink eye.

"Mind telling me what I'm apologizing for?"

"You were supposed to save him!"

"Ah. That." Morgan holds the drink out to me. "This is for you. I thought you might be thirsty."

"No, thank you." Like I'm going to trust an assassin to pour me a drink.

Yeah, I'm taking out my annoyance with Kane on Morgan. Maybe that's not fair, but it's not like he doesn't have it coming. He takes a sip of his drink. "You know, you impressed me.

Not many of the Tuatha would fight a Kellas cat and win. I'm guessing even fewer Dark Worlders could pull it off."

"I did what I had to do to protect Kane. In the book, you save him."

He smirks. "You should be thanking me."

"Thanking you?" I ask in disbelief.

"Of course. Kane already trusts me. He knows I have his back." Morgan pauses to waggle his hand. "More or less." He takes another sip before tipping his glass in my direction. "But you? You were an unknown. A potential enemy. Until you jumped out of the car to fight by his side. Now he believes you have his back, and he knows you're competent in a fight. After all, any girl who can hold her own against a Kellas cat..."

"Yeah. You said that already. You expect me to believe you did this on purpose?"

"I guess it all depends on how smart you think I am," he says with a smooth smile.

In the books, Morgan is very smart. But you never really know if he's on the up and up. Kane may trust him, but he's still an assassin. And a damn good one, if the size and elegance of this house is any indication.

"Cupcake," he says softly. "I'm on your side here. Just like you, I want Kane to go to the island. Just like you, I know he has to rescue the princess."

I suck in a breath. "Did you know this was going to happen?"

"I can travel through time, not see the future."

"What else do you know? Do you know who his mother is?"

"Are you asking if I know his mother is Queen Nerida? I do."

"Then you know he should be king."

"Yes."

There is a hesitancy in his voice that I push right past. "He has to be king," I insist. "Everything in his life has been leading up to this. Together we can convince him—"

"Let's just get him to the island first. We'll worry about what happens next after that."

It's not a comfortable thing, looking at a person who is so unnaturally beautiful, but I force myself to meet his gaze as I ask, "Do you give me your word your goal is to help Kane rescue the princess and the Curator?"

He doesn't even blink. "I'll do everything I can to help."

"Well then, it's a good thing you're rich. Because the two of us can't get Kane to that island on our own. We're going to need to hire people. If you want to help Kane, you can bankroll the operation."

Morgan's perfect lips curve into a wry smile. "Well, you are a clever girl, aren't you?"

"So you'll do it? You'll pay for everything?"

"I did just promise, didn't I?"

"I still don't trust you," I warn him.

"I wouldn't expect you to." He takes another sip of his drink and as he lowers it, he murmurs, "Smart, tough, and naturally suspicious. One would almost think you were Tuatha."

And then, without saying anything else, he leaves.

Excerpt from
Book Five of The Traveler Chronicles:
The Traveler Undone

They say nothing good lasts forever. I guess that's true. No matter how good a bit of magic is, no matter how clever, how refined, or how strong, dawn and dusk always wash it away. Except for some very powerful rune magic, nothing stands up to dawn and dusk. Ancient Tuatha thought there was magic in the pink light of dawn and dusk. Turns out, they weren't wrong. It's something about the UV light spectrum. If you want more info than that, you can ask a scientist. I don't really understand it, but I know this: whatever magic spell you're working on, finish it by dawn. Because once the light changes, you're screwed.

I guess the upside is that if nothing good lasts forever, nothing bad does, either.

CHAPTER TWENTY

Alone in the guest room, I take a minute to emotionally and physically get my shit together.

I find my messenger bag, which also looks like it got the Tuatha-cleaning-service treatment. The spot where the stitching was pulling out has been fixed and the three-year-old Cadbury Crème Egg stain is gone. Besides that, it's fine. All my stuff is still in there.

I put everything back in the bag and sling it over my shoulder before going to look for Kane.

Morgan's house is as big as it seemed at first glance and I wander around, moving through one vast room after another before I catch the sound of conversation and follow it to the kitchen. I pause in the doorway, my nose twitching at the scent of the ocean lingering in the air.

Ro is puttering around in the kitchen. Kane and Morgan are at the table, and they stop talking the second I walk in. There's someone new at the table with them. I recognize him as easily as I did Morgan and Ro.

It's an understatement to describe the newcomer as grubby. His nose is bulbous, his chins numerous. He's wearing a voluminous trench coat and a dingy fisherman's cap.

Yet, there is something likable about him. Maybe it's his friendly smile or the merry twinkle in his eyes. He looks like

Santa Claus, if Santa had retired to spend his days fishing and drinking in Florida.

I've stared at him too long, so I say, "And you must be Mr. Crab."

Before he can answer, Morgan says, "Yes, this malodorous gentleman is indeed Crab. However did you guess?"

Crab stands up and he's hardly any taller standing than he was sitting. He pulls the cap from his head with a nod. "Pleased to meet you, darling. And what might your name be?"

"I'm—"

"You can call her Cupcake," Kane interrupts before I can answer.

Crab smiles as he glances down at my T-shirt. "Ah, yes. Of course. Understand completely. Not offended at all." He rotates the hat in his hands as he speaks. "I'm honored, I am, to be included in an endeavor such as this. Why, I was saying to Mr. Morgan here just a moment ago—"

"Easy there," Morgan says gently.

"Yes, yes. Of course."

He holds out his hand and, when I step close enough to shake it, the briny scent of ocean water clogs my senses.

"Good to meet you, Mr. Crab."

"Just Crab'll do, if you don't mind." Instead of just shaking my hand, he clasps it in both of his.

I expect his skin to be cold, clammy. Instead, it's warm. Despite his obsequious manner, he's charming. Comforting, like a favorite uncle. A pleasant childhood memory. A secret hope held close to my heart.

"I'm so very pleased to be included in this grand scheme of yours, m'dear. Thank you ever so much."

"No. Thank you." He's still talking. Still holding my hand. Still luring me in. And I don't mind. Not at all. I could listen to the gentle cadence of his voice for hours. I've had such a long day. How nice would it be to just relax for a few minutes?

A gentle hand on my shoulder pulls me back a step. "Easy there, Cupcake." Morgan nods to Crab, his expression guarded. "Talk a little less, why don't you?"

Crab blinks innocently. "Now, hey there. You don't think—"

"Talk. Less." Kane stands. "You don't talk to her again." He gives Crab a hard stare as he enunciates each word clearly. "Got it?"

I blink rapidly as I realize what's just happened. Ro's smile is a mixture of amusement and exasperation. Only Kane looks annoyed.

Holy shit. Even knowing exactly what he is, I just got Sirened.

"Wow." I murmur. "That's impressive."

Crab smiles, giving me a nod and wink.

Kane, Morgan, and Crab sit back down. Kane has a notepad at his elbow. Maps are laid out on the table. Ro is still busy in the kitchen, pointedly not taking part in the conversation, but I can tell she's listening.

Neither Morgan nor Crab meet my gaze. And I don't like the defiance in Kane's eyes.

"You're planning my rescue mission without me," I say.

"It's not your rescue mission. It's mine."

"But—"

"I'm the one who lost the princess," he insists. "I'll get her back."

"I told them you'd hate being left behind," Ro says from the kitchen.

"Left behind?" I whirl back to glare at Kane. "You weren't even going to bring me with you?"

"You're a Dark Worlder, which means you're already in danger any time you step outside the wards of this house."

"Oh, hell no. I'm not staying here."

"The wards around Morgan's house are almost impenetrable. You'll be safe."

Safe? I don't want to be safe. I want to make a difference. I want to protect Kane, to keep *him* safe. He's the one who's in danger here...only I can't tell them.

"Smyth is one of the most powerful people in the kingdoms. And you're confronting him in his stronghold, on the island he designed to be a fortress. There's no way I'm letting you bench me."

"Bench you?" Morgan asks.

The frowns on everyone's faces make me realize they are unfamiliar with this term.

"Bench me. It's a sporting term. You know when you accidently kick the ball into the coach's son's face and knock his front tooth out, and then you spend the rest of the season sitting on the bench?"

But I can tell I haven't convinced anyone. This is what I get for trying to use a sports analogy.

"Don't take it personally." Ro gives my shoulder a squeeze. "Kane is always trying to protect other people. It's one of his issues."

"It's not one of my issues," Kane says under his breath.

Ro gives a dismissive wave of her hand. "It is *so* one of your issues. But, Kane, you can't protect everyone. If you don't rescue the princess, she's not going to make it to Saint Lew in time for her wedding. That prince from the Han Court who she's supposed to marry does not seem like the kind of dude who is going to take rejection well. How long do you think it'll be before civil war breaks out?"

Kane sets his jaw at a stubborn angle but doesn't answer.

"Smyth wants chaos among the High Courts. It's the excuse he needs to abolish the Seven Courts entirely and unite the entire kingdom under...I don't know...the Grand Republic of Smyth."

Morgan gives a snort of laughter. "Calm down, sis. I doubt it's as bad as all that."

Kane tips his head in my direction begrudgingly, but still. "What do you think, Cupcake? Is that Smyth's plan? In the books, at least?"

"Pretty much. He thinks the Courts are petty and irrational. Unfit to rule the kingdoms. He doesn't trust anyone but himself with that job."

Ro drops her arm from around my shoulder to square off against Kane on her own. "You need the princess to marry the Han prince. Those two courts together might be strong enough to defeat Smyth once and for all. Unless you know someone else who could unite the courts against Smyth…"

She lets the suggestion dangle.

Does she know that Kane is the king's missing heir? It sure as hell sounds like she does.

"My point is," Ro continues. "If Cupcake wants to help, why not let her?"

Piggybacking on Ro's argument, I pull out the remaining empty chair at the table and sit in it. "You need me, and you know it. You can't even plan this rescue mission without my information."

"If I planned the rescue mission in the book"—he leans back in his chair and crosses his arms over his chest, a cocky smirk settling on his lips—"I can plan it in real life."

God, he's arrogant.

It's a quality I loved in Kane the Traveler.

Being on the receiving end of it, though, is devastating. That smirk makes all my girly parts breathless.

But I don't have time to sit here, fanning myself and swooning. One day, that arrogance may get him killed. If I don't do something, that day is right around the corner.

"Maybe you can get there," I admit. "But in the book, you

waste valuable time. You make a lot of mistakes. Things go wrong. I can prevent that."

"True. But you've already tipped your hand. Back in my workshop, you told me several things about the island. I've got enough to go on that I don't need your help."

They don't understand sports analogies, but poker analogies they get? Great.

No. That's better, actually. I'm good at poker.

"Okay, so you know it's an island," I admit with a shrug. "But you don't know where it is."

Without even looking down at the table, Kane points to one of the maps. "Back at my place, you called it Gull Veston Island. In your world, there is an island off the coast of Houston called Galveston Island. I'm guessing it's there."

I looked down at the maps and realize that one is of the Kingdoms of Mithres and the other is of my world. They are surprisingly similar. Kane is pointing to the map of my world, to the barrier islands that stretch along the entire Texas coast.

"It's not Galveston Island." I'm not even bluffing. I think the island prison is on the much smaller Pelican Island.

He narrows his gaze slightly, leaning forward.

I do the same, feeling like a gunslinger in an old John Wayne movie. "And you don't know about the rest of the magical barriers."

"You mentioned cliffs of insanity."

Aha! At least I have him here. "Which is a reference to a Dark Worlder movie, that you haven't possibly—"

"I've seen *The Princess Bride*."

"You have?"

"We import a lot of Dark Worlder culture."

Huh. I didn't see that coming.

"Yeah, if you think people like Jackson Pollock here, you should see how crazy they are for *Game of Thrones*." Kane lets that sink in a minute before saying, "So I figure the Cliffs of Insanity are just really high cliffs. We can handle that."

"Maybe you can. Or, maybe I have a better way of getting you up the cliffs. A faster way. A safer way." I *am* bluffing here. Sure, I have an idea. But it's a harebrained, crazy-as-hell idea. "And, there are at least two more barriers to the island that I haven't told you about yet."

My gaze never wavers from Kane's. He meets my eyes, without blinking.

"You should at least listen to her," Morgan says in that deep, placating voice of his.

Kane shifts his gaze from me to Morgan. "Whose side are you on here?"

"I'm on the side that doesn't get you killed."

"Fine," Kane says, leaning back in his chair so that it tips back on two legs. "You can help plan the mission."

"Not good enough. I get to come along. I want your promise."

"Fine. I promise."

"A binding promise," I clarify.

At that, Kane laughs. It's the first time I've heard him laugh, and the sound is low and deep, but tinged with bitterness. It does powerful things to all those girly parts I'm having trouble controlling.

That laugh of his hits my emotions even harder. I don't want him to be bitter. I want more than that for him.

"If you think I'm going to tell you my binding name, then you aren't smart enough to be on this crew."

My cheeks burn with embarrassment.

"If I don't have a binding promise from you, how can I trust that you're going to hold up your end of the bargain?"

"If you don't trust me, you probably shouldn't be following me into a dangerous situation."

I meet his gaze, knowing that this is a test. If I waver, if I stumble, he's not going to take me seriously. And if I drop the ball now, I may never get my hands on it again.

I tip up my chin. "I won't be following you. You'll be following me."

His lips twitch just a little. I didn't drop the ball.

And look at that, I can use a sports analogy after all.

Excerpt from
Book Five of The Traveler Chronicles:
The Traveler Undone

I have a lot of friends who… How do I say this without pissing everyone off?

Friends who operate ever so slightly outside the law.

Crab is one of those people.

Not everyone trusts Sirens. Then again, not everyone needs a partner who can talk his way out of any situation and happens to own the fastest damn boat on the continent.

CHAPTER TWENTY-ONE

O kay, so I'm not going to get a binding promise out of Kane. I'll just have to keep my cards close to my chest. To reveal only what I have to, when I have to.

There is one thing we have to discuss, though. My harebrained, crazy-as-hell idea.

I can't pretend this isn't dangerous, so I blurt it out. "To get up the Cliffs of Insanity, we need the Kellas cat."

Morgan looks up. "The Kellas cat?"

I nod. "The one you captured after the fight. Do you still have it?"

"Yeah, it's in a crate in the garage."

"What do you mean 'need'?" Ro asks.

"She'll be a useful ally."

Everyone at the table stills, but Ro's reaction is the most dramatic.

"The Kellas cat? Are you kidding?"

"No, I—"

"A Kellas cat isn't an ally." Her words pour out. "You can't hire her. And unless one of us is a master of cats and hasn't mentioned it, we can't make her work for us."

Ro backs away quickly, her palms raised as if she's washing her hands of us.

Kane stands, holding up his own hands, palm out. "I know

you don't like Kellas cats. No one's going to make you work with her if you don't want to." He steps closer to her and reaches out to touch her shoulder reassuringly. "Let's just hear what Cupcake has to say," Kane says in a soothing tone. It almost makes me wonder if he has a little Siren blood himself. "Agreed?"

After several heartbeats, Ro gives just the slightest twitch of her head.

"Okay, Cupcake, talk us through it."

I lay the plan out as simply as I can.

"Somewhere hidden in the cliffs, there's a staircase. It's carved into the cliffs themselves, made from the same rock. It will be almost impossible to see with the naked eye. That's why we need Ro. She'll be able to touch the rock and use her affinity to calcium to map out the cliffs in her mind. The stairway will be well hidden. Without her, we might not find it."

Kane turns to Ro. Her arms are folded over her chest, holding onto herself for strength. "Does that sound doable?"

"Maybe," she hedges. "It's not easy, but — " She waits a long time before nodding. "I can find the staircase."

Morgan holds up a hand to pause the conversation. "Wait a second. We're going to walk up all those stairs? Exactly how tall are the Cliffs of Insanity?"

"According to Wallace, they go up a mile."

"That's almost six thousand steps."

"Exactly." I take a deep breath and plunge ahead. "We need a way up those cliffs that doesn't involve walking up them. That's where the Kellas cat comes in."

"How does *that cat* help with the stairs?"

"We're going to send the Kellas cat up the steps. Then Kane can create a loop from the boat to where the cat is."

Ro frowns, shaking her head. "He can't just create a loop from any one spot to another. It has to be somewhere he's been before. Someplace he can visualize."

"Yes. That's why we need the Kellas cat."

Kane is squinting at me in confusion. "How does the Kellas cat affect that?"

"You're going to need to form a mental bond with her."

Suddenly, I have the attention of everyone at the table. There's a beat of silence, and then Morgan leans forward and says, "Excuse me?"

"A what?" Kane asks.

"A telepathic bond. If you have a link to the cat, she can show you in her mind exactly where she is. You'll be able to create a loop to wherever she's standing."

Kane is shaking his head. "None of my affinities are telepathic."

"Well, sure but her—" I look around the table and see nothing but confusion reflected back. "You guys know Kellas cats are telepathic, right?"

"What?" Morgan asks.

"I thought you said your mom had a dowt of Kellas cats?"

"She did. I just didn't—" Morgan tilts his head to the side. Then he looks at his sister. "Did you know Kellas cats were telepathic?"

Ro focuses her attention on nibbling on her thumbnail. "I thought they might be," she finally admits.

"Wait a second," Kane says. "If we didn't know Kellas cats were telepathic, how was that in the books?"

I shrugged. "It's not. But, in the Dark World, domestic cats meow only to people, not other cats. Kellas cats are the same. They speak aloud only when they're around humans. Didn't you notice during the fight that they seemed to be communicating without words with one another?"

"I didn't think about it. I was more worried about the cat trying to kill me."

"Well, for my plan to work, we'd better make sure you can form a telepathic bond with her."

Morgan leans forward. "First, we'd better make sure she's not going to kill us all."

"Kane spared her life. She owes him the death-debt. She'll be honor bound to return the favor."

"There's only one way to know if this will work," Kane says slowly. "We'll have to ask the cat."

Ro pushes herself away from the counter, brushing tears from her cheeks as she flees the kitchen.

"Ro, wait."

She stops at the sound of her brother's voice.

"Listen, this plan could work," he says softly. "I know you hate Kellas cats, but you won't be alone this time. We'll all be together. Maybe this is dangerous, but that's never stopped you from doing something before. You're braver than this."

"What is it to you, anyway?" she asks Morgan, her gaze filled with fear. "This isn't your fight."

"You're the one who said that if we don't rescue them, civil war will break out. We need to figure out what Smyth is up to. Kane and I are going to that island. We need you to help us get there."

Ro nods wordlessly, still brushing away tears as she leaves the room.

Well, there goes my one friend in the Kingdoms of Mithres — and I just made her cry. Ro is sweet and kind, but for my plan to work, I'm essentially going to torture her with her greatest fear.

And my mother wonders why I don't have more friends.

Excerpt from
Book Five of The Traveler Chronicles:
The Traveler Undone

Dragons, Kellas cats, hellhounds, and Tuatha all have different native languages. Since most of these creatures don't naturally get along anyway, for most of our history, interspecies negotiations went to hell every time anyone opened their mouths.

Now, nearly everyone speaks some English.

You know why?

TV. Everyone likes Dark World TV.

When you look at it like that, I'm practically an ambassador for peace.

CHAPTER TWENTY-TWO

O nce Ro leaves, silence falls over the room. I'm not great with awkward silences, and I have to fight the urge to make a bad joke to break the tension.

Thankfully, Kane clears his throat and says, "Come on, Cupcake, let's go talk to a cat."

He leads me out of the kitchen and down a long hall.

"So has Ro always been so…" I search around for the least judgy word. "nervous about Kellas cats?"

Kane shoots me a look which implies I've overstepped my boundaries.

I did mention that I wasn't good with awkward silences, right?

"I just…it never came up in the books." Kane doesn't answer. "I mean, Morgan did say, 'You won't be alone this time.' That implies there was some other time when she was alone and when something bad happened. Is that why Ro's afraid of them?"

"What do you think?"

"Is it true the cats in his mother's dowt used to perch on Morgan's chest, hoping he would die in his sleep?"

"The Tuatha stretch the truth, sure. But we don't lie."

I think about when the Kellas cat sat on my chest and remember the uneasy sensation that my soul was tearing loose from my body.

What must have it been like to experience that as a child? Worse still, to know that the creature was your mother's pet.

I shudder.

Kane, who has been watching me, nods. "Exactly."

"Why would his mother keep a dowt of Kellas cats if she couldn't control them?"

"Presumably, she could. Morgan's alive, right?"

"He must have lived in constant fear. Why didn't she stop them?"

"Tuatha aren't exactly known for their parental instincts." We reach the end of the hall, and he opens a door and gestures me through. "And just remember, Morgan was her favorite."

No wonder Ro was terrified of them. "Jesus."

Kane shuts the door behind us and flicks on the light. We are in a garage large enough for multiple cars. The overhead lights only illuminate the spot directly in front of us, which is empty except for a large wooden crate that's impossible to see inside. Sections of the crate bear visible scratch marks, and in other places, the wood is splintered and frayed.

"How long has she been in there?" I ask.

"Since the fight."

"Did you get her any food or water?"

Kane clears his throat. "Well, since we didn't have any spare souls lying around to feed her, no."

Well, there goes my PETA membership.

"Surely Kellas cats don't actually subsist on human souls."

There is a faint click of a door closing behind us, and then Ro says, "Kellas cats eat a high protein diet, just like all other cats."

Ro walks forward. She has a small dish in each hand. One contains water, the other, some sort of flaked meat that smells like fish.

"You don't have to be here," Kane says.

"My brother thinks that if I don't see this with my own eyes, I won't believe it." Ro gives a wry smile.

"Even if we can't use the cat," Kane says. "We need to question her."

"Question her?" Ro asks.

"Yes." His voice is hard and emotionless. "If we play our cards right, we might be able to find out who her master is."

Ro is nearly shaking as she crouches down in front of the crate and sets down both bowls. "An offering to you, cat of the Kells."

A low growl issues from within the crate and, fast as lightning, a paw appears between the slats. Inch-long claws dig in the wood before the paw jerks back, taking a chunk with it.

There's another rumbling growl, then the animal presses her face to the wood, peering through the hole she'd enlarged.

Her green eyes practically glow.

Even knowing it's merely the reflective quality of her eyes, she still looks creepy as shit.

I have to force myself to walk over to the crate.

What am I doing here?

A creature like this one nearly killed me twelve hours ago. But it's not like I have a lot of options. I have to make this work.

So I crouch beside the crate and peer through the gap at the creature within. "How long have you been awake?"

"Long enough," she rasps with an inhuman voice, "to know that you do not know as much about Kellas cats as you think you do."

Her voice grates on my nerves like a cat's tongue on delicate skin.

I meet her gaze. "Then tell me."

She makes a rumbling growl full of hate. "You do not control me, child of the Dark World. You are not my master."

A few years ago, my mom cared for a girl about my own age. Kendal had been treated for cancer on and off since she was five. I didn't have a lot of friends, but Kendal had none. She knew no one except her family. And she knew she wasn't coming out of her struggle alive. That girl had anger like I'd never seen. Bitterness. Resentment. Impotent rage. That was all she had left in her.

This cat reminds me of Kendal.

I have always regretted not trying to befriend her.

The truth is, this cat has every right to be angry.

I shift to sit cross-legged in front of the crate.

"I'm not ordering you," I explain. "I'm asking for information."

"I have no debt with you," she growls.

"No. You don't. But you do have a death-debt with Kane. You are honor bound to protect him."

"To protect him and him alone. Not his dowt-mates."

"True," I agree. "But you and I share a goal. We both want to keep him alive. He will face many challenges in the next few days."

"How do you know this?"

"I have the sight." The words come easily to me, since, I kind of do. I just hope the cat doesn't hear Kane's snort of derision. "If you refuse to help us, he will die." This isn't a lie, and my breath catches on the words as I say them. "If that happens, you will never be free of your death-debt."

She growls again, but this time, I sense it's not aimed at me. It's just a general sign of her displeasure.

I reach for the cage's latch, but pause. "Just so you know, you can't kill me. Or Ro. Or any of the others. If you want to repay your death-debt, we all have to work together. Got it?"

"And then my death-debt will be paid?"

"Yes."

But before I can release the latch, Kane's fingers close around mine.

"Let me." His fingers are warm and strong on mine. His touch is unsettling, but the certainty in his gaze reassures me.

We all hold our breath as the door swings open. The cat moves slowly through the opening, apparently as hesitant to trust us as we are to trust her.

Her whiskers twitch as she sniffs the air for danger. A moment later, she steps, blinking, into the light. She's as big as a dog, maybe fifty or sixty pounds. Her body is a little longer, her legs shorter and more powerful. Her tail curves in an angry *S* toward the ground. In the dark, her fur looked black, but she's actually a brindled mix—charcoal and black, the color of shifting shadows. Her coat is sleek, except for the ruff of fur around her face, almost like the mane of a bobcat. She is as beautiful as she is terrifying.

She continues sniffing the air. Her body tenses and her nose twitches ever so slightly in the direction of the bowls of food and water. I can practically feel her hunger and thirst. With an overt show of will, she turns her back on the offering Ro made.

Ro speaks first. "Tell us, can you reveal who your master is?"

For a long moment, the cat merely stares at Ro, her head tilted to the side, her expression unreadable. "I cannot reveal that information if my master has ordered me not to."

Well that's not much of an answer. "Did your master order you not to reveal that information?"

She flicks her tail in apparent displeasure. "Yes."

"Are you still under your master's command?"

Slowly her head swivels toward me. "Child of the Dark World, you claim to be a seer. And you seem to know much about the laws of honor that dictate how cats behave. Do you not know the answer for yourself?"

"I believe honor dictates you pay your death-debt before

you can return to your master. Am I right?"

"You are correct." She walks over to Kane and sits, sphinxlike before him, bowing her head slightly. "It is to you alone I owe this death-debt. Tell me how I may save your life so that my honor may be restored."

Kane looks slightly disconcerted. He stands and backs up a step. "Cupcake, this is your plan. Why don't you explain to the cat how this is supposed to work?"

"Okay, then. Can you communicate telepathically with a human?"

She turns her green gaze on me. "I have never tried."

"You've never had a death-debt to a human?" Kane asks.

"Obviously," she sneers, with scorn worthy of Snape.

Getting information from this cat is like pulling teeth. On the other hand, she's not slashing the flesh from my body. So at least, there's that.

"And what about your master. Do you communicate telepathically with him?"

"The dowt feels the will of the master. However, we do not share the master's thoughts. We cannot express our own will or thoughts."

"So it's a one-way street. What we need is two-way communication. Can you do that with a human?"

"I can try. If the master were to order me." She tips her head in Kane's direction. "Or if he was to ask it of me."

"Well, then, where do we —"

Before he can finish the sentence, Kane lets out a groan and drops to his knees, clutching his head in his hands.

Shit.

I run to him. "Are you okay?" No. Shit. He obviously is not okay. I whirl toward the cat. "What did you do to him?"

She stalks toward him, never taking her icy gaze from him as he writhes in pain.

"What are you doing to him?" I run a hand across his shoulder. The muscles under my palm are taut and agonized.

She continues toward him. I try to push her away, but she swats a paw out at me.

I look down at my arm, which is miraculously unharmed. She swatted my arm but didn't scratch me. If her claws had been out—if she'd meant to hurt me—she would have shredded my arm.

Whatever she's doing, it's not malicious.

So when she approaches him slowly, I let her.

She slinks past him, rubbing her cheek and shoulder against his head. And then against his shoulder. She circles him, rubbing her cheek against him over and over.

If she were a domestic cat, I would say she is scenting him. Marking her territory.

He twists on the ground, and I move his head onto my lap. He whimpers, and a lock of hair falls across his brow. I brush it out of the way.

She leaps onto his chest and sits there, kneading. A low, rumbling purr vibrates through the room. And, slowly, the pain leaves his body. His muscles stop spasming, the taut tension gripping him eases. I feel him draw sharp, shuddering breaths that leave him shaking and sweaty.

Slowly, his body relaxes.

Apparently satisfied, she springs from his chest and strolls away to go leap onto the top of the crate, where she sits, cleaning her paws.

I glare at her. "What did you do to him?"

She blinks lazily. "What do you suppose I did? I created the mental bond you requested."

"That's all?"

If cats had eyebrows that they could arch disdainfully, that's what she would have done. "It required some…rewiring. You didn't think creating an inter-species mental link would be easy, did you?"

I don't answer, because Kane opens his eyes. He looks exhausted and worn, but his gaze is clear. Sane. Not at all like someone who's had his brain rewired.

Relief sweeps through me, so profound I have to blink away the hot rush of tears. I swallow hard, tracing the lines of his face. Funny, the sharp angle of his jaw no longer looks strange to me. The caramel brown eyes look right. Even the dimples look perfect. Not at all frivolous, like I'd first thought.

And I'm struck by the urge to lean down and kiss him.

Which I cannot do. I know that. He's not mine.

Once he rescues the princess, he's going to fall in love with her. In addition to being the most beautiful girl I've ever seen, she's powerful. Kane's perfect match.

And yet…

Before I can do something stupid, Ro speaks from behind me. "Are you okay?"

I glance over my shoulder to see her looking like she's poised to run. This must have been a nightmare for her.

I repeat Ro's question. "Are you okay?"

"Yeah," he croaks. His voice sounds like he's been gargling Drano. "How 'bout you?"

I nearly laugh. "Me, I'm great. But I'm not the one who apparently had his nervous system ripped out and reinstalled."

His gaze shifts in the direction of the cat before returning to me. For the briefest moment, all kinds of things flicker through his eyes. Relief, exhaustion, fear, embarrassment. I recognize all of it. I've been there. It's awful when someone sees you that vulnerable. It's like being gutted.

"Oh. Is that what that was?" he asks. "I thought I felt a twinge."

The quip falls a little flat, but I give him a pass.

He wedges his elbow under him and pushes up to a sitting position.

Ro takes a tentative step closer. "The connection is formed?"

He nods.

"And it's…everything is okay? Nothing too scary in there?"

Again, he gives a faint nod. "It's—" Then he shakes his head, like he's trying to clear his mind. "Disconcerting. But it's not too bad."

"Do not fear," the cat says. "It should not take long to learn to seal away some of your thoughts. We cats are quite adept at hiding that which must be private."

Wearily, Kane scrubs a hand down his face. "Well, that was fun."

"What do we do next?" Ro asks.

Kane pushes himself to his feet. "Well, now that we know that Cupcake was right about the Kellas cat, we hear the rest of her plan."

"Wait a second, you didn't really believe you'd be able to form a connection with the Kellas cat?"

He shrugs. "It seemed farfetched."

"But you tried it anyway?"

He gives me a clap on the arm as he walks past me to the door back into the house. "I was the only person in danger, so it seemed worth a shot."

Excerpt from
Book Five of The Traveler Chronicles:
The Traveler Undone

It's no secret I don't like Sirens.

I mean, sure. Everybody likes Sirens. It's their thing. They are undeniably the most likeable creatures on earth.

Saying you don't like Sirens is like saying you don't like Girl Scout cookies. (I had an Seelie princess once who hired me to import five hundred and seventy-nine cases of Thin Mints. So I know what I'm talking about here.)

Still, how can you trust someone who can tell you anything you want to hear and make you believe it?

CHAPTER TWENTY-THREE

I catch up with Kane and the cat right as they walk into the kitchen. The cat slows, then stops, every muscle in her body going tense, her tail bristling.

Crab scrambles to his feet.

"It's okay," Kane says aloud. "This is Morgan and Crab. They're friends."

After several wary heartbeats, the cat takes a hesitant step forward, sniffing the air. Morgan holds out his hand. Not to shake, but for her to sniff, the way you would a dog.

The cat blinks in disdain. Then she walks straight past Morgan to Crab. She bumps her head against his calf and weaves between his legs before sitting on her haunches by his feet.

"Cupcake's idea worked?" Morgan asks.

"Well, I'm not dead."

"Obviously."

"We don't know if this link will let him loop-jump somewhere he's never been."

"Right," Kane says, looking at the cat. "You'll need to go somewhere unfamiliar. We'll stay in contact until I can open a loop to where you are."

"You think you can do it?" Morgan asks.

"Sure."

But there's something in his voice. He sounds…wary.

Which, of course, he is.

He just had his brain rewired, although that's something he's obviously not going to mention to the others. Thank you, male ego.

"We should talk more about the plan!" I blurt out.

Everyone turns and looks at me.

Five identical looks of oh-shit-what's-she-up-to-now.

I offer up a bright smile. "We haven't told the cat the plan yet."

Kane quirks an eyebrow, and I get the feeling he sees right through me.

He shifts his gaze to the cat, stares at her in silence for several heartbeats before shrugging. "Okay. She knows."

"Just like that?" I ask.

"Mental communication is efficient," she says. "Though I am unsure how rescuing a meddling old fool and a bratty princess will repay my death-debt, I am willing to participate."

"The Curator is not—" I begin to correct the cat.

"Meddling and bratty were my words," Kane says.

"Oh." Bratty? He thinks the princess is *bratty*? This does not bode well for their epic romance. But that's a plot twist I'll have to worry about after we rescue her. For now, I have to buy Kane enough time to recover. "What about the Crimson Miasma? I haven't told you about that."

Crab walks back to the table and points to the patch of blue on the map of the Kingdoms of Mithres. "There's a bank of mist that floats off the coast here. It's impossible to sail through."

"It's not actually impossible," I say. "But it does confuse and disorient anyone who tries." I plop down in an empty chair. "Sit! I'll tell you all about it."

Morgan meets my gaze—which I keep innocent. After a second, he smiles, like he knows exactly what I'm doing.

He pulls out a chair of his own. "Yeah, let's talk details."

"We should test my connection to the cat—" Kane argues.

"Shh." Morgan waves aside the protest, propping his chin in his hand and gazing back at me with rapt attention. "Cupcake is telling us her plan."

Frankly, I think he's overdoing it a bit. But Kane sighs and then sits. Obviously, he's used to Morgan's antics.

I start at the beginning and launch into a detailed description of the island's location, history, topography. Anything I can think of to draw the conversation out.

I describe the Crimson Miasma, how it confuses people with images of what they most want. Crab chimes in with additional details from his own encounters. It's not until I describe the Everdawn that cloaks the island that Kane stops me.

"Everdawn is a myth. It's not real."

"In the book—"

"I don't care what Wallace says. Nineteen years in this world and I've never seen Everdawn."

The way Wallace described it, magic simply didn't work for the twenty or so minutes of dawn and dusk. Enchantments end, spells break, potions wear off. It was the magical equivalent of rebooting your computer. For forty minutes every day, the Tuatha had no more power than a human.

Theoretically, if you could stretch the moment of dawn, magic simply couldn't be done there.

"I understand why the idea of Everdawn scares you—"

Kane drops his chair back onto all four legs. "It doesn't scare me. Because it doesn't exist."

Ro comes over and pulls out a chair beside me, putting her hand on my arm. "You have to understand, Everdawn is the monster in the closet. It's the boogeyman Tuatha use to scare their children. 'If you don't behave, I'll trap you in Everdawn.'"

I hold up my hands in a display of innocence. "All I know is, it's in the book."

"I get that it sounds cool. A moment in time when no one can do magic, drawn out for all eternity. But it doesn't exist. I've never seen it. I've never met anyone who's seen it. I've never even read an account of it happening. Think about it. Magic, strong enough to freeze time. No one is that powerful."

"Maybe Wallace is wrong, but—"

"You wouldn't have to freeze time," Morgan says softly.

All of us swivel to look at him.

Morgan gives us a *c'est la vie* sort of shrug. "You wouldn't freeze time. You would hold it in a loop, running the same few minutes over and over."

Kane sits back in his chair. "That would take a crazy amount of power."

Slowly, Morgan nods.

"Could you do that?" Ro asks, her voice a surprised hush.

Apparently, this is magic so vast, it's almost unimaginable.

"Not now," Morgan says firmly, shaking his head like he's shrugging off a bad dream. "When I was younger..." He lets the words trail off.

Kane and Ro seem to take this explanation at face value, but I ask, "Why not now? I thought Tuatha got more powerful as they age."

"Most do. Not timekeepers," Morgan says. "Time magic is different. When you alter the timeline, you have to hold that intention forever. If you let it go, reality could shift back to the original timeline. Handling time isn't magic you do once. It's magic you never stop doing. Over the course of the timekeeper's life, he or she might handle dozens, maybe hundreds, of moments. You can't let a single one of them drop. You can't ever let go of them."

Morgan pauses to let that sink in.

So even now, as he was having this conversation, in the back of his mind, Morgan was holding on to all the time magic he had ever done.

"So it's like juggling?" I say. "Every time you add a new ball, it gets harder to keep them all in the air."

Morgan gives a tight nod. Ro reaches out to run a soothing hand across Morgan's shoulder, and his muscles seem to relax infinitesimally.

"Okay, so Everdawn would be hard to maintain," I say. "But it's not impossible."

"The real question," Kane says slowly. "Is why the Council of Sleekers would bother with Everdawn."

I frown. "What do you mean? Obviously, you don't want people doing magic when they're in prison."

"No." Kane shakes his head. "The detention center is just a holding cell to detain Dark Worlders. You don't need Everdawn to imprison them. The only reason to have Everdawn on that island is to imprison Tuathan citizens of the seven High Courts."

"Well, we know he's keeping the Curator and the princess there, right?"

"Yeah, but we've been assuming that the hellhounds came after you, Cupcake—" He gives me a pointed look. "And that they took the princess and the Curator just because they were near you. But if you're right about the Everdawn, if he's gone to the trouble of creating a magical void on that island of his, then taking the princess and the Curator wasn't an accident. He could imprison any member of the Tuathan High Court there. He could take out the courts one by one and by the time anyone notices, it would be too late to stop him."

Deleted from the Advance Reading Copy of
Book Five of The Traveler Chronicles:
The Traveler Undone

Morgan waits until we're alone before he confronts me.
"When are you going to tell her?"
I play dumb. "Tell her what?"
"That you could send her home."
I shrug. "Maybe I could. Maybe I couldn't."
"You know every thin spot in the veil between worlds from Nawlins to Vegas. Don't tell me you couldn't find one of them that she could pass through."
"What's your point?"
Morgan pushes back his chair and stands. "No point. Just making sure you know what you're doing."
Just like that, Morgan drops it and leaves the room. He's an asshole like that.

CHAPTER TWENTY-FOUR

Kane leans back, tipping his chair up on two legs. "If you know what Smyth is doing, now's the time to tell us."

"In the books, he tries to destroy the monarchy. That's why he doesn't want the princess to get married."

"Does he succeed?"

This is it. The perfect moment to tell him how the book ends. With him, dead, on the floor of the great Cathedral in Saint Lew. I can warn him.

But when I open my mouth, the words choke me.

My binding promise to the Curator becomes a physical thing, slithering around my neck and tightening, trapping the words in my throat.

I close my mouth, swallow the truth I want to say, and instead settle for a half-truth.

"You rescue the princess. Smyth is defeated."

"Then we'll deal with him later. We've got enough to worry about among the island prison, the soul-sucking fog, the Everdawn, and probably hellhounds." He drops his chair forward to study the map again. "Have I left anything out?"

Ro crosses her arms over her chest. "We still don't know that the Kellas cat won't rip out our throats the first chance she gets."

The cat, still sitting behind Crab, says, "I will not. That

would be a poor way to repay my death-debt."

"First," Kane interrupts. "We need to test the bond. Make sure I can open a loop to the cat's location."

"You just conscripted her into service against her will," Ro says. "How do you know that once you release her, she won't return to her master, get new orders, and then attack us all over again when she returns?"

I wouldn't say I am an expert at reading the facial expressions of sentient animals, but if I was, I would interpret the cat's facial expression as amused disdain.

"I owe a death-debt to this man. I will return."

"Or," Morgan drawls. "One of us can go with you."

The cat bows her head slightly in his direction. "If it pleases you."

"I'll do it," I say. "It's my plan. If anyone should do it, it's me."

Several beats pass, but no one else argues with me or offers to take my place. I guess only a Dark Worlder is stupid enough to choose to be alone with a Kellas cat.

Ten minutes later, I'm walking back to the garage, Kane by my side.

Morgan has offered to let me use one of his many cars to drive the cat to a location unknown to Kane. He tells me I can pick any car I want.

Oh, great. I'll be driving.

"Just out of curiosity," I ask. "Why can't Morgan send his driver? The one who picked us up."

"Yeah, I don't think that would work." Kane scrubs a hand across the back of his neck. "Cricket doesn't like cats."

"Cricket?"

"The driver."

"Oh. Cricket's a totally normal name."

"No weirder than Cupcake," he says dryly.

"I didn't pick out Cupcake. You did. I would be perfectly

content if you all called me Edie."

"In your world, people may just go around calling each other by their own names. But here—"

"Yeah, yeah. I know. Binding names are important. But, you know, Edie isn't my name. It's a nickname. My given name is—"

"Whoa, whoa, whoa. Don't go telling me your given name. Don't tell anyone that. Don't the books talk about how important binding names are?"

"They do. I just—" I sigh. I just trust him to know my binding name. Which is probably a sign that the line between the Kane in the books and the Kane who is with me now may be a little too thin.

Time to change the subject. "So Cricket doesn't like cats."

Kane gives me a hard look, one that I feel all the way down my toes. It's like he can see straight through me. But, ultimately, he lets me change the subject. "They freak him out. And that was before he had to sit through the fight out on Morgan's lawn."

"Ah. I see."

"Is it a problem?" Kane asks as he opens the door to the garage.

"No," I say brightly. "Not at all."

"You do know how to drive, right?"

"Isn't that what I just said?" See what I did there? How I didn't really answer?

Because, sure, I know how to drive. Theoretically.

I walk down the three steps to the multibay garage. The cat crate is still in the center of the first spot. Kane flicks on an overhead light before walking down the stairs next to me. The light sputters on to illuminate four cars. Closest to us is the limo Cricket picked us up in. I walk past that for obvious reasons. I don't know it for sure, but I suspect driving a stretch limo is tricky.

"Which one should I take?"

"You decide."

Which leaves three other cars to choose from. The first is a gleaming silver vintage sports car. And by "vintage" I mean expensive. There's something vaguely familiar about it. The middle car is a slick black crossover SUV. On the end is a bland-looking sedan.

I stop by the oldest car. "This one looks pretty innocuous."

"Oh, yeah. That one's Morgan's favorite."

Okay then. Moving right along.

But before I make it past, Kane adds, "It was in a movie."

"A movie?"

"Yeah. One of those spy movies Morgan likes."

I side-eye the car. Not Jason Bourne. It's too old for that. Definitely not *Kingsman*.

"James Bond?" I ask.

"Yeah, those movies."

"Huh." I rub my eyes. No wonder it looks familiar. My mom loves those movies. "Just to be clear, this is the actual car that Sean Connery drove? In *the* James Bond movies?"

"Yeah. You want to drive it?"

"No, I don't want to…" My mom would straight up kill me if I took James Bond's car out for a joyride. I shake my head and move down to the car in the last spot. "I'm just going to drive this nice, boring—" But I break off, tilt my head, and stare at the emblem on the front of the car. "Is this a Bentley?"

Kane scratches the back of his head. "Hell if I know. Cars aren't really my thing."

I eye my choices in despair. "So the magical, timekeeping assassin business pays pretty well, huh?"

Kane looks from me to the cars, his lips starting to curve into a smile. "Yeah. I guess it does."

"I don't suppose he has, like, a late model Kia hidden

anywhere? Maybe a minivan?"

He shakes his head.

"Maybe a golf cart?"

Finally, I walk back to the car in the center spot...where the Porsche is parked. This sucks.

"Keys should be in the car," Kane says.

"Keys should be in the car," I mutter under my breath. Because I'm mature like that.

I open the door and sure enough, there are the keys, sitting on the dash. There's only one problem.

"This is a standard." That's me—master of the obvious.

"Yeah. You can drive a standard, right?"

"Oh, yeah. Sure. Of course. Obviously."

I force a grin in hopes of hiding my internal scream of panic.

My mom taught me how to drive a standard when I turned sixteen. Sort of. It was not a happy time in our relationship. I may or may not have made threats of Greek-tragedy-style murder. After three horrible months, we sold the car before moving to Boston.

So theoretically, I *can* drive a standard.

I look longingly at the other cars in the garage. "Just out of curiosity, are any of the other cars automatic?"

"I don't think so. Morgan likes the feeling of power that comes with controlling a big hunk of iron." Kane shrugs. "Why?"

"No reason." I reach into the car and grab the keys off the dash.

"Hey, Cupcake."

"Yeah?"

"Be careful, okay?"

"I'm going to be driving a Porsche. Yeah. I'm going to be careful."

I straighten as Kane walks closer.

"No, I meant—" He stops just beside the open door, so

I'm trapped between him and the car. "Be careful out there. With the cat."

"Oh." I clench the keys in one hand and clasp the arch of the door with the other. "Yeah. Well—"

"I know you think she's trustworthy, but—"

"Don't you know everything she knows?" I ask. "Everything she's thinking?"

"It doesn't work that way." He scratches his fingernails along the scruff on his jaw, where he's got the beginnings of a five o'clock shadow. "I get surface thoughts. I can't dig into her memories. I can't read her intentions."

I just shrug. "We need her, so we have to find out if this works."

"It doesn't have to be you," Kane says softly.

"Hey," I say, forcing humor into my voice. "I thought you said you didn't care if I lived or died?"

He looks up at me and his lips twitch. Taking a step closer to the car door, he puts his hand on the frame, right next to mine. "I said if we weren't working together, I *probably* wouldn't care."

That's a pretty fine distinction to make, but I decide to let him have it. "You're right, it doesn't have to be me. But it's my idea. So it *should* be me."

"Yeah." His pinky moves, just a little, rubbing along the outside of my hand and my thumb. The touch—so faint and gentle—sends a shock wave of sensation up my arm and all the way into my gut. "But of all of us, you're the most vulnerable. Even Ro is more powerful than you."

For a second, it's all I can do to stare at the spot where he's brushing his finger across my skin. It's the first time he's ever touched me seemingly just because he wants to. Not because I'm weak or he's tending to my wounds, but just for the sake of touching me. It's totally messing with my head. And pulse. And breathing.

Basically, all the regulatory systems that keep me alive. No biggie, though.

I clear my throat and force out something like a laugh. "I wouldn't let Ro hear you say that. Somehow, I don't think she'd like it." I try to sound cool. Breezy, even. But I don't move my hand away from his. "Besides, if the Curator is right and I really am an Untethered Sleeker, then I'm more powerful than any of us know."

I say it with bravado I don't feel.

"Powers you don't know how to use yet."

Sure, that's technically true. I decide not to mention the incident back in the warehouse below his loft. After all, I'm not entirely sure that was me using my powers. That was just me really, really wanting something and then it happened. Which—okay, sure—may be what Sleeker powers are all about, right? Sleekers *will* things into being. Events into happening.

Can Sleekers *will* people into feeling things?

Well, *shit*, that's a disconcerting thought.

I pull my hand away from the door of the car. Away from Kane's hand.

I thrust both my hands behind me, wrapping my fingers around the keys, and squeeze.

"For all we know, my powers will magically appear if I'm stressed."

"I'm not joking here." A scowl settles on his face as he stares down at the spot where his hand now rests alone on the doorframe.

Somehow, the scowl doesn't make him any less attractive. It just makes him more intense.

"Yeah, it's the sense of humor thing that you need to work on." My quip doesn't help with the scowl. I inadvertently squeeze the keys too hard and the car bleeps in protest. I jump a little, but the scowl fades from Kane's face, and his lips twitch.

Good. He's amused by me again.

I can be the plucky comic relief. I can't be the girl he cares about. That role in the book is already taken.

The princess is unbelievably, undeniably gorgeous. Even before she glamoured herself into perfection, she'd been gorgeous. She's powerful and brave. She is Kane's perfect match.

In his mind, he may have told the Kellas cat that the princess is a brat, but he won't feel that way forever. He's going to fall in love with her. Being with her will make him happy. It will bring him the peace he needs to become King.

I may be part of this story in a way I never even imagined, but still, my role can be only that of a sidekick. Even if it breaks my heart.

But I'm good at grinning through the pain.

So I summon my most convincing gutsy smile.

"You said it yourself—I held my own in the fight with the Kellas cat," I remind him. "Besides, she won't hurt any of us until she's had a chance to repay her death-debt to you."

"So as long as I'm alive and healthy, everyone else is fine. Has it occurred to you that if something happens to me, she can turn on all of you?"

"Well, then—" I clear my throat. "We'll just have to keep you alive."

After all, that's the whole point anyway.

Excerpt from
Book Five of The Traveler Chronicles:
The Traveler Undone

Importing large items from the Dark World is very hard.

Smaller items aren't that big a deal. Once I find a threshold, it's just a matter of keeping it open long enough to cross over to the Dark World and find what I need.

Big items—things like cars—that's where it gets dicey. It's like threading a hot dog through the eye of a needle.

Or, to be more precise, it's like driving a Porsche Panamera through a hula hoop.

CHAPTER TWENTY-FIVE

I'm still working up the courage to climb into the Porsche when the garage door behind us opens and Morgan enters, the cat by his side.

"So Cupcake, what do you think of my car collection?" He's practically beaming with pride as he asks the question.

I force a smile. "Just out of curiosity, is there any car you don't particularly like?"

Morgan's face splits into a grin at my question. "They are all beautiful, aren't they?"

I end up asking Morgan to back the car out of the garage for me. Somehow, he buys my explanation that garages are bigger in the Dark World and that I'm worried only about dinging his paint job.

Ten minutes later, I slide into the driver's seat, which is like climbing into the pod of some sort of futuristic space shuttle. The cat is on the passenger seat behind me, looking way more comfortable than I feel. The driver-side door is open, and Morgan has braced one arm on it and the other on the roof of the car.

I carefully check the placement of the rearview mirror and the one side mirror I can see. I place my hands at nine and three. My left foot hangs above the clutch, my right above the gas. I barely set it on the pedal and the engine thrums.

"You're good, right?" Morgan asks, panic creeping into his voice.

I manage to pry my eyes away from the dashboard. "Has it occurred to you that hovering over me is not helping?"

"It's just—" He clears his throat, straightens, and takes a microstep away. "Just make sure you come back, okay, Cupcake? We need you."

Before I can answer, he shuts the door. I blow out a long breath, and then look over at the cat. "Are you going to put on the seatbelt?"

She gives me a slow blink of disdain.

Duh. She doesn't have opposable thumbs.

"I mean, I could help. I could…"

I trail off as her look of disdain morphs into one of withering disgust. Seriously. Flowers have shriveled and died under looks less scornful than this.

"Okay then. Off we go."

I tap my foot on the gas pedal, and the engine roars. I ease up on the clutch. A massive shudder shakes the car, and it dies.

If cats had eyebrows, hers would be halfway up her forehead.

I pretend not to notice and say breezily, "I'm just going to try that again."

I clear my throat, mentally say a prayer to God, the Thread, and whatever company produced the Driver's Ed class I took online.

From the corner of my eye, I can see Morgan gesturing, as if he wants me to roll down the window and talk to him.

Yeah, like hearing him talk about how much he loves this car is going to help. The Porsche eases forward, and though neither I nor the cat say anything, I hear us both exhale in relief.

"I'm just going to drive for a while. You can tell me if you sense a location he doesn't know."

"Very well."

For several minutes, I merely concentrate on driving. The roads in Morgan's neighborhood are wide and relatively bare. The few houses that are visible are as large as Morgan's. There are no other cars on the road. The sun is overhead instead of in my eyes. This is all good, because it allows me to concentrate.

After several minutes, I glance in the rearview mirror and see Morgan, Kane, and Ro standing in front of his house, still watching me drive away.

"I believe it would be safe if you wanted to drive faster."

"Yeah. Everyone's a critic," I mutter. I glance down at the speedometer. I'm going thirteen miles an hour. Okay, maybe I could go a little faster.

I speed up but stay on Morgan's street until it T's into another one.

Once we're out of sight of Morgan's house, I work up the courage to shift into second. I don't dare go any faster.

I haven't yet seen another car on the road, but maybe this is normal, since most magic is done at night. Maybe the Tuatha hunker down at home during the day like vampires.

Eventually, the silence wears on me. I've mentioned I'm not good with awkward silences, right?

"So," I say with forced cheer, "You have a name, right?"

"Indeed."

"Well?"

"Well, what?" She blinks, obtusely.

"Well, what is it? What's your name?"

"Wouldn't it be prudent for you to concentrate on the road?"

Chastised, I focus on driving. For a few minutes. Then I add, "It's kind of ridiculous that we're going to be working together and I don't even know your name." She makes a grumbling noise, so I prod, "Tell me your name. Or is it that you don't want to tell me your binding name? If not, that's totally cool."

"Cats of the Kell are creatures of Old Magic. We are bound

by honor and duty. Not by mere names, like the Tuatha."

"Oh." Wallace touches only briefly on the distinction between creatures of Old Magic and the Tuatha. Cats of the Kells, hellhounds, Sirens, the Sköllpada, and dragons were all here long before the Tuatha. They draw their magic from Mithres itself, not from the Thread.

Since I don't know if Kellas Cats are sensitive about that kind of thing, I let the Old Magic vs. Tuatha issue slide on past and ask, "Then why don't you want to tell me your name?"

She stares out the window. "You are a human and a Dark Worlder. Why do you wish to know my name?"

"We're part of a team," I say. "I can't just keep calling you Cat. It would be rude."

"You humans are strange. You killed my dowt-mate. Was that not rude?"

"Your dowt-mate attacked me. Unprovoked. I killed her in self-defense."

Well, this is going great.

After several moments, she speaks, her voice so low I almost can't hear it.

"I do have a name."

I twist to face her, but she's still gazing out the window. "What is it?"

"It would be unpronounceable to humans."

"Can you tell me anyway?"

She makes a noise then. It's not a growl, because there's no anger in it, but it's low and guttural. Sort of a *mreeewreeek* sound.

I try to repeat it. "Mreeeweeek."

She looks at me with disdain. "No."

I try again. "Mreaaweeehk."

"That is not it either."

"Mree—"

"Your attempts are obviously futile."

"Yeah. I guess you're right. It is not pronounceable by humans."

"Indeed." There is another long stretch of silence and then she adds softly, "No Tuatha has ever even attempted it."

"Not even the Tuatha who mastered you?"

"Certainly not."

If the cat has treated me with disdain, she has outright hatred in her voice now. The books don't really go into the whole Kellas cat-Master dynamic, but I'm guessing it isn't pleasant.

We reach the boundary of Morgan's neighborhood. Ahead is a wide road with businesses on either side. The street sign reads LE MARE.

The equivalent of Austin's Lamar, maybe?

Lamar is busy any time of day. Le Mare is almost as empty as the residential streets. I take a right onto Le Mare.

"Then can I call you something else? Something I can pronounce?"

"If you wish to do so."

I think for a minute before saying, "How about Kendal?"

"Ken Dall?"

"Kendal," I correct her. "It's a name. In my world. I used to know a girl named Kendal. You remind me of her."

"Very well," she says disinterestedly.

To try to sell her on the name, I add, "The Kendal I knew, she was tough. Like you."

Kendal had been tough. She'd been mean and bitchy.

She'd also been scared. Alone. Fighting a battle she couldn't possibly win. She'd faced her fate the only way she'd known how.

"Kendal was brave. And a fighter. She was the kind of person who never gave up," I say quietly. "I think the name suits you."

"Very well," the cat says again, but this time, I sense that she is pleased with the name.

Ahead, Le Mare crosses over the river. My gut says it's better to stay on this side of it, so I steer into the parking lot of what looks like an abandoned warehouse. I slide the Porsche into neutral and set the hand brake. "How does this look?"

Kendal looks out the window, studying the parking lot and the building. "It will do."

"Okay," I say, turning the car off. "Let's do this."

But before I can climb out of the car, Kendal says, softly, "I am sorry my Master ordered my dowt to attack you."

I pause and without looking at her, without thinking about how hard this must be for her or how much she must despise me, I say, "I'm sorry, too."

Excerpt from
Book Five of The Traveler Chronicles:
The Traveler Undone

I may be cynical. I may be a criminal. And it's entirely possible that I've never been in a situation that I didn't make worse. But when she looks at me like that, I feel like I could be king.

CHAPTER TWENTY-SIX

The parking lot is shaded by the sprawling oak trees that line the street. In Houston, where the soil is deeper, the oaks tower. Here in the shallow dirt of the Balcones Escarpment, the trees are stocky and stunted. They have to work harder to be who they really are. Knowing the physical landscape of the Kingdoms of Mithres was sculpted to mimic my world by practitioners with an affinity like Ro's, I'm impressed that they exerted the energy to keep even the plant life consistent.

Despite the weeds peeking up through the cracks in the pavement, it's cozy…in a creepy Southern Gothic kind of way. The cat, Kendal, paces around the empty lot in absolute silence.

I don't say anything either, because I don't want to distract her.

Finally, she picks a spot and sits upright, her paws in front of her, her tail snaked around her legs. She closes her eyes. All I can do is stand watch and hope that this will work.

Minutes pass. Five. And then ten. Every once in a while, a car drives past, and I can't help but wonder if they notice me out here. If they do, are they curious what a Dark Worlder is doing out here with a Kellas cat? Of course, they can't tell I'm a Dark Worlder just by looking at me. It's not like there's a neon sign hanging over me, blinking "Dark Worlder, here!" It's not like...

That's when it hits me.

Nobody driving by can see that I'm a Dark Worlder. But a passing hellhound could sure as hell smell it.

Here I am, out in the middle of the day. Completely unprotected.

Yeah, I put on that blue lotion, but I've showered since then.

Why didn't I think of this earlier?

Why didn't anyone else think of it earlier, either?

I glance nervously up and down the street. I don't see anything suspicious, but I remember all too well how quickly those hellhounds can run.

"Um, Kendal?"

She doesn't respond, but her whiskers twitch.

"Remember, you said I could call you Kendal?" Okay, genius, that's not really the point. "Is there any chance you have an ETA on Kane's arrival?"

Still no response.

"Because it occurred to me that this isn't really the best place to just hang out. Since, you know, I'm a fugitive Dark Worlder, and very likely to attract the attention of some rather nasty hellhounds."

She opens only one eye and blinks at me.

"It's just...if you could give me an update on how it's going, that would be awesome."

Finally, she says, "I have maintained the mental connection with Kane."

"That's great news. So what's the holdup?"

Her tail flicks in annoyance. "He is being...difficult."

"Difficult?" Yeah, tell me something I didn't know. When isn't Kane being difficult? "But what does that mean? Can he use the link to transfer here or not?"

"Perhaps. But he will need to allow me more freedom in his thoughts. He's blocking me."

Until now, I wouldn't have thought cats could frown, but clearly Kendal is frowning.

"Why would he do that?"

"There are things he does not want me to know. Something about a girl."

"A girl? Is it the princess?"

"No. Not the princess. Someone else."

Not the princess? Who then?

"Ro?"

"No. Not Ro. Someone else. A girl who is trapped here. A girl from—" Kendal's eyes pop open, and she stares at me in surprise for several seconds, making a distinctly inhuman sound, something between a growl and a purr.

An instant later, she closes her eyes and shifts her body as if she's settling back down. "I will explain the urgency of our situation. I believe that will persuade him that he does not need these barriers between us."

And just like that, Kendal is once again in the world of her own mind.

Me? I'm deeply rattled.

Kane is trying to hide his thoughts from Kendal. Thoughts about the girl from the Dark World who is trapped here.

That has to be me, right? True, Kendal didn't say the Dark World. But how many girls could there be that are trapped here? Which means he's thinking about me, but he doesn't want anyone else to know. What am I supposed to do with that?

How am I supposed to feel about it?

Back in the garage, the faintest touch of his hand sent a flurry of feelings through me.

And, obviously, I have been half in love with him most of my life.

But we are—literally—from different worlds.

There is no way this could end well.

He doesn't belong to me. He falls in love with the princess. He is supposed to be with her.

No matter how I feel. Even, no matter how he feels.

Shit.

Shit.

It's not supposed to be like this.

Before I can finish the thought, I hear a noise in the distance that turns my blood cold. A howl.

I whirl back to face Kendal, only to see that something has already started to happen.

The air above the ground has started to shimmer, like heat rising off blacktop. Then, slowly, the movement shifts. No longer rising vertically, the air beings to swirl and darken, until one spot—no bigger than a dime—is absolute pitch-black. Then, like a hole tearing in a pair of tights, it spreads, expanding to the size of a dinner plate. The hole seems to wobble in midair.

It's not working. In theory, yes. It is a loop-hole. But it's not big enough or stable enough.

Somewhere in the distance, the hellhound howls again.

Kendal and I are going to die.

Unless we climb back in the car and make a run for it.

I take a step closer to Kendal and whisper, "Look, I don't want to distract you, but we need to leave."

Her tail flicks.

"Don't flick your tail at me." There's another howl. Closer this time. "Call this off. It's not going to work. We need to get in the car. And drive like the hounds of hell are chasing us. Which they will be."

And given that I can't drive faster than thirty miles per hour, they will probably catch us. Which I decide not to mention.

Kendal opens one eye and glares at me. "Your lack of faith is not helping."

"Oh, you think my faith would help right now?"

"Indeed, child. I do."

Well, that's just great. We are all about to die, and Kendal wants me to use the power of positive thinking to save us.

You know, for a vicious killer, she's surprisingly touchy-feely.

If I pick her up in my arms and carry her to the car myself, what are the chances that she'll hurt me?

Pretty high. That's my guess anyway.

Since I can't leave her and I can't force her to come with me, I have only one option. To wait it out with her.

I take a step closer to her and the wobbling hole in the universe.

Then, abruptly, as if two huge hands reach through the hole and rip it apart, the hole expands into a swirling elliptic the size of a hula hoop, and Kane comes crashing through.

The second he lands in a heap on the ground, the loop vanishes. I rush to him.

His skin is damp with sweat, his face lined with strain. He is weak and trembling. But he did it. He actually did it.

Which won't matter at all, if we're all killed by hellhounds in the next five minutes.

He opens his eyes and flashes me a tremulous smile. "Look at that, Cupcake. Turns out you're pretty smart after all."

His compliment hits me square in the chest, making me feel all squishy and delicious inside, like someone replaced my organs with homemade chocolate pudding. But he shouldn't be complimenting me, I shouldn't be enjoying it, and we shouldn't be waiting around.

"Great. You can tell me more about how fantastic I am when we're not about to be torn to shreds by hellhounds."

A frown replaces the triumph in his expression, as another howl rends the air.

I crouch down beside him and wedge my shoulder under his to help him to his feet.

"By the way, can you drive? Because I think we'll probably want to go pretty fast."

Excerpt from
Book Five of The Traveler Chronicles:
The Traveler Undone

Some days, it feels like half my job is figuring out who I can trust and who I can't.

The other half is betraying them before they betray me.

CHAPTER TWENTY-SEVEN

I assume it goes without saying that Kane is a better driver than I am.

We are heading off down Le Mare before we even glimpse the hellhounds. Once we are in the well-insulated car and the engine is thrumming, we can barely even hear their howls.

All of which should make me feel better. Only it doesn't.

Squishy, chocolate pudding feelings aside, I still have too many unanswered questions.

Maybe I should have known that the hellhounds would catch my scent that quickly. *Maybe* I should have.

Kane *definitely* should have. So why didn't he warn me?

Why did he leave me unprotected and defenseless?

I'm so lost in my fuming, I don't notice Kane isn't driving straight back to Morgan's until he pulls over.

Outside the window, buildings tower by the shores of Lake Austin. "Where are we?"

"Get out," Kane says instead of answering.

"Why? Because if you're going to leave me here—"

"He is not planning on leaving you here, child." Kendal's answer is surprisingly gentle. "He is trying to make it harder for the hellhounds to track us back to Morgan's. Spreading your scent around town will accomplish this goal."

"Oh." I reach for the door handle.

"It would be beneficial if you could find a tree to rub against," Kendal adds as I climb out of the car.

"I am not marking a tree!" I say before slamming the door behind me.

Not that I could anyway. There are no trees in sight. Instead, I take off my shoes and walk around barefoot for a minute.

Then I climb back in the car. Kane rolls down the windows and drives again. We stop twice more. I repeat the whole barefoot in the grass thing without comment. Finally, Kane rolls up the windows and heads back to Morgan's.

I'm silent the whole time, feeling confused and overwhelmed. I don't want him to care for me, not when he's supposed to be falling for the princess. But I liked it when he at least didn't want me dead.

Kane doesn't let us out of the car in front of the house but pulls straight into the garage and doesn't open the car door until the garage door is back down.

Ro is waiting for us on the steps that lead into the house. She's sitting on the top one, with her head bowed, twisting a sheaf of papers in her hands.

"Oh, thank the Thread," she says when Kane climbs out of the car.

She practically runs down the stairs to him and I expect her to throw her arms around him. Instead, she smacks his shoulder with the rolled-up papers.

"Where,"—she smacks him again—"have you"—Another smack. She must not be putting much force behind it, because he doesn't even flinch. —"been?"

"You done?" he asks.

"No!" She smacks him one more time. Then she drops the papers and throws her arms around him, burying her face against his shoulder. "You should have been back an hour ago."

"It took longer to create the loop than we thought. You

know that. You were here."

He glances at Kendal as he says it and they exchange a brief look. Does he know what Kendal told me? I don't think so, because his gaze doesn't even flicker in my direction.

"So what?" Ro asks. "Once you got through the loop, it should have taken you only another fifteen or twenty minutes to drive back here. I thought you'd gotten lost in the loop. Or that you'd made it through but then—"

She pulls herself off Kane, wiping tears from her eyes, then turns and practically runs from the garage.

Before Ro makes it through the door into the house, Morgan and Crab show up. "What took so long?" Morgan asks.

"Cupcake here was out on the street longer than anyone anticipated."

Morgan studies me. "You okay?"

Kane takes a step closer to me. "Yeah, she's fine. But the hellhounds had caught her scent."

"Got it," Morgan says. "I assume we should get out of here quickly?"

"Definitely," Kane says.

Morgan heads for the garage door. "Okay everybody, grab your stuff. We'll meet in the kitchen in five minutes."

Everyone heads for the door, but Kane stops me with a hand on my arm as I walk past him.

"What?" I ask.

"Can I have a minute?"

"We only have five," I say.

"Then I'll be brief." He glances toward the door and waits until we're alone in the garage before he says, "You wanna tell me what's wrong?"

"Who says anything's wrong?"

"Well, you've barely spoken since I picked you up on Le Mare."

"So?"

"You haven't spoken," he says again more slowly. "At all. And this is *you* we're talking about. So I figure either something's wrong, or hellhounds are the least of our worries, because the apocalypse is starting."

"Oh," I snap. "Because I talk so much, that if I'm quiet for five minutes it must be a sign of the apocalypse. Very funny."

I'm about to storm off, but then I realize I left my messenger bag in the back seat of the car.

"So?"

"So what?" I reach in the car, grab the handle and tug, putting the full force of my anger in that action. But the door must have locked automatically, because the handle slips from my grasp. I tug again. No luck.

"So are you going to tell me why you're so pissed off?"

I glare at Kane. "Can you open the door?"

"You gonna tell me what's wrong?"

That's when I see them. The car keys dangling from his finger.

"Open the damn car."

He jangles the keys. "Tell me."

He's holding them out of reach, so far above my head there's no damn way I can grab them. Goddamn it! I am so tired of being at a disadvantage here!

I lunge for the keys, but Kane grabs me, slinging an arm around my waist. He pulls my back against his chest, lifting me clear off my feet.

I kick at his shins. "Open the car!"

"Tell me what I did to piss you off."

"You want to know what you did?" I yell. "You sent me out there, without protection, when you knew hellhounds would come for me."

Kane's arms loosen around me, and my feet slide to the floor.

"I could have died," I whisper. "You knew and you didn't say anything."

He doesn't let me go, though, but pulls me gently to him. Slowly. Testing me to see if I'll pull away. I don't. My anger isn't gone so much as it's swallowed up by my fear.

And then I feel him rest his chin on top of my head. "I didn't know."

The anguish in his voice flows over me, washing away the blunt edges of my anger. And then he presses the keys into my hand and lets me go.

I click the door open without looking at him and grab my bag from the back seat.

I'm most of the way to the door to the house when he says again, "I really didn't know they would come for you. The lotion usually lasts for days, even if you shower. When Morgan had your clothes and shoes repaired, he had the isotopic frequency of your world wiped clean from them."

"Isotopic frequency?" I ask.

"Yeah, it's what the hellhounds track. It's strongest in metals. That's how they follow the iron in your blood. You should have been safe." His voice cracks. When I glance back, he's standing with his hands on his hips, his head bowed in defeat. "And I don't know what else to do to protect you from them."

Shame burns through me at seeing him like this. I should say something. Forgive him or apologize. Something. But I'm embarrassed. I have never acted like that before. I have never thrown a temper tantrum. I've never—

My thoughts stutter as it hits me. I squeeze my eyes closed, wincing, before I turn on my heel.

Kane is standing right where I left him, his head bowed, his hands hanging limply by his side.

I skid to halt a few feet away. "I'm sorry."

He looks up, relief crinkling the corners of his eyes. "It's okay. You've had a hell of a day."

"No, I mean, not about that. I mean, yes, obviously, I'm sorry. I acted like a brat. And that was inexcusable. But—" I let the messenger bag drop to my feet so I can use my hands to dig around in my pockets. I find what I'm looking for and pull them out. "But mostly I'm sorry about this."

I hold out my hand and open it, so Kane can see the nuts and bolts.

He looks from me to the bolts and back up again.

"What?" he asks.

"I didn't know that thing about the isotopic frequency in metals. If this is what the hellhounds chased…"

His head is tipped to the side, like he's considering. "No, if those are the ones from the Faraday Cage, I'd had them wiped when I brought them over. Do you have anything else metal on you? Anything at all?"

I drop down to my knees and pull my messenger bag over my shoulder, quickly dumping the contents out onto the ground. I quickly separate out a few likely offenders. My cell phone. My keys to the apartment in Austin. My MAC lipstick. My Leatherman. He bends down to watch.

He scoops up the lipstick, the keys, and the Leatherman. "I'll have Cricket wipe these clean and bring them back."

"What about the cell phone?" I ask.

"Nah. We import those all the time. Most have only about one percent iron and the circuits are too delicate to be wiped."

I shove everything else back into the bag, then stand. "There's one more thing. Something that won't be as easy to wipe."

"What?"

And this part? This is where it gets awkward.

My hands are shaking as I reach up to the neck of my Hello, Cupcake! shirt and pull down the neck to reveal the spot, about an inch above my bra, where my scar is. And where, when I turned sixteen, I had a rune tattooed.

For a long moment, he just stares at the tattoo. Then he swallows. "That's my rune."

"Yeah."

The symbol—a spiral of three interlocking *J* shapes—is a rune of deception or disguise. It's embossed on the cover of the every one of the Traveler books. It's printed beneath every chapter head. And it's inked into my skin.

It's the rune Kane's mother marked him with, right before she died.

I let go of my shirt, letting the neckline shift back into place.

But Kane reaches out and pulls my shirt down again.

The backs of his fingers are rough against my chest, and my skin flushes. I can hardly suck in enough air to breathe. Even the most innocent of touches makes it hard for me to concentrate, but, somehow, there's nothing innocent about this touch. Not with his hand where it is. Not when he's staring at me like this. Not when it's his mark that's on my chest.

He swallows visibly, and his voice sounds rough when he asks, "Why is my rune on your chest?"

"I got the tattoo to cover a scar."

Staring at the rune, he traces the tattoo with his fingers, feeling for the raised tissue of my scar beneath the ink.

It's barely visible anymore, but I know its shape as well as the shape of my mother's face. I used to spend hours staring at it in the mirror, trying to wrap my brain around how it had happened. Trying to sort through the jumbled memories. The scar itself is an almost perfect oval in the center with jagged flared edges. Like a sunburst. It would almost be pretty, except it isn't.

"It's a bullet wound," I tell him. "I was shot."

I have a much smaller scar on my shoulder, the entry wound. That one doesn't bother me as much. I don't have to look at it. I don't have to answer questions about it anytime someone sees it. You would be surprised how hard it is to change clothes in gym class without anyone seeing your upper body. Or worse, wear a swimsuit.

"You were shot?" Kane asks, his brow furrowing in confusion.

"Yes."

"Did they remove the bullet?"

"Yes." I don't tell him about the punctured lung. The weeks in the hospital. I'm about to explain the real problem with my scar—the ink in the tattoo that covers it contains metal.

But before I can, he says, "I didn't realize the Dark World was so dangerous. That a girl your age would be shot…" His gaze flickers back to mine. "Did you live in a war zone?"

A bubble of near hysterical laughter rises in my throat. The idea that my mother—who was protective even before the incident—would let me anywhere near a war zone is ridiculous.

"No."

"Then how did it happen?"

Instantly, my throat closes over whatever words I might say. Tears prickle against the back of my eyelids, so hot and fierce that I have to turn aside and squeeze my eyes closed for a moment. I make a show of readjusting the items in my bag and slinging it over my shoulder, hoping he won't notice my discomfort. "It was an accident. I was shot by accident."

This is the part that never gets any easier. The part I will never be better at explaining. The reason I need the tattoo so that I don't have to lie to strangers about what happened.

Except, I have to tell Kane. It would feel wrong not to. I have been unceremoniously thrust into his life. I know things about him that no stranger should know. This will not even things up. I have no illusions about that. But he deserves to know the truth about me.

Besides, there is doubt that lingers in the back of my mind.

Doubt that will always linger in the back of my mind, no matter how many reassurances have been given to me by not one, but three different therapists. What if I am susceptible to the same emotional instability that plagued my father? The doctors say no. They are very good at reassuring me. But I am not very good at believing them.

If I do have the potential to...break the way my father did, doesn't Kane deserve to know what he's getting into?

"My father shot me." I force my hands to still. Force a shuddering breath out of my lungs. Force myself to turn back and meet his gaze. "My father wasn't well. Mentally."

"He shot you on purpose?"

"No. Not..." This is the problem with never telling the story out loud. I don't know how to do it. I don't know how to talk about it anymore. I've never had to explain it to anyone who didn't have my medical records. So I fall back on the most technical language that I know. "He had a psychotic break, characterized by paranoid delusions and hallucinations." That's as far as the medical terminology gets me, but I can tell from Kane's frown that it's not enough information. "He imagined things. He saw monsters. Everywhere. He thought people were after him. That they were trying to hurt him. And me."

Kane's frown deepens, and I find myself rushing to defend my father. "He wasn't always like that. One day, he was fine. Then, suddenly, he saw monsters everywhere. He was trying to protect me from them, trying to keep both of us safe."

"What happened?"

"Somehow he got a gun. I don't know where he found it, because we never had a gun in the house before. Mom and Dad both hated them. He was waving it around. I guess Mom tried to get me away from him. And he shot me."

Kane is frowning again, and his gaze drops back down to the tattoo, which is almost entirely covered by my Hello,

Cupcake T-shirt that has crept back into place. "What do you mean, you guess?"

My thoughts stutter, because that's not the part of the story I had expected him to question. "I…I don't really remember everything very clearly."

"You don't remember what happened?"

"No. The doctor said that was normal though. That it's common to lose memories when something very traumatic happens."

"Who else was there when it happened?"

"Just my parents."

"But your mother remembers? And your father? They remember the same thing?"

Why is he questioning me?

I've embraced my trauma-induced amnesia. I don't want those memories. How my father, who had always been the most loving man I could imagine, who had been kind and gentle, who'd held me on his lap and read to me every night of my childhood, could somehow transform into a monster willing to shoot me? I don't want to remember what that felt like. Or how terrified I must have been.

I don't want to remember being afraid of the person I trusted most. "Yes. She remembered. I didn't. I'm okay with that."

"Is that what your father remembers, too?"

"What does this have to do with anything? It happened. I have the scars to prove it." Defiantly, I jerk down the collar of my shirt again and gesture to the tattoo on my chest. "This definitely happened."

His gaze drops to the tattoo again and then back up to my face. He takes a step closer to me and places his palm over my chest covering the scar. "I'm asking, because that doesn't look like a bullet wound to me."

"Oh, because you have so much experience identifying Dark

Worlder bullet wounds?"

"No, I don't. None. But I do have a lot of experience iden-tifying scars left by Sleekers."

"What? How would a Sleeker scar you?"

He drops his hand from my skin, leaving a burst of searing heat where his fingers were. Then he raises the hem of his own T-shirt. On the left side of his abdomen, an inch or two above the waistband of his jeans, is a small round wound. Almost identical to the wound on my back. Then he turns and lets me see the other side. Like my wound, there's a round hole about an inch across, with scalloped edges. The edges of his wound are more rounded, almost like the petals of a flower. But the two wounds—mine and his—are so similar, they could have been made by identical weapons. By the same gun. Or, if Kane is to be believed, by the same Sleeker.

"I don't understand." I'm shaking my head and I take one step back from him, and then another. "How does a Sleeker do this? It's a bullet hole."

Kane tugs his shirt down. "Sleekers have tentacles."

"Yes, that they use to grab things and pull them closer to them." At least, that's how Wallace described them in the books. "They don't...spear things with them." The image that pops into my head is horrific. "Do they?"

"They do if they're really mad. Or when someone's running away from them. Or, in my case, if they want you to stand really still while they make you watch as they torture someone."

"Smyth did that?"

"Yeah. He made me watch while he tortured my mother. When she refused to tell him what he wanted to know, he killed her."

I remember the scene from the first book, of course, when Smyth kills the High Queen. There's no torture in the book. And Kane wasn't forced to watch. Still, I know how the memory of it has haunted him.

And yet, Kane's voice as he says this is so perfectly blank. So completely emotionless.

Whatever anguish he feels when he remembers his mother's death, it doesn't show on his face. I could take lessons from him about how to talk about trauma.

"And you think my scar is a Sleeker's handiwork? Like yours?"

"Honestly?" He gives his head a shake, his gaze dropping back to my scar. "I can't say for sure. I can't see it well enough beneath the tattoo. And you don't remember. That makes me suspicious, too. Sleekers make wounds that look a lot like that. And Curati can adjust anyone's memories. I would almost guarantee that whatever monsters your dad thought he saw were really there."

My knees give out at his words. I don't fall to the ground, but I feel weak enough that I can't keep standing. The car is behind me, and I slide back against it.

Of all the things that I had imagined he might say, this was nowhere on the list. Maybe my dad wasn't crazy. Maybe there was no psychotic break. Maybe my dad didn't hurt me. Maybe my mom was wrong.

Thoughts tumble through my brain so quickly, I have trouble catching them, let alone sorting them out into any kind of order. My dad has been in and out of psychiatric facilities for the past six years, in court-mandated therapy. Taking court-mandated Thorazine that has left him confused, incoherent, and sometimes drooling.

Seeing him like that... The first time, I cried so much, I threw up. It ripped out my stitches and I still couldn't stop sobbing. I lost a pint of blood before Mom could get me back to a real hospital.

But maybe it hadn't been him who had shot me at all.

Maybe he wasn't crazy. Maybe he was just fine. Maybe when I get back, I can explain, I can make people understand, I can get him out. I can—

No. I can't think about any of that now. Maybe I can do something to help my dad, but not until I get home. Not until I finish what I have to do here.

Saving Kane's life is my one chance to make a difference. To do something big and important. And it's not just Kane's life that's in danger. It's the princess's life and the Curator's. It's the balance of power in this world.

"Okay, what do we do about the tattoo. How do we fix this?"

He frowns at my question. "What? You want to find the Sleeker who did this to you, because—"

"No, I don't care about that." Maybe I should, but I can't. Not yet. "Forget the scar. What do we do about the tattoo?" His blank look doesn't shift into understanding. "In my world, tattoos aren't burned on by magic."

He nods. "I know that. They're inked on."

"Right. And the inks they use contain metal."

He blinks, looking from my face to my tattoo several times, and I can tell it's taking him a moment to process my words. That's how foreign this idea is to him.

Finally, his eyes close and he takes a step back from me.

"Let me see if I've got this right. In your world, people actually inject metal under their skin?"

"In my defense," I argue. "In my world, there aren't ginormous dogs bred to track down and murder anything associated with the isotopic frequency of Dark Worlder metals. So it's a little less weird there."

He gives me a once-over that I think is supposed to be insulting but only makes me feel flustered all over again. "Yeah. I'm still gonna have to guess that your chest looked better without it."

I pull my shirt back into place. "Can you do something about this or not?"

"I have no experience with"—he waves his hand in the general direction of my tattoo—"with this kind of thing."

I blow out a frustrated breath. "What about your actual rune? The one your mother gave you? Couldn't you just duplicate it somewhere on me?"

"First off, rune magic is incredibly difficult. It takes an extremely long time to work. Secondly, I suck at it. The last thing you want is me doing rune magic on your skin. Trust me."

"So then we're stuck with me literally radiating the Dark World?"

"Apparently."

"I should stay here," I say.

"No. We need you on the island with us. You've said that yourself. I'm just going to have to stay between you and the hellhounds and blast the shit out of them."

The others take the news about my tattoo slightly better than Kane.

Kane doesn't tell them why I have the scar. It helps that I don't show them the tattoo. Less embarrassing for me, at least.

But the discussion makes me think of something. "Won't the hellhounds just follow us to Houston?"

"Not if we loop-jump there," Kane says.

Ro stills, a frown of concern marring her features. "You're planning on loop-jumping all of us?"

"Yeah. It'll be the fastest, safest way to get there."

Morgan and Ro exchange a look. Clearly creating a loop steady enough to transport six beings halfway across the state is not as easy as Kane is making it sound.

"Do you still keep *The Blossom* in that slip south of Seaside?" Kane asks Crab, ignoring their obvious concern.

"I do, indeed."

"Then it shouldn't be a problem. We'll loop-jump directly onto *The Blossom*. If Cupcake goes directly from here to there without ever setting foot on the ground in Houston, they'll lose the scent."

This explanation seems to satisfy everyone.

Kane, Morgan, and Ro head off to other parts of the house to gather what they need. Cricket is, presumably, somewhere wiping down the rest of my stuff. Crab and Kendal don't have any belongings with them. My own messenger bag is still where I left it, slung across the back of one of the kitchen chairs, so I have nothing to gather. There's nothing useful for me to do now.

And, just like that, I am alone with Crab and Kendal.

Only then do I think to ask, "Why are we leaving for your boat now? I thought it was almost impossible to do magic during the daylight hours."

"Well now, nothing's impossible, is it? It's really just a matter of managing the energy. Sure, most folks can't really handle the flow during the day. It's too powerful, you see? But Kane? Well, Kane has been using magic in full sunlight as long as I've known him."

The others get back quickly, so I don't have a chance to grill Crab about his statement. But it does leave me wondering if this is one more thing Wallace got wrong. Kane is a Dark Worlder. He's less powerful than most Tuatha, not more powerful. Or is there something I don't know?

Excerpt from
Book Five of The Traveler Chronicles:
The Traveler Undone

All of Saint Lew is accorded neutral territory. There hasn't been an outbreak of violence within city limits in over eighty-seven years, since before the last High King was crowned.

This is undoubtedly why the Red Court and the Han Court agreed to have the wedding there. If the two most powerful courts are going to be in the same place at the same time, they might as well pick the safest place on the continent.

Furthermore, the Great Cathedral is considered the most sacred ground this side of the Atlantean Ocean. There isn't a soul alive who would violate the sanctity of the cathedral.

So naturally, I expect a trap.

Smyth could wipe out two-thirds of the courts in one swoop. If I were in his shoes, that's what I would do.

CHAPTER TWENTY-EIGHT

B ased on Crab's personal appearance—shabby, rumpled, and with the distinct smell of fish—I expect his ship to be similarly unkempt.

I'm wrong.

Whatever his personal hygiene, Crab's ship is as neat, orderly, and cute as a vintage children's toy tugboat.

The Blossom sits high in the water and is made entirely of wood. The hull is bright red, the wheelhouse dark blue. When we land on her deck, we are greeted by the smell of fresh ocean air and wood warmed by the midmorning sun. There is no unpleasant stench of diesel in the air, like there would be in a marina in my world. Instead, at the stern of the boat there is a large paddle wheel.

Crab scrambles up a short ladder and goes straight into the wheelhouse. A moment later he calls out, "Let her loose, Kane."

Kane hops off the stern of the boat onto the dock and unwraps the line from the mooring. Then he tosses the rope onto the boat and leaps back on.

As soon as she's loose, the paddle wheel starts to slowly turn and *The Blossom* eases out of the slip. A few minutes later, we're heading for the open water of the bay. The water is smooth and still, so I get my sea legs quickly. It's a brilliant, clear blue, much clearer than the water of Galveston Bay in my world. I can see all the way to the ocean floor where schools of fish dart among the patches of sea grass. For a few moments, I get lost in the wonder of it all: the crisp, clean salty breeze, the gentle rolling of the ship, the soothing *thud*, *thud*, *thud* of the paddle wheel. Then, just as my heart is beginning to fill with contentment, a dolphin leaps out of the water just behind the ship. And then another.

"They like to play in the wake," Kane says as he joins me at the stern.

"Aren't they afraid to get too close to the boat?"

"I guess they trust Crab."

"Why can't I hear the engine?"

Kane cocks his head to the side with a bemused smile. "This is the boat of a Siren. It doesn't need an engine."

"Doesn't need…" And then it hits me. "He's running it by himself? With his affinity for water?"

Kane nods. "Exactly."

"But I thought he said that when we reach the Crimson Miasma, he wouldn't be able to steer the ship through. If his power is running the boat, what are we going to do?"

"We'll have to crank it ourselves."

Sure enough, there are handles on the paddle wheel so it can be turned by hand. Well, that's not going to be fun. But it's not like I really thought any of this would be easy.

It's a good thirty or forty minutes before we reach the first wisps of fog.

At first, it's just a few tendrils drifting up from the water, like steam rising from a hot tub on a cold day.

"It's starting," Crab calls out. "Everyone get into place."

We had planned for this. I would be up in the boathouse to help Crab steer. Morgan, Kane, and Ro would be at the paddle wheel to turn it by hand.

But none of us expected it to hit so quickly. We're still moving to our prearranged spots when everything changes from one moment to the next. Clear blue skies vanish and a thick, soupy fog rolls over us. I am only a few feet from the bow of the ship, but as the fog spills over the hull, the bow disappears before my eyes. I fight off a burst of panic at the idea of being adrift.

But we won't be lost. I have my phone. It has a compass.

I pull out my phone and open the app. It spins for a minute and then settles on a heading of roughly northeast. Okay.

If we head into the Crimson Miasma heading northeast, then that heading should get us to the island. Southwest should get us out of the Crimson Miasma.

By the time I've put my phone safely back into my messenger bag, the fog has encompassed more than just the bow. Behind me, there's only dense, swirling gray.

It's unnaturally warm and thick enough to choke me. From above, there's a creak and then I hear Crab call, "We're nearing the thick of it. I could use a wee bit of help at the wheel."

"I'm almost there," I call back.

The wooden railing is slick beneath my hand as I make my way back toward Crab. My messenger bag is slung over my shoulder, resting just in front of my body, and I clench my right hand around the strap. Having something solid to hold on to helps.

I can see only eighteen inches from my face. I can hear the creaking of my feet on wooden planks, the *thud, thud, thud* of the paddle wheel—slower now than it was before.

Fear tiptoes up my spine even as a drip of sweat rolls down my temple. I brush it away with the side of my hand as my steps slow and I strain to hear. Anything.

The paddle wheel slows to a *thud...thud...thud...*and then nothing.

The length of the boat stretches endlessly. This must be the Crimson Miasma messing with my head. Making me feel lost, even though I know exactly where I am. I'm on the deck of *The Blossom*. She is no more than forty feet long. That's fifteen of my strides. All I have to do is count my steps.

One…two…three…

My foot slips out from under me, and I land hard on the deck. Too hard.

Excerpt from
Book Five of The Traveler Chronicles:
The Traveler Undone

I'm just going to say it, sometimes, having friends sucks.
You know why?
Because they know when you're being a dick.
Strangers don't always notice, but your friends? Yeah. They notice.
Kinda makes me wish I didn't have any.

CHAPTER TWENTY-NINE

"Are you all right?" asks a voice from above me. I'm on my back, a thrum of pain emanating from my skull.

"Wha—" I start to ask, but the words get stuck in my mouth.

"Are you all right, miss?" the voice asks again.

I blink my eyes open. I'm on the floor. Flat on my back. My messenger bag is clenched in my hand, my only familiar anchor in a sea of the unfamiliar. High above me, white acoustic tiles frame fluorescent lights. There's a guy leaning over me and a girl just behind him. Where am I?

I wedge a hand under me and push myself up to get a better look around. I see tables of books and shelves of tchotchkes. I'm in Book People.

"You fainted and hit your head," the guy says, putting a hand lightly on my shoulder.

"We called 911," the girl interjects.

I've fainted twice in two days. And, no, it's not too much coffee or not enough breakfast this time.

No. That's not right.

I didn't faint. I hit my head.

Or did I?

Another throb of pain pulses through my skull.

"I found a cell phone in your bag," the girl says. She holds up a phone and waggles it in front of me. "I called your mom."

I squint at the phone. It has my cell phone case—a black and white OtterBox, because I kept cracking the screen. I drew diamonds with a silver Sharpie all over the black outside rubber. Definitely my phone.

But how did she get it out of my bag when my hand is still clenched tightly around it?

"No," I say, trying to give my head a shake. "This isn't right."

"You want to see your mom, don't you?" she says, her tone shifting from helpful to soothing.

My mom. My best friend. My lodestone. The one person I can always trust. The one person who would never lie to me.

"Yes," I say. "I want to see my mom."

She can help.

She can explain what's happening. Help me make sense. Help me...

I blink and in the instant my eyes are closed, the air feels thick and sticky. Foggy.

Then I'm back on the floor of Book People.

"I called your mom," the girl says. "She's on her way."

No. That's not right.

"She's in D.C. She can't get here."

"It's okay," the guy says. Like his sister, his tone is soothing. "Your parents will be here in a minute."

"My parents? My dad?"

"Sure," the guy says. "Of course, your dad will be here."

I close my eyes again and take in a deep breath. Of Crimson Miasma. With my eyes closed, I can feel the dampness of the fog on my skin. Feel it creeping into my senses. Faintly, as if from a great distance, I hear the lapping of water against the side of the boat, the creak of boards rubbing against one another as the ship rocks in the still water.

With my eyes closed, I am back in the Kingdoms of Mithres.

But when they're open, I see only what the Crimson Miasma wants me to see.

What it thinks I want.

I open my eyes to see both of my parents leaning over me. I'm in a bedroom with lilac walls and fluttering curtains. It's the house in Cincinnati, where we lived before the incident.

"She's awake," my mom's voice says. "Hey, honey. You've been sick, but you're all right now."

"You really scared us, kiddo," my dad says.

My mom squeezes my hand. I feel it all the way through my body. Her love. Her endless support. How much she needs me.

My dad's gentle fingers brush hair off my face. "I love you so much, kiddo."

Of course, he's always loved me. I never doubted his love. Only his sanity.

But this is too good. Too much of what I've always wanted.

My mother, happy and relaxed. My dad…himself.

Who wouldn't want that?

As soon as I say it, I know the answer. *I* wouldn't want that. I don't want the lie of a perfect world.

The Crimson Miasma may be able to give me a perfect fantasy, but it can't give me what I really want: the ability to make a difference. The ability to control the course of my own life.

To do that, I have to leave the fog.

With my free hand, I reach up and take my father's hand in mine. I pull it away from my hair and hold it up against my heart for just a second.

"I love you, Daddy." I study his face, trying to memorize it as it is right now. "And I forgive you."

I say this last bit for me, because the image isn't my real dad. He doesn't need my forgiveness as much as I need to give it.

I hold his hand tightly in mine for just a moment. Then

I squeeze my eyes closed and stand up on the deck of *The Blossom*.

I keep my eyes closed as I reach out a hand, swinging it through the air until I find a railing beside me.

I just stand there for a moment, getting my feet under me, and listening. I hear only the lapping of the water and the creaking of the boat.

"Hello?" I call out. "Is anyone else still here?"

Maybe the Crimson Miasma has captured them all. Maybe whatever it is showing them is much more enticing than this reality.

Or maybe the Crimson Miasma simply doesn't work on Dark Worlders. Maybe the things we imagine in our deepest hearts are simply too unbelievable.

If that's true, then it will be all on me to steer the ship through the fog.

Panic claws through my chest. "Anyone?"

"Child of the Dark World…" Kendal's low voice drifts to me out of the fog. "I am here." And then, I feel her brush against my legs.

Unable to help myself, I drop to my knees, careful to keep one hand on the hull. I reach out until I feel her beneath my hand. "Thank God."

She comes closer to me, putting her front paws on my thighs and bumping her head against my chin. "I too am glad to hear your voice."

I am tempted to bury my face in her fur. Before I can, she leaps off my lap. But she stays close, my hand still on her back.

"How long did it take you to fight off the Miasma?" I ask.

"The Miasma does not seem to affect Kellas cats."

So all of this time, she was simply alone in this fog?

No wonder she seems so glad to see me.

"Is there anyone else?"

"You appear to be the first one to have fought off the Miasma's effects."

"Any ideas what to do to help the others?"

"We must find a way to wake them, or you and I will have to steer the ship ourselves."

Okay, so we've got to wake some people up.

"Crab said his people were affected strongly by the Miasma. So let's leave him for last. Do you know where everyone else is?"

"I can lead you to my dowt-mate."

"Lead the way. Just go slowly. I'm going to try to hold on to your back so we don't get separated again."

"If you must."

There is something in her voice that sounds almost like relief. I don't think she wants to be alone on this ship any more than I do.

Our progress is excruciatingly slow. I think we're both okay with that.

Finally, she stops and says, "He is here."

I drop to my knees and reach out a hand until I find him.

My hand lands squarely on his chest. I still for an instant. This feels too intimate…touching him while he's vulnerable. But how else can I wake him?

I shake his shoulder. "Kane, you've got to wake up." There's no response. I shake again. "Kane, we need you. You have to wake up." Still nothing. What are we going to do if I *can't* wake him up? Search for Morgan, I guess. But I don't know where he is. "Come on. I know you can fight off whatever it's showing you. You're stronger than this. There are people here in this world who need you."

The muscles of his shoulder twitch under my hand, and I feel like he's trying to fight off the vision. I lean closer. "The princess needs you. The Curator needs you." I hesitate only an

instant before adding, "*I* need you."

The words are barely out of my mouth when he sits bolt upright, something I feel rather than see, since my eyes are still closed.

"Where am I?"

"You're on *The Blossom*. With Morgan and Ro and Crab and Kendal."

"Who the hell is Kendal?" he asks.

"Child of the Dark World," Kendal murmurs. "I do not believe you told Kane you have given me a name."

"Kendal is the cat?"

I can hear him shifting position and imagine that he is standing up. I stand up as well. Kendal bumps against my leg and I exhale in relief.

"Um, yeah. Sorry about that. I thought she needed a name. I just forgot to tell anyone."

"Good point. One question. Why are your eyes closed?"

"Um…" Obviously, his eyes are not closed and yet he's still here. Tentatively, I squint through one eyelid to see what happens. I'm still on *The Blossom*. So I open both my eyes, feeling rather foolish. "Long story. I'll tell you later."

Kane is facing me, standing closer than I could have guessed. For once, there's more in his gaze than just amusement. An unexpected intimacy. Almost as if he is as glad to see me as I am to see him.

Which is undoubtedly a side effect of the Crimson Miasma. Of course, he is glad to see me.

"Okay, Cupcake, what's the plan?"

"First, we wake up Morgan and Ro. Then, some of us need to turn the paddle wheel by hand, and someone needs to get up into the wheelhouse to try to steer. Do you know where the others are?"

I had turned to Kendal, but it's Kane who answers.

"Morgan was near the paddle wheel. Ro was heading up to the wheelhouse to help Crab. That was the last time I saw them, just before the fog rolled in."

"You look for Morgan," I tell Kane. "When you wake him, the two of you will be able to get the ship moving again. I'll find Ro."

Kendal says, "I will be able to find the hull. Kane, if you follow the hull you will find your way back to Morgan. After that, I will lead you to the wheelhouse, child of the Dark World."

"Good plan," Kane says.

"You should both hold on to my back," Kendal suggests. "So that we do not get separated."

I lean down to touch Kendal's back. I have to bend my knees only a little. Kane, who is at least a foot taller than I am, has to nearly bend at the waist.

"Can't I just hold on to your tail or something?"

Kendal flicks her tail with annoyance. "No. You may not."

"All right," Kane says.

"Hold my hand," I suggest.

Kane reaches out and grabs my hand. His hand is so much bigger than mine, and strong. Despite the fog, it isn't cold or clammy, but reassuringly warm. Solid. I have never held a boy's hand before and even though I know this is not a romantic situation, I feel his touch all the way to my very core.

It takes Kendal only a few minutes to lead us to the hull.

"Thanks for waking me up, Cupcake." Even though the fog is too dense for me to see him clearly, I can hear the smile in his voice. "If you can make it up to the wheelhouse, can you keep her on a steady heading?"

"Yes," I say, thinking of the compass in my bag. "I can."

"Then I'll see you on the other side. Good luck." He gives my hand a squeeze, his fingers drifting away slowly, as though he's reluctant to lose contact.

Kendal apparently does not have the patience for long goodbyes, because she immediately walks off in the other direction. I have no choice but to follow or lose her in the fog. I am several steps away when I hear Kane say, "Glad you need me, Cupcake."

"Wait. What?" I can hear Kane chuckling through the fog. "What did he mean by that?"

"Child, he is referring to what you said when you were trying to wake him. That would appear to be obvious to me."

"Sure, it's obvious to you. You can read his mind." I cut myself off abruptly. "Wait. You can read his mind."

Kendal makes a noise almost like a purr. Or she's laughing at me. Either one. "Yes, child."

"Does he—" I cut myself off again. I certainly don't want this conversation getting back to him. "Never mind. Forget I asked."

"In fact, you did not ask."

"Exactly. I didn't ask. I don't want to know."

Yeah, Edie. Way to play it cool. If Kane is listening in to this conversation, I've come off really well. Not at all awkward or needy.

"If you are curious, child, about his feelings for you, you should ask him."

Great. Relationship advice from a cat. This has to be some sort of record low for teenage girls everywhere.

"Well, I'm not going to ask him. Because I'm not curious. Besides which, this is a life-or-death situation. I'm pretty sure we all have more important things to be thinking about than whether or not Kane likes me. Not that I think he likes me. "

Oh my God. Stop. Talking. Now.

"As I said before, child, I do not know how he feels. Kane is ever vigilant in keeping his emotions from me."

Her unspoken message is clear. I need to shut up and keep

my emotions from her as well.

With my free hand, I give her a mock salute. "Gotcha."

I will be playing it cool. Keeping the crazy to a minimum.

"You know, it's not my fault I'm this flustered," I mutter. My life in the Dark World did not prepare me for meeting my book boyfriend. Or for him to have dimples. And honey brown eyes.

I manage to keep my mouth shut until we make it to the wheelhouse. There is a ladder leading up to the small building on the starboard side. Kendal scampers up the ladder with surprising grace.

A moment later, she calls out, "Ro is up here."

I follow Kendal up the ladder and find Ro flat on her back near the entrance. After a quick exploration of the wheelhouse, I find Crab slumped over in a chair.

I make my way back to where Ro is on the floor. Waking her is easy. I lean over and whisper in her ear, "If you don't wake up and help, I'll never be able to tell Chuck Wallace that you're funny."

She sits up so fast, we bang heads.

"Ow!" I run my hand over the spot where her head hit mine.

She scoots back. "Was that supposed to be some kind of a joke?"

"Nope. I just said what I thought would wake you up."

She grins. "Good point. What do we do next?"

"Do you know how to steer a boat?" I ask.

She scrambles to her feet, looking from me to the ship's wheel and then to Kendal. "No. Do you?"

"No. But I have a compass."

"I'll see if I can help down by the paddle wheel."

Ro disappears down the ladder to the main deck, leaving Kendal and me alone in the wheelhouse with the sleeping Crab.

Outside, I hear the paddle wheel creak and then a slow and unsteady, *thump, thump, thump.*

Which means Kane, Morgan, and Ro are turning the paddle wheel by hand. I pull my phone out and open up the compass app. There is a ledge running beneath all of the windows around the wheelhouse. Kendal leaps up to sit on it and stare out the windows into the dense fog.

"Do you know where to go?" she asks.

According to the compass, the ship has drifted so that we are now going just west of north. If we continued to drift on this path, we would slide right past the island and come out on the other side of the Crimson Miasma. I reach past the ship's wheel and prop my phone on the ledge against the window.

"I do."

I grasp the wheel in both hands and turn into the Crimson Miasma. Toward Gull Veston Island.

Excerpt from
Book Five of The Traveler Chronicles:
The Traveler Undone

Oh, you wanna know what the Crimson Miasma showed me?
You wanna know my deepest desire?
    I'd sooner tell you my binding name.
    I'm not a dumb-ass. Despite appearances.

CHAPTER THIRTY

B y the time Crab wakes up, the fog is melting into thin wisps. He groans, struggling to sit straighter in his chair, as he rubs a pudgy hand over his eyes.

"How are you doing?" I ask.

"Well, now, that was quite the display of power. I fancy myself to be in the same general field as whoever created that Miasma. But that was work like I've never seen."

He shakes his head again, and I notice that when he lowers his hand, there is a faint tremor to it.

"Want to talk about it?" I ask.

"Want to talk about what you saw?"

I chuckle. "Nope."

"That's what I thought."

"Who was the first to break through the Miasma?" he asks.

I clear my throat. "Actually, I was."

Crab gives me a slow smile. "I'm impressed. That's quite a trick for a Dark Worlder."

"That's me, defying expectations."

He nods toward the ship's wheel. "I believe I'll take that back, if it's all the same to you."

"She's all yours."

Crab stands and takes the wheel from me. I step aside and Kendal leaps down from the ledge and brushes against my legs once before leaving the wheelhouse.

"She's obviously glad to have you back at the wheel. I don't think she had much confidence in me."

"You did just fine, Cupcake." He squints out the window. The Crimson Miasma has dissipated entirely. Above are clear blue skies. A glance out the back tells me that the sun hangs low in the sky, still several hours away from setting. Ahead, there is maybe a quarter mile of open ocean. Towering out of it, encompassing the entire view, is Gull Veston Island.

With Crab awake, the paddle wheel takes on a powerful, rhythmic *thump*, *thump*, *thump*. It's not long before he slows down and we coast toward the cliffs ahead.

The others join us in the wheelhouse.

"Can you angle in next to the cliff?" Kane asks Crab.

Crab reaches down and pulls out a pair of rubber bumpers that he hands to Morgan and Kane. "Now then, boys, if you'll just go down and drop these over the side of the boat, I'll pull up alongside the cliff."

He hands two more to Ro and me before turning his attention back to the wheel. We all head down the ladder to the deck. I watch carefully as Kane and Morgan wind the rope from the bumper around the cleat on the railing. I do the same, and then drop my bumper over the side.

A moment later, the ship nudges against the cliffs. Crab scampers down the ladder and joins us on the starboard side of the boat.

"Well, Cupcake. What do you think?" Kane asks.

I glance at him. "Looks like the Cliffs of Insanity to me."

Kane nods. "Just like you described. So far, that's two for two."

"Three for three," Morgan corrects. "If you count the Kellas cats."

I glance in Kendal's direction and, uncomfortable with the

reminder of the fight that cost her her dowt, I change topics. "Ro, do you think you can get a reading on where the stairs are?"

"You wouldn't have brought me if I couldn't."

I tip my head back and look straight up at the towering height of the cliff. It's darker at the base, where the water splashes against the stone, but above my head, it lightens to a cream color. And it seems to stretch on forever. I sure hope Ro can find a staircase, because there's no way we're climbing that.

Ro turns to face the wall and reaches out for it. For an instant, she plants her hand flat on the wall, but the waves bump the boat, pitching her forward so she almost tumbles over the railing.

"Any way you can steady the boat?" I ask Crab.

"I can try."

For this, he sits back against the hull, palms flat against the wood. There is a calm, meditative quality to him, as if he is communing with the boat. But his affinity is with water, not wood. More precisely, it is with the oxygen in the water. If it took tremendous power to move the water through the paddle wheel and get the boat here, I can only imagine how much more it must take to calm the waves around us. But slowly, they do calm. Not to a perfect glassy stillness, but they become gentle enough that Ro can plant her hands on the stone to perform her own, much less powerful, form of magic.

I glance over at Kane, who is standing just a little off to the side, turned away. He's looking down at something in his hand. Something gold and round, like a compass or a pocket watch. A second later, Kane looks up, catches me watching him, snaps the watch closed, and puts it back into his pocket.

I can't think of any sinister reason why Kane would be looking at either a compass or a pocket watch. So why didn't he want anyone to notice he was doing it?

Was that his mother's medallion? But if it is, then why did he pretend earlier not to know what I was talking about?

Before I can wonder more, Ro's hands drop away from the wall and she steps back.

"I got it."

Crab's shoulders sag, and the tension holding him taut releases. He gets to his feet, moving slowly.

"There is a staircase that goes all the way to the top. It's maybe a quarter mile around the island from here. It's more than ten thousand steps," Ro says.

I gasp. "Ten thousand steps? That's worse than I thought."

"No. What's worse is that the steps are barely eight inches wide."

"Relax, Ro," Morgan says. "Don't forget. We have a plan for dealing with this."

"Right. A plan that involves Kane loop-jumping onto a narrow step. It's not a plan, it's a suicide mission."

I can do nothing but stare at Ro in mute horror. The idea of Kane loop-jumping onto an eight-inch ledge is terrifying. Especially if he has the same kind of trouble establishing a loop that he did in the parking lot on Le Mare Avenue. Landing on an eight-inch target seems impossible.

"Don't be overly dramatic, Ro," Kane says. "We have a plan. We're going to stick to it."

Ro takes a step closer to him, desperation in her eyes. "This is her plan. So what if she wants to save the princess and the Curator? We got her here. Let her rescue them."

Ro's sudden betrayal stings, but part of me wonders if she's right. My goal here is to save Kane, but I'm putting him in danger.

"She's right, I could go on alone from here."

Never mind that walking up ten thousand steps would straight up kill me. Never mind that I don't know what to do on the island if I encounter any magical creatures. I'll figure it out.

Everyone turns and stares at me.

"I can do it," I repeat. "I can go on alone from here."

"Don't be ridiculous," Kane says. "As you have pointed out, you have the least power of any of us. Driving a Kellas cat around town is one thing. Waltzing into the most secure detention center in our world is another."

"There's Everdawn on the island," I remind him. "No one has power there. So I'll be no different than anyone else."

"You've gotten us this far, and we appreciate the help. But it's time to let the real scoundrels take over," Kane argued.

"Oh, you did not just say that." I take a step toward him. "Don't forget, I'm the Untethered Sleeker. I may be more powerful than all of you combined. So back off. And don't forget, it's my plan. I'm the one who knows where the Curator and the princess are being held on the island."

"It's an island. It can't be that hard to find them."

"Everyone just calm down." Morgan steps between Kane and me, planting a hand on each of our chests. "You're both going onto the island. We got this far by following Cupcake's plans. They'll get us the rest of the way there, too." He levels a hard gaze at first Kane and then me. "Got it?"

I nod reluctantly, and then Kane does as well.

Morgan steps aside and looks to Crab. "Obviously, the solution is simple. Take us around to the steps, and we'll get a look at them." He looks to Ro. "What do the steps connect to? A dock of some kind?"

"Yes, a dock." She wraps her arms around her chest, bumping out her chin with belligerent fear. "And here's the best part. The dock is guarded by two hellhounds."

Excerpt from
Book Five of The Traveler Chronicles:
The Traveler Undone

*Yeah, I get it. Politics is always complicated. Mixing in magic
sure as hell doesn't make it simpler.*

*The Tuatha like to think they have all the power. But there
are plenty of other creatures who have magic of their own. Older,
deeper magic. Magic most people don't even understand.*

*Needless to say, balancing the wants and needs of so many
different magical creatures gets messy. Only a moron would want
that job. So I guess it's a good thing that no one knows I am heir
to the throne. I've done a lot of stupid stuff, but I'm not a moron.*

CHAPTER THIRTY-ONE

Hellhounds. Two days ago, I didn't even know they existed. Now they are the bane of my existence. And they will most likely be the end of it, too.

"Hellhounds we can deal with," Kane says.

"We can?" I ask. "Because before now, I have been under the impression that hellhounds were pretty much unstoppable. So if there's some kind of magical doggie treat that will stop them in their tracks, shouldn't you have mentioned it before?"

Kane's lips twitch. "Unfortunately, you are the magical doggie treat. Fortunately, hellhounds are not terribly smart. I'll open a loop to Houston, you and I will jump through just long enough for them to catch your scent, and then we'll jump back."

"We don't know if you can open a loop to the other side of the Crimson Miasma," I argue. "There's got to be a better way."

It's Crab who speaks up. "Well, m'dear. I think it's obvious what needs doing." After a moment, he nods firmly and takes off his hat. "I think I'd best go in."

"Won't the hellhounds immediately rip you to shreds?"

"Nah. Hellhounds aren't likely to bother me. I can swim up to the dock, pretend to be lost. Talk my way onto the island."

"Hellhounds can't be reasoned with," Kane says.

"Well then, I won't be reasoning with them, now will I? I'll just work a wee bit of me magic and see if I can persuade them."

"Persuade them to do what?" I ask.

Morgan strokes his chin with one hand. "Persuade them to take him into custody."

"How does you being in prison help anything?" I ask.

"Well, those hellhounds will have to take me up the stairs to the island. That will give you a chance to sneak up after me. Don't worry, m'dear. I expect you to come and get me when you rescue the princess and the Curator. I'm not planning to make any grand sacrifice here."

Even without the Siren allure of his words, I know he can do this.

When no one else offers up a protest, Crab adds, "Now, if you wouldn't mind turning away so I could have a bit of privacy to change…"

"Wait!" I say. "We have no way of keeping in touch once you go in. No way of knowing if you're in danger."

He gives me a gentle knock on the chin. "A man like me is in far more danger on land than he'd ever be in the water."

"No," Kendal says quietly. "She is correct. It would be foolhardy for you to venture out with no means of communicating."

He studies the deck in front of him, giving the planking a scuff with his bare foot. "Not much we can do about that now, is there?"

She blinks, looking nonplussed. "You could become my dowt-mate."

He blanches visibly. "Your what?"

"My dowt-mate. I could form a mental bond with you like the one I now share with Kane. For that matter, I can see the benefits of all of us forming a mental link. Shall I initiate a link with all of you?"

Ro, Morgan, and I all take a step back. Kane just laughs. "I think that's a no."

Finally, Crab shuffles forward.

"Well there, then. How exactly does this work?"

It's easier to watch this time, either because I'm not taken by surprise or because Crab isn't wholly human and so his brain works differently.

I try to do what I did for Kane, but racked with pain, Crab waves everyone away. Unable to watch, I go to the far end of the boat and stare off into the mist. When the bond is completed and Crab's groans have stopped, I turn back to see him laid out on the deck, in his true form. Where his legs once were, there is now a massive, finned tail.

The fabric from his pants lays crumpled beside him. His tail is long and tapered and a slick gray, like the skin of a dolphin. Crab moves awkwardly to sit up.

"How do we know if this worked?" he asks.

Kendal stares hard at him and then gives a flick of her tail. Beside me, Kane chuckles under his breath.

Crab looks right into Kendal's gaze. "All right, then," he says and starts unbuttoning his shirt. Looking at Kane he says, "So obviously, I can hear her, but can you hear me?"

"Just concentrate on what's happening. We should be able to keep up." He claps a hand on Crab's shoulder. "Don't do anything heroic."

Crab winks. "I don't think any of us are worried about that."

Crab slips his shirt off his shoulders and holds it out to me. "Hang this up in the wheelhouse for me, will you, m'dear?"

He doesn't wait for an answer but rolls over onto his stomach and pulls himself along the deck toward the back of the boat, his merman's tail swishing behind him. When he reaches the hull, he uses his arms to hoist himself up so he's sitting on the railing.

"Well, then, mates. I'll see you in few, all right?"

Then he gives a jaunty two-finger salute and a wink. For an

instant, with the water sparkling behind him, Crab doesn't look short and plump. He's sleek and strong as he tips backward into the water, his tail arcing over his head for just an instant before he disappears under the waves.

I rush to the side of the boat and peer over, eager to glimpse him in the water—where he's meant to be.

"You won't see him," Kane says quietly beside me.

I glance in his direction. "Oh." I bite down on my lip, feeling weirdly embarrassed.

"Sirens don't surface often. They don't have to."

"I know that."

He shoots me a glance. "You do?"

"Crab can manipulate water, right? So I figure he must have an affinity for oxygen, which lets him pull the oxygen directly from the water."

Kane smiles faintly. "You're pretty smart for a Dark Worlder."

"You'd be stupid to follow me if I *wasn't*."

Excerpt from
Book Five of The Traveler Chronicles:
The Traveler Undone

The last thing my mother gave me before she died was a medallion. It had been her most prized possession. Handed down from one generation to the next in her family for over a thousand years. Imbued with the kind of power most people couldn't even imagine. For four years, I'd guarded that medallion with my life.

Needless to say, the fact that Smyth took it from me pissed me off.

Yeah, he's been my enemy...well, ever since I was born. Sure, he'd murdered my mother. Hunted me. Tormented my friends. But this?

This shit was personal.

CHAPTER THIRTY-TWO

At times like this, the waiting is the worst. Time stretches when you have nothing to fill it with but dread.

I distract myself by thinking about my mother.

If time moves at the same rate here—and I have no way of knowing if it does—then roughly twenty-eight hours have passed since the last time I texted my mother.

Most likely, she's been trying to call me.

I know my mom. After three—maybe four—unanswered calls, she'll turn on the "Where's My Phone" app. Unless that app has a "Lost in a Parallel Universe" function I don't know about, my phone isn't going to pop up.

Yeah. Worrying about Mom? It's not any better than worrying about Crab.

I push away from the railing and go to sit beside Kane. "What's happening?"

"He's almost to the dock."

Kane's entire body radiates tension. Kendal merely swishes her tail. But her claws are slowly digging into the wood of the bench, gouging deep scratches.

Then Kane shoots to his feet, cups his hands in front of him, and pulls a loop.

Kendal jumps down, and, before the loop gets too big, she rears up on her back paws, plants her front paws on Kane's chest, and growls.

Kane stills, looks down at Kendal, and scowls. After a second, he drops his hands.

"Fine. But if they hurt him, it's on you."

Kendal pushes off Kane's chest and lands neatly on the ground. "If Mr. Crab is injured, it is on all of us. However, he did not want you to interfere. We should respect his wishes."

Tail high in the air, she says to the rest of us, "Mr. Crab is being escorted to the surface of the island. I suggest we bring the boat around to the dock. I, for one, am not fond of swimming."

With Morgan, Ro, and Kane manually working the paddle wheel and Kendal and I steering, we take the boat around the island. I am not as skilled as Crab but I get *The Blossom* as close as I can, and then Morgan and Kane leap out and use ropes to pull her the rest of the way in.

Kendal jumps nimbly onto the dock and heads straight for the stairs. Once she is gone, there is more waiting. Finally, Kane pushes away from the spot where he's been leaning against the rock and says, "Looks like I'm up."

Ro, Morgan, and I go to stand near him.

"When I get to the top, I will pull a loop and you can come through," he says, even though we have been over the plan numerous times.

"I don't think you'll be able to get all the way to the top." Kane frowns as he turns to look at me, so I explain. "Because of the Everdawn."

He shrugs. "We'll see."

Okay. So clearly, he still doubts the existence of Everdawn, despite Morgan's opinion that it's possible. He might have doubts, but I don't. He won't be able to pull a loop on the island. He'll have to do it somewhere on the stairs. Which is better than nothing, I guess.

We all nod. He looks at me, and for a second, I think he wants to say something more. Something meaningful. Then he gives his head a shake and says, "Cupcake, I hope your plan works."

"Me, too."

A moment later, he is gone.

Ro, Morgan, and I just stand there. Waiting.

"Well, I guess he made it," I say, clenching my hand around the strap of my messenger bag.

"Yeah. I guess so. Judging by the fact that we didn't hear him scream and see him fall from the sky," Ro said.

"Thanks. That's a helpful image." Like I wasn't worried enough already.

Morgan steps between Ro and me. "There's no point fighting. He made the first jump. He'll make the others. Kane is good. I've seen him make more precise jumps than this." He turns away and leaps back onto the deck of *The Blossom*. "You two need to get along. I'm not going to be there on the island to separate you."

"Wait. What?" I ask. Ro looks just as surprised as I am.

"Why aren't you going onto the island?"

"Someone needs to stay with the boat. Trust me."

Trust him? Trust one of the deadliest assassins this world has ever known?

"You're going to have to do better than that." I follow Morgan down onto the deck, albeit a lot less gracefully. But what I lack in grace, I make up for in persistence. I get right in his face.

"It's cute that you think you can demand answers from me, Cupcake." He reaches out and gives my chin a playful nudge.

I have never hated that nickname more.

"I discussed it with Kane," he continued. "He knows I'm staying on the boat and he's okay with it. You need to be too."

"Not. Likely."

Morgan just smiles. "You know, Cupcake, this is why I've always liked you. You've got spunk."

Before I can reply, Morgan heads up the ladder to the wheelhouse.

Fuming, I sit down on the bench and glare at the deck between my feet.

Suddenly, the space between Ro and me swirls. A second later, the loop opens and, where there was once nothing but boat deck and salty air, there is now a view of brilliant blue sky. And a tiny stone step.

Just like I thought, Kane couldn't open a loop to the top of the island. Damn it, I hate being right sometimes.

"Quickly," Ro says.

She doesn't have to tell me twice. I step through a hole in the fabric of the universe and onto a ledge barely wide enough to stand on. Kendal is a few steps above me and already on the move. Cleaving close to the cliff, I go up several steps before looking back.

I don't need to tell you what a mistake that was, right?

On the upside, Ro and Kane are below me on the steps. We're all here.

We're also all inches from a horrific death.

The steps wind down the side of the cliff, just as treacherous and terrifying as Ro described them. They are tiny. And narrow.

Vertigo rises up to punch me in the gut.

I let out a shaky breath only to find that breathing back in is harder than it should be.

I press myself to the face of the rock and suck in a lungful of air so thin, my head swims.

"Move," Ro pleads from behind me. "Get out of my way, or I swear to Thread, I will push you."

I believe her.

It takes us another forty or so steps to get to the top. Okay, it's forty-three. Yeah. I counted. And even though I know that Kane got us as close to the top as he could, I still resent every damn step.

Forty-three chances to die horribly.

When I stumble to the top, I drop to my knees and crawl away from the ledge. I flop onto my back and breathe as deeply as I can.

I love the sun-kissed ground beneath me. The pokey grass. The solid, firm earth beneath it.

I adore it. I want to hug it forever and buy it flowers on Valentine's Day. I want to doodle "Edie ♥'s Solid Ground 4 evah!"

When I'm done pledging my eternal love to the ground beneath my back, I push up onto my elbows and find myself in paradise.

I don't use the word "paradise" lightly. But the detention center on Gull Veston Island may be the prettiest place I've ever seen.

The air up here—so much higher than the sea level in Houston—is crisp and clear. There's no cloying humidity. No oppressive heat. Just a view that stretches a hundred miles in every direction. Far below, the thin line of the barrier islands stretches down the coast to the southwest. Galveston Bay and the intercoastal waters spread out all the way to Houston.

I draw in deep lungsful of air, but still feel a little light-headed because the air is so thin.

Ro is also sitting on the ground. Kane is a few feet away, head ducked, I suspect trying hard not to look as pathetic as Ro and I do. Finally, he straightens. He turns his back to us but reaches into his pocket and takes something out. A moment later he puts it back. The medallion again? It must be.

Kendal is at Kane's feet, wending in and out of his legs. She alone seems unfazed by the thin air.

The topography of the island itself is unlike anything you'd see in my world. Here, near the cliff's edge, there's a gently sloping field of grass that seems to rim the entire island. Twenty or thirty feet from the cliff, the sloping field gives way to a steep hillside. It's as if the center of the island itself was uplifted even farther, making it seem like a wedding cake. Tiers upon tiers of treacherous height. Yay!

Straight ahead, a footpath zigzags up the hill to a cluster of buildings perched on top. Like a mismatched bridal couple on the top of the cake, the building has two turrets, one tall and lean, the other squat and fat. One of those turrets is the prison. That's where the princess and the Curator will be.

Excerpt from
Book Five of The Traveler Chronicles:
The Traveler Undone

Everything has a downside. Everything.

Call me cynical. Call me jaded. Whatever.

Sure, by most people's standards, I have unimaginable power. But even that power has a price.

In this case, it's overconfidence.

I'm used to working hard for what I want. I'm also used to having the power to back up my threats. The second I step onto the island and into the Everdawn, my power is gone. That's when shit goes sideways.

CHAPTER THIRTY-THREE

J ust as I predicted, on the island it's dawn. Other than the seagulls swirling in the air currents overhead, we are the only signs of life.

Thank God there aren't any hellhounds. None of us seem strong enough to fight them off.

I push myself to my feet, but only because Ro does it first. I refuse to be the weak link here.

Kane is standing a few feet away, his hands cupped in front of him. He's glaring at the empty space between his hands, trying to pull a loop and failing. All his life, he's had power at his fingertips. Now it's gone.

"I did warn you."

"I know." He drops his hands to his side, clenching and unclenching his fists. "But I had to try."

I point to the building on the crest of the hill. "That's the detention center."

Ro, too, is clenching and unclenching her hands, shaking them a little, like someone trying to get blood flowing into a body part that's fallen asleep.

"Okay, I say we split up," Kane says. "Cupcake, you, Kendal, and Ro go up to the fortress. See if you can find a way in. I'll try to circle the island down here, get the lay of the land."

"We don't need to split up," I say. "I know they're being

held in the prison. It matches the description from the book perfectly."

"We'll cover more ground separately. When you come across the princess and the Curator, Kendal can let me know," Kane says, not meeting my gaze. "Somewhere on this island, Smyth must have a timekeeper who is holding this place in Everdawn. If we can find that person and break the cycle, everything will be easier."

Before I can argue further, Kane turns and stalks away.

"You could have led with that," I call out, but he doesn't even glance back.

I turn to Kendal. "What the hell?"

Ro, frowning, watches him leave. "I hope—" Then she shakes her head. When she sees me watching her, she smiles, like she's trying to be brave. "Okay. Let's go."

She marches off toward the path with a perky saunter, like a camp counselor who's realized she's in a horror movie, but doesn't want the kids to know.

I hurry to catch up. "Hey, no worries, okay?" Sure, Kane may have just ditched us, but that doesn't mean we're slasher-film fodder. "We'll find the princess and the Curator. Kendal can let Kane know. And we'll be out of here before you know it."

I know I'm saying it to make her feel better. And I know it's not working. Damn, I never knew how shitty it felt to tell a transparent lie. "Come on, guys. Let's go save a princess."

The three of us head up the path. The trail switchbacks up the hill. It's narrow enough that we walk single file, which is fine by me. I may be great at awkward babbling, but forced optimism is not my jam. By the time we make it to the first turn in the switchback, I am already out of breath.

Then Kendal stops abruptly and I nearly bump into her. Just ahead, the path splits. To the right, it continues up to the detention center on the hill. To the left, it leads around the eastern side of the island.

"Where do you think that goes?" I ask.

Ro looks from me to Kendal and back again. She's doing the nervous hand-clenching thing again. "I'll go look."

Unease creeps into my stomach. "I think we should stay together."

"No, I'll be fine. And Kendal will be here to protect you."

"But—"

Ro pulls me into a quick, tight hug, then she pulls back, a false, too-bright smile on her face. "Be safe."

She turns to leave before I can push any further, hurrying up the path without looking back.

"Look for Crab," I call.

She waves a hand to show me she heard.

As I watch her go, unease skitters across my skin.

I don't like anything about this. Gull Veston Island is supposed to be a high security prison. And yes, we have encountered magical barriers, but we haven't come across any actual guards, other than the hellhounds. We have no idea where Crab was taken. Scattered around the island like this, we're vulnerable.

For all Kane's talk about loving Dark Worlder movies, it's like none of them have ever seen a horror movie!

Shaking my head, I head up the path as it wraps around the hill to the west.

"Did that seem odd to you?" I ask Kendal.

She arches a feline eyebrow. "In what way?"

"Well, for starters, the way Ro—who never wanted to come here—is suddenly comfortable just going off on her own."

"Rowena Geroux is not my dowt-mate."

"What about Kane's weird behavior? He is your dowt-mate. So what's up with him?"

Kendal gives her tail an impatient swish. "Indeed, Kane is my dowt-mate." Her tone drips with censure. "And I will not discuss his motivations or actions with someone who is not."

"Okay then." So that's what it felt like to be verbally bitch-slapped by a cat.

Her expression softens. "I am sorry, child. I forget sometimes that you are not of this world. Do not take my loyalty to my dowt-mate to mean I do not value the compassion you have shown me."

I squint at her. "Did you just read my mind?"

Her tail softens. "I did not. However, after living among the Tuatha, I find your Dark World facial expressions quite…" She tips her head to the side as if considering her words. "transparent."

Great. So much for my poker face.

"Does everyone find my expressions transparent?"

"I am not the dowt-mate of everyone."

I open my mouth, then stop myself from asking, and snap it closed. Honestly, I don't want to know.

Kendal answers the question I don't even ask. "However, I can confirm that both Mr. Crab and Kane find your emotions easy to read."

"Well, I'm glad I entertain them."

"I have offended you?"

"No." Not offended. Just irritated. And not with her. With me. Because I've been wearing my heart on my sleeve this whole time.

We are now high enough up that I can see the entire southwestern side of the island laid out before me. From here, I can see Kane on the path far below. I watch him for a moment before calling out to Kendal, who has passed me.

"Kendal, hold up a second."

Far below us, Kane walks slowly, his head down as he stares

at something in his hands. The medallion? But why would he need to look at it so often?

After a few steps, he pauses to look around and then glances back at what he's holding. He turns slowly in a circle, shaking his head.

Okay then, not a medallion—at least not the one Wallace described. Maybe a compass?

I pull out my phone and open the compass app again. The digital hand wiggles for a second before righting itself. My compass works. West is where west should be. But Kane is behaving as if his compass is broken.

I mutter, "What is he doing?"

Beside me, Kendal says, "I cannot comment on—"

"I know, I know. You can't tell me what a dowt-mate is doing." And I blow out a breath of frustration. "I'm beginning to regret I ever suggested you become his dowt-mate."

"Indeed? On the other hand, I have found the experience to be not entirely unpleasant."

"So," I say, turning on my heel and starting off toward the east. "I guess Kellas cats are considered to be the optimists of the Kingdoms of Mithres."

"I have not found that to be true."

"I was being sarcastic."

"Oh, sarcasm. Kellas cats do not employ sarcasm in our language."

"That's a shame. It's useful."

Kendal does not respond, and she and I are quiet until we reach the eastern edge of the plateau.

From here, we have a view of the path Ro took, which jets sharply off due east. It leads to a bridge, maybe thirty feet across, that spans a narrow chasm between this island and another much smaller, crescent-shaped island.

If I had to guess, I would say the Crescent Island was once

part of this one, before the earth shifters cleaved a gap between the two.

The Crescent Island is just big enough for a large Victorian mansion, complete with a white picket fence and a lush, expansive yard.

Down below us, Ro has nearly reached the bridge. The house on Crescent Island is hard to look at, because the rising sun is just beside it. Then, there is a shift in the air, almost like the chill that creeps over my skin.

And then, the strangest thing happens. One second, the sun is sitting low in the sky, the bottom curve just touching the horizon. The next instant, the sun dips below the horizon with only the tiniest sliver of light peeking out to cast the world in the thick gray of dawn.

So that's it. Whoever was keeping time on the island has reset dawn. But even weirder was what happened on the small crescent-shaped island. The light there never changed. The mansion still gleams in the sunlight. The Crescent Island is beyond the reach of Everdawn. Which means, if we could get there, we could do magic.

I file that away in my mind as a potentially useful bit of info and then turn back to Kendal.

"Come on. We've got to go rescue the princess and the Curator and get out of here."

At the crest of the hill, I crouch down near one of the last scraggly shrubs, hoping to get the lay of the land.

Kendal doesn't take the hint and trots past me.

"Psst," I whisper.

She pauses, looking back at me. "Do you need assistance?"

"No." I gesture for her to come back. "We should hide here to watch for guards."

Kendal sniffs disdainfully. "The prison is currently unguarded."

"But—"

"May I remind you that my sense of hearing and my sense of smell are both significantly more powerful than yours. Now that dawn has been reset, my vision is stronger as well."

"But—"

"Do you not trust me, child?"

"I—" I straighten and step away from the tree. "I suppose I do."

Kendal seems to think this explanation is enough. She does not wait for me but continues up to the top of the hill.

I grumble, "You could have said that before I crouched behind a tree."

"I am unaccustomed to verbal communication."

"Well, sure. If you want to have answers for everything."

The hilltop is a broad plateau. The fortress is perched on the southernmost edge, so that Kendal and I have to cross a lawn of patchy grass before we even reach the doors.

The doors are the massive wooden kind, popular in medieval castles and magic fortresses. Kendal stops and looks up at me.

"What? You think we need to knock?"

She gives me one of those looks. "No. But I believe being bipedal makes you better equipped to use doorknobs."

"Oh! Right." I clear my throat, blow out a breath, and say a little prayer. Then I add on another little prayer to the Thread, in case that's what works here. Finally, I grab the doorknob.

The creak of the doors echoes throughout the empty stone foyer. The second I pass through them, I'm filled with doubts. In the book, it's Kane who rescues the princess. He should be here.

"Wait," I whisper to Kendal.

Kendal pauses, one paw raised, and looks over her shoulder. "What is it?"

"They're here," I tell her.

Something like a frown crosses her face. "How can you be certain?"

"Because this is how it happens in the book. Right down to the creaking door. Contact Kane. Tell him to get his ass up here."

But Kendal shakes her head. "I will do no such thing. We have not found the princess or the Curator."

She turns her butt to me. "Kendal, stop!"

But she keeps going.

Finally, I do the only thing I can think of. I throw myself onto her back, pinning her beneath me. She hisses, squirming, but I've got at least eighty pounds on her. And her poison-tipped claws are pinned under her. That helps, too.

"Listen to me. We can't rescue the princess!"

She growls at me before saying, "But that is why we're here."

"No, what I mean is, we—you and I—can't rescue the princess. It has to be Kane."

Excerpt from
Book Five of The Traveler Chronicles:
The Traveler Undone

There's only one thing I hate more than losing.
Getting stabbed in the back first.

CHAPTER THIRTY-FOUR

Kendal's growling stops and I feel some of the muscles in her back relax. After a moment she asks, "What do you mean, it has to be him?"

"Do you know who Kane really is?"

"Of course. He is my dowt-mate." Then she hesitates and asks, "Do you?"

"Yes! The High King named him as his heir. The power of the throne is his to claim."

"Yes," Kendal says, her voice still taut with suspicion.

I edge off her and squat beside her.

She glares at me through squinty eyes, but she doesn't scratch my eyes out. So there's that.

"And yet," she drawls slowly, "he has not yet claimed that power. He is not King."

"But he should be."

"What should be is irrelevant. He is not King. For reasons of his own, he does not want that power."

Reasons of his own? Because he's a changeling? Or is there something else?

"You have seen his thoughts and read his mind. You tell me. Would he be a good king?"

After a long pause, she says, "He will."

"Then he should *be* King."

"Perhaps. But the next leader of the Kingdoms of Mithres will not be chosen by a dowtless Kellas cat and a child of the Dark World."

"I know that." I talk fast now because I know how crazy I sound. "But if he rescues the princess, they'll fall in love. He may not want the power for himself, but he will claim it to be with her. If they get married, they can rule, side by side, and bring peace to the kingdoms."

She eyes me skeptically. "And you believe this will all happen if he is the one to rescue the princess?"

"I don't just believe it. I know it."

"Why are you telling me this now?"

"Because I'm running out of time." And because I never found the strength to tell Kane himself. "I should have told him." I stand, because I can't look her in the eyes anymore. If he can see what she sees, I don't want him aware of whatever emotions are visible on my face. "Besides, I was hoping it would just happen. That he would be the one to rescue her. That they would just fall in love and I wouldn't have to play a part in it."

"Fine." Kendal says. "I have told him. He is on his way."

"Thank you."

But before I can say more, a voice calls out from somewhere above us.

"Hello? Is someone there?"

Kendal and I exchange a look. "The princess."

"He will be here soon," Kendal says.

"Who's there?" the princess calls out, sounding exasperated. "I can hear you whispering." Kendal just looks at me. I shrug. "I can tell you aren't guards. You have to come get us out! Now! The Curator is wounded. She needs a healer!"

"We should provide assistance," Kendal whispers.

I still hesitate, but I feel Kendal's pragmatism wearing me down.

"Is this love of theirs so fragile, it will not survive a less dramatic rescue?"

"No, I just…" When she put it that way, my gut-deep certainty seemed ridiculous. "Okay, okay," I mutter. Before she can say more, I head off toward the stairs.

The second floor hallway is long and narrow, with jail cells on either side. I instantly know something is wrong.

There's a quality to the air—something more intangible than scent. It feels heavy and fetid and reeks of illness and decay. Every cell I pass is empty until I reach the end of the hall.

"Thank the Thread—" She breaks off. "You!"

Oh good. She remembers me.

And she's clearly super excited that I'm here to rescue her.

Then she points at Kendal and says blandly, "And you've allowed a Kellas cat to sneak up behind you."

"Kendal is with me," I say. "She's helping me rescue you."

The princess huffs. "I wouldn't count on it."

"How is the Curator?"

"Can you get us out?"

The princess is standing at the bars. She isn't touching them, so they must be made of iron. But she's so close, the folds of her dress pour out from between them. The cell is empty except for a lump of what looks like old blankets in the corner.

All the cells I passed were empty. The cell opposite this one is as well. Which means that lump isn't a pile of blankets. It's the Curator.

"How is she?" I ask. "Have you done anything to help her?"

"What could I possibly have done?" The princess's hands flutter in a gesture of futility. "I have none of my powers here. I can't heal her. I can't heal myself."

I step back just long enough to look at the princess. She is in the same rose-petal-covered dress she wore before, but the past twenty-four hours have clearly taken their toll. Her skin is smudged with dirt, the dress torn where the hellhounds grabbed her. She is bruised but not injured. On the other hand, I've seen no more than a faint shuddering from the lump in the corner. The princess may be fine, but the Curator is not.

That sense of unease I had when I turned into the hall condenses into a hard seed in my chest. I need to get them out of here. Fast.

Panicking won't do the Curator any good. I need to focus. I grab the metal bars to give them a shake. The instant I take the metal in my hands, the princess gasps and leaps back. When the bars don't burn me, she leans forward, ogling my hands.

"Oh, right. Your callused Dark-Worlder skin protects you."

She holds out her own hand and examines it, clearly admiring her pale, translucent skin.

There's no easy hack, like the bolts from Kane's Faraday Cage, so I crouch in front of the lock and examine it.

"I am correct, am I not?"

"Yeah. I guess." Does she think this is helping?

She nods, looking satisfied. "That explains why you are so small and stunted."

"I'm not stunted!" I blow out a breath.

I do not have the emotional energy to put up with the princess right now. Not when the Curator is barely moving.

Like the rest of the hardware here, the lock is sturdy but outdated. It's a simple pin tumbler design. The security must rely on the fact that the prisoners can't even touch the lock. "Do you have a bobby pin or something?"

"A what?"

"Anything long and pokey."

The princess frowns, but reaches into her hair. Then she holds out her hand to reveal four long, U-shaped pins. I reach through the bars and scoop them out of her hand. They should do the trick.

I pull my messenger bag around the front of my body and dig through it for a moment before I find my Leatherman tool and flashlight.

"Okay," I say. "Step back."

"Oh! I have read a lot about your many explosive devices in the Dark World," the princess says. "Are you going to blow the door off?"

"No. I'm going to pick the lock." I gesture to her frothy skirt. "You're in the way."

The princess takes a step back. "Oh," she says, sounding disappointed.

"If I had a grenade in my bag, don't you think I would have used it against the hellhounds?"

"I thought perhaps you had made such a device before coming to rescue me."

Restraining an eye roll, I crouch down in front of the lock. I've never picked an actual lock on a jail cell before, but I know the theory. I use the nail file on my Leatherman as a tension wrench and slide it into the lock. I slide the smallest pin in above it and rake it forward, counting the number of pins in the lock. There are only three, and I can feel the first one catch already.

"Are you a thief in your world?" the princess asks.

I nearly laugh, then realize she's serious. "Oh. Um, no."

I slide the bobby pin forward and up, but it slips. My hands are shaking.

I glance at the lump in the corner. She's still not moving.

I have got to get my shit together. I shift so that I'm sitting cross-legged instead of crouching on my haunches. I place the Leatherman and the bobby pins on my knees and scrub my palms on my jeans.

I give my hands another shake to get the tremors out and try again. Slide in the tension wrench, slide the bobby pin in until it catches a pin. Focus on the feel. Don't think about the Curator, in pain, huddled in the corner.

I slide the pick back, then forward, and gently press up the next pin. I exhale and launch into another bout of nervous babbling.

"My mom works for a lot of rich people. People with drivers and paid security and stuff. You'd be surprised the things someone will teach a bored kid. I know how to make a soufflé. How to hotwire a car." I press the final pin up and use the tension wrench to turn the tumbler. "And how to pick a lock."

The gate swings open.

I give a sweeping gesture.

I expect to see gratitude, or at least relief on the princess's face, but she sweeps out of the cell without comment. Kane is right—she is a brat.

But I don't waste time on the princess. The Curator can't wait.

As I move into the cell, that seed of fear cracks and sprouts, nourished by the intangible sense that something is deeply wrong. I crouch beside the lump of blankets, my hand hovering over the peak where her shoulder seems like it would be.

"Curator," I whisper. "We're here to rescue you."

The lump shudders but doesn't rise.

I find the edge of the blanket and peel it back to reveal her face, barely visible in the misty, dawn light. Her temple is marred by a nasty gash. The blood from the wound has dried into the wrinkles on her skin. But that's not what freaks me out. It's the pained shuddering of her breath. The pink foam of blood on her lips.

I put my hand on her cheek. Her skin is blazing hot. Almost tight.

Her eyes roll before settling on me, like she doesn't really see me.

"It's me, Edie," I say.

Her eyelashes flutter, but her gaze doesn't clear.

"We've got to get you out of here."

"No," she mutters again. Then, suddenly, her vision clears. She grabs my arm with surprising strength and she squeezes hard. "You must get back to the Dark World, Edena Allegra Keller. To find the lost *Oidrhe*."

So she does recognize me. I hold her hand tight. "Yes, I will go back to the Dark World," I agree. "I need you to open the threshold for me."

Her grip on my arm tightens as horrible gurgling accompanies her rasping breath. "No. You must open the threshold."

"I can't open the threshold."

"Yes. You can. You did it before." Again, her gaze seems to sear mine. "I release you from our first binding promise."

Behind me I hear footsteps. Kane skids to a halt behind me. Ro must have followed him in, because she's right behind Kendal and the princess, who are just outside the doors of the cell.

I look at Kane. "Her injuries are bad. We have to get her back to the boat. Or Crescent Island. The princess can heal her there."

But the hand on my arm clenches with unexpected strength, pulling me closer.

"I waited for you…" There's another horrible bubbling sound, as her gaze meets mine. "Edena Allegra Keller, promise you will find the lost *Oidrhe*."

"Yes, of course! I will, but—"

"Your word."

"Of course, I give you my word. But—"

Her hand is barely strong enough to grip my arm, but, still, I feel it. The magic that courses between us. The moment I give my word, she pushes the last of her will through the thread between us to bind the promise.

From behind me, I hear the princess gasp.

Okay, so I didn't imagine it. That promise really was knock-me-on-my-ass powerful.

"Step aside," Kane says from behind me. "I'll pick her up. We can be at the boat—"

"No," the Curator says. "Tell them, Edie."

Her gaze holds mine for another heartbeat—for another agonizing, shuddering breath—and then her eyes flicker closed.

I look over my shoulder at the others. They're impatient. They're not willfully blind, just ignorant.

The Tuatha live long lives. They get wounded in battle, but their wounds are healed by magic. They don't have Ebola or AIDS or famine. They don't have cancer. They don't know death.

Not like I do.

I know death. I have seen it haunting my mother's eyes. I have felt it whisper past my room in the night. I have heard it rattle at the window and seep in under the door.

I know death. It's not always the enemy. Sometimes, it's a blessing. It's a relief.

I lean over the Curator. "I will do it," I murmur. "I'll find the lost *Oidrhe*. I promise. I'll restore order to the Kingdoms of Mithres."

This promise isn't a binding promise. Not like the last one. I give it freely. Not because I have to, but because it's the right thing to do.

A thin-skinned hand reaches toward my face. Instinctively, I grasp it and cup it to my cheek.

"My child," she murmurs. "It is your destiny."

Then before I can do anything else, her hand goes limp in mine. She is gone.

That seed of panic in my chest blooms into a full-grown

plant, big enough to push a sob out of me.

I feel hands on my shoulders. Kane pulls me to my feet. I try to wrench myself from his grasp, but he holds tight to my shoulders and pulls me against him.

"Shit," I mutter. "How the hell am I supposed to get home now. Let alone find the lost *Oidrhe*."

"We'll figure it out."

"I hate to be the one to interrupt this touching display of grief," the princess says with cool disdain. "But shouldn't we leave before the hellhounds come tearing in here and rip us to shreds?"

"Shut up," Kane says over his shoulder.

I look from her to Kane and back again.

Oh, crap.

This isn't how it was supposed to go. He was supposed to rescue her. This was the moment when they were supposed to start falling in love.

And I've buggered it.

I pull away from Kane. "No. She's right. We need to go."

We move quickly after that. I push aside my despair and fall in line beside Kane, who seems to have some idea about where we're going, even though I don't. We race through the abandoned wing of the prison and out into the misty sunlight of dawn.

And find ourselves surrounded by hellhounds.

Excerpt from
Book Five of The Traveler Chronicles:
The Traveler Undone

*"Did you get the princess?" Morgan asks as soon as the loop
closes behind me.*

    I step to the side to reveal the princess.

    *Morgan nods. He heads back to the wheelhouse, pausing
halfway there. "You run into any trouble?"*

    "I always run into trouble, don't I?"

CHAPTER THIRTY-FIVE

I've mentioned how terrifying hellhounds are, right?

I mean, I've never been a dog person to begin with, but these things are so damn big. And muscly. And drooly.

Yeah. Really, none of it is okay.

We all skid to a halt right outside the doors to the fortress, Kane thrusting out his arms like he can somehow protect us from them. The princess gasps and takes a step back. Kendal growls low in her throat.

A single hellhound would be bad enough to make me pee my pants. But now, we're facing nearly a dozen of them spread out, two deep, in a semicircle around the door.

No, wait—I do some quick counting—thirteen.

A baker's dozen.

Which is a lot.

"Anyone else notice they aren't moving?" Kane asks, sotto voce.

Sure enough, they are still, their muscles taut and poised, but unflinching.

"Um…yeah," I whisper back. "The lack of having my throat ripped out would be hard to miss."

"What's wrong with them?" the princess asks.

"What is wrong with them," a voice calls out, "Is that I have ordered them not to attack."

The only movement is from a single man wending his way through the hellhounds.

Like all the Tuatha, he is tall and thin, impeccably dressed in a gray pin-striped suit. His crisp white dress shirt is buttoned all the way up. His features are fine-boned, almost elegant, despite the pinched quality around his eyes.

Kane tenses. "Smyth."

Of course. Smyth. The leader of the Council of Sleekers. Kane's most powerful enemy.

Mine, too, since he is, undoubtedly, the man who has dispatched hellhounds to attack me not once, not twice, but at least three times.

"What do you want?" Kane asks.

Which is pretty ballsy, considering.

"What do I want?" Smyth taunts. "Interesting question, considering you have come to my home. You have removed one of my guests from the safety of her confinement. And worst of all"—he pauses as his lips curl in disgust—"you had the unmitigated gall to bring with you this Dark Worlder." His voice rises sharply. "To my island!"

The hellhounds lean forward, drawing closer to his rage.

Smyth pauses and takes a deep breath. And then he says, noticeably more controlled, "All of which I might have overlooked…if you were not obviously attempting to renege on our bargain."

Kane's shoulders slump, almost imperceptibly.

"Wait! What?" I ask. I look from Smyth to Kane. "Your bargain?"

Smyth's nose twitches and for the first time, he looks at me. "Yes. Bargain." He nods at Kane. "Did you fail to tell her that you were in my employ?"

"I don't work for you," Kane growls.

"I disagree," Smyth says smoothly. "I hired you to keep the

princess from her wedding. When that job is complete, I will pay you in an agreed-upon currency. That is the very definition of employment."

"Wait! What?"

I'm repeating myself. Yeah. I get that.

I take a step away from Kane. "You were hired to keep the princess from her wedding? I don't — "

My mind stumbles over this new information.

But Smyth is clearly unconcerned by my confusion. "Lucky for you, I am a forgiving man. And you happen to have something I want."

Kane's gaze narrows. "I do?"

Smyth tips his head. "Indeed, you do. So, Mr. Travers, I will strike you a second bargain. One you will find more than fair."

"I'm listening," he says.

"You, the princess, and the rest of your companions may leave this island unharmed. Your Siren has already been returned to the boat." He pauses, tipping his head ever so slightly in my direction. "And in exchange, you will leave the Dark Worlder with me."

"Not. Likely."

"Then you will all die," Smyth says simply.

Then, as if he's tired of the conversation, Smyth turns away. The hellhounds inch forward.

"Wait!" I yell.

Smyth raises a clenched fist in the air, and the hellhounds freeze again. Slowly he turns back around, his gaze on me.

I step forward without thinking. What else can I do? I can't let my friends be killed. I can't let Kane die, not after all I've done to save his life.

"I'll go with you. But I need a moment. To talk to Kane," I add hastily.

Smyth studies me for a moment as a chilling smile crosses

his face. "Very well."

I glance back at the princess and Kendal. Kendal seems to know what I am thinking because she nudges against the princess's legs and then the two of them step back, giving Kane and me space.

Smyth is not as polite. I put my hand on Kane's arm and lead him a few steps away from the others.

Kane talks before I do. "I'm not leaving you here."

"It'll be okay. Smyth isn't going to hurt me. I know this."

"Really? More knowledge from the books?"

"No." Surprise flickers over Kane's expression. "Remember? I'm Sleeker born. Smyth isn't going to want to kill me. I'll be fine."

I almost even believe it. But the truth is, I have no idea what Smyth's intentions are. I know only that I have to get Kane and the princess off this island. That's why I'm here.

And I'm running out of time.

"But before you go, I have to tell you—"

"I know."

I must look confused, because Kane continues. "I know that I'm supposed to fall in love with the princess. That I'm supposed to marry her and take my place as High King. Kendal told me."

"Good." I nod, squelching my own feelings. That's how the books are *supposed* to end. "But that's not what I need to tell you. When you go to St. Lew, don't trust anyone. There's an assassin at the church. You'll be shot."

I blurt the words out, relieved to be able to voice them now that the Curator has released me from my binding promise.

Kane doesn't even have the good grace to look surprised. "An assassin?"

I can't tell from his expression if he believes me or not. "Yes. If you know what's going to happen, you can—"

"Enough!" Smyth barks the word like in order. "Your time is up."

"No." I hold out my hand to ward him off. "Just another—"

"Enough," Smyth snarls again. And this time, before I have a chance to protest, Smyth's arms stretch out toward me. He keeps his feet planted firmly on the ground but his arms reach for me. Not his human arms, but something else. They sprout from his shoulder blades, undulating toward me, their movement more like the limbs of an octopus than those of a person—human or Tuatha. Instead of hands, they end in flat, spade-like paddles, like the head of a flatworm. There is an elegance to his movements, a sinuous grace. Then, in an instant, their movement changes from lazy undulations into rapid, whiplike snaps. I barely have time to ram my own arms between them and my body as the great loops snake around me.

His massive Sleeker arms yank me off my feet and drag me to him, across the coarse grass and rocks of the plateau.

See? This is what I get for thinking the hellhounds were the threat here.

"No!" Kane roars.

Smyth's arms twist as he sets me upright directly in front of him. Kane's expression twists in anguish. And I know he's reliving the moment Smyth killed his mother in front of him.

Kane whips out his blasting rod and aims it right at Smyth.

Smyth doesn't even flinch, but raises one of his paddle-hands and wags it in front of Kane in a gentle chiding.

"Do not be a fool," he says softly. "We have a bargain. The lives of all your people for the life of this single Dark Worlder."

I'm sure Kane is going to argue. He won't abandon me here.

Kane stares at Smyth, hard, for a moment, the muscle in his jaw twitching, the arm holding his blasting rod so tense, it quivers. "All my people?"

The faintest smile twists Smyth's lips. "All your people on this island."

After a long moment, Kane lowers his blasting rod.

Kane's betrayal is like a kick to the gut, but what did I really expect?

He's told me all along that he didn't care if I lived or died. That there was no honor among thieves. I'm just the fool who didn't believe him.

Deleted from the Advance Reading Copy of
Book Five of The Traveler Chronicles:
The Traveler Undone

*I always expect to run into trouble, but this was more than even
I expected.*

Morgan frowns. "Wait. Where's Cupcake?"

*"Smyth took her. There's another island. One with no
Everdawn. That's where he took her."*

"What are you going to do?"

"I'm going back for her."

*"So," Morgan says with a nod. "You're going to Crescent
Island."*

*Morgan's smile tells me he knows more than what he's
admitting. Which just goes to show that you can't trust anyone.
Even your best friend.*

CHAPTER THIRTY-SIX

O kay, Kane and the others may have left me here to face a monster alone, but that doesn't mean I'm going to let the monster win.

One of Smyth's broad flatworm hands clamps around my mouth.

Oh…and while we're on the subject of not giving in to bullies—no one tries to shut me up and gets away with it.

I claw the edges of his Sleeker paddle to pry it loose from my mouth. This thing is gross.

But I have bigger problems as he drags me away from Kane and the others, down the rocky slope to the path that switchbacks across the island. I stumble multiple times, trying to keep up.

With every step, my mind races. Will Smyth uphold his end of the bargain? Will he really let Kane and the others go?

I do *not* believe that I am all he wants. Why would he want me at all?

The Curator wanted me to come here because she believed that, as someone of Sleeker blood who was not tethered to this world, I could move freely between worlds and find the lost *Oidrhe*.

If the Curator is right and I am destined to find the lost heir, then maybe Smyth wants to take me out before I can?

When we reach the split in the path, he drags me east, toward Crescent Island.

Still struggling to keep up with Smyth, I catch only a glimpse of Kane and the others as hellhounds escort them toward the stairs that lead down toward the ocean. Once they're all on the boat, they can leave. Kane and the princess will be fine. They can continue their journey to St. Lew. They can fall in love. And maybe, just maybe, I have saved Kane.

Even as I cling to the hope, I have doubts. Smyth shouldn't be here. But then again, neither should I.

The path evens out enough for me to see the bridge that connects Gull Veston Island and Crescent Island.

Smyth's paddle-hands loosen just enough that I am able to pull them off.

"Are you kidding me?" I ask, looking at the bridge.

It's the kind of bridge that would give Indiana Jones nightmares. Made of thick rope and crumbling planks of wood, it spans a distance of at least fifty feet, sagging low in the middle like the belly of a donkey. If it was connecting two sections of a child's tree house, I wouldn't cross it. Given that the drop is at least a mile of rocky cliffs, I am more than hesitant.

Vertigo crawls its way up through my belly, threatening to drag up my sad, half-eaten Luna bar with it.

"You cannot be serious!"

Apparently, Smyth is not much of a joker.

I dig in my heels.

He drags me closer to the bridge of death.

"Okay, I get that you people don't like using steel, but I think you need to seriously rethink your building codes!"

Smyth's flat-worm paddle slaps back onto my mouth, cutting me off.

Well. That's rude.

I guess that's the thanks I get for trying to keep him from

plummeting to his death. And dragging me with him.

There is no way this thing can support our weight.

Bridge maintenance in the Kingdoms of Mithres is obviously underfunded, because these ropes are way too loose. The second he steps on the first plank, our weight shifts the bridge's center of gravity over to our side of the canyon so that it's almost a vertical drop straight down. The planks slip out from under my feet. Only Smyth's Sleeker arms keep me from falling.

Thank God the hellhounds stop just short of the bridge. They line up along the cliff, shoulder to shoulder, so close to the edge that the claws on their massive paws curl over the edge and dig into the side of the rock. But at least they stay there.

Smyth must be used to crossing this bridge, because he barely seems to notice the way the bridge vibrates and sways with every step. The wooden planks creak and moan. Wind whips up from the gully between the two islands, like nature itself is trying to keep me away.

Only Smyth's boa-constrictor arms keep me moving forward. I have to keep moving, but I can't look down. His arms are so big around my chest, I can't see my feet. I stumble. A gap between boards catches my left Converse and for one panicky second, I'm stuck.

Then Smyth gives me a yank and my foot wrenches out of the shoe.

And Smyth keeps moving.

Maybe I should be thankful. If Smyth hadn't dragged me along behind him, I never would have made it across.

But those planks of wood are old. And without my shoe, splinters stab my sole.

And this asshole just keeps walking.

Because I'm nothing to him. Dark Worlder trash. Something to be thrown out.

I let my body go limp. He barely notices, his arms hefting my weight so he's carrying, rather than dragging me behind him.

No matter what he thinks, I am more than just another Dark Worlder.

I have value, even here. Especially here.

I am Sleeker born. I have powers, even if they don't match his.

Yeah, okay. I can't use my powers to fight him. I'm not stupid.

I'm untrained. Even if I have the ability to grow creepy Sleeker arms like his, I don't know how to use them. How to fight with them the way he obviously does.

All I know about being a Sleeker is what I've read in books. Books that I'm now thinking are *not* accurate enough!

Okay, I also know what the Curator has said. That I was made to want things beyond my reach.

Well, right now I want my damn shoe.

If I'm going to have any hope of protecting myself against Smyth, I need my shoe. Besides, it's *mine*.

I want it back. Even if it is beyond my reach.

I want so many things. So many things beyond my reach. So many things I can't have. I want my father back. That intrinsic sense of safety that his mental instability stole from me. I want him whole and healthy and normal. I want other things, too. Silly things. A permanent home. Thicker hair. A high school boyfriend. A prom date. A best friend.

I want all of those things.

Some of them are truly forever beyond my reach.

But that damn shoe is not.

And just like that, I feel my will reaching out for it.

Because I am Sleeker born and Sleeker bred. Just like the Curator said.

My Sleeker arms don't feel anything like I thought they would.

I thought…I don't know. That my body would stretch and pull and grow. But that's not how it works. They aren't my cells somehow stretched and reformed. They are pulled from the air around me. A physical manifestation of my will. They don't grow out of me. They materialize.

And there's only one of them. Maybe because I'm reaching for only one shoe?

I only know that I want the arm to be there and suddenly it is. Long and undulating, slender and elegant. Instead of Smyth's spade-like paddle, my "hand" has willowy fingers.

Fingers that snatch the shoe from the spot where it's wedged.

Triumph surges through me as my Sleeker arm snakes back around and carefully slides the shoe onto my foot before dissipating into nothingness. With any luck, Smyth never even saw me do it.

As we near Crescent Island, the bridge does that wonky center of gravity thing again, so that he has to climb the remaining planks like a ladder. One of his Sleeker arms unwinds from my torso to snake up to the rope and leverage us up.

The moment we touch land, the sun above us shifts to a spot just west of overhead. Time flows normally on Crescent Island. Magic can be done here.

I want to drop to my knees and kiss the lush green grass—clearly Smyth pays more for landscaping here on Crescent Island than he does on Gull Veston Island. Even the air feels richer. Laden with more oxygen as well as more power. But Smyth doesn't give me the chance to relish the feeling of solid ground beneath my feet. He drags me across the lawn toward the Victorian mansion nestled against the outer curve of the island.

Like something out of a gothic novel, it's planted right on

the edge of the cliff, so close, it looks like it could tumble off at any moment. The house is a three-story monstrosity hewn of gray stones and draped in creeping ivy.

I am not going to lie. I am more than a little relieved he doesn't take me inside. Instead, he stops on the lawn. His long Sleeker arms turn me to face him and the paddle hand that has been covering my mouth snakes away, trailing across my cheek in a gesture that is almost loving.

I ask the question that has been bugging me since he grabbed me on Gull Veston Island. "How were you able to take me with your Sleeker arms while you were still in the Everdawn? Magic can't be done there."

Smyth shakes his head, making a disappointed clucking sound. "A Sleeker's arms are not part of his magic. Yes, Sleekers have magic. We use magic to open the threshold between worlds. But our arms are part of us, part of who we are. They don't materialize out of the air, no matter what you may have thought when you used your arm to grab your sneaker."

"Oh." So he noticed that, did he? "Okay then."

That sucked. For a minute there, I thought I had a trick up my sleeve—powers he didn't know about.

But obviously, he knows I am of Sleeker blood. It doesn't seem to impress him.

I bump my chin and take a step forward, prepared to bluff and stare him down. "I am a Sleeker like my father before me. And I have powers you cannot possibly know."

For a second, he blinks, as though surprised. Then he tips his head back and laughs. This dour, humorless man laughs.

Actually, it's more of a cackle.

"Oh that is… What is that word you Dark Worlders use? Oh, right. Cute. That is cute. You think your father was a Sleeker."

Suddenly my mind is racing. "But my father—"

"Your father was a weak and mewling Dark Worlder. With

no power whatsoever."

"But... But..."

If my father wasn't a Sleeker, then...

"No. My father was a Sleeker. He was tall and thin. He wore suits like yours. Gray. Meticulous. He was a Sleeker."

A smile teases at Smyth's lips, as though this idea pleases him. "Perhaps your mother has a type."

"No!" My panic is choking me, rising so fast, I don't process his words. "I am Sleeker born and Sleeker bred. The Curator told me so. I am Untethered."

"In this world, genetic power is passed from mother to child."

No. He's wrong. That doesn't make sense.

The image of my father flashes through my mind. His lean frame. His elegant features.

"My father was a Sleeker," I say again, more weakly this time.

"From mother to child," Smyth says again, more slowly.

"No. My mother was human."

My mother couldn't possibly be a Sleeker. She couldn't possibly be, because...because she's my mother. She tells me everything.

"She was born in Indiana." My words rush out in a flood of proof. Concrete proof. She couldn't possibly be what he is saying she is. "Her parents were Bill and Julie Staller. She was an only child. She grew up on a corn farm. She was a cheerleader. She had a beagle."

"Oh, did she?"

But I don't need Smyth's sarcastic question to raise my doubts.

Because suddenly, all of this proof doesn't feel like proof at all. All of these things she told me about her childhood seem so completely, perfectly all-American. The corn. The beagle. It's too perfect.

Panic clutches my heart as my breath comes in rapid bursts.

Suddenly, my mind is racing through my own childhood. Looking for clues. There had been pictures of my grandparents. Two of them, one framed and on the mantel next to the photo of my parents' wedding. The other on my mother's dresser.

But why weren't there pictures from her childhood?

"No." My protest is barely above a whisper. I can't believe it. My mother would never have lied to me. Not about anything, let alone something like this. "No. It's not possible."

"But of course it is, you ridiculous child. Why else would I even bother with you?"

"You're a fanatic," I say numbly, repeating what I know of him from the books. "You hate all Dark Worlders. You believe we are a blight on the Kingdoms of Mithres."

"Well," he says, his tone amiable. "That is certainly true. You are a blight. But think about it."

He steps closer to me and his thin, Sleeker arm slithers up, cupping my cheek with his flatworm paddle.

"Think. About. It," he repeats, the tip of his not-a-hand tapping against my cheek with each word. "Think of the planning that it took to get you here. This has been years in the making. I manipulated the Curator into going to look for you. Convinced her that you had to be found. That the lost *Oidrhe* could save the kingdoms—all without her realizing I was behind it. All so that she would find you and bring you here. To me."

"All along, you needed me here? Am I...am I the lost *Oidrhe*?"

"The lost *Oidrhe*? The lost ruler who will once again unite the Kingdoms of Mithres?" Smyth laughs again. That same blood-chilling cackle. "Don't be ridiculous!"

"Oh." I didn't really believe it, of course. There is nothing about me that screams long-lost ruler. "But then...why? Do you need me to find the lost *Oidrhe*?"

"No, you are useless to me." Then he takes one ominous step closer to me. "Or rather, mostly useless."

The slender arms encompassing me tighten ever so slightly, pulling me closer to him, until he reaches out with his human hands and grabs a lock of my hair.

"Wait. What?"

Before I even know what he is doing, there is a flash as one of his Sleeker arms morphs into a long razor-thin blade and slices downward, cutting off my hair.

"I don't need you at all. All I need is a lock of your hair." He waggles the chunk of hair before me. "With this, I will be able to track down your mother."

"My mother?" I ask, but Smyth has already turned and is walking away from me, his long arm beginning to unwind from around me as he leaves.

The same mother that he claimed was a Sleeker?

Why does he want her? Is she in danger?

If my mother is a Sleeker...

It's a betrayal so deep, I can't even think about it now. But Smyth, who has raised more questions and given me almost no answers, is already walking away from me. He got what he needed from me.

But I am not done with him.

Even though he's wrong about my mother—I'm sure he's wrong—he can still use my hair to track her, to hurt her.

I walk after him. His arms are loose enough around me that I am able to peel them off, stepping out of them as they pool around my feet.

"What do you want with her?" I call out. He doesn't even glance at me. "I have to know."

His stride slows ever so slightly, so I know he heard me.

He is just deciding whether or not I am worth the time it takes to answer.

I pick up my pace, closing the distance between us. "If I am Sleeker bred, and I was made to want things forever beyond my reach, what I want now is answers."

He stops but still doesn't face me.

"I may not understand how to use my powers. I may barely have begun to tap into them. But right now, you have two options. You can answer my questions for me. Or you can leave me wanting more. If I know one thing about this world, it's that a Sleeker who wants things is a dangerous enemy."

Finally, he turns to face me. For the first time, there is something like respect in his expression. Unfortunately, there is also amusement. "You have your mother's spirit, but you do not know who you are messing with. Compared to me, you are barely a dust mote on the breeze. You are as small and insignificant. As powerless. And about as much of a threat." He takes a slow menacing step toward me. "But if you want answers, I will give them to you, because it amuses me to do so. And because, apparently, your mother cares for you. And the thought of bringing pain to something she loves pleases me."

He takes another step closer, and now we are facing each other. He looks down at me, his face refined, so handsome he might be a plastic surgeon's finest work. Somehow, I know he is studying me, taking in all the minor physical imperfections of my very human body. No doubt, wondering how my Sleeker mother could possibly love such an insignificant weakling.

"I want your mother, quite simply, because she was mine first."

His?

He must have the wrong person. Despite that, his words send a chill through me.

I swallow. "You were mated?"

"No. Nothing so human. We were partners. Sleekers work in pairs. She and I were curated to be the perfect pair. Bred for it. Raised from birth. For decades, we guarded the thresholds between our worlds. We were the best, the most efficient pair of Sleekers this world has ever known."

"And then she met my father." Somehow, I know this is what changed things. My mother always said he was unlike anyone she'd ever known.

"And then she met your father. She left this world to hide in yours." His gaze softens, as if remembering the events from the past. "Even when I found her, she wouldn't return. Even though I need her to help me sever the threads between our worlds. But she'll return now." He nods as he studies me. "Yes, she will return now."

With a sudden, sinking dread, I understand. He's not just going to use my hair to find my mom. He's going to use me as bait to lure her back here. That's why he didn't simply take a lock of my hair and let me leave with Kane. He needs me to still be here when he brings her back. That's how he'll control her. How he'll trap her here.

Kane himself said it. Gull Veston Island was not made to trap Dark Worlders. It was built to contain Tuatha.

He built a prison, just for her.

Rattled, I'm desperate to keep him talking.

"Why cut all the threads between worlds?"

"Not all the threads. All but one. So only I will have power."

For the first time, I see true emotions in his expression. I see the fevered light of fanaticism. I see passion and faith, twisted by molten rage.

Which, for the record, it is a lot scarier than you might think. Especially when it's gleaming in the eyes of the most powerful being you've ever faced. Especially when that being just compared you to a dust mote. I'm not gonna lie, if I'd had enough water to drink in the past twenty-four hours, I probably would've peed my pants.

Thankfully, I'm saved from that humiliation by two things. The first—I am dangerously dehydrated right now. The second— Smyth once again turns and walks away. He may have enjoyed his monologuing, but he's already moving on.

His Sleeker arms retreat into his back as he leaves. This time, I don't follow him. The time for Q&A is over, and I'm okay with that. As he walks, he swirls his hands in the air before him. A threshold opens and he steps through it without breaking his stride.

When Kane opens a loop, there is tension in his arms and muscles. He's physically pulling space apart. Smyth's motions are gentler, more elegant. He is willing the doorway into being. Smyth's threshold is an arch of light and space big enough to drive a Mack truck through. And for a moment, I can see my world on the other side, hanging there in the space above the green lawn of Crescent Island. I catch a glimpse of a city street, passing traffic, and red brick buildings.

I run toward it. If I can get there, if I can follow him through. I can stop him. I can find my mother before he does.

But it snaps closed before I reach it.

Just like that, I am all alone on Crescent Island.

Excerpt from
Book Five of The Traveler Chronicles:
The Traveler Undone

I have one rule of thumb. Never trust anyone who appears to be defenseless.

CHAPTER THIRTY-SEVEN

I don't have a lot of panic attacks, but the second the threshold closes behind Smyth, my anxiety ratchets up by about 200 percent.

I am trapped here. I could do magic, if I actually knew how to control my powers. Of course, so far, my powers consist entirely of ward removal and shoe retrieval. I have no idea how either of these skills is going to help me here.

And frankly, right now, there are a lot of things I need to do.

I need to get off this island.

I need to find a way to open a threshold of my own so I can return to the Dark World.

I need to find my mother before Smyth does.

And then I need…

I need answers.

How could my mother be a Sleeker? After all these years of it being just the two of us against the world, how could she have lied to me?

I could believe my father was of Sleeker blood. That explained everything. His trouble connecting to the "real world." His emotional fragility. His ultimate breakdown. That made sense.

But if my mom was a Sleeker… If she defected to the Dark World, knowing what she was… If Smyth came after her…

Then, my dad's breakdown wasn't a breakdown at all. Smyth had found us and attacked my dad and me. Dad hadn't shot me at all. Smyth had...*punctured* me.

Then, somehow, a member of the Curati had altered our memories.

But my mother must have known the truth. If she had been Smyth's partner, she would have known what he was capable of. She would have known the difference between a bullet wound and a Sleeker wound. Even if no doctor in the Dark World knew, she'd know.

She'd let me think my father was crazy... She let him think he was crazy. All this time. He's been in and out of mental hospitals for the past six years.

She knew the truth. She let this happen.

Oh God.

This is all too much to take in. I need to sit down.

Slowly, I walk back to the steps of Smyth's mansion and lower myself onto the lowest one.

Except, instead of easing onto the bottom step, I bump into another Jell-O barrier, practically bounce off it, and slide down onto my ass.

"Great. That is just fan-fucking-tastic."

This world has knocked me on my ass. Again. Literally and metaphorically.

I don't know how to process this new information about my mom.

The person I trusted most in the world is a monster. An actual monster.

But she's also my mother. I don't want Smyth to kill her.

Is there anything I can do to stop it?

I shift to look up at the mansion. He has wards around it. Of course, he does.

Damn paranoid asshole.

Not that I wanted to go into his house. It just would've been nice to sit on the porch while I plotted how to get out of here.

So instead, I stretch my legs out in front of me and lean against the Jell-O.

Okay, what are my options?

The only non-magical way off this island is over the bridge of death. Which, incidentally, leads right into the mouths of those hellhounds.

I glance in that direction, just to verify they are still there. They are. Big gaping mouths, butcher-knife-sized teeth, buckets of drool. I think one of them just licked his lips.

Obviously, I'm not crossing that bridge. No way.

That leaves me with two options. Either I wait here for Smyth to get back and beg for mercy. Or I open a threshold of my own.

Okay. How hard can it be? I watched Smyth do it. From behind. I couldn't see his hands, but I remember what his elbows did.

I push myself to my feet and dust off my hands. Just in case it makes any difference at all, I walk to where he opened the threshold. After all, there are places where the veil between worlds is thinner. That's the whole point of those doors at Book People.

I stand right where he had planted his feet and I close my eyes.

Back when dawn first broke on the island, I felt magic in the air. I felt it dance along my skin just before the timekeeper set time back to Everdawn. If I'm going to open my own threshold, I need to find that thread.

After a minute of standing there, I feel the faintest bit of magic dance along my skin.

I raise my arms in front of me and mimic the motion I saw Smyth use. The action is different than what Kane does to pull a loop. Smyth isn't wrenching anything open. He's brushing away a veil.

I move first one hand and then the other in front of my face in a circular motion. Nothing.

I do it again with my fingers held in a different position. I try a peace sign. The finger wiggling Benedict Cumberbatch did as Dr. Strange. I even try it with Spock's "live long and prosper" sign. Nothing.

Which is what I expected. I'm not trained to do this. All I know is that I can't stay here on this island when my friends are in danger. While my mother is in danger. While a sociopathic wannabe dictator uses my genetic material to hunt down someone I love.

And just like that, I feel the magic snag on my fingers.

A subtle resistance to the air, as if I'm touching an actual veil.

Of course.

My power stems from my will. My intention. The things I desire that are beyond my reach.

The more I yearn for them, the more tangible the threshold becomes.

I repeat the swirling motion until the veil feels as heavy and weighty as a velvet curtain.

With my right hand, I draw the veil aside. Only then do I open my eyes.

I immediately stumbled backward.

Yeah, I've opened the threshold. To this exact place in my world.

On this side of the veil, there is the solid ground of Crescent Island. Twelve inches in front of me, there is nothing but blue sky and what I can only assume is a mile-long drop to Pelican Island in my world.

I swipe my other hand in front of the air, pulling the

threshold closed.

And I stumble back several more steps before dropping to my knees, shaking.

What is it with this world and terrifying heights?

Every time I turn around, I nearly plummet to my death.

"That's not a bad threshold," says a voice from behind me. "For your first try, anyway."

I whirl around to see Kane standing behind me. I scramble to my feet. "You came back!"

I have to fight the urge to throw myself into his arms. *You came back* feels like the kind of thing you should say while throwing your arms around someone. So I'm pretty proud of the restraint I show in not doing that.

"You came back," I say again, trying to sound slightly more chill.

"Of course." Kane's mouth twists in a bemused smile.

I realize coming back for me was his plan all along. I underestimated him. I believed him to be the arrogant, selfish Kane that he had been pretending to be ever since I arrived in the Kingdoms of Mithres, instead of the person I know him to be from years of reading about him.

He fooled me. Or, maybe I let myself be fooled. Because this Kane, this kind and decent and selfless guy, will be much harder to walk away from.

"Let's get you out of here," he says.

Nodding, I cross to his side as he pulls a loop. A minute later, we are standing together on the deck of *The Blossom*. As Smyth promised, Crab is there, once again in his human form. He crosses to me and claps a hand on my shoulder. "Glad to have you back on board, missy."

"Are you okay?" I ask. "The hellhounds didn't hurt you?"

"Don't you worry about me. I have ways to protect myself from hellhounds."

I smile, barely able to believe that we all made it off the island alive. This motley crew of comrades fills my heart with an overwhelming sensation of peace and affection.

But the moment is short-lived. I know what they don't. We don't have time to relax, because we still need to stop Smyth.

"I figured out why Smyth built a prison capable of holding a Tuatha. He's going to try to cut the thread between worlds."

The princess sucks in a breath. "That's not possible."

"He believes he can do it if he—" I cut myself short. I'm not ready to tell anyone about my mom. Not yet. "Trust me. He thinks it will let him rule the Kingdoms of Mithres. Is he right?"

The others exchange worried looks, but it's the princess who answers. "We all rely on the thread to fuel our magic. Without it, no one could do any magic. Not even Smyth."

Without the thread of magic, Smyth may not be able to do magic, but... "There's no magic on the island, but he can still use his Sleeker powers."

"Exactly." Kane bites out the word.

"So only the Sleekers would have power. They would control everything. We have to stop him. We have to get back to Austin so we can follow him into the Dark World."

So I can stop him from finding my mother.

Even as I say the words, it hits me that the boat isn't moving. We should have set sail for Houston as soon as Kane and I got back.

"Why aren't we going?" I ask Kane, even though it is a question I could just as easily ask Crab. Somehow, I know in my gut that it is Kane who has the answer. "We should be heading back to Houston. Why aren't we?"

"You will. I just wanted—" He runs a hand through his hair, not quite meeting my gaze. "You're going to be fine. Morgan's with you. Kendal, too. You already have Crab wrapped around your finger."

"What are you talking about?"

"When you get back to Austin, Morgan can get you back to The Volume Arcana."

"Why would Morgan need to find me a threshold? Why won't you be there?" Kane isn't meeting my gaze, so I look around at the other people standing awkwardly on the deck of *The Blossom*. "What's going on?" Suddenly, everyone seems to have something else to do. "Somebody answer me."

"I'm going back to the island."

"What?"

"I'm going—"

"I heard you." I cut him off. "Why would you go back there?"

"I have unfinished business."

"Unfinished…" I can't even finish the sentence. Literally everyone else has scattered. "Something more important than stopping Smyth? And we're supposed to just leave you trapped here?"

"I'll follow when…" He hesitates, swallows, and then seems to find the end of his sentence. "When my business is finished. I should be able to pull a loop back to Austin."

"*Should? Should* be able? In other words, you have no idea if you can pull a loop back to Austin from within the Crimson Miasma at all."

"Kendal is going with you. If I can't pull a loop, she'll know. She can tell Crab to come back for me."

"This is the stupidest plan I've ever heard." He just stares blankly at me, so I elaborate. "Crab can't come back for you because he can't make it through the Crimson Miasma on his own. So if you can't pull a loop back to Austin, you'll be trapped here."

"I'll figure something out."

"You'll *figure something out*? Do you even realize how ridiculous that sounds?" Apparently, he does, because instead of responding, he ignores me. He takes a step back and cups his hand in front of him to pull a loop. I don't let him. Instead, I close the distance between us. I get right in his face.

He looks down, fuming. "Get out of my way."

"Yeah. That's not gonna happen." I give his chest a poke. "You didn't leave me here. So I'm not leaving you here. I didn't come all this way, didn't devise a plan to rescue the princess from Gull Veston Island, and didn't learn how to use my powers, all so that you could die on that stupid island."

"Trust me, I don't have any intention of dying."

Before I can argue, Morgan says, "He's going back to rescue his sister."

Morgan's words are so soft, it takes a moment for them to register.

He is standing a few feet away, one foot on a bench as he stares off the port side into the distance.

I whip back around. Kane doesn't meet my gaze but scratches at the back of his head, looking guilty.

"What?"

"He is going back to rescue his sister." This time, Morgan speaks more clearly.

"What?" I repeat again dumbly. "He doesn't have a sister." I turn to Kane again. "You don't have a sister. Right?"

"I…" He doesn't finish the sentence.

I look from him to Morgan and back again. Ro nibbles on her lip, her smile knowingly sympathetic. Crab looks bemused. The princess just looks bored. Only Kendal looks unsurprised, maybe even resigned.

I take a few steps back until I feel a bench hit the back of my knees. I sink down onto it, dropping my head into my hands.

How could he possibly have a sister that I didn't know about? A *sister*?

It doesn't seem possible, and yet…

Is this the mysterious girl from the Dark World that Kane was trying to hide from Kendal? It must be. But to form the loop, he had to let Kendal fully into his mind. And so she knows.

If he *does* have a sister, if she is on this island, then it explains a lot—why he was so desperate to come here, but then so disinterested in rescuing the princess.

The strange conversation between Kane and Smyth.

Whatever that device is that he keeps taking out of his pocket and looking at, it's clearly something he's using to search for his sister.

Still, I can't believe it.

I blow out a breath. "You have a sister I don't know about?"

He wraps a hand around my arm and pulls me to standing. We're facing away from the others, so that our words drift out to sea rather than back to their ears.

"Look, until five minutes ago, there were only five other people in the world who knew I had a sister. Morgan, Ro, Smyth, Kendal and the Curator. That's it."

"But the books—"

"The books didn't get everything right. Travers. Not the Traveler. And I'm not gonna fall in love with the princess."

"You *do* fall in love with the princess."

"In case you haven't noticed, the princess and I don't get along."

"Sure, but—"

I cut myself off. Why am I arguing for this? It's going to happen. He'll see.

"But a sister? Why didn't you say anything?"

"Her survival depends on her existence being a secret. So yeah, when someone showed up out of nowhere and brought hellhounds and Kellas cats down on us, and all kinds of trouble, no, I didn't open with 'By the way, I have a secret sister no one knows about.' It's not the kind of thing I tell strangers."

"But—" I cut myself off again. Damn his logic for being so...logical. "Okay, whatever. You didn't want to tell me. I get that. But how do you have a secret sister at all? You are an only child."

"Obviously, I'm not. I gather from what you've said that you think I'm a changeling. A Dark Worlder, like you. I'm not. My father was a Dark Worlder. My mother was the High Queen."

"Your father—"

But he doesn't give me a chance to voice my surprise. He keeps on talking.

"You want to know why I haven't taken power? That's it. I'm a halfling. A halfling has never sat on the throne of the Kingdoms of Mithres. But my birth status wasn't that big a deal. At the time, it wasn't shocking for the queen to take a lover, even one from the Dark World. After I was born, my Dark Worlder father rejected her. He ended it. She never quite recovered. When I was nine, the High Queen got pregnant again. This time by the king. It was a girl—the child who should have succeeded them as queen. But she was sickly. It just so happened that my Dark World father had a newborn daughter as well. Lucy. My mother changed the sickly Tuatha baby for Lucy. She's the changeling."

"When you were nine," I say numbly.

In the books, he was nine when his mother left the king and went on the run. When they began living in hiding.

Only a few years later, they are found by hellhounds, who bring them all to Smyth. The queen is killed trying to protect Kane from Smyth.

This new information he has given me dovetails seamlessly with the story that I do know. If Kane is a halfling, hellhounds would not hunt him. Not if he had lived in the Kingdoms of Mithres his whole life. But if Lucy is a true child of the Dark World, then the hellhounds would always hunt her.

"But the king acknowledged you. He bestowed power on you."

"The queen bestowed power on me. It was a formality. To tie me to the throne, in case she had no other children. She was young and healthy. No one expected her to die without an heir. No one thought a halfling would actually take the throne."

I fold that information into what I know about the politics of the kingdoms and set it aside.

"And, ever since your mother's death, you've been protecting Lucy. Keeping her safe."

"Trying to. But then Smyth found out about her. He kidnapped her to try to get me to betray the princess. If the princess died before the wedding—"

"Then the Council of Sleekers could take control."

"Exactly."

I have so many more questions. How has he kept Lucy safe all this time? How did Smyth find out about her? How does Kane plan to protect her, now that Smyth knows?

I shove all my questions aside. They're inconsequential right now.

Now, we have to get Lucy back.

Still, I hesitate. Somewhere, in the Dark World, Smyth is hunting my mother. And if he finds her, then Smyth will be able to cut the thread of magic between worlds. He'll control everything.

Yeah, we could leave Kane here. It is the fastest way for me to return to my world.

Crab will take me because it is what he was paid to do. The princess will return to Houston as well. Based on Morgan's expression, I'm guessing Kane asked him to make sure I get home. He doesn't look happy about it, but he will obey his friend's wishes.

That leaves Ro and Kendal. I can't guess what Ro will do, but my gut says she'll stay with her brother. That leaves Kendal.

Kendal cannot repay her death-debt until she saves Kane's life. So she'll go with him.

One man and a Kellas cat versus all of those hellhounds. The odds aren't good.

If they go back to Gull Veston Island alone, they're definitely going to die.

And I can't let that happen.

Deleted from the Advance Reading Copy of
Book Five of The Traveler Chronicles:
The Traveler Undone

*There she was, all alone, trapped on that damn island with a
psychotic monster, and she held it together.*

*This tiny little Dark Worlder went up against one of the most
evil bastards in the Seven Kingdoms and she didn't back down.*

Damn. I think I'm in love.

CHAPTER THIRTY-EIGHT

I have a choice. I can save Kane or I can save my mother.

Kane's danger is immediate. If I don't do something, he will die. Everything I've done to protect him will be meaningless.

My mom, on the other hand, well, she's managed to stay ahead of Smyth for years. Decades. She knows he's a threat, and the fact that I've disappeared has likely made her suspect he's up to something. So I'm guessing she can manage a little longer.

Yeah. I know what you're thinking. That I'm just pissed because she lied to me my whole life. Lied about who she was. Who I am. About what happened to my dad.

My dad, who's been in a frickin' insane asylum for nearly six years because of her. When he's not really crazy at all.

This is like the worst version of gaslighting in history.

So yeah, I'm pissed at my mom. But I'm not choosing Kane *over* her. She can take care of herself. At least for a few more hours.

"Okay then." But my voice sounds wobbly with doubt. I clear my throat and try again. "Obviously, we're coming with you."

"What?" Kane asks.

I'm not gonna lie. It's nice to have someone else playing the part of the confused bystander.

"Obviously," I say more slowly. "We are not going to let you go back by yourself. That place is a death trap. Besides, you're going to rescue a defenseless ten-year-old girl. Anyone who would let you do that by yourself is a monster."

I don't look at the others as I say this.

In my heart, I know they were ready to let Kane go on his own. But I'm hoping—okay, *really* hoping—that now that I've laid it out like this, they'll be on board.

My instincts pay off. Almost as soon as the words are out of my mouth, both Ro and the princess step forward. Neither of them wants to look that bad. Maybe there's some good in public shaming, after all.

Kane gives me a wry look as if to say, *I see what you did there.*

I give him a smile back and quirk an eyebrow. *You're welcome.*

Ro speaks first. "Obviously. We're not letting you go alone. If Cupcake thinks she can help, then I'm sure I can help as well."

The princess gives a disdainful snort. "Well, then I am sure my meager talents will come in handy."

I cannot imagine her talents are meager. She's the heir to the Red Court. Her family would have spent a fortune making sure she had useful skills. But kudos to her for at least trying to be modest.

Only Kendal doesn't say anything, which confirms my theory that she intended to go all along.

Kane looks at each of us. "I'm not going to ask any of you to sacrifice yourselves for me or my sister."

"You're not asking," I argue. "And you can't stop us."

"That's where you're wrong, Cupcake. I control the loop. I control who goes through it."

I cross my arms over my chest. "Fine. If you refuse to take us, we'll just walk up the stairs. We'll arrive weakened and vulnerable. Your choice."

Kane says nothing, but glares at me.

I take this to mean that my argument won him over.

I turn to the others. "Okay, here's the plan. Kane will open a loop to Crescent Island. We all go through." I pause for a fraction of a second to see if he's still going to argue with me. He doesn't. "On Crescent Island, we search for the timekeeper. Once that person is out of the equation, you'll be able to do magic on the island, which should help with our hellhound problem. Then we find Lucy." I look at Kane. "I assume you have some way of finding her?"

"I do."

"Once we have Lucy, Kane opens a loop back to the boat and we're on our way. And then we deal with Smyth." And I would have to deal with my mother. "Any questions?"

Ro looks around nervously. "If we need to take out the timekeeper, why didn't we do that the first time around?"

"Before we went to the island, we had no idea where the timekeeper might be," I say. "Now that we've been there, it's obvious. He or she is in Smyth's house on Crescent Island. It's the only building there. Any other questions?"

No one has any questions. Doubts, however, appear to be plentiful if the expressions on everyone's faces are an indication.

Yeah, their confidence in me is awesome.

But what other choice do I have? Even if I could let Kane and Kendal face certain death, I'm not going to leave a ten-year-old girl at Smyth's mercy.

Deleted from the Advance Reading Copy of
Book Five of The Traveler Chronicles:
The Traveler Undone

She may be tiny, but damn, that girl can fight.
I've got to admit, I like that in a woman.

CHAPTER THIRTY-NINE

Just for a moment, when we first land on Crescent Island, everything seems peaceful.

That should have been my first sign that shit was about to go very bad.

Because suddenly, the howls of hellhounds rend the air.

I whirl around. There's a row of them lined up along the cliff of Gull Veston Island.

"Well, this should be fun." Ro pulls a hair band from her pocket and starts scraping her hair back into a ponytail.

The hellhound closest to the bridge creeps forward. He puts his front paw on the first board, testing it. The wood creaks under his weight. He loses his balance, tipping over the rope railing of the bridge and tumbling over the side. His anguished howl as he falls seems to echo up through the canyon.

"At least they can't cross the bridge," I say cheerfully.

But as soon as I say it, one hellhound starts eyeing the gap between the two islands. Sure enough, he backs up several steps and then runs forward. His powerful back legs spring off the edge of Gull Veston Island as he launches himself to Crescent Island. He lands with an earthquake-inducing thud, his front paws on firm ground, his back paws clawing to gain hold. His back legs flail, digging into the rock. Anger and desperation war within his bloodshot eyes as he struggles to climb to solid land.

Kane raises his blackthorn rod and shoots a burst of red-hot energy toward the hellhound. Before he can use it again, the princess steps forward. She holds both her hands palm out toward the hound. Even from a few feet away, I feel magical energy pouring through the air from her. The force knocks the hound back, his claws gouging deep trenches in the earth before he finally tumbles over the side, pulling a chunk of limestone with him.

The princess dusts off her hands, as if this is the kind of thing she does every day. For all I know, it is.

She says, "I'll keep the hellhounds at bay. You go find the timekeeper."

"I'll stay here," Ro says, crouching down and placing a hand on the ground. "I don't like the way the ground shook when that hellhound landed. I'll do what I can to stabilize the island from within. But you should hurry."

"And I," Kendal adds, "will stay here as the communication link."

She nods slightly in Kane's direction as she says this.

Kane nods back, then he and I head for Smyth's mansion.

The mansion is only a hundred feet away, but still we run, urged on by the increasingly frantic yelps and howls of the hellhounds. There is another earth-shaking thud as we reach the steps of the mansion. I glance back to see the princess sending another hellhound to its death.

"She's good," I say as I pause at the steps, expecting to hit the jello barrier.

But instead, Kane waves his hand and the barrier that should be there…just isn't. Which is pretty powerful magic for a guy who supposedly needs a wand to do spell work. Before I can mull on that tidbit, Kane responds to my comment about the princess.

"Yeah, she is good," Kane says, a note of surprise in his voice. "I didn't expect that."

That note of admiration in his voice? No, I don't notice it.

Okay, barely notice it.

Of course, she's good in a fight. I knew she would be. And of course, that impresses Kane. I knew it would.

This is good news. After all, admiration could be the first step to love.

"Do you want to stay together?"

Kane's words snap me out of my thoughts. "Wait. What?" Do I want to stay together? "No. I mean, I have to go back."

Kane smiles, looking a bit bemused. "I meant, do you want to search together or split up and cover more territory?"

"Oh." I can *feel* myself blushing. "Yes. We should split up. We'll get more done. Definitely."

Oh God. Now I am blushing and babbling. It's a good look, I'm sure.

"On second thought, I think we should stick together. You seem distracted."

The front doors of Smyth's mansion lead directly into a long, wide hall with a massive staircase at the end. Kane takes off down the hall, assuming I'm going to follow him. I do, obviously. There are doors leading off on either side. Kane heads into the first room on the right.

It's a Victorian sitting room, complete with fireplace, camelback sofas, and knickknack-laden tables everywhere. No timekeeper here.

The room to the left of the front door is a library with dark wooden bookshelves and old, leather-bound books. For someone who claims to despise the Dark World, Smyth certainly has a taste for Victorian decorating.

The other two rooms on the first floor are similarly

uninteresting. Everything looks as though the cast of *Downton Abbey* just left.

As we creep toward the staircase, I ask Kane, "Do you think this is magicked? Maybe the timekeeper is here and we just can't see him?"

Kane pauses halfway up the stairs and glances back at me. "No. Sleekers aren't good at illusion."

Huh. What exactly did that mean? Was that some kind of jab at my inability to hide my emotions?

Of course, if it was, I probably deserve it.

And if I get killed on this island because I'm distracted, worrying about whether Kane *likes* me likes me, then I deserve that, too.

The stairs continue up to a third floor, but we stop on the second. Kane is nearly to the first door on the right, when I hear a faint *thump-thump* from a room at the front of the house. I stop Kane with my hand, then nod in the direction.

And there it is again. *Thump-thump.*

He frowns and gives his head a little shake.

Yeah, it's faint, but how can he not hear it?

Thump-thump.

I jerk my head in that direction a second time, shoot him a "follow me" glance, and then head toward the thumping sounds.

The room is at the front of the house, facing Gull Veston Island. I guess we're feeling cautious, because we both pause in the doorway. A pair of large windows flank a door that leads out onto a balcony. It's a bedroom, maybe once a child's bedroom, based on the murals of delicate fairies and toadstools painted on the walls. Whatever it once was, it is now empty of furniture, except for a single chair—a big, comfy padded armchair, covered in butter yellow fabric. And sitting cross-legged on it is a boy.

He can't be more than nine. Maybe even seven or eight.

He doesn't glance up when we enter. Not even a flicker of awareness mars the concentration in his expression. He is focused entirely on the two balls that he is juggling in his hands.

The balls are smooth and glassy, with swirls of gray and misty blue, like marbles the size of tennis balls. They are almost too large for his small hands. He throws one straight up into the air. It hovers for an instant at the apex before falling to land in his open hand. Then he throws the other straight up into the air and catches that one. It's not really juggling. Until his face contorts into a frown of extra concentration and he throws both balls at the same moment and catches them with the opposite hand.

This time, the instant he catches the balls, the sky outside his window darkens. He has just reset dawn.

"Whoa," I murmur. "I did not expect Morgan's metaphor to be so…unmetaphoric. He really is juggling time."

Kane shuffles forward a step so that his shoulder almost touches my back. He leans closer to me to murmur, "Juggling?"

His breath brushes my ear and I have to suppress a shiver as I glance back at him. "What else would you call it?"

"Weaving."

Weaving?

He is clearly not weaving. Unless…

"Do you think manipulating time is something so"—I search for the word—"so intangible that it looks different for every person who sees it?"

Kane's face is so close to mine, we are mere inches apart. I swallow and struggle to find my train of thought. "I see juggling because that's how he described it to me. And you see weaving because—"

"Because that's how I always imagined it."

"Is that possible?"

"Anything is possible."

Is anything possible?

I close my eyes, just for a second, wanting the thing I can never have. Then, I open my eyes and step fully into the room of the timekeeper.

Excerpt from
Book Five of The Traveler Chronicles:
The Traveler Undone

Here's the short list of things that really piss me off:
Bad tippers
Guys who let their dogs shit on other people's lawns
Anyone who picks on kids.
You wanna guess which one Smyth is guilty of?
I'll give you a hint. Unless you count the hellhounds, he doesn't own a dog. And I've sure as hell never sat down in a restaurant with him long enough for the bill to arrive.

CHAPTER FORTY

The magical energy around the timekeeper is so thick, I feel it pressing against my skin. The timekeeper's magic streams out from him toward Gull Veston Island. It is so thick directly in front of him, I stop trying to move through it and instead approach from the side.

The boy looks sickly and unkempt. His hair is too long. What should be thick curls is matted and dirty. His skin, which should be the color of amber, instead appears a jaundiced yellow.

I crouch down beside him, placing my hands on the fat arm of his chair.

"Morgan?" I say softly.

How did I not guess this before?

Timekeepers are incredibly rare. It's some of the most powerful magic around. Plus, it explains why Morgan refused to come to the island. There's a crap ton I don't understand about timekeeping. But not having two versions of yourself in the same time, at the same place, seems like a no-brainer.

"Morgan," I repeat.

Kane comes to stand behind me and puts a hand on my shoulder.

Finally, Morgan's gaze flickers in our direction. "Shh." He throws up one of the balls, frowning before catching it. "This is very hard," he whispers. "Don't distract me."

"Yes," I say. "I can see that it's hard. Why don't you take a break, just for a few minutes?"

"I can't," he says, frowning.

"Yes, you can."

His frown deepens, and I feel my heart tugging hard. He is so serious. So worried. So unlike the Morgan I know that it breaks my heart just a little.

"I can't," he insists.

"Why do you think you can't stop weaving?" Kane asks, crouching down beside me.

"Because he said I couldn't."

Kane and I exchange a glance. We don't need to ask who the "he" is in that sentence.

"Did he say why you can't stop?" I ask.

Morgan concentrates for a few more seconds, throws the ball, watches it hang in the air, and then catches it again. Following his movements, I can almost—almost—see how this could be considered weaving. Smoothing down the strands. Every once in a while, the flick of his wrists intertwining them.

"If I stop…" Morgan pauses once again to throw and catch the ball. "Bad things will happen."

"What bad things?" Kane asks.

"Bad things will happen to my sister." Morgan glances at us lightning fast, and there is anguish in his gaze. "She's only six. And she's my best friend. If I stop juggling, bad things will happen to her."

And just like that, the tug at my heart becomes an overwhelming crash. The weight on my chest is so heavy, I can hardly breathe, let alone talk, to reassure him.

"If I stop keeping time, she will die. Within twenty-four hours, she dies. That's what he said."

God damn it.

And I thought Smyth was evil before. I had no idea. He has kept this boy, this child, trapped here in this room for more than a decade, doing his dirty work, with the threat that his sister would die within a day if he stopped.

I don't know whether or not keeping time is painful. The adult Morgan didn't say. But I know it's hard. I know it's exhausting. And this child, this innocent child, has been doing it nonstop for years, all so that Smyth could have absolute control over this one tiny slice of the world.

What kind of monster does that? What kind of monster allows a child to be in pain for his own benefit?

The kind of monster that Smyth is. The kind of monster who doesn't look monstrous at all.

I don't know how to make peace with being a Sleeker. I don't know that I will ever be comfortable knowing that I was made to want things beyond my reach.

I'm not good at wanting things. Certainly not things for myself. Because of my mom's job, I've seen way more people die than most kids my age. I've seen people, better people than me, die painfully, horribly. It seems beyond selfish to want anything for myself beyond what I already have.

I don't know that I will ever be comfortable wanting things for myself.

But in this moment, the thing that I want most is Smyth's death.

Because a man that evil cannot be allowed to live, let alone stay in power.

And bringing down Smyth? It starts right here. In this moment. With freeing Morgan.

"That man lied to you," I say. "Your sister doesn't die when you stop this. I know your sister. I know Ro." I do some quick math in my head based on how old the grown Morgan is now. The number that I come up with is another blow to my heart.

"You've been doing this for thirteen years. You have protected your sister long enough. She is still alive, all these years later. She doesn't die when you stop. She goes on to live a long and full life."

And, I realize as I say it, that she must never know the sacrifice he made for her. If she knew that he had lived like this for thirteen years to protect her, it would kill her.

I swallow down the anguish threatening to overwhelm me. "You've done enough to protect her."

Morgan looks at me, his frown deepening. "She's alive?"

"Yes." I nod.

He must not believe me, because next, he looks at Kane. "And if I stop keeping time—" He pauses long enough to throw and catch a ball again. "What will happen to me?"

I have been so focused on Morgan, I hadn't so much as glanced at Kane until now.

The anguish I feel is reflected in Kane's expression, in the pain in his eyes and the tightness of his jaw. "I don't know. Not for sure. But I have a theory."

Morgan throws and catches the ball again. Cocking his head just slightly to the side he asks, "What do you think will happen to me?"

"I think that if you stop keeping time, you will go back to when this all started."

"And Ro will still be alive?"

"Yes. I know you when you are grown. You've been my friend for years. Ro has been my friend for years, too. And you never…" Kane pauses, and I am close enough to hear him swallow. "You never said anything." He nods as if resolving the matter in his own mind. "I think you have to keep holding on to this moment. I think you have to let this happen. But you can choose to go back to the life you left when Smyth took you. You can still have your childhood. With Ro and your parents."

"I don't know if I believe you," Morgan says softly. He looks down at the balls in his hand, frowning as if he is trying to decide what to do with them. The muscles in his arm tense, and I can tell that he is preparing to throw them again.

"Ro may be your sister, but when you're grown up, I'm going to be your best friend. I wouldn't lie to you." Kane reaches out and places his hand on the little boy's arm. "You can rest now."

"That sounds nice." Morgan looks up at Kane. "I am very tired."

"Yeah. I bet."

Morgan looks back down at the balls in his hands. After a long moment, he brings his two hands together. There is a moment of resistance when the two balls touch, and then they melt into each other to become one.

Morgan looks back at the two of us and says, "I'll hold on to this one."

Then, there is a pulse of magic through the air, almost like a shockwave, strong enough that it nearly knocks Kane and me back a step. When I get my feet under me again, Morgan is gone.

The chair is empty. Every surface in the room is covered with years' worth of dust. And outside the window, the sun is shining on Gull Veston Island.

Kane continues to crouch beside the chair, his hands braced on the arm, his head ducked, his shoulders hunched against the burden today has placed on him.

I have never been good at wanting things for myself, so when I reach out and place my hand on his shoulder, smoothing away some of the tension there, I tell myself that I am comforting him as well as myself.

"All that time—" Kane shakes his head. "He never said anything. Never once."

"No, I don't suppose he would've."

I think back over the events of the last few days, of the

things that have happened since I met Morgan. He must have recognized me the moment I climbed into that limo.

No wonder he wanted me and Kane to get along. No wonder he wanted us to rescue the princess. He knew everything was leading to this moment, here on Crescent Island. This was his endgame all along.

After a long moment, Kane pushes himself to his feet. The past few minutes have aged him. Maybe not the way they have aged this room, but close.

"What now?" I ask.

Before Kane can answer, reality crashes back through the room, as the ear-piercing howl of a hellhound rends the air. Followed quickly by a crash so powerful, it shakes the floorboards beneath our feet.

Excerpt from
Book Five of The Traveler Chronicles:
The Traveler Undone

At the risk of sounding like a smart-ass...
   Oh, who am I kidding? Everyone knows I'm a smart-ass.

CHAPTER FORTY-ONE

K ane and I share a look. "Hellhounds," we say at the same
time.

We both run for the door as the entire house rattles.

I skid to a halt almost as soon as my feet touch grass.
While we were inside, three hellhounds made it on to Crescent
Island.

The princess is battling one close to the bridge, blasting it
repeatedly, as it slides back toward the bridge of death.

Beside her, Ro is crouched on the ground, both hands flat
on the grass. A few feet away, a hellhound is perched on the
cliff, desperately trying to get a footing. Ro's eyes are closed
as she ignores the hellhound just a few feet away. His massive
paws dig into the earth. He snaps at the air threateningly.

As we watch, Ro's whole body tenses, and then the chunk of
earth the hellhound is clinging to breaks away, and he tumbles
to his death with an earsplitting howl.

Kendal is fighting a third hound.

The fight is a blur of fur and blood and claws and yelps of
pain, so violent, it's hard to see, let alone follow. It is the stuff
of nightmares. The kinds of noise that are like jagged nails on
the chalkboard of your soul.

There is a spray of blood, a crunch of bone, the snapping
of jaws, and then Kendal seems to break free from the fight,

landing several feet away—fur damp, back arched, tail straight in the air.

The princess dashes to Kendal's side, hands raised, ready to blast the beast, though Kendal's paralyzing venom already seems to be working on the hound. The beast sways, giving its massive head a shake as if trying to clear its vision.

The princess blasts it, but it's not quite enough to knock it over the cliff edge. Instead the enormous beast stumbles back a step before falling with an earth-rattling thud to its knees.

An earth-rattling thud.

A crack ripples across the jetty the princess and Kendal are standing on. It slices right through the ground between us.

A tremor shakes the entire island as a chunk of land pulls away. The fissure widens as the earth and stone seem to growl and screech with pain. The entire cliff threatens to fall away, taking the princess and Kendal with it.

I run toward them, but make it only a few steps before Kane's arm wraps around me and jerks me back.

"Let me go."

"No!" Kane yells. "Ro, do something!"

There is no response from Ro. She is still on her hands and knees, palms still planted on the ground, as she does what she can to stabilize the splinter of land.

The princess and Kendal whirl around. They both move toward us, but every step they take shakes the ground.

Across the chasm, the hellhounds seem to realize that something has gone horribly wrong. They yelp with delight, and one of them lunges forward, planting his paws on the end of the bridge that is connected to Gull Veston Island. His action jerks the bridge toward them, pulling the chunk of Crescent Island with it.

The ground tilts out from under the princess's and Kendal's feet. They fall forward, scrambling to reach solid ground.

I watch, hopeless, as they fall into the chasm between the islands.

I wrench myself out of Kane's grasp.

No.

I am *not* helpless.

I am a Sleeker, like my mother before me.

And I don't just want things beyond my reach—I can reach for things beyond my reach.

My Sleeker arms, long and sinewy, snake out from my back and snatch the princess and Kendal from the air.

I have them.

But then they reach the end of the length of my arms and they snap out of freefall. I lurch off balance, landing on my hands and knees with a bone-jarring thud. Their falling motion pulls me forward and I slide along the grass. I dig in the heels of my palms trying to stop myself but it does little good. I slide, inexorably, closer to the edge of the cliff.

The weight of them is tremendous. I feel as though my shoulder blades are going to be ripped from my body.

My Sleeker arms are strong, stronger than I ever could have expected, strong enough to hold the weight of a Tuatha princess and a Kellas cat, but not strong enough to lift them.

Not strong enough to bring them to safety.

Behind me, in the corner of my mind that is not overwhelmed by the wrenching, burning, pain of holding the princess and Kendal in my arms, I hear Kane yelling something to Ro.

And then I feel him behind me, wrapping his arms around me. Somehow, he lifts me up, gets in front of me, so that his weight blocks my momentum toward the cliff.

"You have them," he murmurs. "You can do this."

He believes this. He has faith in me.

I close my eyes against his faith. Because I know the truth.

I don't have them. I can't hold them both.

Distantly, I hear the princess screaming, but the burning in my muscles blocks out everything but the pain.

And then, there is a sharp burst of new pain in my brain.

And I hear a voice—Kendal's voice—speaking in my mind, "You cannot do this, child. You cannot hold us both."

"I can." I don't know if I'm saying the words aloud or speaking only to her. "I'm not losing you. I'm not letting you die."

"But you must. If you can save only one of us, child, you know who it must be." Somehow, Kendal's voice is calm and soothing in my mind. "The princess must be protected. She must become Queen so that Kane can become King."

But I don't want her to soothe me. I don't want her to be logical. And I don't want her to die.

"Child, my death would be a small price to pay if the next ruler of the Kingdoms of Mithres could be chosen by a child of the Dark World and a dowtless Kellas cat."

There is an ominous popping noise from the area of my shoulders, like a bone being wrenched from its socket. The searing pain of muscle strain becomes a blazing fire in my joints.

And still I cannot make myself let go of Kendal.

But she makes me let go.

For an instant, she is not only deeply in my mind, but I am in hers, and I see through her eyes. I see my dark Sleeker arm wrapped around her torso, tightly enough that she can barely breathe, but her legs are free. Her claws are free. In a moment filled with selfless love, and with endless loneliness, she reaches out a claw and scratches the arm that is holding her. And then licks it.

I feel the venom in her saliva as it begins to work. Numbness creeps through the muscles of my Sleeker arms. I struggle to tense them, to will strength back into them, but my control is nothing compared to her venom. The loops around her body uncoil. She exhales and slips from my grasp.

I am in her mind as she falls.

It feels endless.

Somehow, she pushes me out enough so that I do not feel the moment she hits the water below. I do not feel any of the pain as her body is smashed. I know only the moment she is gone.

I feel her absence, sudden and abrupt. Brutal.

In the void created by her absence, I feel the rush of her venom again, pulsing up my Sleeker arm into the rest of my body.

If I don't get the princess onto firm land, the venom will spread into my other arm and I will lose her, too. I can't let that happen. I will not let Kendal's death have been in vain.

If she died solely so that the princess could live and rule this land by Kane's side, then I will make sure that happens.

I pull the princess toward me, my arm looping around her over and over again to close the distance between us. Then there is a scrambling, a frantic yelling.

"I've got her!" Ro yells.

"She's safe," Kane says. "You can let go of her now. We've got her."

I push myself up. My Sleeker arms are still coiled around the princess. Muscles trembling, adrenaline pounding through my veins, I sit up on my haunches, my head sagging, my hands on my thighs, as I suck in deep breaths.

I can't believe it. I can't believe Kendal is gone. That I dropped her. That I let her go.

My mind races, playing the moment over and over again when I felt her slipping through my grasp.

What could I have done differently? How could I have held on to her?

I can't stop thinking about it. But I can't keep thinking about it, either. There's too much to do, because I have to do something. We're still in danger. Kane's sister needs to be rescued. And we have *got* to get off this damn island.

So I force myself to block out the image of Kendal falling, to concentrate on the people still here with me.

My Sleeker arm uncoils from around the princess and I will it back into nothingness. There's an odd throbbing pain in my shoulders that I mentally shove aside. I'm not hurt, but others are. The princess rolls out of my grasp to land on her hands and knees, pulling air into her lungs.

She struggles to her feet, one hand clutched to her side as her chest heaves. Bright blue blood is just beginning to seep from the scratches along her arms, but it's the bit of blood bubbling at her lips that sends fear spiking through me.

She sways on her feet, and for a moment, she seems to shimmer in midair, as if she is gathering her magic to glamour her appearance. But she can't muster the magic for it. The air around her stills as she clutches her ribs and sags.

Her obvious pain, her undisguisable wounds, are enough to finally force energy into my shaking muscles. I push myself to my feet and stumble toward Kane.

"The princess," I gasp.

He looks up, coming to his feet. By the cliff's edge, Ro stands as well. She looks as shell-shocked as I feel. She jerks in one breath after another, but it doesn't dispel the sickly tint of her skin.

"I think I cracked one of the princess's ribs," I say. "She needs a healer."

"Ro?" Kane calls. "Can you help her?"

Ro steps forward, eyeing the princess. She reaches out a trembling hand, then snatches it back, clenching it tightly and tucking it under her arm, as though she can't bear to have anyone else see her weakness.

This has shaken her, deeply.

"If she cracked a rib, I can heal that." She gives a shaky nod in my direction. "But if she punctured a lung, there's not much I can do."

The certainty in her voice hits me hard. This wasn't what I wanted. I never meant to hurt anyone. I know firsthand how serious a punctured lung is.

"If you can," the princess says, before pain flickers over her face, "heal the break, I can do the rest. I have no skill with bones, but I can manage tissue."

Kane looks at the princess. "You can heal yourself after she gets that rib out of your lung?"

She gives a weak nod. "I can."

"Okay, Ro, get to work. Heal the princess and then wait in the house. Cupcake and I are going to go find Lucy and come back for you."

Kane nods toward Ro and the princess, and then shifts his attention back to Gull Veston Island. On the other side of the chasm, there are still four hellhounds pawing at the earth.

Obviously, the hellhounds who are left are more cautious. None of them seem to be eager to jump across the chasm and risk death.

On the upside, that means Ro has a safe place to try to heal the princess. On the downside, Lucy is still on Gull Veston Island. Kane and I have to find a way to get past those monsters if we're going to find her.

Excerpt from
Book Five of The Traveler Chronicles:
The Traveler Undone

Chaos loves a power vacuum.

The High King may have been a dickhead, but at least he kept the chaos at bay.

Now that he's gone and there's no heir to fill the void, the entire Seven Kingdoms are like a bar full of drunken frat boys — one clumsy shot away from an all-out brawl.

You might say I'm a total dick for not stepping in to take power — seeing as how I am the High King's heir.

I've thought about stepping up. Taking one for the team.

The truth is, I'm smart enough to know I'd be a shitty King. I may have the brute power, but I have none of the diplomacy that it takes to be a leader. And frankly, nobody likes me enough to follow me.

When a bar fight is about to break out, you need someone to come in, crack a few jokes, and send everyone home in a good mood. You don't need the guy no one likes, storming in and throwing punches. So if you think I should try to wrestle power and become King, then you obviously haven't been in as many bar fights as I have.

CHAPTER FORTY-TWO

A s Ro and the princess head to the house, Kane and I stare across the chasm at the hellhounds pawing at the ground. "What's the plan?"

"There are too many to fight one-on-one. We need some way to divide them up. Something to distract them."

"Can't we just jump to the far side of the island and hope they don't notice?"

Kane shakes his head. "We'll be upwind of them. They'll smell you within seconds."

Again, my blood is screwing up everything. Unless I can make it work for me.

Five minutes later, I've convinced Kane my plan will work. "You ready?" he asks.

I nod.

"You sure?"

I nod again.

For an instant, a smile plays at his lips. Then Kane closes the distance between us and slips his hand under my hair at the nape of my neck. I suck in a breath, sure he's going to kiss me. Instead, he presses his forehead to mine.

"Thank you."

"For what?"

He squeezes his eyes closed before he answers. "For helping

me save my sister."

I nod, closing my eyes, too. Standing there, breathing in the warm, deep scent of him, prepping myself for the danger ahead, I want to stand here forever. Just him and me.

Except we're not alone. Lucy is imprisoned here somewhere. Ro and the princess are back in Smyth's house and Morgan is waiting for us on the boat a mile down below. And I'm pretty sure he would warn me about the dangers of stopping time.

Still, it's hard to let Kane go when he pulls away. Harder still, not to imagine that his lips brushed against my forehead.

Excerpt from
Book Five of The Traveler Chronicles:
The Traveler Undone

According to Ockham's razor, the simplest explanation is always the most likely. So if a guy hires you to kidnap his rich wife and leave her in the Dark World, it's probably because he wants her money.

If a woman hires you to put a tracker rune on her husband, it's probably because she thinks he's cheating on her.

If a lower member of the Council of Sleekers hires you to import five hundred and twenty-three human ears, it's probably because…

Ah, hell. I got nothing.

I have no idea why anyone would need those. And I sure as hell don't know how to get them.

But this is the kind of crap I'm talking about. Do you believe me now when I tell you I work with the scum of the earth?

CHAPTER FORTY-THREE

B y the time we land on Gull Veston Island, the sun is low in
the sky. We've been here most of the day. Soon it will be
dusk, magic will stop again, and we'll have to wait until nightfall.
We have about forty-five minutes to kill the hellhounds, find
Lucy, and get the hell out of here.

Kane has dropped us at the far northeastern edge of the
plateau. Below, the hillside slopes sharply down to the cliff
where the hellhounds are perched, staring at Crescent Island in
confusion. Behind us is the expanse of the prison lawn. Farther
beyond that are the prison and the southern cliffs.

The island looks different now that the sun is overhead,
instead of sitting right on the horizon. Things should look
better in the light of day, right? If you take away the shadows,
the monsters turn back into trees, right?

A gust of wind hits us from behind. A moment later, the
hellhounds below us tense. Then, as one, they turn toward us
and howl, then throw themselves up the cliff. With every leap
up, they slide down, struggling to gain footing. Once they reach
the open land of the plateau, they'll be unbelievably fast.

There is no way I can outrun them. I'd have to be stupid
to try. Or desperate.

Apparently, I'm both.

Beside me, Kane mutters a curse and then says, "I'm going

to drop you midfield. Remember the thread lines cross the ground, deep in the earth. Stay as close to those lines of magical power as you can, because when the loop appears, that's where it will be."

"Yeah. Okay."

"You ready?" he asks.

I give my calves one last stretch. "Yeah. Let's do this."

Kane opens a loop in front of me. I step through. When it snaps closed behind me, I'm midfield, right where he said he'd drop me.

I land right on a thread line, and I can feel its energy through the soles of my shoes.

I whirl around, bobbing up onto the balls of my feet, ready to run. But the hellhounds are still thundering toward Kane.

He's still there.

The plan was for him to immediately pull a second loop and land ahead of me, but he must be struggling to do that.

Hellhounds don't hunt him, but that doesn't mean they won't kill him if he's in their way.

I watch in dread as they close in on him.

They're twenty feet from him. He's stretching his hands apart.

Ten feet. The loop is the size of a dinner plate. Not big enough.

"Hey, over here!" I jump up and down, waving my arms. "I'm over here, you big dumb dogs."

One of the hounds sees me and issues a sharp bark. The other hellhounds skid into wide turns and head my way.

My heart catches as the full reality of what I'm doing hits me. Then, I run like hell. At first, there's only the strain of my muscles and the slap of my feet on the ground. The brittle weeds scrape my ankles. Rocks jab through the soles of my Converse, but I keep running. Every time one of my feet lands, magic pulses into my soles from the thread line.

But damn, they're fast. Soon, too soon, I can hear them closing behind me. The pounding of their feet on the hard ground behind me fills my ears. How many are there? Four, I hope. I pray.

I don't dare look back to check. Please, please, please let it be all four. If Kane didn't make it through the loop in time, then he's already dead, and I will be very soon. They're close enough that I can hear the strained bellows of their breathing.

Something wet and warm lands on my back. Something I can only imagine is a giant glob of slobber. This is it. I'm dead.

Then, just in front of me, a loop stretches into existence. The shimmer of ground through the loop is different than the ground in front of me. I don't see Kane. Just the loop. I jump and dive through it, landing in a roll as it snaps closed behind me.

Distantly behind me, a hound yelps in frustration. I pop back up, exhilaration pulsing through me. This is going to work.

I'm already running again as I glance over my shoulder. I catch a glimpse of Kane waving me on. He's already trying to pull another loop to get himself ahead of me. The hellhounds are behind me, maybe a hundred yards back now. They stumble in confusion before picking up my scent.

I concentrate on running. I trust Kane to keep me safe, because all our lives depend on this.

I keep following the thread line, putting one foot in front of the other until, suddenly, there's a tree directly in front of me — a scrub oak with spindly branches that dip low to the ground. I veer to the right, then angle back, trying to triangulate where the thread is, but I don't find it. Shit.

I hear the hellhounds, right behind me now. And this time, I don't have the energy from the thread line pulsing up through my shoes, giving me that extra burst of energy. I'm dead. Because they are right behind me, and there's no way I can outrun them.

There's a scrub oak just ahead to the right. I curve off toward it, while the thumping sounds of massive hellhound feet follow me. I head straight toward the tree. At the last possible instant, I dive into a roll under the branch. I scurry out on the other side of the tree. The hellhound is too close to turn away and slams into the trunk. The second hellhound crashes into the first. I skitter back as the force of the beasts rips the roots of the tree from the ground and the whole mess topples over in a mass of tree limbs and dog.

I dance from foot to foot, searching for the zip of energy from the thread line. I never find it. Thankfully, I do see a loop open maybe twenty feet to my right. And I dash toward it.

When I land, maybe forty feet away, the hellhound wheels about in confusion. He sniffs the ground under the closed loop.

I keep running and I make damn sure I don't lose the thread line again. I barely see Kane. He is either always behind me or in front of me, closing and opening loops, keeping me just ahead of the hellhounds. Then, abruptly, I drop out of a loop to find the edge of the cliff only a few feet away. There's nowhere else to run.

I take two tentative steps forward and peer over the side. Just like Kane promised, there is a ledge, maybe twenty feet down—way too far to jump. But the hellhounds are thundering toward me.

Too fast to slow down or stop. Which is exactly what we wanted.

I wait as long as I dare, until the closest hellhound is so near, I can see the hate in its mindless eyes, and then I step off the edge of the cliff and fall, trusting that Kane has the loop open for me and that I'll land on my feet.

I drop only a few feet before I feel rock under me. Kane is there to catch me and keeps me from tumbling over the side.

An instant later, the first hellhound reaches the edge of the cliff above us. Rocks and pebbles tumble over the edge as he tries and fails to gain purchase with his claws.

Kane pulls me to him, sheltering me against the side of the cliff. Above us, the hellhounds howl in a wild cacophony of fear and anger. More rocks slide off the cliff above us, landing on our ledge and then bouncing away into the abyss below. There's a panicked yelp that ends in a howl that we hear fly past us. Then another.

I squeeze my eyes closed, trying to block out the sounds of the second hellhound tumbling to its death. Above us, I can still hear at least one dog fighting to stay on the cliff. More rocks shower down on us. Kane lets out a grunt of pain. One of them must have hit him on the back. Then another anguished yowl. From above of us comes the hair-raising screech of nails sliding along rock. The last hellhound is right above us, trying to hold on to the cliff. He's not going to make it. And when he falls, he's going to fall right on top of us.

Kane picks me up and spins me around, holding me to him. I hear the dog slide past us. There's a horrible minute when I can feel him digging into our ledge, but he's got too much momentum and he's just too big. And then he's gone. Off the side of the cliff and into the nothingness below.

When I finally open my eyes, it's to see my own feet dangling above thin air. Kane turns again and sets me back on the ledge, which is now considerably smaller. So small, in fact, that it's barely big enough to hold us both. I instinctively suck in a breath.

"It's okay," Kane says. "I've got you."

"Yeah. You do." The adrenaline pumping through my veins has left me dry mouthed and shaky. Thank God he's still holding me, because I'm not sure my legs could support me. Somehow, my crazy-ass plan actually worked. My life was quite literally in Kane's hands, and he saved me. "Am I the only one surprised that it actually worked?"

He chuckles, his eyes closing briefly as he drops his forehead to mine. "Let's get off this ledge." Then, after a second, he lifts his head and takes his hands off my back, holding them out in front of him. "What is all over you?"

I cringe, plucking the damp fabric of my shirt away from my skin. "I think it's drool."

Excerpt from
Book Five of The Traveler Chronicles:
The Traveler Undone

Now that we're out of danger, I take a good look at her.

She's a little worse for wear. Her silky hair is tangled. Dirt smudges her face, the parts of it not already darkened by exhaustion, anyway. Slashes to the fabric of her clothes reveal tempting bits of pale skin. I'm not gonna lie: it's a good look on her.

She doesn't let her guard down for a minute.

I really like this woman.

CHAPTER FORTY-FOUR

When we return to the plateau, the prison looks different. At first, I think it's a trick of the light, but it's not.

The main building looks like it's been bombed. The entire west wing has collapsed in on itself. The east wing has multiple broken windows. But what is most interesting is a small squat building peeking out from behind the rubble of the west wing. It's the kind of temporary building schools use as portable classrooms.

"That wasn't there before, right?" Surely, I would've seen it. "Smyth must use the glamour to hide it, but how did he do that during the Everdawn?"

Kane shakes his head as he and I walk toward the prison. "The building is new. Think about it. Morgan was holding this island in the past. When you and I were here before, it was thirteen years ago. Sometime recently, Smyth came here, stopped Morgan from keeping time just long enough for him to move this building in. He did it to keep my sister here."

"Which explains why you couldn't find your sister earlier today on the island. She wasn't here then because that was thirteen years ago. You couldn't find her, because she hadn't even been born yet."

"Yes."

"Is she here now?"

Kane looks down at his hand, where the compass is held in his tightly clenched fist. Something like fear flickers over his expression. This guy—this guy who has faced down hellhounds and demons and monsters I can't even imagine—this guy is afraid to look at the compass. And I know instinctively why. What if we're wrong? What if we've gone through all of this and she's not here? Because then, he has no idea how to find her.

I cup his hand in both of mine and gently pry the compass open. His mouth twists in a wry smile that I take as a thank-you.

I squint at the compass. Inside, there are three layers of glass. One like a compass shows N for north. The middle has a single hash mark that rotates around the center. The top layer is etched with a rune I don't recognize. Like the compass layer, the rune face rotates slowly every time Kane moves it. It's constantly aligning and realigning itself to Lucy, who, if the compass is working, is in the building. We both breathe a sigh of relief.

"Okay, let's go get her."

Before I can move, Kane stops me.

"You didn't really think it was going to be that easy, did you?"

"This was easy? Seriously."

He shrugs, kneeling down to inspect something on the ground. I kneel, too, and see a line of gray powder. It looks exactly like the line of gunpowder cartoons pour when they're planning to blow something up. Only this doesn't go from a box of explosives to a lit match. Instead it circles the building.

Kane trails his finger just above the powder. "This," he says.

"What is it?"

"Inactivated bluestone."

"It's not blue like the bluestone from your workshop."

"It's inactivated bluestone. It won't turn blue until it's mixed with water. When it touches your skin, it will pull that water from your blood to mix with it and to bind with the copper in the powder. It will become brilliant blue. Then it will eat away at your flesh and boil your blood. Because Tuatha and halflings have copper in our blood—"

"It doesn't affect you the same way."

"Exactly. A Tuatha would probably have to drink it to have the same effect."

"That sounds extremely painful."

"It is."

"Oh." I take a big step away from the line of inactivated bluestone.

Except…it's a really small line. No more than an inch tall or wide.

Then it hits me. "Oh!" I stare down at the line of powder. "Goofer dust."

"What?"

"In the books, Kane encounters something called goofer dust. It's used as a binder in certain potions. Plus, it acts as a poison for Dark Worlders."

"Goofer dust?" Kane asks with obvious disdain. "That's a stupid name."

"I didn't make it up." But I do have a much more vivid idea of the kind of pain it can cause. "But, can't we just—I don't know—step over it. It's an extremely tiny line—"

As I'm talking, I raise my knee to step over the line of dust… only to get knocked on my ass and blown back about ten feet.

Wincing, I push myself up on my elbows.

"You okay?"

"You could have told me it was going to do that."

"You could have given me a chance to."

"Fair enough." I suppress a groan as I sit up.

"Bluestone is also a fairly stable magical conduit. So you can use it to draw a circle, infuse it with a little bit of magic, and—"

"Instant force field, perfect for knocking Dark Worlders on their asses."

"Exactly."

"So we can find a way past this, right?"

"Oh sure. We just need something to disrupt the magic barrier. If we break the circle of bluestone, we break the circle magic. The barrier goes down. The trick is to not stir it up in the air. Trust me when I tell you that you do not want—"

"To breathe that in," I finished the sentence for him. "Yeah. That happened to a guy in Book Two. Gave me nightmares."

Kane scans the plateau. "I'll go get a branch from one of the trees near the house."

"That'll take too long," I say. "I have an idea." I pull my Hello, Cupcake T-shirt up over my head and wrap the still-damp cloth around my hand. I try not to think about the fact that I am now standing in front of Kane wearing only my bra.

Which is totally no big deal. I mean, a bra is basically a bikini top, right? And at least it's my cutest bra. Green with pink polka dots. You know, just in case Kane was starting to think I'm a badass.

I suck in a deep breath and hold it, before kneeling. I inch my cloth-covered knuckles closer to the line of bluestone. Gently I brush it out of the way. I feel the same resistance I felt when I tried to step over the barrier, but it's not knock-me-on-my-ass strong.

"Be careful," Kane murmurs.

I can't answer—since I'm busy not breathing.

After only a few seconds I have worn a spot in the line of Bluestone maybe an inch wide. Hopefully just enough to knock out the barrier. I don't even exhale until I'm standing again and have taken a big step back. "Is that enough?"

Frowning, he extends his hand until it passes above the line of bluestone. "Looks like it worked."

I waggle the shirt. "All due to the protective powers of hellhound drool." I carefully unwind the shirt from my hand. There are spots on it now where the bluestone has turned brilliant, almost glowing, sapphire blue. "It's really lovely."

"Yeah. Until it starts eating away at your flesh." Kane grabs the corner of the shirt in one hand and examines it. He glances at me and then quickly away before clearing his throat. "You know you can't put this back on."

"Oh. Okay." I carefully fold the shirt so that any remaining bluestone is folded in on itself. So far Kane has politely avoided looking below my chin. I can't help but shiver, probably from the cold, but possibly because I'm standing here in my bra. And, believe it or not, I'm not as cool as I pretend to be.

Kane sees me shivering, slips out of his coat, and holds it out to me. "Here. If you can't put your shirt back on, at least take my jacket."

I don't argue. The leather is soft and surprisingly supple. Just sliding into it makes me feel safer.

Yeah. That's much better. I just needed to be warm. And wrapped in something that smells like Kane.

That's a train of thought I can't afford to hop on. So instead, I comment, "It's not a good defense, is it?"

Kane tests the barrier again to make sure it's still down and then takes a wide step over the bluestone. "What isn't?" Then he gallantly holds out his hand for me to take as I step over it. "Be careful here. You don't want this on the bottom of your shoes, either."

I nod to let him know I've heard him, before answering his question. "Someone went to a lot of trouble to erect that barrier. Why go to all the trouble of laying all that bluestone if someone trying to break in can just brush the bluestone aside and the spell is broken?"

"It's a question of knowledge, not difficulty. Lucy is ten. Not a lot of ten-year-olds would know about bluestone."

The implication being that Lucy does.

"She's lucky to have you."

Kane shakes his head, looking like he wants to disagree. There's a pair of steps that lead up to the door of the building. For some reason, Kane grabs my arm as I walk past.

"There's something you need to know about Lucy before you meet her."

"Okay."

"She's…" Kane presses his mouth into a hard line, his gaze fixed on some spot off on the horizon. "Lucy is not lucky to have me. I am not the fantastic older brother you seem to think I am. Lucy is—"

But Kane breaks off as the door to the portable building opens. He looks up, pain and then relief flickering over his face. A second later, he takes a half step back, as if something invisible has slammed into him.

"Hey, kiddo," he mutters, bending down enough to scoop the invisible something into his arms.

It takes a moment—a rather long moment—for what I'm seeing to sink in. Or rather, what I'm *not* seeing.

His last sentence hangs between us.

Lucy is…

"Invisible?" I ask. "She's invisible?"

But Kane doesn't seem to hear me. He has his hands crossed in front of him, like he's holding a child on his hip. His head is bent down as he murmurs something I can't hear, even though his lips move.

His words are magicked out of my range of hearing.

They are not meant for me.

In fact, as I watch, the whole scene seems to blur at the edges. I can feel the magic trying to pull it out of my mind. If I so much as blink, I won't even remember that Lucy is here.

I don't blink.

Kane. This guy who is so tough. Who I have doubted and questioned and loved and wanted, and maybe even feared. This guy who has fought hellhounds and demons and monsters. This guy loves his sister. And all of this has been to protect her.

If I even blink, I won't ever remember the truth about him.

Okay. So I don't know if that's how the magic really works. I'm just guessing. Because it already feels like this moment is slipping away from me.

Then Kane looks up at me. "I can introduce you."

"Okay."

"But I'll need to know your name. Your binding name."

"Okay," I say quickly.

"You shouldn't just give that out. You have to be sure you want me to know it. Because it will give me power over—"

"Edena Allegra Keller," I say quickly. And then, remembering that with binding names, pronunciation is everything—I repeat it. More slowly. Perfectly. The way my mother always said it to me—lingering on the -ena, rolling the r in Allegra. "Edena Allegra Keller."

Kane nods. "Edena Allegra Keller, I would like you to meet my sister, Lucille Marie Teegan Travers. Lucy, this is Edie. You can call her Cupcake."

Then she fades into my vision. Slowly, like her molecules are coalescing out of thin air. "Holy…" I manage to restrain my f-bomb, but just barely.

There she is, this tiny, feminine version of Kane. He sets her down and she immediately slips behind him so that she's looking at me from under his arm. Her hair is a mass of dark curls. Her eyes, like his, whiskey brown. Her gaze serious.

I squat down beside her. "Pleased to meet you, Lucy."

She cocks her head to the side, looking at me with open curiosity. I've never met an invisible person before, but I'm guessing they don't get out a lot.

She looks back up at Kane. "I didn't touch the bluestone."

He runs a hand over her hair. "Yeah. I noticed. Good job, kiddo."

"And I stayed away from the hellhounds." She frowns, considering. "But I didn't try to escape. I knew you would come for me. Was that the right thing to do?"

For an instant, Kane looks pained. I imagine that he is thinking of all the ways this rescue plan could have gone wrong. All the ways in which Smyth could have been successful. Imagining his sister trapped here indefinitely, always waiting for him to come for her. And when he answers, his voice is thick. "Yeah. I'm here now, right?"

Before she can respond, he scoops her up in his arms and walks back to the line of bluestone. He steps over it before extending a hand back to help me over as well. Only once we're both over does he set her down.

He squats down to her level and takes one of her hands in his. "I'm going to open the loop to a boat," he says. "I'm not going to introduce you to everyone there. So I want you to be quiet and stay close to Cupcake. She can keep you safe. But first, I need to talk to Cupcake, okay?"

She nods, giving me another one of her too-serious looks. Then she walks maybe fifteen feet away, keeping Kane in her line of sight.

Kane watches her carefully before looking back to me. "Don't look at me like that."

"Like what?"

"You know what I mean. Like I'm that guy. Kane the Traveler."

"I hate to disappoint you, but you are *so* Kane the Traveler. You have never been more Kane the Traveler than you are at this moment."

"No, I'm not. You want to know why Lucy is invisible? That's my fault. I tried to replicate the rune magic my mother did on me, and this is what happened."

"How old were you at the time?"

"Does that matter? I screwed up. I did magic beyond my reach, and she will have to pay for it. Forever."

"So how does that work exactly? She's invisible to everyone?"

"Yeah. If someone knows she's there," he continues. "They might be able to see her residual impact, but until I've introduced them with binding names, she's invisible."

Residual impact. So that was why I could *almost* see her.

"You can't blame yourself. You couldn't have been more than thirteen or fourteen when you did that magic. It was far beyond your skills. And even if it didn't work, it's kept her alive. That counts for something."

"Look," he says harshly. "I'm not telling you this because I want you absolving me. Now that you know, now that you've been introduced, you could introduce her to someone else." He scowls at me. "I'm trusting you not to do that."

His voice may be hard, his gaze even harder, but I hear the truth behind his words. His sister is the most important thing in the world to him, and he has placed her life in my hands.

"Got it," I say simply. "No introductions. Ever."

A moment later, we are back on the deck of *The Blossom*, and Lucy is sitting beside me on one of the benches while Kane goes to rescue the princess and Ro from Crescent Island.

While we wait, my mind races.

If Smyth was able to kidnap Lucy, that means someone introduced her to him, and I doubt it was Kane.

If Kane didn't do it, that means someone else did. Someone Kane trusts.

Maybe even the same person who is going to try to kill him.

Excerpt from
Book Five of The Traveler Chronicles:
The Traveler Undone

Every once in a while, everything works out. You save the girl. Save the kingdom. Bring peace to the world.

Maybe you even make a little money for your trouble.

I could tell this was going to be one of those days. I could feel it in my bones.

Turns out my bones are lying bastards.

CHAPTER FORTY-FIVE

L ucy and I haven't been back on *The Blossom* long when Crab comes to sit beside me.

Feeling unexpectedly weepy, I have to fight the impulse to throw myself into his arms. "I'm glad you're okay."

He claps a hand on my leg. "Well there, missy. I'm glad of that, too. I can't say I'm going to miss this place, but I sure will miss you."

Frowning, I say, "But aren't you coming back with us to Austin?"

"I don't believe I am." He gives his head a solemn shake. "I suspect that your lot will be wanting to get on just as soon as we cross over this barrier. So this is probably goodbye for you and me."

I can't help but feel that when we cross through the Crimson Miasma, I will be more vulnerable.

I'm one step closer to home. Once we cross through the barrier, Kane will open a loop back to Austin, and we will all return to Morgan's house. Then I'll have no reason to stay in the Kingdoms of Mithres. I'll open a threshold to the Dark World—presumably one closer to the ground—and return to my home. Return to the unanswered questions about my mother. About the lies she has told me my whole life.

I want answers. I need them.

But some part of me wishes I didn't. Some part of me wishes I could return home and forget everything I learned about my mother and myself.

Almost as though Crab senses this, he wraps an arm around my shoulder and strokes my hair. "You're going to be okay, Cupcake. Yes. You're going to be just fine."

I know that he is *talking* to me, using his Siren skills to comfort me. And I don't even care. Instead, I reach out my free hand and brush it on Lucy's arm. She leans her head against my arm, and I let Crab's reassurances flow through me into her. We both need this.

"I'm going to miss you, Crab," I say.

"Yes, you will."

I have to laugh at Crab's absolute confidence. But, maybe that's another one of his Siren skills. There is a kind of magic in believing in yourself that much.

Then I stop laughing when Crab adds, "But not as much as you're going to miss him."

Crab nods toward the bow of the boat where a loop forms. A moment later, Kane, the princess, and Ro step through onto the deck of the boat.

I don't answer Crab. I wrap Kane's jacket more tightly around my body.

I will miss Kane for a long time after I return to my world. Maybe for my whole life.

Excerpt from
Book Five of The Traveler Chronicles:
The Traveler Undone

I live in a world of monsters, demons, and criminals. Everything and everyone is either trying to kill you or trying to betray you for money.

Sometimes, just walking away alive is enough to put a check in the win column.

Other times, you want a little more than that.

Today, I wanted her.

CHAPTER FORTY-SIX

C rossing back through the Crimson Miasma to the
outside world is far easier than it was going in. Maybe
because we know its tricks. Maybe because we have less to
escape now.

A few moments after we make it through, we are back on
Morgan's front lawn. Since Morgan is with us, Kane is able to
open the loop directly at his house.

We stumble across his lawn and into the house, a bedraggled
and exhausted group. Only the princess looks as though she
has not been dragged across multiple magical barriers, fought
hellhounds, and been rescued from a magical prison. She, of
course, looks like she just walked away from a *Vogue* fashion
shoot. She has magicked her hair back into perfect curls and
donned a black silk pencil skirt and white ruffled blouse. She
has even conjured a pair of black Louboutin pumps. Despite
that, her bright red lipstick bleeds slightly at the corners, as if
she forgot to magic on lip liner.

I like her better for it.

Lucy, who has stayed by my side ever since we landed on
the boat, still holds my hand. I give it a squeeze and nudge her
in Kane's direction. I understand his expression to mean that he
wants me to distract the princess so he can talk alone with Lucy.

"Princess—"

She turns to me, her expression dismissive.

Well, I guess that's the thanks I get for saving her life.

"I mean, your highness." Her expression softens slightly. "Can you look at my shoulder." I give it an exaggerated roll, not bothering to hide the wince when pain spikes through it. "I think I might've pulled something."

The princess's lips curve into an unpleasant pout that highlights her imperfect makeup application. "Very well. I'll take a look at you. I suppose I have some magical powers to spare."

"Excellent," I say with way more enthusiasm than I'm feeling. "I know right where the guest bedroom is." As I walk past her, I snag her elbow in mine and head down the long gallery. "Any chance you can magic my clothes while we're at it? I still have dog drool on my T-shirt. And bluestone, for that matter."

"T-shirt?" the princess says with disdain thick enough to spread on crackers. "Well, throw it away then."

"I like T-shirts." I give the princess's high fashion outfit a once-over. That shit cannot be comfortable. "You should try them sometime. They're cozy."

I chat about T-shirts all the way down the hall to the guest bedroom, partly to distract myself, but mostly to keep her attention on me. By the time we get there, the princess is so clearly exasperated, she says, "Oh, for the love of the Thread, enough. I will fix your clothes if you will just stop talking."

It's wrong, isn't it, how much I enjoyed irritating the princess?

I open my mouth, but she cuts me off with a decisive swipe of her hand. "You must be silent."

Instead, I nod. I turn away from her and slip out of Kane's jacket. The leather is soft and supple in my hand as I carefully fold and place it on the end of the bed. My fingers linger on it only for a moment, before I shake off the feeling and face the princess. I make an elaborate gesture toward my shoulder blade, trying to mime what I think is wrong with it.

She rolls her eyes in exasperation and then says, "Very well. You may talk. But only about your injuries."

"I must've pulled something when I caught you. It still aches."

She grabs me by my shoulders and gives me a once-over. "Are all human girls this bony?"

I fold my arms over my chest defiantly. "No. Just me."

My annoyance doesn't even register. She turns me around so that she's eyeing my shoulder blades. "Well, obviously you still have the venom from the Kellas cat afflicting your blood. Only the fact that your Sleeker arms are noncorporeal at the moment has saved you from the effects."

"But why does it still hurt? My arm isn't there anymore."

She sighs. "Did your Sleeker parents teach you nothing about your powers? Your Sleeker arms are always with you. They are a part of you. Just as much as your will is."

"But—"

"Yes," she says again with exasperation. "They are not physically there, obviously. Not everything that is real has a manifestation in this world. You think love is a physical thing? You think duty, honor, hope are tangible? These are not physical things, yet they are real, are they not?"

"I—" I twist my head to look at her. She doesn't strike me as the kind of person who cares about those things. Perhaps duty and honor, but not love and hope.

She gives my head a tap with her hand. "Do not fidget while I am trying to heal you."

Her fingers move lightly over my shoulder blades, as if she is searching for the socket that is out of joint.

"You mentioned love, but—"

She gives my head another tap. "Be still."

"I… I just—"

Her movements slow and then I hear her pull in a long breath. When she speaks, her voice is full of resignation. Of duty. "You think I do not know what I must do? Of course, I do. I must marry Kane. You are right. As much as it pains me to say so. This world needs leadership that only Kane and I can provide. I know that. And I know that you have made it clear to him, as well. I will do my duty. It is what I have always done."

It was as simple as that. And as complicated.

There are twists and turns to this story I never would have anticipated. But I know how it ends.

I feel a burst of pain in my shoulders, and then suddenly, it abates. I give my shoulders an experimental roll, but there is no stab of pain, not even a throb.

"Thank you," I say softly. "That is much better."

"Of course it is. I'm an excellent healer."

And modest, too.

"Now, turn around. Let me see what I can do about your appearance."

But before I can protest, she grabs me by my shoulders and forces me around. She closes her eyes and waves her hand over my head, down my shoulders and arms, and then over the rest of my body. When her eyes open, she asks, "Does that feel better?"

She's cleaned the smudges of dirt, and all my superficial scratches are healed. I reach a hand up to my hair, which should be matted and gross. It slips smoothly through my fingers as if it's been recently washed and dried.

"I don't suppose you would let me do something about that, will you?"

"About what?"

"Your hair. Or, in your world, is it common for girls to have hair as short as a boy's?"

My hand automatically goes to my wedge.

"No. It's not common. But I rather like it like this." And then, after nibbling on my lips for a second, I add, "Unless you could make it just a little bit thicker?"

"Of course I can. Like I said, I am an excellent healer."

A moment later when I run my hand through my hair, it's thick and springy.

By the time I am done admiring my new hair, the princess has cleaned up my Hello, Cupcake T-shirt and is handing it back to me. "Now, unless there are any other menial jobs you have for me to do..." she says regally.

There's an ironic quirk to her lips. Like maybe she doesn't take herself as seriously as she seems to.

"You know, you're not quite as bitchy as you want people to think."

"I am a princess of the Red Court." She tips her head as she says this. Her tone holds none of the arrogance I have grown accustomed to hearing from her. Only quiet resignation. "It is my duty to maintain the illusion of power, grace, and perfection."

"That doesn't mean you can't also be kind," I say gently.

"I do not know how things are in the Dark World, but in this one, kindness can be mistaken for weakness. And until the Kingdoms of Mithres are truly at peace, a princess cannot be weak."

I may not like her, but the sorrow in her voice makes it impossible to hate her.

I put my hand on her arm. "Maybe..."

I don't get a chance to finish. The bedroom door opens and Ro walks in carrying a tray with a pitcher and three glasses.

The princess shakes off my touch and straightens, her

vulnerability sluicing off her like rainwater off a duck.

Ro stops short, looking from me to the princess as if she's surprised to have found us together. "I brought drinks," she chirps.

"How provincial. I am to align myself with a man who has very few resources of his own. Even the wealthiest family he knows can't afford servants, but instead fetch refreshments for themselves." She bumps up her chin, giving the impression that she's looking down on Ro, me, and the entire household. "Well, sacrifices must be made for the good of the kingdom, I suppose."

She sweeps out of the room, making a large arc around Ro so that the edge of her skirt doesn't touch the other woman.

It's a dick move, even by the princess's standards.

But it's a dick move that I see through.

The princess may have shown me a single moment of vulnerability, but she's not about to let Ro see it.

I look at Ro, who is frowning and shaking her head. "She makes it really hard to like her."

Deleted from the Advance Reading Copy of
Book Five of The Traveler Chronicles:
The Traveler Undone

What do you want me to say? That I don't want to let her go?
Fine. I don't want to let her go.
But it's the right thing to do. Save my sister. Save the kingdom.
Bring peace to the world. Yeah, all that bullshit.
So what if I don't want to let her go.
At the end of the day, it's not my choice. It's hers. And I'm
not the kind of guy who begs.

CHAPTER FORTY-SEVEN

Ro turns her plucky little scowl on me. "You can't really believe that she's right for Kane."

"I do."

There are so many things that don't seem as clear to me as they once did. It's harder to sound confident now. I lower myself to the edge of the bed and my hand grazes against the soft leather of Kane's jacket. "It's how the story is supposed to go. They fall in love. Together, they rule the Kingdoms of Mithres."

I run my hand down the front of his jacket, one finger tracing the soft, supple leather, the other, the jagged edge of the zipper.

Now that Kane knows about the assassin waiting for him in Saint Lew, he can protect himself. I did what I came here to do.

Ro sits beside me, Kane's jacket between us, and takes my hand in hers. "I know that's what you believe, but Wallace was wrong about other things. Who's to say he's not wrong about this, too?"

"What difference would it make?"

I'm sure she's trying to be comforting, but even if I have Sleeker blood, I belong in the Dark World. And Kane belongs here.

"I'm sorry." Ro gives my hand a squeeze, and her touch is

unexpectedly warm. "I really wanted us to be friends."

"We are." I give her a smile that I hope passes for plucky rather than pathetic. "Friendship is more than proximity."

Ro doesn't meet my gaze. Instead she shakes her head a little sadly and says again, "I'm so sorry. I didn't want it to be this way." She puts her other hand on my arm. "I really am so sorry."

Except, she doesn't sound sorry. She doesn't sound sad.

Instead, her tone is fretful. Worried.

Freaked out.

Like she sounded back on the island, after the cliff destabilized and Kendal fell to her death. After the princess had finally made it to safety.

"What do you mean?" Suddenly her hands are not just warm, they're uncomfortably hot. "Ro. Look at me."

She shakes her head. "I didn't want it to be like this."

"Ro. What are you doing?" I pull my arm away from her, but her grip is tight. And she is Tuatha, far stronger than I am. "You're hurting me."

I give my arm another wrench and this time she lets go, skittering back across the bed, as if I'm a big nasty spider she's trying to escape.

She pulls her knees up to her chest, burying her head in her hands. "I'm sorry. I'm so sorry. I don't know what else to do."

"Okay." I rub my arm where she'd gripped me. My skin feels tender and hot, like I've been beaten with a baseball bat and then scalded with steam. My hand feels even worse. I flex my fingers but can't shake out the achiness.

"I'm going to go get Morgan. He can help."

But as soon as I take a step toward the door, Ro looks up, her expression tortured.

"Please. Please, don't get my brother. He wouldn't understand. He'll never forgive me."

"Understand what?" Her gaze drops to my arm. I must be twenty kinds of idiot. She hurt me on purpose. She didn't accidently grab my arm too tightly with her Tuatha superstrength. She used her elemental affinity to calcium to bruise my bones.

But Ro wouldn't do that. She's my friend. She's the nicest person I've met in the Kingdoms of Mithres. She's Snow White steeped in chamomile tea.

Unless she's not. Like every other person in the Kingdoms of Mithres.

I edge backward toward the door. "Whatever's wrong, we'll sort it out. I can help."

"Yes," she says, nodding, hope shining through her tears as she raises her gaze to mine. "I want what you want. It's all I've ever wanted. I want the story to have the right ending. I want Kane to become King. I want him to marry a Tuathan princess. I want them to rule the kingdom together. That's what we both want, right?"

"The story?"

My steps falter. Of all the people I've met in the Kingdoms of Mithres, I am the only one who thinks about this as a story. I am the only one who has read the books.

"Ro, have you read the books?"

"Yes. I have." She nods eagerly, like I'm finally getting it. "I found copies imported in The Volume Arcana. Kane never even saw them. How weird is that?"

"Pretty weird." Especially since she never mentioned reading them to me, even when we talked about how Wallace portrayed her.

"But that last book." Her tone goes hard. "That last book is all wrong. He can't marry princess Merianna."

"Then who is he supposed to marry?"

"Me." She scrambles off the bed and clasps my hands in

hers. "Don't you see? I am the princess he is supposed to marry."

"He is supposed to marry a princess from the Red Court," I say, sounding way calmer than I feel. Her touch isn't burning me this time, but I don't want to take any chances.

She waves her hand. "That's just one of the details Wallace got wrong. Like the way he wrote me so that I'm not funny. It's a mistake." Her voice rises sharply. "Just a mistake."

Wow. Ro isn't just conniving. She's unhinged.

She clutches my hands again, more tightly this time. "And I can get things back on track. Kane can marry me. We'll rule the kingdoms together. He has to share all that royal power with someone. It might as well be me."

"You want to marry him for his power? You don't even love him?"

Okay, I'm not going to pretend that my logic here is…well, very logical. But *this* is what pisses me off.

She's trying to take over the story, to force herself into the role that is supposed to be played by Princess Merianna. And she's not even doing it because she loves Kane?

Oh, hell, no. I have not worked my ass off for the past thirty-six hours to try to get this story back on track only for her to hijack it.

I yank my hands from hers. "I'm sorry, Ro. But that's not how this story ends. Kane falls in love with Princess Merianna of the Red Court. Not you." I spin on my foot and march toward the door.

"No."

She moves with Tuathan speed that I can't hope to duplicate to reach the door before I do.

"I can't let you talk to Morgan. I said that already." Her tone flips from fierce to pleading. "He would be so disappointed. He doesn't understand."

"You could make him understand. He loves you."

"No, he doesn't. He feels guilty. He feels obligated to look after me because I'm this weakling with no useful powers. But when I marry Kane, all of that will change." Suddenly she glares at me. "You've ruined everything." Then she grabs me by the arms, hatred suddenly blazing in her eyes. "Ever since you arrived, you've mucked up the story. You see that, don't you?"

"Yes." Well, if you can't beat them, placate them. "My being here has messed things up. Once I leave, the story can get back on track."

Well, Ro will clearly still be crazy, but at least I won't be in danger. I'll find some way to come back and warn Kane.

And Morgan. Oh, Jesus. Morgan's going to be devastated when he learns the truth. But I can't think about that now. I have to focus on getting free from Ro. Right now, saving myself is the only way to save Kane.

It's not much of a plan, but I run with it.

"If you just let me go, I'll return to my own world. You'll never see me again."

"You think I haven't thought of that? That was my plan all along. Rescue the Curator, send you home. Then we'd never hear from you again. But you messed that up, too." Her hands tighten around my arms as she gives me a hard shake. "You went and made a binding promise with the Curator to find the lost *Oidrhe*."

"I won't do it. I won't look for the lost *Oidrhe*. I promise."

"That's not how binding promises work. You can't just decide not to fulfill one. You're bound by magic to do it."

She takes another step into the room, farther away from the door and my only escape route.

"Even if you don't search for the lost *Oidrhe*, you will find her. The binding promise will draw the two of you together. And then Kane won't become king. And I'll have to spend the rest of my life without any magic but this useless alkaline affinity.

I won't do it. I just won't."

"I don't understand," I say. "What is it you want me to do? Do you want me to make a binding promise to you?"

She seems to consider my offer but then shakes her head. "No. Only death breaks a binding promise." She gives me another shake. Her gaze is desperate. "The lost *Oidrhe* must remain lost. It's the only way I can convince Smyth to spare Kane."

"Smyth," I whisper the name, as the truth takes shape in my head. "You're working with Smyth."

She blinks, seeming to see me for the first time in several minutes. "Well, yes."

"He's staging a coup to take over the Kingdoms of Mithres. How can you be working with him? He's going to cut the Thread of power."

She shakes her head in a bless-your-heart gesture. "That's just what he told you."

"No, Ro, it—"

"He doesn't want Princess Merianna to marry Kane, either. We worked together to devise the plan. He would kidnap her. I would send the Kellas cats to attack Kane. They weren't supposed to hurt him, just wound him enough that he wouldn't rescue the princess himself. I would nurse Kane back to health and he would fall in love with me. I had it all worked out."

"You sent the Kellas cats?"

"Of course I did. It's the one talent I come by naturally."

"Because your mother was a master of cats."

I had guessed someone close to Kane must have betrayed him, but I never guessed it was Ro. Sweet as chamomile tea Ro. She must also be the one who introduced Lucy to Smyth. And why hadn't I thought to ask Lucy as soon as I met her? Everything had happened too fast.

Well, all of this made sense, in some weird, crazy way.

Except the part where she thought she could kill me. That part, I'm not so excited about.

And I suddenly realize that Ro's been backing me up, step by step, and now we're almost to the bathroom.

"Smyth is using you. I don't care what he told you. He wants power. He will do anything to get it."

"Don't you see? Once Kane and I are married, I can control him. Smyth won't need to cut the thread, because I'll have all that power. It's all going to work out fine."

If the full-blown crazy blazing in her eyes was any indication, she absolutely believed that. Me? Not so much.

"You can't get away with this," I tell her, trying to sound reasonable. And not afraid. "You can't murder me in your brother's own house. Kane and Morgan know you're with me. When they find my dead body, they'll know what happened."

"See, everyone underestimates me. There won't be a dead body. I'll just tell them that you opened a threshold to the Dark World, and you disappeared from our lives. Easy. As. Pie."

"You don't honestly think I'm going to open a threshold so that you can toss my dead body through once you kill me?"

"Of course not. I'm going to kill you and then dispose of your body myself."

She gives my arm another twist, and her touch burns me from the inside out.

"I don't have much magical power, but I have an affinity for the alkaline elements. Have you forgotten that?"

"No."

She had knitted my bones together. Could she unravel them as well?

"Yes, I can see you get it now." She gives me a tug, pulling me closer to her. "I can dissolve the bones in your body." She takes a few more steps toward the bathroom. I try to dig in my heels, but it does no good. "That's what an alkaline mage can do. It's not a skill most people admire, but it certainly does come in handy when you want to kill someone."

She shoves me through the bathroom door and then closes and locks it behind us.

I look down at the floor. Hard tile. Oh yes, this will make it much easier for her to clean up my body once it's dissolved into a puddle. Fantastic.

She stalks toward me, pushing me toward the shower stall.

"Okay," I say, stalling. "Once you dissolve my bones, what are you gonna do with the rest of me?"

Almost as soon as the question is out of my mouth, I regret it. Do I really want to know?

"Oh, that's why I brought an entire pitcher of activated bluestone. It'll dissolve your skin and flesh." She pauses, tilting her head to the side as if she's considering an interesting problem. "I hope I brought enough."

Somehow, that's what kicks my fear into high gear. She is absolutely going to kill me. If I don't do something to save myself, she's going to kill me, and then she's going to kill the princess. She'll marry Kane, get all the power she's always wanted, and maybe eventually kill him, too.

Ah, crap. She's probably the one who tries to assassinate the princess. Duh. That makes perfect sense. It is her I have been working against all along.

If I don't stop her, she'll ruin everything.

Besides, being dissolved from the inside out doesn't sound like much fun, so I'm going to have to do something about *that* anyway.

I look around, desperate for anything that I can use as a weapon. Unfortunately, Morgan's austere, modern decorating style doesn't leave much for me to work with.

But I've had less. Against bigger, droolier opponents than her. At least with her, I know where her vulnerabilities are.

She takes another step closer to me and once again grabs my wrist.

"Yeah," I say. "I may be gullible, but I'm not a pushover."

With my free hand, I reach up and grab her hand, pinching my thumb hard into the soft tissue between her hand and her thumb, and wrench her hand off my arm. Then I slam the back of my fist into her nose and quickly follow it up with an elbow to her temple.

She doesn't crumble, but she stumbles forward, which gets her close enough for me to wrap my hands around the back of her head and slam my knee into her face over and over.

But humans are physically weaker than the Tuatha. Besides, she's already damaged my left wrist. When she stumbles back, wrenching herself out of my grasp, I can't hold on to more than a clump of hair in my right fist.

"Stop it," she growls.

I follow with a crescent kick to her head. She stumbles back again, hitting the sink, but then throws her full weight at me. Her shoulder rams into my chest, and we both go flying back against the wall.

Here's where she has the upper hand. All she has to do is touch me. I need space to punch and kick. She doesn't. She wraps her hands around my throat. I bring my arms up between her forearms and force them apart, then slam my head into her nose.

Tuatha may be naturally stronger than humans, but someone can take only so many blows to the nose before it starts gushing blood.

The broken nose only pisses her off. Her doe eyes blaze and become predator-like as she grabs my shoulders. My joints instantly burn. Her blood drips onto the floor, bright dots against the white tile. I snake my foot out, wrap it around the back of her legs, and pull.

We both go down, sliding across the floor and landing with a bone-jarring thud. We roll over once, twice. I make it back on top. Crippling pain pulses down from my shoulders to my arms. It's unlike anything I've ever felt. What the hell is she doing to me? Even if I stop her, even if I could kill her now, I might not make it. I wrench her hands from one part of my body, only to have her grab me somewhere else. Every defense I have against her, she matches. And that's when it hits me. She's going to win.

She is stronger than I am. Physically, I am no match for her. Even with all my years of Tae Kwon Do. Even with my indomitable will to live, she is stronger.

I will die here. My mother will never know what happened to me.

What will she think? That I ran away? That I was kidnapped? That after all she's done to protect me from the dangers of the Kingdoms of Mithres, I got kidnapped by some human serial killer and my bones are rotting in a grave somewhere?

And what about Kane? If I die here, will he believe Ro's lies? That I left without saying goodbye? Will he still take the throne? Will Ro eventually convince him to marry her? I don't accept that. I don't accept either of those things.

I wasn't made to want things beyond my reach. I was made to reach for the things I want.

I want to live.

I want to go home.

I want to save Kane.

Isn't that what I thought when I first came here? That saving Kane was what I was made to do. Then, by God, I'm going to do it.

I may not be able to keep her from touching me with my human hands, but those aren't the only hands I have anymore.

I stretch out my Sleeker arms, and I wrap them around her

arms and pull them off my body.

"You may be able to kill me, but you're not going to do it today." She fights me, struggling to get her arms free from my Sleeker hands, but I keep pulling them, inch by inch, away from my skin. "You may be stronger than the parts of me that are human. But my humanity makes the parts of me that are Sleeker stronger than you."

Ro stares up at me. She knows she's beaten. But she still has so much rage in her that she can't admit it. Instead, she spits in my face.

"Nice," I say. I struggle to my feet, keeping my Sleeker arms wrapped around her. And when she tries to pull free, I wrap them around her again and again, pinning her own arms to her sides.

Holding her away from me, I struggle to my feet, pulling air into my lungs, trying to soothe my suddenly racing heart.

I take a step toward the bathroom door, and my legs nearly buckle. I feel myself sway.

How much damage has she done to my body? My bones feel barely strong enough to support my weight.

I stumble backward. Only the strength of my Sleeker arms keeps Ro within my grasp.

"You are weak," she sneers.

"Not too weak to defeat you."

"You've gained nothing. You won't live long, now that I've dissolved most of your bones. If you even trip, you'll break."

"I've saved Kane. I might live long enough to make it home to my mother. I'll warn her about Smyth. If I do die, I die on my own terms." I use my Sleeker arms to tug her a little closer to me. "And I'll die knowing you didn't win."

I reach behind me and open the bathroom door. I stumble out, keeping one shoulder to the wall to support me as I drag her along.

I gaze across the vast distance of this guest room. Once I make it to the door, I have that long as hell walk down the gallery. And then I have to find Kane, Morgan, and the princess.

Goddamned rich people and their goddamned big houses.

Before I can even summon the strength to take the first step, the door flies open and Kane and Morgan rush into the room, the princess on their heels.

"Ro—" I am weaker than even I knew, and I can barely gasp out the words. "Tried to kill me. She's working with Smyth."

"We know," Kane says. "I know. I know everything."

I want to ask what he means by that. But instead, I fall to the floor. And I break.

Excerpt from
Book Five of The Traveler Chronicles:
The Traveler Undone

I've gotten into a few fights over the years. I've been hurt. I've been beaten. I've been knocked so hard on my ass, I didn't think I could get back up.

But seeing her hurt, seeing her broken…that just about killed me.

CHAPTER FORTY-EIGHT

I wake in unimaginable pain.

Turns out, there is nothing as bad as having your bones almost dissolve, and then breaking most of them.

Having them healed again, one by one, is no picnic either.

That's the pain that wakes me up. I'm screaming, struggling to get up, but unable to, since, as I mentioned, the bones in my arms are all broken.

Once again, I am lying on the bed in Morgan's guest bedroom. Once again, someone is weaving the calcium back into my bones.

"What?" That's all I'm able to get out.

"Don't move," Kane says from beside me where he's sitting on the bed, his hip by my shoulder.

He reaches out a hand and brushes my hair out of my eyes.

"Ro?"

"Morgan is holding her in another room." Kane closes his eyes briefly, and I sense all of the things he doesn't say aloud.

That Ro's betrayal is as hard on him as it is devastating to Morgan. Everything Morgan has ever done since he was seven has been to protect Ro.

I cannot imagine what this will cost him.

Somehow, I know this is one more thing that Kane will torture himself over. Saving his own sister cost Morgan his.

I know Ro would call that weakness—Kane feeling guilt about something that he had no control over—but I don't. I call it humanity. I call it empathy. And it is what makes Kane... well, Kane.

"Then who is healing me?"

Kane's lips twist in a wry smile. "Remember all of those shifters that Ro berated?"

"The earth shifters?"

"Exactly. They have the same powers that she has. They can all heal bones. What she did to you was unconscionable, but thankfully, the people who can fix it are a dime a dozen."

"What will happen to her?"

"She tried to kill you. She tried to kill the princess. She plotted to overthrow the government. Even in our world, those are grave offenses."

"She'll go to prison?"

"We don't have prisons. We have only punishments."

I nod, closing my eyes. And I can't help but think that what Smyth told Morgan all of those years ago was true after all. Within twenty-four hours of him letting go of time, his sister would die.

With that thought, I close my eyes and will myself to sleep, partly to avoid the physical pain, mostly to hide from what I have done to Morgan. I promised him that his sister would be safe. I had no idea I was lying.

Excerpt from
Book Five of The Traveler Chronicles:
The Traveler Undone

I hate killing chaos demons.

Every time you snuff out one of them, it creates a vacuum, and two more demons rush in to fill the void. Then they fight for dominance and create that much more chaos. If you're really unlucky, they'll kill three or four more in the process.

Basically, you kill one chaos demon and it all goes downhill from there.

Chaos loves a vacuum.

CHAPTER FORTY-NINE

When I wake, the room is dark and I am alone. The good news is, the agonizing pain of 206 broken bones has been replaced with a dull throbbing ache and a ravenous hunger. Probably dehydration, too.

I roll to the side of the bed and push myself into a sitting position, swinging my legs over the edge. I sit there for a minute, making sure that I don't feel any ill effects from being broken and then healed.

In the bathroom, Ro's bright blue blood has been scrubbed from the floor. I turn on the water faucet and take several long drinks, cupping my hands. I am almost afraid to look in the mirror. I'm sure the last two days have taken a toll. But it's not as bad as I expected. Besides, my hair looks cute. That counts for something, right?

I go back to the bedroom and find my messenger bag sitting on the bench. Beside it is Kane's coat. Why didn't he take it with him earlier?

I sling the messenger bag over my shoulder, then dig through it to find my phone and check the time. It's early Sunday morning. If I'm going to get home before my mother, now is the time to do it.

I toy with the idea of trying to open a threshold here. It might be easier—sneaking out in the dead of night.

I close my eyes and hold my hands in front of my face the way I did the one time I was able to open a threshold on Crescent Island. I wait for the tingle of magic to dance across my skin. But when it does, I drop my hands and let it go.

It would be easier, but way more cowardly.

"Don't go yet," Kane's voice says from behind me.

I whirl around to see him standing in the open doorway, his shoulder propped against the doorjamb.

"I wasn't going to."

Kane raises his eyebrows. I drop my gaze to the latch on the front of my messenger bag and fiddle with it.

"Well, I had just decided not to."

Kane walks into the room, crossing to stand so close, I can smell the clean, leathery scent of him. How does he still smell like leather when he doesn't have his jacket? That doesn't seem fair.

I wait for him to say something. Anything. When he doesn't, I finally look up at his face and meet his gaze.

"I know you have to go," he says, his voice rough. He leans down, pressing his forehead to mine and closing his eyes. "But I wish you didn't."

"Don't say that," I whisper, squeezing my own eyes closed against the tears.

He pries his hands off me, holding them stiffly, like he doesn't know what to do with them now. "I know what I have to do. Kissing you isn't going to make it any easier."

"I'm sorry," I say softly, even though I'm not sure what I'm apologizing for.

He turns back, running a hand through his hair. "No. I'm the one who's sorry. I wish…" He turns away and walks over to the wall of windows that looks out into the night. "I know I have to marry the princess. That I have to accept the power of being High King. It's what you want."

I almost laugh at that, the sort of panicked, frantic cackle that accompanies hysteria. "It's not what I want. It's what has to happen. Together, you and the princess can stop Smyth. There are more important things than you and me."

"And you can just accept that?"

"I have to accept it. It's what's right. If we ignore the good of the Kingdoms and do whatever we want, we'll be no better than Smyth."

Kane just looks at me for a moment, his expression intense. Then his mouth twists in a smile, and he says, "Yeah, well, nobody wants that, do they?"

It takes me a moment longer than him to see the humor in the situation. Finally, I chuckle. "No. They don't."

After all, he wouldn't be Kane if he didn't joke his way through every shitty situation.

"That's not why I came here, though," he says.

"It's not?"

"No. I need a favor."

"Anything," I say without hesitation.

"I want you to take Lucy with you."

"What?"

"She's in constant danger here. And you're right. As long as Smyth knows her binding name, he will use her against me. Or someone else will. I'm vulnerable as long as she's here."

I swallow hard and force myself to nod. "I understand."

He gives my arm a squeeze. "It's not forever. I'm going to stop Smyth. Even if I have to become King to do it. Once I'm King I can change things. Besides, I—" He ducks his head. "I'm hoping you'll check in on me occasionally. When things are more stable, you can bring her back."

"Yes. Of course." My heart thuds in my chest. This isn't goodbye forever, even if it's goodbye to my deepest wishes.

"I know I'm asking a lot."

"I'll do it," I say automatically. I don't let myself think about the logistics of this. About how I will explain this to my mom, or how I will make a life for Lucy in my world. I'll worry about that when we get there.

Kane looks at me again. "I trust you to keep her safe."

Again my breath catches. Because I know what this means to him. I know what a big deal it is, this thing he's asking of me. "I will. Absolutely."

He turns and walks toward the door, but I stop him before he reaches it.

"I have another question."

He turns back, arching one eyebrow.

"When Ro and I were fighting, how did you know to come? Did the princess tell you something was wrong?"

"No. You did. I heard you call out to me in my mind."

I think back, to the moment on Crescent Island, when I was trying to save Kendal. When I felt her in my mind.

Finally, I nod my understanding. "When Kendal was falling off that cliff, when I was trying to save her… Did she make me her dowt-mate?"

"I think so."

"And now—" The words stick in my chest, because the possibility for excruciating embarrassment is profound. "And now, we're dowt-mates, too? You can hear everything I think?"

He shakes his head. "I don't think the connection is that strong. Not without Kendal here keeping the link open."

"Is that why I can't read your thoughts?"

"I think I heard your thoughts only because you needed me." He gives me another one of his hard, impenetrable looks. "If you ever need me again…" He lets his words trail off, shaking his head. "I mean, I know you won't."

He's almost out the door when I reach him, stopping him with a hand on his arm.

"Kane, it's not that. It's that—"

"It's that you think I belong with the princess."

"I *know* you belong with her."

"Why?" he asks bluntly. "What makes you so damn sure she's the one?"

"You mean besides the fact that she's gorgeous? And perfect? And—"

"*You're* gorgeous. *You're* perfect."

"No, I'm not! I'm not what you need."

"And you're so sure you know what I need?"

"Yes, I am." Though I wish I wasn't. "The Kingdoms of Mithres need you. They need you to be King, because if you don't take the throne, Smyth will steal it. Before your mother took you into hiding, the king named you heir. That means you can claim the throne all on your own, without the princess by your side. But you still need someone to help you. Someone who is powerful and respected. Someone who will watch your back. The princess can do all that in a way I never could."

I can see my logic working its way into his mind. I'm convincing him, even though I wish I wasn't.

Then he steps forward and cups my face in his hands. "You want to know why I won't fall in love with the princess? It's because I'm already in love with you. I won't ever love her. I will never feel about her the way I feel about you. Which is ironic, I guess, since you'll never feel about me the way you feel about him."

"Him?"

"Kane the Traveler." His gaze meets mine. "I've been in your mind, Edie. I know how you feel about him. And I know what you've said to Kendal about him. The noble hero. The only hope for the Kingdoms of Mithres. And I know I'm not him." His voice is bitter.

I grab both of his arms, wanting to shake him to make him

understand. "You don't know anything."

"I know I'm a disappointment. You can't love me the way you love him." He pauses, his gaze moving over my face like he wants me to contradict him. "But if I could rewrite the story of my life to be the kind of guy who deserves you, I would."

I let go of his arms and reach up to cup his jaw. "No, Kane. You're not less than he is. You are him. In all the ways that matter to me, you are him. And in the ways you're not, you're better than he is. Kane the Traveler didn't want to be King because he was afraid he wasn't worthy. You don't want to be King because you are protecting someone you love. I would never fault you for that. I would never wish that part of you away. I would never wish Lucy away."

He kisses me. And I can feel him pouring all of his heart into it. I can taste the hope. The longing.

Which makes it that much sadder for me. Because I know how this story ends.

When he lifts his mouth from mine, he says just one word. "Stay."

That one word pierces my heart to the core. Suddenly, I have a new understanding of what it means to be a Sleeker. Because this is yet another thing that is beyond my reach.

"I can't. This isn't my world. I have to go back to my world. To my mother. And you have to become High King. It's your destiny."

"It could be your destiny, too. I'm a better man when I'm with you. I would be a better King with you by my side."

"I may be Sleeker born, but I'm still a Dark Worlder. The people of the Kingdoms of Mithres would never accept a halfling on the throne."

"I am halfling."

"Maybe, but you're also the rightful heir of the previous High Queen. You grew up here. You pass for Tuatha." I gesture to his height. "You're even as tall as a Tuatha. I could never pass. I'm too stubby, remember?" I add with a gentle tease.

Instead of laughing at my joke, he runs the back of his fingers down my cheek. "You're perfect."

I want to make another joke, but the words get stuck in my throat.

I have to step away, and I shove my hands deep in my jean pockets to keep from reaching for him again. "Besides, eventually, you'll forget about me. You'll fall in love with the princess. I know it."

"I will never feel about the princess the way I feel about you. But if you want me to, I will try to fake it."

"I don't want you to fake it. I—" God, it about kills me to say it out loud. "I want you to actually love her. I want you to be happy. I want you to let her make you happy."

Slowly, his gaze searching my face, he nods. "Okay. I will."

I try to be satisfied with his answer, even though grief is crushing my soul.

This is the right thing to do. It's the right ending for this story. It's a happy ending.

It's just not a happy ending for me.

Excerpt from
Book Five of The Traveler Chronicles:
The Traveler Undone

I'm no good at goodbyes.
When it's time to leave, I just disappear. It's better that way.
Besides, if you know my binding name, you'll always be able to summon me.

CHAPTER FIFTY

Somehow, I make it through the next couple of hours on adrenaline alone.

Sure, I eat a few bites of something that Morgan puts in front of me while we are waiting for Kane to explain what's going to happen to Lucy.

Surprisingly, Tuatha food is bland and uninteresting. I expected a lavish feast, but instead, I get food that looks pretty but has little flavor. I don't know if their taste buds are different than ours, or if this is another area in which they are just not as creative as we Dark Worlders are.

Morgan doesn't say much to me as I eat. And I have too many things to say to him to say any of them.

Morgan sits sprawled in his chair, his legs spread wide. Though his posture isn't that different than the last time we sat at this table, previously his sprawl seemed the result of his arrogant confidence. Now, he seems almost unable to support himself, as if his grief is too big for his body and it's seeping out of him.

We have been alone for almost an hour when he says, "I don't blame you."

I don't need to ask what he's talking about. Instead, I force myself to meet his gaze. I owe him that much, at least. "I blame me."

"You shouldn't. You didn't know what would happen. You didn't know who she would become." He leans back in his chair, looking out into the distance.

After a long moment, he says, "I know you are eager to get home, but if you have time, may I tell you a story?"

I'm not sure what to say, so I simply nod.

"I think it is a story you'll want to hear." Apparently, it's not an easy story to tell, because he pushes himself from the chair with an obvious effort of will and crosses to stand before the wall of windows that looks out on the lake.

"It is a story about the time I spent on the island you have been calling Crescent Island. Those years, those long thirteen years, passed mostly in a blur. Not a quick blur—actually, it was a slow, agonizing blur—but a blur, nonetheless. Every day, the same. Every moment, the same. With no hope that things would ever change. Until you and Kane showed up and rescued me."

As he speaks, I cannot help but remember the younger Morgan that I met on that island. He was so unlike the Morgan I have known in this timeline. So fragile and pained. So heartbreakingly serious.

"After you rescued me, I returned to the moment just after Smyth had taken me. To the life I had known before. I had spent thirteen years on Crescent Island. My brain and my body had not developed. I was still a seven-year-old boy. And yet I had lived all those years, lived as no sentient creature should have to live. I need not tell you, I was never the same."

He pauses, glancing over his shoulder at me, before looking out the window.

"I was safe. I was with my family and my sister again. I should have been at peace, and I became very good at pretending that I was. But I knew better than most that no timeline is fixed. No destiny is so firm that it cannot be changed. I knew that in sixteen years, I would be rescued. Or rather, I hoped I would. I waited eleven years never knowing what my fate would be.

"Then when I was fifteen, I met Kane. He seemed impossibly young compared to the man I remembered. But I recognized him instantly. From that moment on, I had the hope that one day Kane would rescue me. But I knew it couldn't happen until you showed up. I was haunted by the possibility that the timeline in which I had been rescued would not happen."

He turns back to face me, his hands shoved deep into his pockets, his expression drawn.

"So you see, I knew who you were the moment I met you in that limo. I knew you had finally come to save the boy I was. I manipulated Kane into trusting you. I brought you to the island. The events of these past few days are the result of years of me willing them to happen."

Something must be showing on my face, some hint of my surprise or my confusion, because he adds, "Remember, Edie, in this world, will matters. Even for those of us with no Sleeker blood."

"Did you know how this was going to end?"

"None of us really know how this is going to end, Cupcake. Not even you."

I am still struggling to wrap my brain around everything he has told me. "So then, I really am part of the story?"

He crosses to stand in front of me, seeming impossibly tall. And for the first time this morning, his grief softens into something else. Something warm and affectionate. "My dear, you have *always* been part of my story."

. . .

Just before dawn, Kane opens a loop back to his loft above
The Volume Arcana. Since this is the threshold through which I
entered this world, it should be the easiest one for me to open.
Besides, The Volume Arcana lies upon the intersection of six
powerful lay lines. Even a newbie like me should be able to
pick up the power and open a threshold.

Once we're there, Kane and Morgan exchange a look.
Before I wonder why, Morgan takes Lucy by the hand and leads
her down the hall to one of the rooms I never saw, leaving me
alone with Kane. In his living room. With that stupid Faraday
Cage still sitting there.

I start to babble. I can't help it.

"The first time I ever heard of a Faraday Cage was when
my dad read me *The Postman*."

"Cupcake—"

"By David Brin. You ever read it? No? You should. It's a
classic. It—"

"Edie."

I stop talking, slowly turning to look at him. "That's my
name," I whisper.

"Yeah. I know."

"You don't usually say it."

I don't know that he's ever said it, and the sound of my
name in his voice does things to my insides that make it hard
to breathe and harder still to think.

"I get it," he says, closing the distance between us until
he's right in front of me. So close he's almost touching me.
"You think I'm going to fall in love with her. But you're
wrong. I'm not gonna fall for her. How can I when I'm in
love with you?"

"You're—"

But before I can get the words out, he presses a finger to
my lips. "Shut up. For once, just let me do the talking."

I'd be insulted if it wasn't for the playful glint in his eyes as he says it.

"You thought you knew my story, but you were wrong. About a lot of things. You were wrong about Morgan. About Ro. About Lucy. There are just too many things you didn't know."

It's on the tip of my tongue to protest, but I stop myself. Why am I still arguing with him about this?

"What if you're wrong about this, too?" he asks. "What if I'm not supposed to fall in love with her? What if I'm *supposed* to love you?"

"I don't know what the right answer is here," I admit. Saying it aloud is harder than it feels like it should be. I don't like not knowing things. It's terrifying. "I know you'll be a great King. And I know you can't do that with me by your side."

"Edie—"

"Let me finish. This isn't me just babbling. This is important."

His lips—those perfect, too-full lips of his—curve into a wry smile that shows off his dimples and melts my resolve. But he doesn't interrupt me again. He just tips his head, waiting for me to continue.

"I can't choose my own happiness over the safety of this entire world. I just don't have it in me to make that choice." I pause, looking off into the distance, running my teeth over my bottom lip as I consider my words, scared to say this out loud. In a world full of monsters and enemies, hope may be the most dangerous thing of all. "But if there was another way…if there is another person who can rule…"

"You mean, if the lost *Oidrhe* is real."

I meet his gaze and try not to lose myself in it. "Yeah."

My answer sounds breathless, my voice made delicate by holding so much hope.

Kane grins. "If she's real, you'll find her."

"You've never believed she's real," I counter. "You told the

Curator she was a fairy tale."

He shrugs. "True. But you made the binding promise. If she's out there, you *will* find her."

"Maybe," I say, hesitantly, still not quite willing to give myself over to hope. "If she lived, she'd be Lucy's age. Way too young to rule. And who knows how long it will take to find her?"

His hand slips up to cup my cheek, tipping my chin up so I meet his gaze. "I'm patient."

I study his face, taking in every detail, all the features that are exactly what I expected. All the ones that aren't. All the tiny things that make him, *him*, and not that other Kane. I don't know when I'll see him again—and I don't want to forget anything. I only know that I *will* see him again. "All I'm saying is…don't give up on me yet."

"Ah, Cupcake. If you thought I was going to give up on you, you don't know me as well as you think you do."

He nuzzles his nose against mine, and when I tip my face up, he leans forward and whispers something in my ear. Something only for me. Then he kisses me. His lips are warm against mine. I feel myself rising up on my toes to get closer to him. His hands cup my cheeks and his fingers are in my hair. And I want the moment to go on and on. I want it to last forever. I want that so badly, I'm afraid of wanting it too much. I am afraid that I will somehow make the world stop turning, just so that I can keep this moment a little longer.

It's terrifying to want something this much, but maybe it shouldn't be.

I've spent so much of my life hiding from the real world. Maybe it's time to stop hiding and take my place, whether it's in this world or in mine.

• • •

The future may be terrifying, but it turns out, opening a threshold isn't. I feel the magic pulse from beneath my feet and into the air around me. The magic is so strong right here that I don't even need both hands to open a threshold into the Dark World. I don't look back at the world I am leaving behind. Instead, holding Lucy's hand, I step through, out into the early morning light in Austin, Texas.

I don't feel the nausea or dizziness I felt crossing from my world into theirs, but suddenly, I feel the absence of something. Like when you yawn after a flight and the pressure equalizes in your eardrums.

The air is crisp and cool and oddly flat. Free of the magical pulse I felt in the Kingdoms of Mithres.

I crouch down beside Lucy. Her eyes are closed, her lips pressed together, still trembling. She looks as bad as I felt when I first crossed over. After a minute or so, she seems to get her legs under her, and she opens her eyes to look around.

Lucy says nothing, but stares, wide-eyed, at the buildings, so different from the ones in her world.

"We're going to be okay," I tell her. "I'm going to take care of you. And we're going to find the lost *Oidrhe* together. And when we do, then we can go back to the Kingdoms of Mithres together."

She just presses her lips in a line and nods. But I can see that the idea calms her down. Giving her a purpose has given her strength.

I don't even dare take my phone out of airplane mode in case my mother is tracking its location. Thankfully, the buses still run on a Sunday morning. One of them gets us across the interstate to the neighborhood where the Bufords live. Lucy and I have to walk the last mile or so, but neither of us seems to mind. It's nearly seven a.m. when I let Lucy into the apartment I share with Mom.

Somehow, it seems even smaller than it did when I left.

Lucy, who is beyond exhausted, falls asleep almost as soon as she lies down on my bed. I tuck blankets around her and then return to the living room. I forage around for a snack, grabbing an apple and a jar of peanut butter, as well as a drink, before settling in on the sofa to wait for my mother to come home. Only then do I pull out my phone and take it out of airplane mode. The battery is at 5 percent, so I plug it in as I wait for my mother's texts to pour in.

As I suspected, there are a ton of them.

I'm trying not to helicopter, but your phone seems to be off. Check in when you turn it back on, okay?

OK?

I know I said you could ignore my texts, but it'd be great if you could just check in quickly.

Edie, this isn't like you. Check in. Pls.

Why aren't you answering your phone?

Answer. Right now.

Are you even getting these?

You're not even showing up on the Find iPhone app.

Where are you?

The most recent one floods me with relief.

Boarding the plane now. I'll be home by 11:30. You better be there.

So as of this morning at seven thirty, Smyth hadn't found her.

For now, she is safe.

I quickly text her back so that she'll have a message when she gets off the plane.

Sorry, phone was off all weekend. Long story. Will tell you when you get here.

Of course, now that I am back in Austin, I can no longer ignore that other possibility—the possibility that none of this really happened at all. I look down at myself. All of my wounds have been healed. I have no physical evidence on my body of anything that happened…other than slightly thicker hair. My clothes are clean. My Hello, Cupcake T-shirt is a couple inches shorter, but otherwise the same. Those missing two inches of fabric are the only tangible proof I have that what happened wasn't all in my mind.

You would think that having Lucy with me would be reassuring. Except…she is invisible. And having an invisible friend has never been a sign of mental stability.

The truth is, I'm not sure exactly what I've accomplished. I have way more questions than answers. Kane now knows enough to avoid the assassin in Saint Lew. But as long as Smyth is around, he's still in danger. Have I saved his life, or merely postponed his death?

For now, I will have to wait for answers. I will have to find my way back to his world at some point. But first, I have to wait until my mother comes home.

I need answers from her.

I need to know if she really is a Sleeker, what her relationship with Smyth really is, and why she hid the truth from me for so long.

Of course, that's assuming she gets home to me before Smyth gets to her. I wish there was some way to warn her. For now, all I can do is send a text. One she most likely won't even see until she gets off the plane.

But what do I say?

There is no short and easy way to ask these questions. In the end, I merely write:

Can't wait to see you. Be careful.

Then, I curl up on the sofa and let my eyes close, relishing the secret Kane whispered to me right before he kissed me.

He told me his binding name. When I'm ready, I know

how to summon him. I don't know yet when I'll use it. Maybe after I find the lost *Oidrhe*. Maybe sooner. But before that, I need to rest.

The last thing I think about before I fall asleep is what Morgan said to me.

No one knows how this story is going to end.

Not even me.

ACKNOWLEDGMENTS

No book is easy to write, but some are harder than others. Some are a trip down a familiar path, where you can't always see the way ahead, but you know in your heart the ground is beneath your feet and there's just enough light ahead you know you'll make it out the other side. Other's are like running uphill, through the brambles, trees snagging your clothes, hellhounds snapping your heels, until you finally break through only to realize you're teetering on the edge of a cliff. There's no way back. You can only leap and pray you sprout wings.

That was this book for me.

My wings were made up of a lot of people. So sorry, but these acknowledgements are long. That's just the way it goes when it takes seven years from story conception to book delivery.

In (roughly) the order that you stepped in to help out in one way or the other.

Tracy—you were there there moment this story was born. I was having just the worst day and locked you out of our hotel and probably traumatized you forever. It was the moment in my life when I most wanted to escape to another world. If our friendship can survive that, it can survive anything.

Robyn—you're my partner in crime, my oldest writing friend, and the person who introduced me to Jim Butcher's Harry Dresden books. I love my husband, but if I could cross over into another world and find Harry, we might have a problem.

Skyler, Karen, & Jax—I can't thank you guys enough. From the initial brainstorming, to the fabulous beta reading, to the encouragement and friendship. I am so damn lucky to have you guys!

Madeline—I trusted you with one of the earliest drafts of this book. It was total crap at the time. I bet you gave up reading forever after that. But thank you! And I hope you'll give this story another try now that it's less crappy.

Brandi—honey, I adore you. You also saw this when it was pure crap. You offered so many great ideas and totally changed the direction of the book. You're amazing!

Sherry—I don't even know if you remember this, but you gave me some blunt feedback when I really needed it. And you also sent me an amazing letter when I was down and didn't even know that I needed the lift. Thank you.

Shellee—you are always there to give me a swift kick in the ass when I need it. Plus, I love that sometimes I get to see what a marshmallow you are on the inside.

Dr. Hsieh—when I was struggling and thinking about giving up writing forever, you told me exactly what I needed to hear. Thank you!

Avyu—through sheer kismet, you needed a ride on day when I needed some brainstorming. Your ideas were awesome.

Daven—thanks for reading this book and telling me that it was indeed something teenagers would want to read, but it was a bit long. It's shorter now, so hopefully that helps.

Misty—I love that you love this book so much. I feel like you really get it and that's amazing!

Brenda—I am so lucky to get to work with you again!!! I love that you were able to share my vision and guide me and make the book the book is always wanted to be.

Stacy, Liz, Bree, Nancy, Curtis, Heather, and anyone else at Entangled that I haven't yet met but helped with the book—thank you so much for helping to make the book of my heart a book I can hold in my hands.

GET READY FOR BESTSELLING AUTHOR MARLENE PEREZ'S SNARKY, HILARIOUS TAKE ON THE VAMPIRE ROMANCE NOVEL.

I didn't even want to go to the party.

Seriously, I'd rather have stayed home with my librarian-witch grandmother and her mystical book club than go. But my best friend Skyler begged me. So I went.

And it was the worst party of my life. The last party of my life.

Not only was the band downright horrible, but the lead singer bit me afterward. And then stole Skyler.

Now I'm chasing down a band of angry vamps with my other best friend Vaughn in tow—and a buttload of feelings between us we can't even begin to address. And worse, I'm changing into something else…

Let the afterlife begin.

Let's be friends!

🐦 @EntangledTeen

📷 @EntangledTeen

📘 @EntangledTeen

📰 bit.ly/TeenNewsletter

entangled teen

an imprint of Entangled Publishing LLC